THE ULTIMATE
DRAGON

Wishing you all
the very best, Dave
Olive, Fred & Ross

Christmas
1995
x

OTHER **ULTIMATE BOOKS**
FROM **DELL**

THE ULTIMATE ALIEN
THE ULTIMATE DRACULA
THE ULTIMATE FRANKENSTEIN
THE ULTIMATE WEREWOLF
THE ULTIMATE WITCH
THE ULTIMATE ZOMBIE

THE ULTIMATE
DRAGON

BYRON PREISS
JOHN BETANCOURT
& KEITH R.A. DeCANDIDO
EDITORS
▼▼▼

ILLUSTRATED BY
LARS HOKANSON
& FRANCES CICHETTI

A BYRON PREISS BOOK
A DELL TRADE PAPERBACK

A Dell Trade Paperback

Published by Dell Publishing, a division of Bantam Doubleday Dell Publishing Group, Inc., 1540 Broadway, New York, NY 10036

Special thanks to Jeanne Cavelos, Eric Wybenga, and Leslie Schnur

Book design by: Fearn Cutler

CONTENTS

INTRODUCTION
▼▼▼

TANITH LEE

Glimmering and shadowy, they stand in the caves of legend. Almost every mythos of the world contains them—in some form, probably all. They sleep under rivers and in the bellies of volcanoes, they rule the clouds and shake the earth. They are the symbols of sexual energy and eternal life—and they are the destroyers, whose flights of poisonous, fire-breathing terror easily rival any (somewhat) limited nuclear strike.

Dragons.

They have a lair now in our brains, so intent, they are nearly like a memory. From where do they come?

The dinosaurs, those scaled and gorgeous beasts, may be at the root of some of it, perhaps. Who knows what race recollection or genetic imprint remains from some early fossil sighting of our ancestors? Or, could it be that, contrary to the dictates of science, a few dinosaurs survived the mass extinction, somehow lingered on in a world that had, by then, produced the rudiments of humanity? And if such a thing were possible, conceivably they, or a handful of descendants, continued into subsequent eras. The physical eye-witness accounts of dragons persist staunchly late into the seventeenth century, and debatably later than that.

Something, certainly, gave rise to this being that is the symbol of an ultimate and unique power. Its origins are impressive. In Mesopotamia, the Chaos dragon, Tiamat, was slain by a hero to bring about order. In China, the fundamental dragon is a guardian and weather-maker, propitiated by lotuses. In the Norse, the dragon gnaws the World Tree and must be defeated in the last twilight by a master god. In Egypt, the subterranean dragon Apep battles with the sun deity, Ra, by night, in an attempt to destroy the return of day—and is always overcome. For the Christian epoch, it is the Fallen Angel, Satan himself, the serpent from the Garden. Arthur's knights fight victoriously with dragons, just as Beowulf did—while in the Orient, women too may turn out to be apt and agile dragon-slayers.

Of course, evidently, whatever else, the dragon is a creature of the Id. The medieval maps give the clue to this with their labeling of all unknown places: *Here be dragons.*

And like all the species that come from the dark of the human brain-moon, the dragon has duality. It is wicked, devouring, unreasoning, and savage. It is beautiful, graceful, cunning, wise, and potentially holy. The old stories, though they abound mostly in images of the dragon's evil and disgusting nature, are not always immune to the glamor and nobility, or to the mystical quality of the dragon. Like its Satanic counterpart, it too may encircle supernatural trees, guarding the precious apples or fleece. Only the most perfect or deserving hero can slay it—a Heracles, a Jason. It becomes then the dark shadow of fear, the erroneous lusts, which must be conquered in order that the bright fruit of knowledge and delight may be achieved. The dragon's hoard comprises exquisite gems and articles of gold and silver—these too, the prize of conquering heroes. But has the dragon stolen such items only in the way of the thieving magpie, attracted by their glitter, or is it a connoisseur of the special and the lovely—the priestly guard of the finest things that men create?

The maiden too, where she is the sacrifice, must—like the hero—be of the very best, the most charming, pure, and divinely-fashioned. So we give up the best of ourselves to serve the dark monster within us . . . or is it that the dark (that is, the *unknown*) side demands of us the most wonderful, our utmost, drawing it from us reluctantly and with pain and outcry, refusing to settle for less?

Maybe that, then, too, is what a dragon is, what we, in the dark of ourselves, tear from our hearts and minds, triumphs of courage and perfection that otherwise we would never rise to.

I doubt there is one of us who never has, or will, stand like Louis MacNeice's hero before the Dark Tower wherein the dragon lies. In whatever way or by whatever means, we all sound the gold or silver horn, and the demon will come forth. We are braver than we know, all of us, and the dragon has taught us how to be.

Dragons are the power inside us, externalized, obviously, because that is the way we do things. For such a reason, dragons have been the symbol of power for centuries, perhaps forever. The standards of Roman armies, the souls of the longships of the Vikings, battle gages, the crests of kingdoms. They are magnificent and almost indestructible. And, as time has gone by, they have lent themselves to a fascinating and rewarding extension and analysis.

Writers, as storytellers, have always been drawn to investigate and to represent dragons. In recent years the dragon has gained breadth and depth and a psychology of its own. As with the terrifying, and yet curiously almost suburban Smaug of Tolkien, a creature horrifying and nightmarish, and yet self-blind as some smug, rich businessman. And, alternatively, the luminous, intelligent and persuasively benign dragons of Anne McCaffrey's Pern, a ground-breaking excursion into ethnic alienism. While even on film, the dragon has reached new heights—in Disney's *Sleeping Beauty*, for example, where it is the appalling and perhaps *male* alter-energy of the enchantress Maleficent. And in *Dragonslayer*, with the marvelous Vermithrax, a beast that combines beauty with hideousness, glory with revulsion—and ultimately touches the heart as it—*she*—bends above her slaughtered children.

We have come a long way with our dragons—for, I dare to suggest, they do belong to us in some secret and magical form. As with all the things that humankind does well (and we must never forget, we are very good at very much), we are working and delving and finding. And our stories, once told about low, smoking fires, still expand and burn, and call the shadows of the night.

We all have our dragon within us, as each of us has our angel, and the whole winged pantheon of the possible. May this book therefore inspire you to dream dreams, and perhaps to fashion visions of your own. For be sure, we are not done with them . . . nor they with us.

HERE be dragons:

AGE
▼▼▼

TANITH LEE

AUTUMN was dying now. The brown and bronze valleys, where, fifty years before, nothing would grow, were thick with trees that had lost their density, turned sere and pale grey. The rain washed through them. The birds had flown. There had been no birds once. The birds had amused him: Such little things, yet able to fly. Long days, he lay and watched them playing.

From the mouth of the cave high in the hill, he could see too the track on which the fallen leaves lay thick, gleaming with wet. Up this track, a month ago, people had come. As in the old days. They had brought him a maiden. From inside the cave he watched. She did not scream, not then. She was drugged and wreathed in flowers, and wearing a white dress. Her long hair was the color the leaves were then coming to be. They chained her to the iron post and ran off in frightened silence.

It was his fault, this waste. There had been a long hot night when he had howled aloud in pain and in a kind of rage. And they—they had heard him, in their huts and hovels. They had said, *the dragon is awake again.* They had gone back to the old formulas, to feed and appease him. And once she was chosen, they brought him the young virgin girl, for his pleasure.

The dragon shifted a little. Even to do this hurt a great deal. He stared away along the track, but no longer saw it.

Fifty years back, and before that, the valleys had been black and barren from his fire. He kept them so, to mark his territory and his fastness. He had lived in the cave a century, for it suited him. Then again, before that time, he had roamed.

When he had been young. Blacker he was than the blackness his fire induced, black as a starry night. He had seen himself often, and known himself, reflected in the lakes of the world. Silver edged his scales, and he was limber as a big cat. His teeth were white, sharp as swords. He had bitten swords through with them.

How many times—he had soon lost count—the bold or terrified men came to challenge him. Often, for the pure joy of it, he would not blast them with the fire, but toyed with them. And their blades clanged harmless on his opalescent midnight obdurate hide. At last he would crunch them in two. He would eat them on the open hillsides, in the woods, where they had sought him. Their mail he bit off to expose their lean white flesh. Their horses he tried to spare, letting them go cantering free, neighing in fear. Sometimes though the horses were caught in the fire. But that was very quick.

He rarely harmed anything but man. Man and woman. Sometimes he took a deer to feed him, or fish from a river or the sea, swooping down to spoon the waters and their creatures up in his shining mouth.

But man was his staple diet. What did him the most good. He took them as he wished. There had been nights he had flown above their villages and roasted them in their beds, alighting in the after-smoke to pick them out, his baked meats, from the embers. But then again, he did not care to roast their cattle or their domestic beasts, and as he matured, he did not do anymore this thing, this flying over and burning.

He preferred to come out on them from his place, some cave or crook of a hill. They would stand in astonishment, for a moment too startled even to be afraid. Then the shrieks would commence. They would try to run. He always caught them. He ate them sometimes alive. They tasted best that way. Children he left. They were unformed. They would wander crying on the roads, above the bloodied bones of their parents.

He felt sorry for them, then. And, after a while, he did not kill men and women who traveled in the company of children.

In all areas, once they knew that he was there, they brought him the young girls dressed in white.

Some were conveyed drunk or full of herbal stuff, but others they had not troubled to quieten, or had not known how to, and these ones screamed and wailed and wept.

This uproar went on until the people had gone away. When he emerged from his cave or cover, they fell silent, the young girls. Some fainted, it was true, but others stared. And he came close and gently breathed on them. It was the magic underbreath of the fire. It did something wonderful to them. Their faces filled with light and sweetness, and they stretched out towards him, calling him, ready, full of love. Only then did he use the fire. They died in ecstasy, cooked to a turn, delicious as no other thing ever was.

He ate them slowly, savoring, keeping morsels back for two or three days.

But when had it—when had *this*—begun with him? Oh, the first seeds were perhaps there even when he chose this cave above the valleys, and settled here, and did not fly away. Flights he still took, to subdue the people round about, and for the sheer delight of it. To feel his strength, which it seemed to him now he had only truly felt at that era, doubtless as it began to wane.

The vast wing-beats, and the moon that came no nearer yet revealed its face, white and serious as the face of a virgin. The land beneath, the mirrors of its waters and the banks of its forests, mountains and hills, the glowing settlements of men, that now he did not light more brightly. But now and then, a joke perhaps, a ruined barn, a scarecrow in a field—he breathed and they burned, a mound, a golden cross. *The dragon*, they would say, and bring him another maiden.

His eyes cleared, slowly, as they did now, and he looked and saw, not the past but the present, the iron post to which they had tied the last maiden, the girl with amber hair.

Such a pity, such a loss.

Not for three hours did she come to herself enough, and then she started. She screamed and roared until her throat gave out. Then she croaked. And he, he had had to lie here in the cave, listening to her crying and her ceaseless terror. Her terror that he could not ease or end.

He had had a hoard once, and in the hoard were gems as green as her eyes and amber and bronze like her hair. Glass he had collected too, and mirrors. Ivory and medallions of gold. He had gathered these things where he found them, in the wreckage of houses he destroyed, from champions that he killed, caravans he arrested. But he had finally lost interest in the hoard, abandoned it. He had pondered who would dare, eventually, risk that place and steal it. Perhaps no one ever, for even when he had gone away, his spirit haunted those spots that had been his. They were avoided, he knew, spoken of with dread.

He had even learned a few words of the language of men. By force of repetition. He knew his own name among them, and used it now of himself. *Dragon*.

And *maiden*. He knew that word also.

It made him—it made him ashamed.

There had only been, at first, a little stiffness, on waking. And later, in the rainy winters, and when the snows came and turned

the valleys white as the moon. And presently he ached. But with
the summer these things went away, and he forgot them, until
the first dapple of the cold put into him—what could he say it
was? A sort of *fear*.

Yes. He came to fear. No other thing. Not man nor beast.
But himself. Of himself, as for all those centuries others had
been, he was now afraid.

His body betrayed him. Villainous, it grew worse and worse.
Decline seemed to come in great leaps, until each day some
new thing was taken from him, as if it had been subtracted while
he slept. One morning he woke and his eyes did not see the
pebbles under his foreclaws, only a sea of mist, and when he
looked across the valleys, minutes passed before his vision cleared
sufficiently to let him know the view.

He did not hear anymore the higher notes of the birds as they
danced in the air. The birds did not fear him. Nor the foxes,
who came to tidy up the bones and offal that he sometimes left
below the slope.

He did not grudge them their lives, their play, their vigor. He
had lived far longer.

He had lived so long, so long. And as he began to remember,
it seemed to him that the centuries doubled, as if he had lived
forever. And so he knew that he was tired. Exhausted mostly by
his aching rock-hard body, that now he could barely move along
the floor of his cave. Exhausted by his sore jaws, from which the
teeth had one by one dropped out, black and rotten, on the
stone. Lapping at the little stream that ran there, he thought of
the enormous scoops of lake and river. In the stream he was not
reflected, but he knew himself even so. He was grey now. His
white teeth had gone black and his black scales whitened.

He had not left the cave for a year. Could not. And in the
late summer night, when the heat, which no longer helped him,
had pressed upon him like his own vanished fire that he could
no longer summon, he had howled in horror at himself, as all

those decades ago men had howled at him. And men heard. And they brought him the girl.

She died on the second day. He reasoned what had happened. A sharp part was in the chain that held her left wrist, and she had struggled so violently. He saw the blood, or made it out, dripping. The chain had been merciful.

He had not been able to go to her. He could barely reach his stream. And if he had gone to her, his breath was foul now, and he had no fire.

Dead, he could only observe her rotting. He had no teeth. How beautiful she had been, he would have loved to taste of her. And in his sleepless dozing state, he almost dreamed of it, her welcome and the fire and her toothsome skin. But that was as near as he could come to Paradise.

And she had died meanly and in vain.

Though, not quite in vain. For at length the birds began to feed from her, and the foxes came, careless of him, and pulled delicacies from her body.

In the end she would be bones, and they would say, *The dragon ate her.*

He lay quietly. He closed his eyes. They burned as if fire was still in him, but it was not. Soon the rain would give way to snow. And he would lie here in the raw and tortured coffin of his body. He thought that this winter might finish his life, for now his life was only like a thread.

He slept a little then, the first sleep he had known for half a year. And in his sleep he saw the maiden waiting for him, holding out her arms in love. When he woke, perhaps it would be time. He would look with his half-blind eyes, and see the initial whisper white of snow, falling like tears through the aching air. His soul would go out of him like a sigh. He would sleep forever in the arms of love.

TIN LIZZIES
▼▼▼

CHELSEA QUINN YARBRO

EVERYONE in Deer Crossing knew that old Mick McCullough was a bit of a nut, and never more than when he found a new crackpot theory to espouse: twenty years back he had developed a passion for the odd, beginning with a bout of research on Bigfoot and Yeti; he went on to explore the accounts of dowsing for metals; a decade ago it had been flying saucers and abductions; then it was the origin of those weird wheatfield markings in England; next it was out-of-body experiences; and now it was dragons.

"Of course they were real; there's always something real behind myths. Everyone knows that, and it couldn't've been dinosaurs—they're too old for that, gone long before us—so it has to be dragons," he insisted over coffee in the Sagebrush Diner, off of Second Street; Deer Crossing had only three numbered streets, and they, with Washington, Jefferson, and Clay, constituted most of what passed for downtown. "Probably some kind of aliens who came here five, six thousand years ago. Maybe a little earlier, a little later."

"In spaceships, Mick?" asked his old fishing buddy, Arnold

Makepeace. It was a fine spring morning, and already turning hot.

"They might not've needed 'em," suggested Elihu Manners, the town's oldest black citizen—one of four. "Could've been able to fly here with their wings. That'd work."

"Not in outer space, Elihu," protested Jack Cramer, who had a PhD in math and had come to Deer Crossing twenty years ago in the wake of some academic scandal. Now pushing seventy, he had become the Town Intellectual, and in that capacity was expected to challenge everything he heard, saw, or was told. "Wings flapping won't do any good in outer space. You need air to make flapping wings work."

"Maybe they didn't flap them. Maybe they coasted like buzzards," said old Mick, gamely continuing. "Could be that dragons wasn't really *dragons*, not meaning like animals, but maybe they was the spaceships of the aliens." His own, old, faded-hazel eyes lit at the possibilities.

"Why would any species intelligent enough to go into space make a ship that looks like a dragon? What would the design achieve?" Jack asked at his most reasonable.

"Why should we make spaceships that look like humongous hard-ons?" asked Arnold Makepeace. He was enjoying himself thoroughly, as he did every morning when this group assembled for coffee and conversation.

"They made 'em the way they liked them, the way that they worked best." Mick thrust his jaw out pugnaciously.

Ruthie, who had inherited the place from her brother Sam nine years back, refilled all their coffee cups, flirting with Jack as she did. She put out a small tray of doughnuts. "Take your pick, guys." She relied on their presence as the pacing of her day. Two hours every morning after the breakfast crowd was gone, these five or six men would gather and keep the place occupied until shortly before lunch.

Arnold Makepeace took the single jelly doughnut and stuffed

half of it into his mouth, leaving a trail of red on the underside of his moustache. Ever since he retired from his job at the mine, he had stuck to his routine of a single jelly doughnut in the morning, with coffee. He was trying to say something more but could not speak around the mass, so contented himself with chewing.

"Listen," Mick went on, his enthusiasm increasing, "can you think of another way to account for all those legends of dragons, all over the world? Why should all those ancient cultures think up huge, flying, *noisy* lizards if they hadn't seen one. There weren't many big lizards, flying or grounded, in Europe, not after the Ice Age, anyway." He took a hasty slurp of coffee and went on. "They had to have seen something like that to start talking about one. And those dragons in China, the Chinese dolled 'em up differently, but they're sure as hell the same critter."

"Or spaceship," said Jack, laughing in spite of himself. "I tell you, Mick, you are a very inventive fellow. Too bad we didn't have you in the paleontology department back at CNSU."

"Paleontology, shit," said Ben Horner, the old contractor who still occasionally put up a new building in town and who rarely said more than a dozen words in a whole day. "Anthropology, maybe, or creative writing."

The others laughed at this, even Mick, who was good-natured about the ribbing he took for his interests.

"Okay," said Jack as he finished his coffee, "why should creatures who looked like or who traveled in ships shaped like what we call dragons come here? What would we have to offer that they should visit this planet?"

"How can we figure out what aliens think?" asked Arnold, and was endorsed by Elihu.

"Sure. Maybe it'll tell us why we don't got tourists comin' here." He reached for a last doughnut and left three dollars on the table at the same time. " 'Bout time to get on with it."

"That it is," said Jack, leaving three-fifty for Ruthie as he stood up. He reached for his neat straw hat to put over his bald head. He nodded to Mick. "I'm looking forward to what you come up with tomorrow."

"Thanks," said Mick, and it was impossible to tell whether he was being sarcastic or genuine.

"See you fellas tomorrow," Ruthie called out as they went out into the street.

▼▼▼

These days, Mick spent most of his afternoons wandering around the abandoned junkyard on the north side of the Deer Crossing. He had convinced himself that there had been a major Indian settlement there, three or four thousand years ago, and that they were somehow connected with dragons. He knew he could discover proof of this if he kept looking.

As he picked his way between rusted frames of automobiles that had rolled off production lines half a century ago he was whistling to himself; he moved aside the fragmented treads of sixty-year-old tractors. The shine of broken glass made the dusty earth shimmer, which only served to increase his certainty that there was something very special about this place. "It's like things were left out here as . . . offerings," he had suggested to Jack Cramer two months ago.

"For the dragons," Jack had suggested, to save Mick the trouble.

"Right. *Right.*" Mick had grinned at this implied endorsement. "That's just it. I bet the Indians did the same thing."

Jack had tried to interject a note of reason. "But the Indians used to stay out of here. You know what the Papagos and the Western Pueblos say about this region. And the Navajos now avoid the place."

"I know; it isn't a good place to live," Mick had responded at once. "That's my *point.* There was something *here*, something they respected and feared. They wouldn't have anything to stay away from if there weren't a good reason for it, don't you see? The Indians are very pragmatic people. They don't go where it's dangerous to be, where bad things can happen to them. And they don't try to make sense out of everything, they just accept what it is." His determination had caught Jack's attention in spite of himself.

"I see what you're driving at," he had said, and gave up the debate as useless. "Good luck with it." By which he meant he washed his hands of the whole thing, though he offered one parting shot. "Most Indians don't have dragon myths, you know."

"Aztecs have flying serpents, and the Navajos have a great winged lizard," Mick reminded him.

Recalling this encounter, Mick felt renewed energy and purpose as he moved some of the wreckage aside, watching for snakes and scorpions as he did. It wouldn't do to get poisoned while he worked to unearth the secret. He was confident it could not be long now before he found it, the proof that would show them all that dragons had been here.

At the north end of the junkyard the oldest cars surrendered to oblivion, and it was here that Mick came, his determination so great that he almost quivered with purpose. He found his way to where a Model A and a Model T Ford leaned together, their frames partially collapsed against one another. The sight of these two always brought a touch of sadness to Mick, as if he were watching two ancient comrades leaning on one another even in death, soldiers fallen together in battle. He went to the hood of the Model T and carefully tried to move the door aside.

A shriek of rusted metal rose like the howl of an injured animal.

Mick jumped back, swearing as he did, and fell heavily against the front fender of a black de Soto. It nearly knocked the wind out of him, and he sat there, dazed, for several minutes, attempting to gather his wits once again.

Then he noticed something under his hand, and he brushed

away the dust to see it better. It was a curved section of metal, about as wide as his palm and much the same shape. It shone in the brilliant sunlight, as if it had been dropped there yesterday, for there was no sign of rust or dent in the metal. Puzzled, Mick turned it over and noticed a kind of engraving on the back—at least he thought it was the back—in what might be Arabic script, or ornamentation, or the result of sand scouring the metal. He pondered it, and then slipped it into his pocket. He would show it to Jack Cramer later and find out what it was.

He got to his feet and began to walk past the old Fords, making his way with care toward the bits of rubble strewn across the desert. "Something's here, I know it." He shaded his eyes and squinted, and looked for irregularities in the ground. He had read somewhere that late in the day and early in the morning you could see things on the flat of the desert that would not show up except when the shadows were long. He had a good two hours to sunset and he was determined to make the most of them. With great determination he began to trudge his way around the limits of the junkyard, pausing from time to time to peer narrowly at the expanse of pale tan dust, looking for any-thing casting a shadow, no matter how insignificant. Once the sun dropped below the horizon, he would have to wait until the next evening to continue his search, and this gave him the impe-tus to keep at his self-appointed task. Every rock, every bit of half-buried gear, every hillock or hump in the sand was investigated.

Mick was not easily discouraged; he had the tenacity of one who knows he is right. His painstaking effort brought no reward that day, nor the next, nor the next.

Then, as the usual gang gathered for their morning coffee and conversation, he remembered the odd piece of metal, and he fumbled in his fishing-vest pocket for it, holding it out so the others could see it. "Well, what do you make of that, eh?" he challenged them all.

"It's metal," said Jack, glancing at it once. "Where'd you find it?" Then he went on without giving Mick a chance to answer. "Out in the junkyard, right?"

"Right," said Mick with a tight grin. "Not rusted or nothing. It was under the sand. Looks something like a *scale*, doesn't it?" He took a long sip of coffee to show his satisfaction at his discovery.

"It could be a scale, or a medallion off a bumper," said Jack, turning the thing over in his hand. "It's very light. No obvious corrosion." He lifted the thing and angled it this way and that. "The incising seems to be regular, of a uniform depth." Now he frowned. "Do you mind if I show this to the guys at the assayers office?"

Mick's attitude was cordial to a fault; he nearly bowed on his stool. "Go right ahead, Doc. Be my guest, and welcome. Just tell me what they say when they're done, no matter what it is. And make sure I get it back." He smacked his lips before he bit into a doughnut. "Ruthie, another round of these for my friends. On me."

Ruthie shook her head in disbelief and rolled her eyes upward in good-natured resignation. "All right," she said. "Whatever you want, Mick."

"And see that they all get their favorites. Let Elihu have one of those cream-cheese things he likes so well." He was feeling magnanimous, relishing the success he anticipated with the metal. "I bet those assayers can't identify that metal, Jack."

"Don't bet on it," said Jack, who was willing to indulge Mick only so far. "But it would be interesting to know what it is." Metallurgy was not his field, but he had a healthy respect for what the assay office could do, and he doubted this lightweight metal would offer them much of a challenge.

Ruthie put down the cream roll Mick had ordered for Elihu.

"Thank you kindly," said Elihu, who had been listening with a growing sense of excitement. "Say, Mick, when you go back out there, could you use some help?"

"You mean in looking for more of those things?" he asked. "I sure could."

"Think I'll tag along with you, then," said Elihu, and took a healthy bite of his roll.

"Good Lord, now we'll have to listen to two of 'em," moaned Arnold Makepeace, throwing his hands up in dismay before helping himself to a second jelly doughnut.

▼▼▼

Bill Eli was waiting at the edge of the junkyard when Mick drove up with Elihu the next day. As usual, he was dressed in jeans and a flannel shirt, wearing a silver-belly Stetson and boots from Roper Sam. His Navajo features looked almost Korean. He leaned against his Jeep Renegade and motioned Mick over to him. "You're poking around again," he said, no condemnation in his voice.

"Yep," said Mick with pride. "And I got some help now."

"It's not a safe thing to do," Bill Eli told him, his tone level and unthreatening.

"Has been so far," said Mick.

Bill stared out over the desert. "You're taking a big risk, Michael." He only used Mick's given name when he was determined to make a point.

"I'm not afraid, William," Mick responded, turning to wink at Elihu.

"Don't get cheeky on me, my friend," said Bill. "The Papagos don't like you messing around out here. This land is considered dangerous by their people and mine. And I'm concerned for your welfare.'

"Well, I thank you for your trouble, but you got no call to be worried about me. All that's out here is Tin Lizzies. Everyone knows that. Everyone says so." He indicated the bed of his pickup. "No shovels back here. Just brooms. You tell the Papagos that I won't bother the old gods sleeping under the desert."

"Tin Lizzies." Bill glanced toward the pickup and sighed in exasperation. "You could be messing with things you can't handle, Michael. And that's all I'm going to say to you." He climbed into his Renegade and started the engine. "But if you get into trouble out here, remember you're on your own."

"Fine by me," said Mick, and signaled Elihu to join him as he watched Bill drive off, leaving a swirling wake of dust.

"Navajos're superstitious," said Elihu as he reached into the back of the pickup for one of the brooms. "Everyone knows that."

Mick shook his head, his eyes narrowing as he looked out over the junkyard. "They *know* something about this place, the Navajos and Papagos. And they don't want anyone else to find out. That's why they didn't mind when the town put the junkyard out here. They figured it'd cover up whatever it is that's down here." His face shone with purpose. "But we'll find out what's going on here."

"You bet," said Elihu, but with less enthusiasm than Mick showed.

▼▼▼

"We got another half-dozen of those metal things," Mick boasted over coffee two days later. "Elihu and me, we just kept sweeping until we found some more, all laid out nice and proper, like a kind of river under the sand."

There was a single, vertical frown line between Jack's brows at this announcement. "You found them in the same place?"

"Out in the junkyard, at the north end," Mick confirmed smugly. "Thirty-seven of the things, in a real nice pattern, like they was laid down special. And tomorrow I'm going out there again and look for more of 'em."

"Why not today?" asked old Ben Horner, breaking his usual silence earlier than usual in their meetings.

"Today I want to find out if I can fit these things together, make 'em go back into the pattern I saw out there. The way we found them, it looked like they could do it, in a nice, neat pattern, you know, like *part* of something." He chuckled in anticipation. "Like scales, maybe, on a dragon."

"Not *that* again," Ruthie exclaimed as she poured more coffee. "Don't you *ever* get tired of that old saw?"

"Did you take any photographs of how they looked?" asked Jack. His frown had deepened as he listened.

"Nope; never thought of it. Didn't have a camera," said Mick, and gave Jack a chagrined look. "I guess we should've."

"It might be useful," said Jack slowly.

"For Lord o' Mercy, don't encourage him," exclaimed Arnold Makepeace, who had been listening to all this in skeptical delight. "Things are bad enough as they are, with him exploring around those Tin Lizzies. He'll get it into his head that he's got a major discovery out there, and none of us will be able to stand his crowing about it."

Mick shrugged, and then asked slyly, "What did the assay office have to say, Jack?"

This question caused Jack Cramer some consternation. "I haven't heard back from them yet," he admitted.

"Thought so," Mick declared. "They can't figure out what the metal is, right?"

"I don't know," said Jack, knowing all the while that the report was long overdue. Ordinarily this would not bother him, but now it gave him a qualm or two. "Think I'll call over there this afternoon and find out what's holding them up."

"You do that," approved Mick. "And let me know what they tell you."

"You'll be the first to know," said Jack, who was suddenly uncomfortable with the entire subject. "If you do any more exploring, take pictures."

"Told you—I don't have a camera," said Mick, dismissing the suggestion lightly.

"You can borrow mine," Arnold offered. "It's got about twelve exposures left on the roll. You can have those. If you want to take more, buy your own film. Then we can get this settled."

"That's mighty generous of you, Arnold," said Mick, pleased that his fishing buddy was taking his project so seriously. "If you'll bring it with you tomorrow morning, I'll take it out to the *site* with me. I'll get all the evidence I need to convince you Doubting Thomases. You can see for yourselves what it looks like."

"*Anything* to settle this thing, so we can get back to the way things were before," said Arnold, who missed his fishing expeditions with Mick. "It focuses itself, does all the adjustments. All you got to do is point it and push the button. You don't have to know any more than that. Just point it and shoot. Don't fuss with any of the knobs or the focus, or anything. I got it set on automatic."

"Sounds good to me," said Mick, anticipating success.

"Anyone see the news last night?" asked Miles Hawthorne, the oldest of the men, who was now over ninety and as active in mind as he was frail in body. He was anxious to change the subject to something he found interesting.

"Nope," said Arnold. "Why don't you tell us all about it?" His question was laconic and rhetorical. He sat back and prepared to listen to Miles rail at whatever governmental shenanigans had been reported the evening before.

▼▼▼

Jack Cramer was not at the Sagebrush Diner the next morning. "He's gone over to the county seat," Ruthie told the others. "Called here before he left. Said he'd be back tomorrow or the next day."

"Assay office is at the county seat," Mick said, lifting his head in pride.

"There're lots of reasons he could go there," Arnold reminded him. "He's a Pee-aich-dee, and he could have things to do there, like research, or—"

"He's gone to the assay office," said Mick, fully confident he was right. "When he gets back, he'll tell us what the report is on that dragon scale I found." He had a second doughnut in celebration of this vindication of his theory.

"It's *not* a dragon scale," said Arnold, who was tiring of the game. "It's just some piece of metal that fell off one of the old cars, that's all." He was sorry now he had remembered to bring his camera. He was getting tired of indulging his friend in his lunacy.

"Then what is it?" Mick challenged, enjoying himself hugely. "If it was off a car, why wasn't it rusted?" Why weren't any of 'em rusted?"

"Maybe there's a coating on 'em," suggested Ben Horner. "We got all kinds of coatings for metals."

"Sure. Now. But back when the old Model As and Ts were out there, they rusted up real good. Go out and look at 'em for yourself if you don't believe me," said Mick. "You wait and see. Jack will have a report that makes it plain these things weren't anything that ought to be in that junkyard."

"How can you be so sure?" asked Ruthie, who rarely interjected such a question. "I mean, why does it have to be dragons?"

"Because I *open* my eyes. I don't start off saying: this stuff can't be there, so it has to be something other than it is. I look around and try to see what's *there*, not what I expect to be there."

"But you admit you're looking for proof that dragons existed," said Arnold. "That means you look for them, doesn't it? Which makes you as bad as the others you're complaining about." He folded his arms and looked deep into his coffee as Ruthie refilled his cup and handed him the metal creamer.

"Because I have my eyes open enough to see there *had* to be dragons." He braced his elbows on the counter and leaned forward. "If you just stop trying to make the dragons something they're not, and understand that they're dragons, real dragons, then you know there has to be some record of them somewhere." He tossed his head.

"But here in Deer Crossing," protested Ben Horner.

"That's just *it*! Everywhere else they've been lost. Cities got built on top of 'em, or rivers changed course and drowned them, or they fell into the sea, or they got broke up in earthquakes and tornadoes and tidal waves. If there's any record left at all, it would *have* to be a place like this, where nothing's disturbed the land for generations."

"Ain't it convenient that you just happened to go looking for 'em here in Deer Crossing? They might have been somewhere like the jungles of the Amazon," said Arnold, trying not to be disgusted.

"They probably are there, too, but no one's found 'em," said Mick, undaunted. "You wait until Jack gets back. We'll hear something. I bet those scales cause real scientists to get curious." He stood up, putting on his old straw hat. "I'm going back out there now. Anyone want to come with me? Elihu?"

"Don't think so, Mick," said Elihu apologetically. "I don't like the feel of that place."

"You mean Bill Eli scared you off?" asked Mick in disbelief. "With all that Navajo superstition?"

"Nope. Not him. The place is . . . eerie. Indians don't like it for a *reason*; and I respect that. I don't want to go back out." He shook his head to punctuate his refusal. "I don't think you should go out there, either."

Mick laughed aloud. "Old places don't spook me, Elihu. I'm kind of surprised it scared you. Nothing but Tin Lizzies, right?"

"And them things in the sand," muttered Elihu unhappily.

"Yeah," said Mick, his eyes shining. He reached for Arnold's camera. "Jack's right. Pictures'll help. I know, just point and shoot. Don't mess with the settings." He tossed a five-dollar bill onto the counter and headed out the door, leaving the others staring after him in puzzlement and dismay.

"Mick McCullough is a crazy man," said Arnold.

"Wonder what it'll be after he's finished with dragons," mused Elihu.

"Don't ask," said Ben Horner.

▼▼▼

"They say the Papagos had a legend of things like dragons," Mick announced to the air at large as he began to sweep at the hard earth, looking for more of the strange, scale-shaped pieces of shiny metal under the junkyard. He had chosen the stretch of land just beyond the place where he had found the few bits of metal before; the area he hoped was most likely to yield something of interest covered a little less than a quarter of an acre, big enough to include many possibilities, but small enough to be workable for one seventy-three-year-old man. He was panting, in part from eagerness, in part from his own satisfaction with the job he had set for himself. Exertion had not yet caught up with him, but would as the sun rose higher over the hard land. "It wouldn't surprise me at all to learn they had stories about visitors from far away. Strange visitors." He noticed a lizard skittering away from the widening swath of his broom's path, and chuckled, thinking it a fine joke that such a creature would be witness to his activities. "You keep at it, you lizard. I'm gonna find one of your ancestors, or something like one." He pushed his hat back on his head and took his dark glasses out of his shirt pocket. He hated wearing anything that could impede his vision, but at the height of the day the reflection off the desert was blinding.

In an hour he was sweating freely and his back was sore with the effort he demanded of himself. He paused to drink more of the water he carried, his face flushed with the effort of his activity. "I don't know," he muttered to the blank sky. "It has to be here. I can feel it in my *bones*."

By noon the relentless sun forced him to stop his labors and drove him into the shelter where he busied himself reading the most recently acquired book in his collection, an account of the sightings of unusual creatures throughout history. The style was popular and credulous, but Mick loved it, saying that amidst the most sensationalized accounts a grain of truth would remain to make the effort of digging for it worthwhile. He napped in the comfortless seat of his pickup, and woke in the middle of the afternoon, when the worst of the heat was past and the air felt like a dragon's hot breath scorching over the land.

He had swept another large plot of earth, and it was nearing sundown, when he caught the glint of sun off shiny metal. With a shout of gratification, he discovered his fatigue had vanished and he was able to redouble his efforts, sweeping away the hard-packed dust until he had revealed a long, sinuous pattern in the sand, the impression of a long, snaky tail so overwhelming that he stared at it, his eyes bright with unshed tears as he began to walk up and down the length of his find.

Belatedly he remembered the camera in his pickup, and hurried back to get it, fumbling with the lens cap as he rushed to take his pictures while the sun was still making the pattern shiny and clear. Peering through the viewfinder, he could not get the scales to show up the way he wanted, so he fiddled with the focus, to make it as sharp as he could, and did his best to change the exposure time to make the most of the shine off the metal; he shot the entire roll, and cursed himself for not buying more film before coming out to the junkyard. "Next time," he promised himself, wishing now he had had the foresight to bring a six-pack as well. He wanted to celebrate as much as he wanted to cool off.

He climbed back into his truck half an hour after sunset, trying to make sure he had got pictures of everything he had unearthed. Let the guys at the Sagebrush Diner laugh at him now, he thought, ready to crow at his accomplishments. "They're gonna get the shock of their lives when they see these pictures. They'll be laughing out of the other side of their mouths." With a victorious whoop, he drove off in the general direction of the highway, making his way between heaps of discarded appliances and abandoned cars, paying little attention to anything more than avoiding them in the fast-encroaching darkness.

▼▼▼

Jack Cramer was waiting for Mick when he arrived for his morning coffee and conversation, a deep frown puckering his brow. "I have to talk to you," he said, keeping his voice low so that the others would not overhear their conversation. "Not here."

"Okay, but I got to get back out to the junkyard this afternoon." Feeling proud of himself he added, "You might want to come out with me, and have a look around. No telling what you could find there."

Jack did not laugh. "I might," he said grimly, his eyes hardening.

"Good." Mick approved, and went to sit on the stool next to Arnold. "Thanks for the loan of the camera," he said by way of opening. "It came in real handy yesterday."

"You found something?" Arnold said with a wink to Elihu at his side.

"You bet I did," Mick declared, loudly enough that even Ruthie looked at him.

"All right," said Arnold, knowing what was expected of him. "Let's hear the whole fish story. What did you find?"

"More scales. 'Cause that's what those are," he said, sounding a bit defensive in spite of his best intentions. "There's a whole tail out there, I bet, just lying there under the dirt. Still nice and shiny. That's what I got pictures of yesterday."

"Good for you," said Arnold, no longer able to prod his old friend.

"I took the film by the pharmacy on my way here. So you can all have a look day after tomorrow. And then you'll see." He held up his cup to salute his friends. "You won't be able to dismiss dragons as myths again."

"If you're so certain they're scales, you might want to dig a few more up," said Miles Hawthorne, wheezing as he chortled at the idea. "Better do it fast, though; they said on the news last night we could be in for a real storm tonight: rain, wind, all of it."

Ben Horner swore. "I got to get that roof finished over at the all-night store. I don't need bad weather now."

Mick had paled. "When's the storm supposed to get here?"

"They're saying late afternoon, but you know what they're like at the weather bureau," Ruthie told them all. "I'd say we won't have any real rain until near sundown."

"God, this is terrible," Mick whispered, staring down into his cup, his face set into deep lines of distress.

"Can't be helped," Arnold said. "And if you really got something out there, it'll last a bit longer. According to you, it's been there for thousands of years."

"Yeah," said Mick with emotion. "But *protected*. Under the sand. I dug it up, and now anything could happen to it. I have to make sure it's not lost." He drank the last of his coffee in sudden decision and stood up. "I better get out there right now, do what I can to make sure it doesn't wash away."

"But what?" asked Elihu. "I seen how big that thing is. You ain't gonna have time to cover it all up, no sir."

"Maybe, maybe not," said Mick in real determination. "I don't know what I'll do yet, but I gotta try. I gotta do *something*." He tossed three bucks onto the counter, grabbed up his hat and started for the door.

Jack Cramer intercepted him. "We have to talk. Today, Mick. It's urgent."

"So's protecting my dragon," he said, and pushed past the retired professor.

"Now what?" asked Ben Horner, in mild irritation.

"Somebody better call Bill Eli," said Ruthie, trying to come up with a practical suggestion. "He should be able to do something."

"That's right," Miles approved. "Get the Indians on it." He reached out with palsied hands for another doughnut, enjoying himself hugely.

"He's over at the Public Lands office, isn't he?" said Arnold. "Think I'll mosey on over and have a word or two with him after we finish up here."

"I'm going after Mick," Jack Cramer announced, leaving his second doughnut unfinished, to the amazement of his friends.

"Did you ever see the like?" said Miles.

"Don't think the professor's given up on a doughnut in twenty years, 'cept that time when he had that flu thing." Arnold deliberately turned away from the window so he would not have to watch Jack drive off in his Trooper II.

"It's probably something about the assay office," said Ben, biting into his second doughnut. He rested his elbows on the counter. "He don't want to embarrass Mick, talking to him about it where we can all hear."

"How do you figure that?" asked Elihu, accepting more coffee and adding extra cream to it. He was beginning to feel oddly guilty about leaving Mick on his own. " 'Bout it being embarrassing, I mean."

"Probably the metal is some kind of hoax—you know, a fake thing put out there to fool someone like Mick." Ben shrugged, as if uncomfortable at talking so much.

"But who'd *do* that?" asked Elihu with increasing apprehension.

"I don't know; Indians, maybe," said Ben, and fell silent.

"Don't make much sense to me," Miles remarked. "Arnold, you know Mick best: what'd he want out of a fake dragon?"

Arnold hunched his shoulders higher. "I don't think Mick

wants a fake anything. If he thinks there's a dragon—" the word came awkwardly and he coughed after he said it "—he wants it to be the real thing. If he found out it was fake, it'd bother him a lot." He took a long sip of coffee. "And he'd find something else to get hooked on."

"That's it then," said Elihu. "Someone's trying to get him off the dragon thing."

"But why?" asked Arnold, who was fast coming to dislike the whole thing. "What would be the *point*?"

"Maybe someone doesn't want him poking around in the junkyard?" said Miles, and warmed to his own notion. "Maybe someone's got something hidden out there they don't want anyone to find."

"Like what?" asked Elihu.

"I don't know. Money, maybe." Miles rubbed his hands together. "Back in Prohibition times, didn't some of the old gangsters used to hide out here from time to time? Maybe some of 'em brought something with them, and hid it where they junked their cars. Maybe someone knows about it and doesn't want an old coot like Mick looking around, because he might find something they'd just as soon keep secret."

"You were here in the Twenties," Ruthie pointed out to Miles. "You ever hear of anything like that when you were a kid?"

Miles shook his head slowly. "Can't say as I did. But folks around here kept pretty mum about the gangsters. They was 'fraid of 'em, don't you know. Indians might know something. Kept to themselves back then." He finished his coffee, got off his stool and reached for his cane. "Those Tin Lizzies out there in the old junkyard belonged to gangsters, though. That's what I heard when I was a kid."

Arnold defiantly ate a third doughnut.

▼▼▼

Huge cumulus clouds were piling up overhead, great castles in the sky. Dark on the underside, they glistened white where they towered over the desert. A wind had sprung up in the last hour that was growing stronger as the morning slid into afternoon.

Jack Cramer found Mick McCullough busily trying to gather up all the shining metal he could find, stacking it in the rusted remains of the Model A and Model T. He was working at a furious pace, and did not welcome Jack's intrusion.

"Can't stop now, Doc," said Mick, breathing hard as he bent over, scooping another four of the scalelike metal plates into his hands.

Jack saw that Mick's knuckles were bleeding and his nails were ragged. "You want any help?"

"Depends on what you mean," said Mick. "Trouble is, this is just the top part of the dragon. The rest is still underground." He stumbled as one scale stuck hard in the earth.

"I mean I think you may have something worth investigating here." His answer was meant to be cautious, but it caused Mick to stop working and grin.

"You mean that I'm right? That there's something weird about this metal?" Mick's satisfaction was tremendous. "They told you it couldn't come from Earth, right?"

"Not exactly," said Jack with the same circumspection he had encountered at the assay office. "They did say that the alloy was one they had not encountered before. It's the Cesium content that has them a little puzzled."

" 'A little puzzled'," Mick quoted with intense pleasure as he pulled another scale from the earth. "You mean they're flummoxed."

"I mean they're puzzled," Jack insisted, moving out of the way as Mick carried another armload back to the rusted out cars and shoved the scales through the empty windows. "They're talking about coming out to investigate this site."

"They could be a little late," said Mick. "If I don't get these things dug up."

"Let them take care of it, Mick," Jack recommended, looking upward at the thickening clouds. "It's gonna pour."

"Think I don't know that?" Mick challenged. "It's the dragon-makers. It's how they keep the ships hidden. When someone uncovers enough of the ship, it starts sending a signal, and they do something about it." He had a fixed determination about him now.

"Mick," Jack said, attempting to be reasonable, "you know yourself these low washes can be dangerous in a rainstorm. Get out of here before we have a flash flood." He pointed away toward the mountains where the first rain was falling. Thunder cracked and crumbled like a distant vehicle collision.

"I won't wait much longer," Mick assured Jack, continuing to work frantically.

"The storm'll be overhead shortly. You better leave now." He pointed as lightning cracked. "It's not safe to be around all this exposed metal."

"I'll get out of here as soon as the rain starts," he said. "If you're worried, you can leave now. Let me get on with this."

Reluctantly, Jack left Mick at his desperate, self-imposed task, and made his way to the place he had left his Trooper. He found Bill Eli waiting there, arms crossed.

"He's still at it, isn't he?" Bill asked.

"Yes," said Jack.

"I guess it's useless to order him out of there," said Bill, squinting as the first spattering of rain struck.

"I guess; I couldn't," said Jack as he hastily scrambled into the Trooper and started the engine. Without waiting to see what Bill Eli might do, he shoved the gears into first and drove away.

Bill Eli waited a bit longer, then, as the break between lightning and thunder narrowed, he, too, left the old junkyard.

▼▼▼

"Shame about Mick," said Miles the next week as the men gathered at the Sagebrush Diner for the first time since Mick's body was discovered, half-covered in mud at the far end of the junkyard.

"Shame, hell," said Arnold, still angry at his friend for dying so foolishly. "He knew better'n to stay there once the storm began." He had to make himself swallow his coffee against the tight constriction in his throat.

"Maybe he didn't have any choice," said Elihu, his dark eyes filling with tears. "A place like that could make a man do . . . things."

"What's that supposed to mean?" Arnold demanded. "What kind of things?"

"All kinds," Elihu muttered.

"Anyone seen the pictures he took yet?" asked Ruthie, hoping to find a bright note in the otherwise gloomy occasion.

"Yep," said Arnold. "Most of 'em're out of focus. All you can see are bright patches. Could be anything."

"Maybe broken glass," Miles confirmed. "There's lots of that out there."

Jack Cramer, who had been silent until now, said, "Cesium is an excellent conductor of electricity, and those scales he found had Cesium in them."

"And that's why he got hit by lightning?" asked Ben Horner, cocking his head to the side. "I don't believe that. Maybe it was all the metal in them Tin Lizzies. That'd do it."

"According to Mick, dragons was Tin Lizzies," said Elihu.

"Then what about what the Indians are saying?" said Arnold, stung to make a retort.

"And what's that?" asked Ruthie, offering extra doughnuts to them all.

Arnold cleared his throat. "That the dragon got him."

Only Jack Cramer did not laugh.

ULF THE WYRM
▼▼▼

LOIS TILTON

DEEP beneath the cold gray waves off the island of Hlesey
lay the gleaming hall where Aegir, the sealord, dwelled with his
wife Ran. Its roof and beams were all made of shining gold, and
carved into the lintels were the fantastic images of many beasts:
seals, fishes, monstrous whales. On the highest roof-beam of all
was carved the coiled shape of Jormungandr, the world-serpent,
greatest of all wyrms.

There were always many servants in Aegir's hall, and the lowest of these was Ulf, the thrall. All the meanest tasks were left
for him: to haul in firewood when Aegir brewed mead in his
huge cauldron, to haul the ashes out to the midden afterward.

Aegir's feasting hall was often full, with the gods and goddesses
of Asgard crowded onto the benches for mead and good fellowship. The gods all loved Aegir's bright, foaming mead!

Of course, for the servants, the feasts only meant more work,
running here and there to fill the guests' drinking horns. The
largest horn of all was reserved for the god Thor. The weight of
it was enough to make Ulf groan as he carried it, brim-full, to
the bench of the huge, red-bearded god. Thor often bragged that

he had once come close to draining the ocean, so thirsty he had been on his visit to the hall of the giant-king, Utgard-Loki.

But that was only one of Thor's many exploits. Ulf had heard them all. At every one of Aegir's feasts the gods all took their turns to boast about their adventures: the giants they had overcome, the monsters, the dragons they had slain. And when they weren't bragging, they were listening to the skalds and poets sing the songs they had made in praise of the gods and their great deeds. The more they drank, the finer the verses, for Aegir's mead had the power of inspiration.

Hearing the songs, Ulf would often dream of taking up a sword or a spear and slaying some fearsome monster—a feat to make all the poets celebrate his name. But all he ever did was run back and forth from the mead-vat to the benches, answering the incessant calls for *mead, more mead!*

▼▼▼

After one feast, when Thor had astonished all the gods with his feats of deep-drinking, Aegir looked into his mead-vats and saw that they were emptied to the very dregs. There could be no more feasts until they were refilled.

"Time to brew more mead," he announced, and shouted to Ulf, "Thrall! Bring me my net!"

Staggering under the weight, Ulf dragged the vast, knotted net to his master, and Aegir flung it over his shoulder. "While I'm gone," he ordered the thrall, "I want you to clean out the big cauldron. Scrub it inside and out. It should be gleaming bright by the time I return."

The god strode from his hall and waded out into the sea for miles and miles, until the waves rose above his knees and broke foaming against his thighs. Standing there, he cast his wide net, so broad that as it rose in the air, it cast a shadow over the sea.

Then he hauled it in, and caught up in the broad mesh were a multitude of long, dark, wriggling forms.

The sealord threw the full, dripping net over his shoulder and brought his writhing catch back to his hall. "Thrall!" he bellowed, and Ulf came running. While Aegir was gone, he had crawled into the depths of the huge cauldron to scrub away the thick, clotted dregs at the bottom. He had cleaned and polished it, inside and out, until his face was reflected in the bright surface.

Now his master tossed the heavy, dripping net at him. "Take these eels, cut off their heads, and drain the blood into the cauldron. Then gut them and toss their hearts into this basket." He frowned at the thrall like a threatening stormcloud. "There are a full nine hundred of them, and not one of their hearts must be missing when you are done."

Leaving Ulf to his gory task, the sea god went in to take his pleasure with his wife, Ran.

Sighing morosely, Ulf pulled the thrashing, sinuous length of the first eel from the god's net. It hissed and bit at him with needle-sharp teeth, and Ulf thought that it was different somehow from all the other eels he had seen. But, as his master had ordered, he cut off its head and held the writhing, slippery body as its blood spurted, seething hot, into the polished cauldron. When the blood was quite drained he slit the carcass open, but when he pulled out the eel's heart it burned his hands.

This is an uncommon eel, he thought, tossing the heart into the basket.

One after the other, he cut off the heads of the eels, until the cauldron was brimming full of blood and the basket heaped high with their nine hundred hearts. When Aegir returned to the hall the god counted the hearts jealously to make certain they were all there, and then skewered them onto a spit and placed it at the hearth to roast.

But Ulf's work was not done. Armload after armload of wood must now be brought into the hall to stoke up the fire in the pit, and after that he must sweep away the offal and carry it out to the midden while Aegir brewed his mead.

"I still think," the thrall grumbled to himself, "that these are very uncommon eels. Since when do eels have blood so seething hot, or hearts that burn at the touch? See! Even without their heads or hearts, they're still twitching, almost as if they were alive."

But as he picked up one headless, gutted carcass to toss it onto the midden, a single drop of blood fell onto the back of his hand. It was still so hot that it burned his skin, and Ulf reflexively licked at the place.

At first, his tongue felt as if it were burning, and then the heat spread throughout his entire body, until he felt light-headed. Just then a pair of gulls flew overhead, mewling, attracted to the heap of fresh offal. But, to his surprise, Ulf discovered that he could now understand their speech.

"Look!" cried the first gull, "a feast for us! A heap of fresh eels, already gutted."

But the second said, "Those are no eels, Brother. Those are the spawn of the Midgard serpent, the wyrm Jormungandr! And if any man, even that thrall there, would consume the heart of even one such, he would obtain wisdom beyond all measure."

Now, it is well-known that the blood of wyrms and dragons and other wise serpents has the power of bestowing wisdom. This, Ulf realized, was the secret of Aegir's inspirational mead, the mead of the gods: it was brewed from dragon's blood.

Now, also, he knew why Aegir had ordered him to save the dragons' hearts, why the sealord had counted them so jealously. Had not the Allfather Odin hung nine days and nights to obtain wisdom? Had he not given one of his eyes for a single drink from the well of inspiration?

If I could only consume the heart of even one of these wyrms, Ulf thought to himself, *then I might become like one of the gods!*

Gathering his courage, the thrall crept back into Aegir's hall. There the sealord, bare-chested and sweating from the heat, was standing over the huge steaming cauldron, stirring the mead as it boiled and seethed over the fire. But on the spit above the hearth, the nine hundred dragon hearts were roasting. Ulf smelled the savory aroma and licked his lips, but he feared his master's wrath.

Yet, he told himself, *Aegir counted all the hearts as he skewered them on the spit. Surely he will not count them again.*

But just as he reached the hearth where the hearts were roasting, Aegir looked down at him and bellowed, "What are you doing, Thrall?"

Ulf felt himself shaking in fear, but he ducked his head as a thrall must do, and said, "Sweeping the ashes, Master, as you ordered."

"Oh," said the god, and he turned his attention back to his bubbling cauldron.

Ulf took up his broom and plied it industriously, but when he was certain that Aegir's head was turned away, he bent down and plucked one of the dragon hearts from the spit where they were roasting.

Oh, how it burned his hand! But Ulf clutched it tightly and would not let go. As soon as he was out of his master's sight, he put the dragon heart in his mouth and swallowed it whole. Once again, he felt as if he had swallowed living fire. Then his mind reeled as he came to understand all the lore of the great wyrms: the mysteries of storms and tides, the secrets of transformation and flight.

He now had the power to become, not a god, but a wyrm himself!

Hurrying to the midden, he pulled the largest carcass he could find from the heap and skinned the wyrm carefully. Then he flung the cloak of dragonskin over his shoulders, and in that instant he was transformed. He, Ulf the thrall, was now a mighty wyrm!

Exulting, he plunged into the sea. His sinuous, powerful body swam smoothly, cleaving the waves. His mighty head rose above the foam. Soon he had left the island of Hlesey and Aegir's hall far behind him.

Ulf gloried in his new form. No longer a thrall, he feared no creature in the sea. Even the whales regarded him with respect. When he was hungry, all he had to do was snatch a fish from the water, or a seal. How much better than the constant drudgery of his previous life!

And yet, Ulf thought to himself, *there could be more. There could be riches, gold.* He imagined himself in a great hall of his own, on a high seat, with gold rings on his arms and around his neck. Gold heaped up at his feet. Poets singing verses in praise of his might. Thralls scurrying to heap logs onto his roaring fire. And bare-armed maidens to fill his drinking horn with foaming mead.

Imagining the maidens, Ulf's mouth watered. His thoughts and lusts were half wyrm's and half man's.

Now, against the horizon ahead, he spotted the billowing square sail of a ship. Breasting the waves, he swam swiftly toward it. This was a Viking ship, with a high, carved dragonhead rising fiercely at the prow.

But a hotter ferocity burned in Ulf's heart. He reared up his head, his crest rose, and he lashed the sea with his tail. The ship's lookout saw him and cried out an alarm. The rowers bent at once to their oars, churning the sea to a white foam. The wake surged up around the stern as the longship picked up speed. But Ulf in his serpent-form was faster. Relentlessly, he bore down on the fleeing ship.

As he drew near, he could see these indeed were Vikings — grim, scarred raiders, ready to do battle. But Ulf was undismayed. It was only more likely that their ship would be filled with treasure looted from some nearby coast.

One Viking, a berserker with a thick red beard, gnawed at the rim of his sword and shook his spear, howling out a challenge to the wyrm. Then a warrior in the stern let fly an arrow at the approaching wyrm, but it shattered harmlessly against the tough scales of his neck. Ulf bellowed in rage, and the heat that smoldered in his heart erupted in a gout of flame. The Vikings cried out in alarm, but these were hardened warriors. More arrows flew toward the wyrm.

Then Ulf bellowed again, and the flames roared out of his mouth, catching the longship's sail. In moments, it was blazing like a torch. Even then, the oarsmen continued to pull, while the rest of the Vikings bent their bows or stood ready with swords and spears.

Ulf lashed his tail and struck the longboat's hull amidships. Strakes splintered and broke, oars were shattered, and the hungry sea poured in through the breach. Waves tumbled the broken bodies of rowers and the once-proud carved dragonhead that had stood at the prow.

But where it had been, the berserker stood with his legs braced, drew back his arm and flung his spear with the desperate strength of battle-madness. The broad iron blade penetrated Ulf's scales, and his hot blood spurted. The wyrm thrashed his tail in pain and rage, striking the ship again, and the impact sent men flying into the water, where the cold gray waves claimed them. Then Ulf reared up with the spear still piercing his neck and seized the berserker in his jaws. The Viking only had an instant to cry out to Odin to receive his soul in Valhalla before the wyrm's maw closed on him.

By that time the longship was a shattered hulk, with the burned rags of its sails dangling from the broken yard. Drowning men struggled as the weight of their armor dragged them down, and soon the broken ship capsized and sank. Whatever treasure it had held now rested on the seabed.

▼▼▼

When Aegir, in his hall, had finished brewing his mead, he took the spit full of dragon hearts from the hearth where they had roasted and heaped them onto a platter. He counted as he consumed every savory mouthful, but when he had finished eight hundred and ninety-nine, the platter was empty. Then a hot rage seized him, for the nine hundredth heart was missing.

At once, he shouted for his thrall, but Ulf never answered his summons. Then the sealord knew who had stolen his dragon heart. He took up his net and his spear and strode out into the open sea, vowing to avenge his loss. With each step he took, vast waves surged up, capsizing boats, drowning harbors. He cast his net far and wide, dragging the seafloor, bringing up sunken ships and the drowned bodies of sailors. Great fish filled his net, and spouting whales, but Aegir tossed them all aside.

But whenever his net caught up one of the Midgard serpent's spawn, he thrust his spear through its heart, hoping each time to discover his treacherous, thieving thrall. But each time, the wyrm turned out to be only a wyrm, writhing and dying on the end of his spear. Nine hundred times nine hundred, one after the other, he dragged them from the depths of the sea, stabbed them to the heart, until the sea boiled red and hot with their blood.

But the seas of the world are vast. And in the deepest, darkest trenches of the seafloor, the Midgard serpent lay: Jormungandr, second-born of Loki, the fire-giant, the shape-changer, the sky-traveller. The gods had cast him down into Midgard, the world of men, there to grow until his length encircled the whole earth.

Now, when the seething blood of his spawn began to fill the seas, the father of all wyrms released his tail from his jaws and lifted his head. All was not well. His offspring were being slaughtered.

Slowly, the vast form of the world-serpent rose. The seabed groaned and cracked, mountains split, and tidal waves rose up to engulf the coasts of Midgard. Jormungandr's head broke the surface of the water, looking like a monstrous island, dripping with weeds. Then his neck rose to the level of the clouds, until he could survey all the seas that lay below. And there he saw Aegir, the sealord, casting his net into the waves.

Aegir was mighty among the gods, but Jormungandr's girth was greater than the trunk of the world-tree, and his strength was such that even the powerful Thor had twice been unable to defeat him. Now the wyrm loomed over Aegir, and his breath was a flaming, poisonous gale. "The seas of Midgard are red. They boil with the blood of my spawn. What do you here, little god, with your net and spear?"

Aegir trembled at the hideous sight of the world-serpent. He felt it best that Jormungandr did not learn how he brewed mead for the gods. "I am seeking a treacherous thrall. He has killed a wyrm and eaten its heart. Now he flees from me in dragon form, using its skin as a cloak."

Then, in his anger, the huge wyrm lashed his tail. The Earth trembled, molten rock and fire burst forth from its depths, and even the gates of Asgard shook, so that the gods in their golden halls looked at each other and said, "The serpent is restless."

But Jormungandr only said, "I will find this thrall."

▼▼▼

Now, Ulf had tasted man-flesh and decided that he liked it well. Ship after ship he attacked, until even the boldest Vikings would no longer venture out onto the seas for fear of the wyrm. Now he had a rich hall, filled with the gold he had plundered from the sunken longships. Thralls he had in plenty, who brought him maidens to devour, for men in their terror had offered them in sacrifice, to save themselves from his fiery wrath.

But Jormungandr, who knew his own spawn, searched all of Midgard until he found Ulf's hall. Then he rose up, until his vast girth blotted out the sun.

In the sudden darkness, Ulf trembled. His servants fled, screaming as Jormungandr tore the roof from his hall and exposed him, coiled among his heap of gold.

"Miserable thrall!" the world-serpent roared, and the beams

of the hall burst into flame from the heat of his breath. "You are no spawn of mine!"

The vast monster opened his jaws to devour him, but Ulf in his fear transformed his fins into wings and took flight. High he flew, and swiftly, far from the flaming ruins of his hall. Men below cried out in terror at the sight of the fiery wyrm flying overhead.

But Aegir the sealord also saw the wyrm in flight. He cast his net high, into the clouds, and Ulf was caught up in the thick mesh. His wings were trapped, and no matter how he twisted and writhed, he could not break free, for no living being can escape the sea god's net.

Then Ulf fell into the sea, and Aegir brought up the net with its catch entangled in the mesh. "Thieving, treacherous thrall!" he said, holding the tip of his spear above the wyrm's heart, ready to flay the skin from him.

Ulf thrashed desperately, but he was held tight and could not escape. As the god's spear pierced his skin, he tore off his dragon-skin cloak, and once again he was only Ulf the thrall, weeping and pleading for mercy.

But Aegir closed one hand around Ulf's belly and squeezed it tight until the dragon heart burst out of his mouth and fell into the sea. Then he brought him back to his hall beneath the waves, and there he beat his thrall with the spit from the hearth, until Ulf could barely crawl.

While he had been gone, plundering the seas in dragon-form, a vast mountain of ashes had built up in Aegir's firepit. Now, as his punishment, Ulf must sweep them all up and carry them to the midden outside the hall, and the heap of ashes was so high that he is still at the task, even to this day.

SHORT STRAWS
▼▼▼

KEVIN J. ANDERSON

YES, a dragon was terrorizing the land, so the king had offered his daughter in marriage to any brave knight who slew the foul beast. Same old story. I was new to the band of warriors, but the others had heard it all before. This time, though, the logistics caused a problem.

"We could split a *cash* reward," said Oldahn, the battle-scarred old veteran who served as our leader. "But who gets the princess?"

The four of us sat around the fire, procrastinating. Though I was still wide-eyed to be part of the group—they had needed a new cook and errand runner—I'd already noticed that the adventurers liked to talk about peril a lot more than actually doing something about it. I was their apprentice, and I wanted for us to go out and fight, a team of mercenaries, warriors—but that didn't seem to be the way of going about it.

We knew where the dragon's lair was, having investigated every foul-smelling, bone-cluttered cave in the kingdom. But we still hadn't figured out what to do with the princess, assuming we succeeded in slaying the dragon. It didn't seem a practical sort of reward.

Reegas looked up with a half-cocked grin. "We could just take turns with her!"

Oldahn sighed. "One does not treat a princess the way you treat one of your hussies, Reegas."

Reegas scowled, scratching the stubble on his chin. "She's no different from Sarna at the inn—except I'll wager Sarna's better than your rustin' princess at all the important things!"

"She is the daughter of our sovereign, Reegas. Now show some respect."

"Yeah, sure, she's sacred and pure . . . Bloodrust, Oldahn, now you're sounding like *him*." Reegas shot a disgusted glance at Alsaf, the Puritan.

Alsaf plainly took no offense at the insult. He rolled up the king's written decree, torn from the meeting post in the town square, and stuffed it under his belt, since he was the only one of us who could read. Alsaf methodically began polishing the end of his staff on the fabric of his black cloak. He preferred to fight with his staff and his faith in God, but he also kept a sword at hand in case both the others failed. Firelight splashed across the silver crucifix at his throat.

Reegas spat something unrecognizable into the dark forest behind him. Gray-bearded Oldahn chewed his meat slowly, swallowing even the fat and gristle without a word, mindful of worse rations he had lived through. He wore an elaborately-studded leather jerkin that had protected him in scores of battles; his sword was notched, but clean and free of rust.

I sat closest to the campfire, nursing a battered pot containing the last of the stew, letting my own meat cook long enough to resemble something edible. "Uh," I said, desperately wanting to show them I could be a useful member of their band. "Why don't we just draw straws to see who goes to kill the dragon?"

Alsaf, Oldahn, and Reegas all stared as if the newcomer wasn't supposed to come up with a feasible suggestion.

"Rustin' good idea, Kendell," Reegas said. Alsaf nodded.

Oldahn looked at all three of us. "Agreed, then. Luck of the draw."

I scrabbled over to my bedding and searched through it to find suitable lots. I still preferred to sleep on a pile of straw rather than the forest floor. The straw was prickly and infested with vermin, but it reminded me of the warm bed I had left behind when running away from my home. The straw was preferable to the cold, hard dirt—at least until I got hardened to the mercenary life.

I took four straws, broke one in half so that all could see, then handed them to Oldahn. The big veteran covered them in a scarred hand to hide the short straw, and motioned for me to draw first.

Tentatively, I reached out, unable to decide whether I wanted the honor of battling the dragon. Sure, being wed to a princess would be nice, but I had barely begun my swordfighting lessons, and according to stories I had heard, dragons were vicious opponents. But I wanted to be a warrior instead of a shepherd's son, and a warrior faced whatever challenges he encountered.

I snatched a straw from Oldahn's grasp, and could tell from the others' expressions even before I glanced downward that I had drawn a long one.

Alsaf came forward, holding his staff in his right hand as he reached out to Oldahn's fist. He paused for a long moment, then pulled a straw forth. His black cloak blocked my view, but he turned with a strangled expression on his face, looking as if his faith had deserted him. The short straw fell to the ground as he gripped his silver crucifix. "But, my faith—I must remain chaste! I cannot marry a princess."

Reegas clapped the Puritan on the back. "I'm sure you can work something out."

Alsaf was pale as he shifted his weight to rest heavily on his staff. He nodded as if trying to convince himself. "Yes, my purpose is to destroy evil in all its manifestations. A divine hand has guided my selection, and I will serve His purpose." Alsaf's eyes glinted with a fanatical fury as he strode to the edge of the camp.

"Take care, and good luck," said Oldahn.

Alsaf whirled to face the three of us, holding his staff in a battle-ready stance. "I shall be protected by my unquenchable faith. My staff will send the demon back to the fires of Hell!" He looked at the skeptical expressions on our faces, then changed the tone of his voice. "I shall return."

"Is that a promise?" Reegas asked, and for once his sarcasm was weak.

"I give you my word." The Puritan turned to stride into the deep stillness of the forest night, crunching through the underbrush.

It was the only promise Alsaf ever broke.

▼▼▼

"For our honor, we must continue." Oldahn held three straws in his hand, thrusting them forward. "Come, Reegas. Draw first."

Reegas cursed under his breath and reached out to grab a straw without even pausing for thought. A broad grin split his face. He held a long straw.

I came forward, looking intently at the two straws, two chances. One would pit me against a scaly, fire-breathing demon, and the other would give me a reprieve. Knowing that the dragon had already defeated one warrior, I decided the princess wasn't so desirable after all. Alsaf had seemed so strong, so confident, so determined. I hesitated, hoping the Puritan would return at the last possible moment. . . .

But he didn't, and I picked a straw. It was long.

Oldahn stared at the short straw remaining in his hand. Cold battle-lust boiled in his eyes. "Very well, I have a dragon to slay, a death to avenge, and a princess to win. I have thought it too late in my life to settle down in marriage—but I will adapt. My brave exploits should be sung by minstrels all across the kingdom."

"Our kingdom doesn't have any minstrels, Oldahn," I pointed out.

The old warrior sighed. "I should have volunteered to go first anyway. I am the leader of our band."

"Our band?" Reegas said, sulking in his crusty old chain-mail shirt. "Rust, Oldahn—with you gone we aren't much of a band anymore."

Oldahn patted his heavy broadsword and walked stiffly across the camp. It was a beautiful day, and the sun broke through in scattered patches of green light. Oldahn looked around as if for one last time. He turned to walk away, calling back to us just before he vanished into the tangled distance, "Don't be so sure I won't be coming back."

By nightfall, we were sure.

▼▼▼

The campfire was lonely with only Reegas and me sitting by it. Oldahn had fallen, and the fact that he was the best warrior in our group (old mercenaries are, by definition, good warriors) didn't improve our confidence. I could hardly believe the great fighter I had revered so much had been *slain*. It wasn't supposed to be this way.

I looked at Reegas, fidgeting in his battered chain mail. "Well, Reegas, do you want to wait until morning, or draw straws now?"

"Rust! Let's get it over with," he said. His eyes were bloodshot. "This better be one hell of a princess."

I picked up two straws, one long, the other short. I held them out to Reegas, and he spat into the fire before looking at me. I masked my expression with some effort. Reegas reached forward and pulled the short straw.

"Bloodrust and battlerot!" he howled, jerking at the ends of the straw as if trying to stretch it longer. He crumpled it in his grip and threw it into the fire, then sank into a squat by my cookpots. "Aww, Kendell—now I can't teach you some things! I meant to take you over to the inn one night where you would—"

I looked at him with a half smile, raising an eyebrow. "Reegas, do you think Sarna takes no other customers besides yourself?"

Wonder and shock lit up his craggy face. "You? . . . Rust!" Reegas laughed loudly, a nervous blustering laugh. He clapped me on the back with perverse pride. "I won't feel sorry for you anymore, Kendell." He drew his sword and leaped into the air, slashing at a branch overhead. "But I'm gonna get that rustin' princess for myself. Maybe royalty knows a few tricks the common hussies don't."

He turned with a new excitement, dancing out of camp, waving farewell.

Alone by the campfire, I waited the long hours as the dusk collapsed into darkness. The forest filled with the noisy silence of a wild night. As the stars began to shine, I lay on the cold ground with my head propped against the rough bark of an old oak. I gave up sleeping on straw in fear that I would have dreams of dark scales and death.

The branches above me looked like the black framework of a broken lattice supporting the stars. The mockingly pleasant fire and the empty campsite made me feel intensely lonely; and for the first time I felt the true pain of my friends' losses. I had wanted to be one of them, and now they were all gone.

I remembered some of the stories they had told me, but I hadn't quite fit in with the rest of the band yet. I was a novice, I hadn't yet fought battles with them, hadn't helped them in any way. And now Alsaf and Oldahn were gone, and Reegas had a good chance of joining them. . . .

Since I had talked my way into accompanying the band, nothing much had happened. Until the dragon came, that is.

Of course, if I had known my first adventure might involve a battle with a large reptilian terror, I might have put up with my dull old life a little longer. My father was a shepherd, spending so much time out with his flocks that he had begun to look like one of his sheep. Imagine watching thirty animals eat grass hour after hour! My mother was a weaver, spending every day hunched over her loom, hurling her shuttle back and forth, watching the threads line themselves up one at a time. She even walked with a jerky back and forth motion, as if bouncing to the beat of a flying shuttle.

Me, I'd just as soon be out fighting bandits, dispatching troublesome wolves, or chasing the odd sorcerer away under the grave risk of having an indelible curse hurled at me. That's excitement—but slaying a dragon is going a bit too far!

I couldn't sleep and lay waiting, listening to the night sounds. At every rustle of leaves I jumped, peering into the shadows, hoping it might be Reegas returning, or Oldahn, or even Alsaf.

But no one came.

Finally, at dawn, I threw the last long straw on the dirt and ground it under my heel. I had only ever used my sword to cut up meat for the cook fires. I was alone. No one watched me, or pressured me, or insisted that I too go out and challenge the dragon. I could have just crept back home, helped my father tend sheep, helped my mother with her weaving. But somehow that kind of life seemed worse than facing a dragon.

I stared at the blade of my sword, thinking of my comrades. Alsaf and Oldahn and Reegas had been my friends, and I was the only one who could avenge them. Only I remained of the entire mercenary band. I had been with Oldahn long enough, heard his tales of glory, seen how the group worked together as a team. I couldn't just let the dragon have its victory.

Muttering a few curses I had picked up from Reegas, I left the dead campfire behind and set off through the forest.

The forest floor was impervious to the sunshine that dribbled through the woven leaves. A loud breeze rushed through the topmost branches, but left me untouched. I knew the boulder- strewn wilderness well, and my woodlore had grown more skillful since my initiation into the band. While we had had no serious adventures to occupy ourselves, there was still hunting to be done.

My anxiety tripled as I crested a final hill and started down into a rocky dell that sheltered the dragon's den, a broken shadow in the rock surrounded on all sides by shattered boulders and dead foliage. The lump in my throat felt larger than any dragon could ever be. The wind had disappeared, and even the birds were silent. A terrible stench wafted up, smelling faintly like something Reegas might have cooked.

I crept forward, drawing my sword, wondering why the ground was shaking and then I saw that it was only my knees. Panic flooded my senses—or had my senses left me? Me? Against a dragon? A big scaly thing with bad breath and an awful prejudice against armed warriors?

The boulders offered some protection as I danced from one to another, moving closer to the dragon's lair. Fumes snaked out of the cave, stinging my eyes and clogging my throat, tempting me to choke and give away my presence. I could hear sounds of muffled breathing like the belchings of a blacksmith's furnace.

I slid around a slime-slick rock to the threshold of the cave. I froze, an outcry trapped in my throat as I found the shattered ends of Alsaf's staff, splintered and tossed aside among torn shreds of black fabric. I swallowed and went on.

A few steps deeper into the den I tripped on the bloody remnants of Oldahn's studded leather jerkin. His bent and blackened sword lay discarded among bloody fragments of crunched bone.

On the very boundary of where sunlight dared to go, I found Reegas's rusty chain mail, chewed to a new luster and spat out.

A scream welled up as fast as my guts did, but terror can do amazing things for self-control. If I screamed, the dragon would know I had come, the latest in a series of tender victims.

But now, upon seeing with utmost certainty the fates of my

comrades, my fellow warriors, anger and lust for vengeance poured forth, almost, *almost* overwhelming my terror. The end result was an angered persistence tempered with extreme caution.

Leg muscles tense to the point of snapping, I tiptoed into the cave where I stood silhouetted against the frightened wall of daylight. The suffocating darkness of the dragon's lair folded around me. I didn't think I would ever see the sun again.

The air was thick and damp, polluted with a sickening stench. Piles of yellowed skulls lay stacked against one wall like ivory trophies. I didn't see any of the expected mounds of gold and jewels from the dragon's hoard. Pickings must have been slim in the kingdom.

I went ahead until the patch of sunlight seemed beyond running distance. My jerkin felt clammy, sticking to my cold sweat. I found it hard to breathe. I had gone in too far. My sword felt like a heavy, ineffective toy in my hand.

I could sense the lurking presence of the dragon, watching me from the shadows. I could hear its breathing like the wind of an angry storm, but could not pinpoint its location. I turned in slow circles, losing all orientation in the dimness. I thought I saw two lamplike eyes, but the stench filled my nostrils, my throat. It gagged me, forcing me to gasp for air, but that only made me gulp down more of the smell. I sneezed.

And the dragon attacked!

Suddenly I found myself confronted with a battering-ram of fury, blackish green scales draped over a bloated mass of flesh lurching forward. Acid saliva drooled off fangs like spears, spattering in sizzling pools on the floor.

I struck blindly at the eyes, the rending claws, the reptilian armor. The monster let out a hideous cry, seething forward, fat and sluggish, to corner me against a lichen-covered wall. My stomach turned to ice, and I knew how Alsaf, Oldahn, and Reegas must have felt as they faced their deaths—

▼▼▼

Let me digress a moment.

Dragons are not exactly the best-fed of all creatures living in the wild. Despite their size and power, and the riches they hoard (but who can eat gold?), these creatures find very little to devour, especially in a relatively small kingdom like our own, where most people live protected within the city walls. Barely once a week does a typical dragon manage to steal a squalling baby from its crib, or strike down an old crone gathering herbs in the woods. Rarer still does a dragon come across a flaxen-haired virgin (a favorite) wandering through the forest.

Hard times had come upon this particular dragon. Only impending starvation had driven it to increase its attacks on the peasantry, forcing the king to offer his daughter as a reward to rid the land of the beast. The future must have looked bleak for the dragon.

But then, unexpectedly, a feast beyond its wildest dreams! This dragon had greedily devoured three full-grown warriors in half as many days, swallowing whole the bodies of Alsaf, Oldahn, and Reegas.

And so, when the dragon lunged at me in the cave, it was so *bloated* and overstuffed that it could barely drag its bulk forward, like a snake which has gorged itself on a whole rabbit. Its bleary yellow eyes blinked sleepily, and it seemed to have lost heart in battling warriors. But it snarled forward out of old habit, barely able to stagger toward me. . . .

I won't, by any stretch of the imagination, claim that killing the brute was easy. The scales were tougher than any chain mail I could imagine, and the dragon didn't particularly want its head cut off—but I was bent on avenging my friends and winning myself a princess. If I could just accomplish this one thing, I could call myself a warrior. I would never have to prove myself again.

Alsaf, Oldahn, and Reegas had already done much of the work for me, dealing vicious blows to the reptilian hide. But I still can't begin to express my exhaustion when the dragon's head finally rolled among the cracked bones in its lair. I slumped to the floor of the cave, panting, without the energy to drag myself back out to fresh air.

After I had rested a long time, I stood up stiffly and looked down at the dead monster, sighing. I had won myself a princess. I had avenged my comrades.

But perhaps the best reward was that I could now call myself a real warrior, a dragon-slayer. I imagined I could think of a few ways to make the story more impressive by the time I actually met my bride-to-be.

The monster's head was heavy, and it was a long walk to the castle.

PLEASANTLY PINK
▼▼▼

MIKE RESNICK AND
NICHOLAS A. DICHARIO

LES wasn't exactly a young man anymore, but he wasn't too old to enjoy success. As he walked through the kitchen, his chefs were sweating and singing, as they always did in a busy restaurant—and Pleasantly Pink was as busy as restaurants got to be. People stood three deep at the bar. The waiters and waitresses ran back and forth, huffing and puffing.

Les entered his cramped office.

"How are we doing?" he asked.

His wife glanced up from the desk and smiled her handsome smile. Les had only enough room in the office to fit Blanche and her desk, one chair and two fat filing cabinets. Blanche was a whiz with the calculator. "Never better." She winked. "How's the dragon?"

"I was just going to check on him. Did you stop in and say hello?"

Blanche frowned. "He makes me nervous."

"Without the dragon—"

"I know."

Blanche, somewhat younger than Les, had been sturdy through several spoiled restaurant ventures. Les went over and kissed her on the forehead.

Back through the kitchen he marched, with a spring in his step, and into the storage area at the rear of the building. "How are you feeling tonight, my little friend?" said Les.

The dragon, perched upon a pillow atop a small table, stretched out his short wings and short legs, and scratched behind his ear with one of his sharp talons. "I want a raspberry Snapple iced tea," he said in a whiny voice.

"Coming right up," said Les. He called to his errand boy. "The dragon wants a raspberry Snapple iced tea!"

"And a Ho-Ho," added the dragon.

"And a Ho-Ho," said Les. He handed the boy some money. "Hurry up about it."

The boy ran off.

A waitress nudged her way into the storage room carrying a tray with four dinner specials (New York strip steaks smothered in mushrooms). She set the tray on a stand in front of the dragon.

The dragon yawned. "I don't think I can perform without a Snapple and a Ho-Ho."

"Can't you at least give it a try?" said Les. "The Snapple and the Ho-Ho will be here in just a few minutes. I guarantee you the boy is fast. He's on the high school track team."

The dragon shrugged. "Ooooooh, I suppose." He leaned forward, breathed deeply into his lungs, and puffed out a heavy breath through his nostrils. A delicate pink mist wafted over the tray of food and settled like a fresh, odorless dew atop the steaming steaks.

Les stepped forward and breathed in a bit of the dragon's discharge—so fine a mist it was barely perceptible to his senses— yet he felt intoxicated by it in a perfectly indescribable way. He picked a mushroom off one of the plates and tasted it. The flavor exploded in his mouth. "Succulent!" The dragon's magic mist never failed! It could reach into a mushroom, or a piece of beef or chicken or fish, or a salad or a fruit torte, and extract its purity, its essence, and introduce it to the taste buds as if for the first time, as if one had never before tasted anything like it.

"Les!" Blanche called from the kitchen. "Mr. Tsang Fu is here to see you."

"Tsang Fu?"

"To interview for the new cook's position, remember?"

"Oh, of course, show him back." Les was hoping Blanche would come back with him, but no, Mr. Fu appeared in front of the storage room without her.

"Mr. Fu," said Les. "Come in, come in."

Mr. Fu was an old, wrinkle-faced Chinese man. As soon as he entered the room, the smile washed away from his lips.

The little dragon reared up on its haunches and hissed. His scaly skin turned from mauve to crimson. His forked tongue lashed out, his fangs dripped dark pink saliva. The dragon fanned his wings and his long ears stood on end, trembling.

"*Tsai hai lung! Tsai hai!*" screamed Mr. Tsang Fu, tripping over his feet as he tried to back out of the room.

"Get him out!" screeched the dragon.

Les didn't have to worry about getting Mr. Fu out. By the time his initial shock passed, Fu was gone.

The dragon settled down uneasily onto the small pillow atop its table.

"What was all that about?" Les had broken into a sweat. "Are you all right?"

"Where's my Ho-Ho?" whined the dragon.

A waiter entered the room with another tray of entrees.

"The boy will be back any minute," said Les. "Now if you could just—"

"I'm too upset now! Don't ever bring a Chinese person near me again! Are you crazy?"

"I had no idea it would upset you."

"The Chinese hate me, you imbecile!"

The boy entered the storage room, out of breath. Les grabbed the paper bag from him and rustled it open. He popped the Snapple cap. The dragon snatched the bottle out of his hand and slurped it down.

"This isn't raspberry!" he screeched.

"What?" Les turned on the boy. "What did I tell you about getting the exact items!"

The boy's face flushed. "But the store didn't have any raspberry, so I got—"

"Then you should have gone somewhere and found raspberry! You're fired!" Les turned back to the dragon. "I'm sorry. But we have the Ho-Hos." He held out the package enticingly. The dragon curled his tongue around the Ho-Hos and they disappeared down his throat, wrapper and all. "I'll go out and get the raspberry Snapple myself," said Les.

"Never mind." The dragon coiled his long thin tail beneath him and lay down on the pillow. "I'm not thirsty anymore."

"But the entrees—"

"Get them out of my sight," replied the dragon. "And I think *you* should get out of my sight, too."

Les stormed into his office and kicked the door closed. He could feel the blood rush to his head. "That temperamental little beast! I hate it when he won't mist the food!"

"Calm down," said Blanche. "You know how he is."

"Yes, I know how he is: a goddamned three-and-a-half-foot-tall prima donna."

Blanche sighed. "Is he really worth all the trouble?"

"Would I put up with him if he wasn't?" retorted Les. "Look what we've done with this place because of him."

"Success isn't everything. We still have each other." She reached out and held his hand.

Les nodded. He wanted to say, "We've had each other for

twenty years, but we've never had money or success." But he
didn't say it because he didn't want to hurt Blanche's feelings.

▼▼▼

The dragon refused to mist the food for the rest of the evening.
After closing, Les paced the storage room, apologizing about the
Chinese man, and for the raspberry Snapple blunder.

"The whole point," he was saying, "is that the food without
your mist is very good here, but I've lost restaurants before when
the food was very good. A *lot* of restaurants have very good food.
Only a few restaurants have *exquisite* food. And no restaurant
anywhere else in the world has the kind of food your mist can
provide. Saturday is an important night in the restaurant business.
Tomorrow night, being Saturday, we expect our biggest crowd
yet, and I'm sure I can count on you to—"

"Shut up!" The dragon stamped its hind foot on the table. A
bit of filmy slop escaped his jowls. "The whole point, Mr. Big
Shot Restauranteur, is that we had an agreement. You would
satisfy my cravings, and I would mist your food. Does that
sound familiar?"

"Yes, but—"

"Have my requests been too demanding?"

Les shook his head. "No, of course not." In fact, the dragon
had been very reasonable. He was a snack-food junkie, requiring
different varieties of chips and dip, Big Macs, ice cream in various exotic flavors, pizza blanca with extra cheese, chocolate bars,
Hostess cupcakes and fruit pies, doughnuts, cheesecakes and past-
ries, Taco Bells. And he loved soda pop, the occasional iced tea,
or a Kenyan or Bolivian coffee from time to time—and of course
Yoo-Hoo chocolate drink (though he would occasionally settle
for Chocolate Soldier). Oh, and cockroaches, too, which he
would snare himself, and the occasional mouse.

Les had stocked most of the usuals, but the dragon was unpredictable, and Les couldn't stock everything. Once the little beast had demanded a pair of black leather shoes. He chewed them to bits and pieces (in order to clean his teeth, he later told Les) and then flossed with the shoelaces.

"I can always take my talents elsewhere," said the dragon petulantly, as his forked tongue flicked out.

"No!"

"Then you'd better shape up."

"Certainly!"

"Good. Now I want something else."

"Just name it."

"A cat."

"A cat?"

The dragon seemed to smile. (It was always difficult to tell, but Les liked to think of it as a smile whenever the dragon showed his teeth.) "I've heard them mewing out in the back alley. I want one."

The dragon's tongue flicked and flicked. He stared at Les but said nothing. The dragon had such menacing eyes. They were shaped like half-moons, black as a sealed tomb.

Les hesitated. Blanche loved the alley cats. She always put out scraps of food, and milk and water for them. She had done this at every restaurant they'd owned together. "The children," she called them. Les and Blanche had never had children of their own.

"A cat," repeated Les dully. He went to the back of the storage room, picked up the baseball bat he kept in case of prowlers, unlocked the door, and stepped out into the alley. Several cats nudged each other out of the way for Blanche's scraps. The poor things were homeless and starving. What kind of a life was that, anyway?

One of the cats rubbed up against Les' leg. The animal was filthy and smelly. Les raised the bat, but couldn't bring it down. Instead, he bent over and scooped it up. The skinny animal wriggled in his grasp. He came back inside, closed and locked the door behind him, dropped the animal on the floor, and strode out of the storage room without looking back at the dragon.

The last thing Les heard from behind the door was the soft mewing of a cat, and its claws scratching at the door.

▼▼▼

"I'm worried about the children," said Blanche, looking up from the desk. "Some of them haven't been coming back."

"What?" Les felt his heartbeat jump. Leave it to Blanche to notice something like that. Who cared which ones came back? The dragon had been asking for cats every night for the past week.

"You know how it is," said Les with what he hoped was a nonchalant shrug.

"Oh, I know. It's dangerous out there. They have no one to care for them. There's so much traffic. And people can be so cruel sometimes. I wouldn't put it past some people to hurt those poor cats intentionally."

"It's awful," agreed Les. He got to his feet. "I'm going to check on the dragon."

Les marched into the storage room and closed the door behind him. "I can't do it anymore. I can't keep feeding you cats. You don't need to eat them."

The dragon sighed. "Ooooooh, I suppose you're right. I've sort of lost my appetite for them, anyway." He belched.

Les let out his breath. (He hadn't realized he'd been holding it.) What would he have done if the dragon had insisted upon more cats? Would he have been able to stand his ground?

"I want something else," said the dragon.

"What?"

"Blanche."

"Blanche?" said Les uncomprehendingly.

"Your wife," said the dragon. "I want to have sex with her tonight."

"You're joking!" exclaimed Les. "That's preposterous! And disgusting! Not to mention impossible. Besides, Blanche would never agree to it."

"She doesn't have to agree to anything. I can hypnotize any human who is in a state of sleep or deep relaxation. I promise that she'll never know what happened to her." The dragon lowered his voice conspiratorially. "Now, here's the plan. I'll follow you home—I can fly, you know, these wings aren't just for show—and when Blanche goes to bed, tell her you'll join her in a few minutes, and then let me in the house. I'll take care of the rest."

"Why would you want to do such a thing?"

The dragon shrugged. "A craving."

"No!" said Les, "I won't allow it."

Someone knocked on the door. Les cringed.

"We have six entrees that need to be misted out here," said a voice.

The dragon flicked his forked tongue. "Well, of course, it's your business," he said with a grin.

▼▼▼

The plan remained the same every night for three-and-a-half weeks. Les would drive home; the dragon would follow; Les would let him in; and the dragon would take care of the rest.

Les thought that the dragon would tire of Blanche, just as he had tired of the cats, but in fact he showed absolutely no sign of tiring.

One night, after Les had let in the dragon, he went out for a drive. He drove to Pleasantly Pink and went inside. Empty and dark, it seemed no more than a building. There was nothing special at all about it. Les thought about how hard everyone had been working, and how happy his employees were. And the customers! He should have been glowing with pride. It was the people that made a place special—the people who worked there and the people who ate there. That had always been the way of it in the restaurant business. How was it that he had forgotten such an important truth?

He should have known right from the start the dragon would be trouble. He'd found the little beast just sleeping in the corner of the storage room after he'd bought the place. If the dragon had been worth anything at all, the previous owner never would have failed. Why hadn't he seen that before? Dreams of success had blinded him. And perhaps something else had blinded him too: the dragon's mist. He'd breathed in an awful lot of the stuff in the few months he'd known the dragon. Could that pleasantly pink mist have given the beast some hidden power over Les?

He went into his office and searched the files until he found the address of Mr. Tsang Fu, and then he drove to Chinatown.

▼▼▼

Mr. Tsang Fu's son, or perhaps it was his grandson, invited Les into the living room and asked him to sit. A short time later, Mr. Fu entered. They sat in silence while the youngster brought them tea. Les noticed a game board of Go set up on an end table in the corner of the room, its black and white stones shining like polished gems.

"Grandfather understands a fair amount of English," the boy announced, "but he doesn't speak it very well. I will speak for him."

"Does he know why I'm here?" said Les.

Old Fu nodded.

Les stared at him. "Why did you run out of my restaurant in such a fright?"

"Tsai hai lung," said Fu.

"The evil dragon," the boy said.

Les leaned forward in his chair. "What can I do to stop the beast?"

Fu looked sad, then spoke again in Chinese.

The boy listened and nodded and turned to Les. "Grandfather says, your dragon is very bad, and probably cannot be stopped. According to Chinese folklore from the archives of Weihaiwei, there was once a terrible dragon born of a mortal man and woman. The dragon's ugliness grew more terrifying every day, so his father decided the dragon should be slain. His love for his son proved less strong than his fear of what the dragon-boy would become. So one day after the infant fed from his mother's milk, he tried to chop off the dragon's head."

Old Fu made a chopping motion with his arm and hand.

"But the dragon's instincts were far greater than his father's," continued the grandson, "and when the father's sword lashed out it bit nothing but air. The dragon, with his mighty forked tail, seized his mother and flew away with her. The legend says that they lived together happily, and, some say, became lovers. Grandfather says that because the father plotted against the dragon, the dragon never trusted human men again, and now the dragon's descendants wander the earth, and plot against all men, great and small."

There was a long silence as Les sat and thought about the tale. Was he a victim of the Chinese dragon in Fu's legend? He was certainly a small man, who could feel his self-esteem becoming smaller day by day, and the dragon had surely plotted against him.

Old Fu spoke again.

"Grandfather wants to know if the dragon has killed."

Les nodded reluctantly. "He's eaten some cats. And some cockroaches."

"Is that the worst he's done?"

Les didn't know how to answer that. He felt choked up. He

started to weep. The two men let him cry until he could cry no more.

"Grandfather says, don't feel bad. Only the Chinese can tell an evil dragon from a good one. The Chinese can feel a dragon's life force, dark or light, yin or yang. You could not have known."

"Is there something in the dragon's mist that helps him control men?" asked Les.

"Dragons have always controlled men, by whatever means necessary."

"How can I kill it? I want the beast dead."

Old Fu shook his head and spoke again in Chinese.

"Grandfather says, do not try. A mortal man cannot kill a dragon, and if he attempts such a feat, it will only make matters worse. Once you have opened yourself to the dragon, he will take what he wants, and leave only when he feels you have nothing left worth taking."

Les stood up and paced the floor. "Surely there must be something I can do."

Fu thought about it for a moment, and spoke to his grandson.

"You must accept your fate," said the boy.

Les thanked the Fus, and left.

▼▼▼

He drove back to Pleasantly Pink. After all, where else *could* he go? Certainly not home. Home was too painful for him with Blanche and the dragon there. How had things gotten so complicated? He had only wanted a little success.

Finally he fell asleep on the chair in his office, and woke to the sound of Blanche's voice:

"—up, Les, wake up. Have you been working all night?"

Les blinked at the light. "How did you get here?"

"I saw your note and took a cab."

"My note?"

"Yes, that you would be working at the restaurant."

"Oh." The dragon must have written it. Les stood up and stretched out his stiff muscles. He was too old to be falling asleep in chairs. He looked at Blanche. She seemed so distant. He reached out and stroked her short brown hair. Reliable Blanche. He had never loved her more than he did right at this moment. He wanted to tell her that he was sorry, and that he truly loved her with all the love he could give, a love he knew to be pitifully inadequate when compared to hers—but then she would ask him all sorts of questions, and how would he ever begin to explain what he had done?

No, there was only one thing for him to do, and that was to kill the dragon. He didn't care what old Tsang Fu had said about accepting his fate. He had been less than a man for too long, and now, at the risk of becoming a caricature of one, he had no choice but to defend what sense of honor and righteousness yet remained alive in him.

Les washed his face and combed his hair at one of the kitchen sinks, then walked into the storage room.

"Well, look who's here," said the dragon. "The mighty Lessssssssss-ter, come to try and kill poor little *Tsai hai lung.*"

How did the dragon know? Was his despair so obvious? It didn't matter. In fact, it was preferable this way. A duel. Les closed the door behind him. He walked to the back of the storage room and picked up the baseball bat.

The dragon showed his fangs. Was he sneering?

Les gripped the bat in both hands and began to warily circle the beast. The dragon remained still, and flicked his tongue.

Be careful, Les told himself. *The beast can fly. And those small legs of his are powerful. He can leap at a moment's notice. And watch out for that mist!* The sweat beaded on his forehead. For the first time he noticed how sickly sweet the dragon smelled, like something gone rotten.

Les stepped closer. The dragon didn't move. How close could

he get? The dragon hadn't turned crimson yet, as he had with old Tsang Fu. Was the beast *that* unafraid of him?

He heard a knock at the door. "Les?"

"Blanche—stay out of here!"

"What are you doing?" She opened the door.

"This is between me and the dragon. Stay clear."

"No! Don't you dare harm him!" She came up behind Les and grabbed his shoulders.

Les shrugged her off. He saw his moment of heroism slipping away. He lunged at the dragon and swung with all his might.

The dragon cackled deep in his throat. He didn't move a muscle. He was going to take the blow—

No! Faster than the human eye could follow, he dodged the bat. Les fanned. Hopelessly off balance, he whirled around and fell to his knees. He felt the dragon's long tail wrap around his arms and chest and waist and squeeze him. He dropped the bat. He couldn't breathe. And then he was face to face with the dragon's fangs.

"Blanche! Run!" These would be his last selfless, heroic words, thought Les. But the dragon's fangs did not strike. Instead, the dragon hissed and released him.

Blanche ran up to Les.

No—Blanche ran *past* Les.

She picked up the dragon and held him to her bosom. The dragon draped his tail around her and licked her face with his forked tongue.

"I love him, Les," said Blanche. "I know it sounds crazy, but no one has ever made me feel so wanted, so needed. I felt like you'd abandoned me, and suddenly the dragon was there. I can't really explain it."

Les coughed and gasped. "No, Blanche! The dragon has hypnotized you, or misted you, or something. The dragon has all sorts of powers we humans can't begin to understand. He's a *Tsai hai lung*, an evil dragon. Don't give in to him!"

"Don't be ridiculous, Lester."

The dragon seemed to smile. "I have no special power over human beings, except for the power that human beings *give* me over them."

Blanche looked at Les with what could only have been pity. "He has more love in him than anyone I have ever known."

Les felt the full brunt of that remark. It stabbed at his deepest insecurity, plucked it from the dark cavity of his soul, and exposed it to the light. It was something that the dragon must have known all along. Les did not know how to love; indeed, he had thrown love away for something as meaningless and ephemeral as success.

"Besides," Blanche said, scratching behind the dragon's ear, "I think I might be pregnant. Isn't it wonderful!"

"Oh, God, no!"

Les sat on the floor, remembering old Tsang Fu's tale, and seeing clearly for the first time his role in the retelling of it.

The dragon and Blanche walked out of the restaurant together, and Les never saw either of them again.

▼▼▼

Les converted Pleasantly Pink to The Chinese Dumpling House, an Oriental eatery featuring the cuisine of Master Tsang Fu. He didn't get rich, but he managed to make ends meet. Within months he had moved to Chinatown, and was never seen anywhere without being in the company of a man or woman of Chinese descent.

He promised himself that one day he would feature dragon on his menu, but of course he never did.

THE RULE OF NAMES
▼▼▼

URSULA K. LE GUIN

MR. Underhill came out from under his hill, smiling and breathing hard. Each breath shot out of his nostrils as a double puff of steam, snow-white in the morning sunshine. Mr. Underhill looked up at the bright December sky and smiled wider than ever, showing snow-white teeth. Then he went down to the village.

"Morning, Mr. Underhill," said the villagers as he passed them in the narrow street between houses with conical, overhanging roofs like the fat red caps of toadstools. "Morning, morning!" he replied to each. (It was of course bad luck to wish anyone a *good* morning; a simple statement of the time of day was quite enough, in a place so permeated with Influences as Sattins Island, where a careless adjective might change the weather for a week.) All of them spoke to him, some with affection, some with affectionate disdain. He was all the little island had in the way of a wizard, and so deserved respect—but how could you respect a little fat man of fifty who waddled along with his toes turned in, breathing steam and smiling? He was no great shakes as a workman either. His fireworks were fairly elaborate but his elixirs were weak. Warts he charmed off frequently reappeared after three days; tomatoes he enchanted grew no bigger than cantaloupes; and those rare times when a strange ship stopped at Sattins Harbor, Mr. Underhill always stayed under his hill—for fear, he explained, of the evil eye. He was, in other words, a wizard the way walleyed Gan was a carpenter: by default. The villagers made do with badly-hung doors and inefficient spells, for this generation, and relieved their annoyance by treating Mr. Underhill quite familiarly, as a mere fellow-villager. They even asked him to dinner. Once he asked some of them to dinner, and served a splendid repast, with silver, crystal, damask, roast goose, sparkling Andrades '639, and plum pudding with hard sauce; but he was so nervous all through the meal that it took the joy out of it, and besides, everybody was hungry again half an hour afterward. He did not like anyone to visit his cave, not even the anteroom, beyond which in fact nobody had ever got. When he saw people approaching the hill he always came trotting out to meet them. "Let's sit out here under the pine trees!" he would say, smiling and waving towards the fir grove, or if it was raining, "Let's go have a drink at the inn, eh?" though everybody knew he drank nothing stronger than well-water.

Some of the village children, teased by that locked cave, poked and pried and made raids while Mr. Underhill was away; but the small door that led into the inner chamber was spell-shut, and it seemed for once to be an effective spell. Once a couple of boys, thinking the wizard was over on the West Shore curing Mrs. Ruuna's sick donkey, brought a crowbar and a hatchet up there, but at the first whack of the hatchet on the door there came a roar of wrath from inside, and a cloud of purple steam. Mr. Underhill had got home early. The boys fled. He did not come out, and the boys came to no harm, though they said you couldn't believe what a huge hooting howling hissing horrible bellow that little fat man could make unless you'd heard it.

His business in town this day was three dozen fresh eggs and a pound of liver; also a stop at Seacaptain Fogeno's cottage to renew the seeing-charm on the old man's eyes (quite useless when applied to a case of detached retina, but Mr. Underhill kept trying), and finally a chat with old Goody Guld, the concertina-maker's widow. Mr. Underhill's friends were mostly old people. He was timid with the strong young men of the village, and the girls were shy of him. "He makes me nervous, he smiles so much," they all said, pouting, twisting silky ringlets round a finger. "Nervous" was a newfangled word, and their mothers all replied grimly, "Nervous my foot, silliness is the word for it. Mr. Underhill is a very respectable wizard!"

After leaving Goody Guld, Mr. Underhill passed by the school, which was being held this day out on the common. Since no one on Sattins Island was literate, there were no books to learn to read from and no desks to carve initials on and no blackboards to erase, and in fact no schoolhouse. On rainy days the children met in the loft of the Communal Barn, and got hay in their pants; on sunny days the schoolteacher, Palani, took them anywhere she felt like. Today, surrounded by thirty interested children under twelve and forty uninterested sheep under five, she was teaching an important item on the curriculum: the Rules of Names. Mr. Underhill, smiling shyly, paused to listen and watch. Palani, a plump, pretty girl of twenty, made a charming picture there in the wintry sunlight, sheep and children around her, a leafless oak above her, and behind her the dunes and sea and clear, pale sky. She spoke earnestly, her face flushed pink by wind and words. "Now you know the Rules of Names already, children. There are two, and they're the same on every island in the world. What's one of them?"

"It ain't polite to ask somebody what his name is," shouted a fat, quick boy, interrupted by a little girl shrieking, "You can't never tell your own name to nobody my ma says!"

"Yes, Suba. Yes, Popi dear, don't screech. That's right. You never ask anybody his name. You never tell your own. Now think about that a minute and then tell me why we call our wizard Mr. Underhill." She smiled across the curly heads and the woolly backs at Mr. Underhill, who beamed, and nervously clutched his sack of eggs.

" 'Cause he lives under a hill!" said half the children.

"But is it his truename?"

"No!" said the fat boy, echoed by little Popi shrieking, "No!"

"How do you know it's not?"

" 'Cause he came here all alone and so there wasn't anybody knew his truename so they couldn't tell us, and *he* couldn't—"

"Very good, Suba. Popi, don't shout. That's right. Even a wizard can't tell his truename. When you children are through school and go through the Passage, you'll leave your childnames behind and keep only your truenames, which you must never ask for and never give away. Why is that the rule?"

The children were silent. The sheep bleated gently. Mr. Underhill answered the question: "Because the name is the thing," he said in his shy, soft, husky voice, "and the truename is the true thing. To speak the name is to control the thing. Am I right, Schoolmistress?"

She smiled and curtseyed, evidently a little embarrassed by his participation. And he trotted off towards his hill, clutching his eggs to his bosom. Somehow the minute spent watching Palani and the children had made him very hungry. He locked his inner door behind him with a hasty incantation, but there must have been a leak or two in the spell, for soon the bare anteroom of the cave was rich with the smell of frying eggs and sizzling liver.

The wind that day was light and fresh out of the west, and on it at noon a little boat came skimming the bright waves into Sattins Harbor. Even as it rounded the point a sharp-eyed boy spotted it, and knowing, like every child on the island, every sail and spar of the forty boats of the fishing fleet, he ran down the street calling out, "A foreign boat, a foreign boat!" Very seldom was the lonely isle visited by a boat from some equally lonely isle of the East Reach, or an adventurous trader from the Archipelago. By the time the boat was at the pier half the village was there to greet it, and fishermen were following it homewards, and cowherds and clam-diggers and herb-hunters were puffing up and down all the rocky hills, heading towards the harbor.

But Mr. Underhill's door stayed shut.

There was only one man aboard the boat. Old Seacaptain Fogeno, when they told him that, drew down a bristle of white brows over his unseeing eyes. "There's only one kind of man," he said, "that sails the Outer Reach alone. A wizard, or a warlock, or a Mage . . ."

So the villagers were breathless hoping to see for once in their lives a Mage, one of the mighty White Magicians of the rich, towered, crowded inner islands of the Archipelago. They were disappointed, for the voyager was quite young, a handsome black-bearded fellow who hailed them cheerfully from his boat, and leaped ashore like any sailor glad to have made port. He introduced himself at once as a sea-peddlar. But when they told Seacaptain Fogeno that he carried an oaken walking-stick around with him, the old man nodded. "Two wizards in one town," he said. "Bad!" And his mouth snapped shut like an old carp's.

As the stranger could not give them his name, they gave him one right away: Blackbeard. And they gave him plenty of attention. He had a small mixed cargo of cloth and sandals and piswi feathers for trimming cloaks and cheap incense and levity stones and fine herbs and great glass beads from Venway—the usual peddlar's lot. Everyone on Sattins Island came to look, to chat with the voyager, and perhaps to buy something—"Just to remember him by!" cackled Goody Guld, who like all the women and girls of the village was smitten with Blackbeard's bold good looks. All the boys hung round him too, to hear him tell of his voyages to far, strange islands of the Reach or describe the great rich islands of the Archipelago, the Inner Lanes, the roadsteads white with ships, and the golden roofs of Havnor. The men willingly listened to his tales; but some of them wondered why a trader should sail alone, and kept their eyes thoughtfully upon his oaken staff.

But all this time Mr. Underhill stayed under his hill.

"This is the first island I've ever seen that had no wizard," said Blackbeard one evening to Goody Guld, who had invited him and her nephew and Palani in for a cup of rushwash tea. "What do you do when you get a toothache, or the cow goes dry?"

"Why, we've got Mr. Underhill!" said the old woman.

"For what that's worth," muttered her nephew Birt, and then blushed purple and spilled his tea. Birt was a fisherman, a large, brave, wordless young man. He loved the schoolmistress, but the nearest he had come to telling her of his love was to give baskets of fresh mackerel to her father's cook.

"Oh, you do have a wizard?" Blackbeard asked. "Is he invisible?"

"No, he's just very shy," said Palani. "You've only been here a week, you know, and we see so few strangers here. . . ." She also blushed a little, but did not spill her tea.

Blackbeard smiled at her. "He's a good Sattinsman, then, eh?"

"No," said Goody Guld, "no more than you are. Another cup, nevvy? Keep it in the cup this time. No, my dear, he came in a little bit of a boat, four years ago was it? Just a day after the end of the shad run, I recall, for they was taking up the nets over in East Creek, and Pondi Cowherd broke his leg that very morning—five years ago it must be. No, four. No, five it is, 'twas the year the garlic didn't sprout. So he sails in on a bit of a sloop loaded full up with great chests and boxes and says to Seacaptain Fogeno, who wasn't blind then, though old enough goodness knows to be blind twice over, 'I hear tell,' he says, 'you've got no wizard nor warlock at all, might you be wanting one?' 'Indeed, if the magic's white!' says the Captain, and before you could say cuttlefish Mr. Underhill had settled down in the cave under the hill and was charming the mange off Goody Beltow's cat. Though the fur grew in grey, and 'twas an orange cat. Queer-looking thing it was after that. It died last winter in the cold spell. Goody Beltow took on so at that cat's death, poor thing, worse than when her man was drowned on the Long Banks, the year of the long herring-runs, when nevvy Birt here was but a babe in petticoats." Here Birt spilled his tea again, and Blackbeard grinned, but Goody Guld proceeded undismayed, and talked on till nightfall.

Next day Blackbeard was down at the pier, seeing after the sprung board in his boat which he seemed to take a long time fixing, and as usual drawing the taciturn Sattinsmen into talk. "Now which of these is your wizard's craft?" he asked. "Or has he got one of those the Mages fold up into a walnut shell when they're not using it?"

"Nay," said a stolid fisherman. "She's oop in his cave, under hill."

"He carried the boat he came in up to his cave?"

"Aye. Clear oop. I helped. Heavier as lead she was. Full oop with great boxes, and they full oop with books o' spells, he says. Heavier as lead she was." And the stolid fisherman turned his back, sighing stolidly. Goody Guld's nephew, mending a net nearby, looked up from his work and asked with equal stolidity, "Would ye like to meet Mr. Underhill, maybe?"

Blackbeard returned Birt's look. Clever black eyes met candid blue ones for a long moment; then Blackbeard smiled and said, "Yes. Will you take me up to the hill, Birt?"

"Aye, when I'm done with this," said the fisherman. And when the net was mended, he and the Archipelagan set off up the village street towards the high green hill above it. But as they crossed the common Blackbeard said, "Hold on a while, friend Birt. I have a tale to tell you, before we meet your wizard."

"Tell away," says Birt, sitting down in the shade of a live-oak.

"It's a story that started a hundred years ago, and isn't finished yet—though it soon will be, very soon.... In the very heart of the Archipelago, where the islands crowd thick as flies on honey, there's a little isle called Pendor. The sealords of Pendor were mighty men, in the old days of war before the League. Loot and ransom and tribute came pouring into Pendor, and they gathered a great treasure there, long ago. Then from somewhere away out in the West Reach, where dragons breed on the lava isles, came one day a very mighty dragon. Not one of those overgrown lizards most of you Outer Reach folk call dragons, but a big, black, winged, wise, cunning monster, full of strength and subtlety, and like all dragons loving gold and precious stones above all things. He killed the Sealord and his soldiers, and the people of Pendor fled in their ships by night. They all fled away and left the dragon coiled up in Pendor Towers. And there he stayed for a hundred years, dragging his scaly belly over the emeralds and sapphires and coins of gold, coming forth only once in a year or two when he must eat. He'd raid nearby islands for his food. You know what dragons eat?"

Birt nodded and said in a whisper, "Maidens."

"Right," said Blackbeard. "Well, that couldn't be endured forever, nor the thought of him sitting on all that treasure. So after the League grew strong, and the Archipelago wasn't so busy with wars and piracy, it was decided to attack Pendor, drive out the dragon, and get the gold and jewels for the treasury of the League. They're forever wanting money, the League is. So a huge fleet gathered from fifty islands, and seven Mages stood in the prows of the seven strongest ships, and they sailed towards Pendor.... They got there. They landed. Nothing stirred. The houses all stood empty, the dishes on the tables full of a hundred years' dust. The bones of the old Sealord and his men lay about in the castle courts and on the stairs. And the Tower rooms reeked of dragon. But there was no dragon. And no treasure, not a diamond the size of a poppyseed, not a single silver bead. . . . Knowing that he couldn't stand up to seven Mages, the dragon had skipped out. They tracked him, and found he'd flown to a deserted island up north called Udrath; they followed his trail there, and what did they find? Bones again. His bones—the dragon's. But no treasure. A wizard, some unknown wizard from somewhere, must have met him singlehanded, and defeated him—and then made off with the treasure, right under the League's nose!"

The fisherman listened, attentive and expressionless.

"Now that must have been a powerful wizard and a clever one, first to kill a dragon, and second to get off without leaving a trace. The lords and Mages of the Archipelago couldn't track him at all, neither where he'd come from nor where he'd made off to. They were about to give up. That was last spring; I'd been off on a three-year voyage up in the North Reach, and got back about that time. And they asked me to help them find the unknown wizard. That was clever of them. Because I'm not only a wizard myself, as I think some of the oafs here have guessed, but I am also a descendant of the Lords of Pendor. That treasure is mine. It's mine, and knows that it's mine. Those fools of the League couldn't find it, because it's not theirs. It belongs to the House of Pendor, and the great emerald, the star of the hoard, Inalkil the Greenstone, knows its master. Behold!" Blackbeard raised his oaken staff and cried aloud, "Inalkil!" The tip of the staff began to glow green, a fiery green radiance, a dazzling haze the color of April grass, and at the same moment the staff tipped in the wizard's hand, leaning, slanting till it pointed straight at the side of the hill above them.

"It wasn't so bright a glow, far away in Havnor," Blackbeard murmured, "but the staff pointed true. Inalkil answered when I called. The jewel knows its master. And I know the thief, and I shall conquer him. He's a mighty wizard, who could overcome a dragon. But I am mightier. Do you want to know why, oaf? Because I know his name!"

As Blackbeard's tone got more arrogant, Birt had looked duller and duller, blanker and blanker; but at this he gave a twitch, shut his mouth, and stared at the Archipelagan. "How did you . . . learn it?" he asked very slowly.

Blackbeard grinned, and did not answer.

"Black magic?"

"How else?"

Birt looked pale, and said nothing.

"I am the Sealord of Pendor, oaf, and I will have the gold my fathers won, and the jewels my mothers wore, and the Green-stone! For they are mine.—Now, you can tell your village bob-bies the whole story after I have defeated this wizard and gone. Wait here. Or you can come and watch, if you're not afraid. You'll never get the chance again to see a great wizard in all his power." Blackbeard turned, and without a backward glance strode off up the hill towards the entrance to the cave.

Very slowly, Birt followed. A good distance from the cave he stopped, sat down under a hawthorn tree, and watched. The Archipelagan had stopped; a stiff, dark figure alone on the green swell of the hill before the gaping cave-mouth, he stood perfectly still. All at once he swung his staff up over his head, and the emerald radiance shone about him as he shouted, "Thief, thief of the Hoard of Pendor, come forth!"

There was a crash, as of dropped crockery, from inside the cave, and a lot of dust came spewing out. Scared, Birt ducked. When he looked again he saw Blackbeard still standing mo-tionless, and at the mouth of the cave, dusty and disheveled, stood Mr. Underhill. He looked small and pitiful, with his toes turned in as usual, and his little bowlegs in black tights, and no staff—he never had had one, Birt suddenly thought. Mr. Under-hill spoke. "Who are you?" he said in his husky little voice.

"I am the Sealord of Pendor, thief, come to claim my treasure!"

At that, Mr. Underhill slowly turned pink, as he always did when people were rude to him. But he then turned something else. He turned yellow. His hair bristled out, he gave a coughing roar—and was a yellow lion leaping down the hill at Blackbeard, white fangs gleaming.

But Blackbeard no longer stood there. A gigantic tiger, color of night and lightning, bounded to meet the lion. . . .

The lion was gone. Below the cave all of a sudden stood a high grove of trees, black in the winter sunshine. The tiger, checking himself in midleap just before he entered the shadow of the trees, caught fire in the air, became a tongue of flame lashing out at the dry black branches. . . .

But where the trees had stood a sudden cataract leaped from the hillside, an arch of silvery crashing water, thundering down upon the fire. But the fire was gone. . . .

For just a moment before the fisherman's staring eyes two hills rose—the green one he knew, and a new one, a bare, brown hillock ready to drink up the rushing waterfall. That passed so quickly it made Birt blink, and after blinking he blinked again, and moaned, for what he saw now was a great deal worse. Where the cataract had been there hovered a dragon. Black wings darkened all the hill, steel claws reached groping, and from the dark, scaly, gaping lips fire and steam shot out.

Beneath the monstrous creature stood Blackbeard, laughing.

"Take any shape you please, little Mr. Underhill!" he taunted. "I can match you. But the game grows tiresome. I want to look upon my treasure, upon Inalkil. Now, big dragon, little wizard, take your true shape. I command you by the power of your true name—Yevaud!"

Birt could not move at all, not even to blink. He cowered, staring whether he would or not. He saw the black dragon hang there in the air above Blackbeard. He saw the fire lick like many tongues from the scaly mouth, the steam jet from the red nostrils.

He saw Blackbeard's face grow white, white as chalk, and the beard-fringed lips trembling.

"Your name is Yevaud!"

"Yes," said a great, husky, hissing voice. "My truename is Yevaud, and my true shape is this shape."

"But the dragon was killed—they found dragon-bones on Udrath Island—"

"That was another dragon," said the dragon, and then stooped like a hawk, talons outstretched. And Birt shut his eyes.

When he opened them the sky was clear, the hillside empty, except for a reddish-blackish trampled spot, and a few talon-marks in the grass.

Birt the fisherman got to his feet and ran. He ran across the common, scattering sheep to right and left, and straight down the village street to Palani's father's house. Palani was out in the garden weeding the nasturtiums. "Come with me!" Birt gasped. She stared. He grabbed her wrist and dragged her with him. She screeched a little, but did not resist. He ran with her straight to the pier, pushed her into his fishing sloop the *Queenie*, untied the painter, took up the oars and set off rowing like a demon. The last that Sattins Island saw of him and Palani was the *Queenie*'s sail vanishing in the direction of the nearest island westward.

The villagers thought they would never stop talking about it, how Goody Guld's nephew Birt had lost his mind and sailed off with the schoolmistress on the very same day that the peddlar Blackbeard disappeared without a trace, leaving all his feathers and beads behind. But they did stop talking about it, three days later. They had other things to talk about, when Mr. Underhill finally came out of his cave.

Mr. Underhill had decided that since his truename was no longer a secret, he might as well drop his disguise. Walking was a lot harder than flying, and besides, it was a long, long time since he had had a real meal.

SIRINITA'S DRAGON
▼▼▼

LAWRENCE WATT-EVANS

"**Y**OU'RE going to *kill* him?" Sirinita said, staring at her mother in disbelief.

Sensella of Seagate looked at her daughter with surprised annoyance.

"Well, of *course* we're going to kill it," she said. "What else could we do? In a few weeks it'll be eating us out of house and home—and in a year or two it might very well eat *us*. Just *look* how big it's getting!"

Sirinita looked.

She had to admit, Tharn *was* getting large. When he had first hatched she could sit him on her shoulder, with his tail around her neck, and almost forget he was there; now she could barely pick him up with both hands, and he certainly didn't fit on her shoulders.

And he *did* eat a lot.

"Really, Sirinita," her mother said, "you didn't think we could keep a full-grown dragon around the house, did you?"

"No," Sirinita admitted, "but I thought you could just let him go, somewhere outside the walls—I didn't know you were going to *kill* him!"

"Now, you ought to know better than that," Sensella said. "If we turned it loose it would eat people's livestock—and that's assuming it didn't eat *people*. Dragons are *dangerous*, honey."

"*Tharn* isn't!"

"But it *will* be." Sensella hesitated, then added, "Besides, we can sell the blood and hide to wizards; I understand it's quite valuable."

"Sell *pieces* of him?" This was too much; Sirinita was utterly horrified.

Sensella sighed. "I should have known this would happen; I should never have let you hatch that egg in the first place. What *was* your father thinking of, bringing you a dragon's egg?"

"I don't know," Sirinita said. "Maybe he wasn't thinking anything."

Sensella chuckled sourly. "You're probably right, Siri. You're probably just exactly right." She glanced over at the dragon.

Tharn was trying to eat the curtains again.

Sirinita followed her mother's gaze. "Tharn!" she shouted, "stop that this instant!"

The dragon stopped, startled, and turned to look at his mistress with his golden slit-pupiled eyes. The curtain, caught on one of his fangs, turned with him, and tore slightly. The dragon looked up at the curtain with an offended expression, and used a foreclaw to pry the fabric off his teeth.

Sensella sighed. Sirinita almost giggled, Tharn's expression was so funny, but then she remembered what was going to happen to her beloved dragon in a few days' time, and the urge to giggle vanished completely.

"Come on, Tharn," she said, "let's go outside."

▼▼▼

Sensella watched as her daughter and her pet ran out of the house onto the streets of Ethshar.

She hoped they wouldn't get into any trouble; both of them

meant well enough, but the dragon did have all those claws and teeth, and while it couldn't yet spit fire it was beginning to breathe hot vapor; and sometimes Sirinita just didn't think about the consequences of her actions.

But then, that was hardly a unique fault, or even one limited to children. Sensella wondered again just what Gar had thought he was doing when he brought back a dragon's egg from one of his trading expeditions.

One of the farmers had found it in the woods while berry-picking, Gar had said—had found a whole nest, in fact, though he wouldn't say what had happened to the other eggs. Probably sold them to wizards.

And why in the world had she and Gar let Sirinita *hatch* the egg, and keep the baby dragon long enough to become so attached? That had been very foolish indeed. Baby dragons were very fashionable, of course—parading through the streets with a dragon on a leash was the height of social display, and a sure way to garner invitations to all the right parties.

But the dowagers and matrons who did that didn't let their children make playmates of the little monsters! The sensible ones didn't use real dragons at all, they bought magical imitations, like that beautiful wood-and-lacquer thing Lady Nuvielle carried about, with its red glass eyes and splendid black wings. It moved and hissed and flew with a perfect semblance of life, thanks to a wizard's skill, and it didn't eat a thing, and would never grow an inch.

Tharn ate everything, grew constantly, and couldn't yet fly more than a few feet without tangling itself up in its own wings and falling out of the sky.

And Sirinita adored it.

Sensella sighed again.

▼▼▼

Outside, Sirinita and Tharn were racing side-by-side down War-gate High Street, toward the Arena—and Tharn was almost winning, to Sirinita's surprise. He *was* getting bigger. He was at least as big as any dog Sirinita had ever seen—but then, she hadn't seen very many, and she had heard that out in the country dogs sometimes grew much larger then the ones inside the city walls.

Much as Sirinita hated to admit it, her mother was right— Tharn was getting too big to keep at home. He had knocked over the washbasin in her bedroom that morning, and Sirinita suspected that he'd eaten the neighbors' cat yesterday—though maybe the stuck-up thing was just hiding somewhere.

But did he have to *die*, just because he was a dragon?

There had to be someplace a dragon could live.

She stopped, out of breath, at the corner of Center Street; Tharn tried to stop beside her, but tripped over his own foreclaws and fell, in a tangle of wings and tail. Sirinita laughed, but a moment later Tharn was upright again, his head bumping scratchily against her hip. If she'd been wearing a lighter tunic, Sirinita thought, those sharp little scales would leave welts.

He really did have to go.

But where?

She peered down Center Street to the west; that led to the shipyards. Tharn would hardly be welcome there, especially if he started breathing fire around all that wood and pitch, but maybe somewhere out at sea? Was there some island where a dragon could live in safety, some other land where dragons were welcome?

Probably not.

There were stories about dragons that lived in the sea itself, but somehow she couldn't imagine Tharn being that sort. His egg had been found in a forest, after all, up near the Tintallionese border, and he'd never shown any interest in learning to swim.

The shipyards weren't any help.

In the other direction both Center Street and Wargate High Street led to the Arena—Wargate High Street led straight to the south side, four blocks away, while Center looped around and wound up on the north side after six blocks.

Could the Arena use a dragon?

That seemed promising—after all, dragons were impressive, people liked to look at them.

At least, in pictures; in real life people tended to be too frightened of adult dragons to want to look at them.

But Tharn was a *tame* dragon, or at least Sirinita *hoped* he was tame; he wasn't dangerous, not really. Wouldn't he be a fine attraction in the Arena?

And she could come to visit him there, too!

That would be perfect.

"Come on, Tharn," she said, and together the girl and her dragon trotted on down Wargate High Street.

There wasn't a show today; the Arena gates were closed, the tunnels and galleries deserted. Sirinita hadn't thought about that; she pressed up against a gate and stared through the iron grillwork at the shadowy passages beyond.

No one was in there.

She sat down on the hard-packed dirt of the street to think; Tharn curled up beside her, his head in her lap, the scales of his chin once again scratching her legs right through her tunic.

People turned to stare as they passed, then quickly looked away so as not to be rude. Sirinita was accustomed to this; after all, one didn't see a dragon on the streets of Ethshar every day, and certainly not one as big as Tharn was getting to be. She ignored them and sat thinking, trying to figure out who she should talk to about finding a place for Tharn at the Arena.

There was one fellow, however, who stopped a few feet away and asked, "Are you all right?"

Sirinita looked up, startled out of her reverie. "I'm fine, thank you," she said automatically.

The man who had addressed her was young, thin, almost handsome, and dressed in soft leather breeches and a tunic of brown velvet—a clean one, in good repair, so Sirinita could be reasonably certain that he wasn't poor, wasn't a beggar or any of the more dangerous inhabitants of the fields out beyond Wall Street.

Of course, people who lived in the fields rarely got this far in toward the center of the city. And there were plenty of dangerous people who didn't live in the fields.

She had Tharn to protect her, though, and she was only a few blocks from home.

"Is there anything I can help you with? You look worried," the man said.

"I'm fine," Sirinita repeated.

"Is it your dragon? Are you doing something magical?"

"He's my dragon, yes, but I was just thinking, not doing magic. I'm not even an apprentice yet, see?" She pointed to her bare legs—if she was too young for a woman's skirt, she was too young for an apprenticeship.

In fact, she was still a month short of her twelfth birthday and formal skirting, which was the very earliest she could possibly start an apprenticeship, and she hadn't yet decided if she wanted to learn *any* trade. She didn't think she wanted to learn magic, though; magic was dangerous.

"Oh," the man said, a bit sheepishly. "I thought . . . well, one doesn't see a lot of dragons, especially not that size. I thought maybe it was part of some spell."

Sirinita shook her head. "No. We were just thinking."

"About the Arena? There's to be a performance the day after tomorrow, I believe, in honor of Lord Wulran's birthday, but there's nothing today."

"I know," Sirinita said. "I mean, I'd forgotten, but I know now."

"Oh." The man looked at them uncertainly.

"Do you work in the Arena?" Sirinita asked, suddenly realizing this might be the opportunity she had been looking for.

"No, I'm afraid not. Did you want . . ." He didn't finish the sentence.

"We were wondering if Tharn could be in a show," Sirinita explained.

"Tharn?"

"My dragon."

"Ah." The man scratched thoughtfully at his beard. "Perhaps if you spoke to the Lord of the Games . . ."

"Who's he?"

"Oh, he's the man in charge of the Arena," the man explained. "Among other things. His name is Lord Varrin."

"Do you know him?" Sirinita looked up hopefully.

"Well, yes," the young man admitted.

"Could you introduce me?"

The young man hesitated, sighed, then said, "Oh, all right. Come on, then."

Sirinita pushed Tharn's head off her lap and jumped up eagerly.

Lord Varrin, it developed, lived just three blocks away, in a mansion at the corner of Wargate High Street and, of course, Games Street; a servant answered the door and bowed at the sight of the young man in velvet, then ushered man, girl, and dragon into the parlor.

A moment later Lord Varrin, a large, handsome man of middle years wearing black silk and leather, emerged and bowed.

"Lord Doran," he said. "What brings you here?"

Sirinita's head whirled about to look at the man in velvet. "Lord Doran?" she asked.

He nodded.

"The overlord's brother?"

"I'm afraid so."

"But I . . . um . . ."

"Never mind that," Doran said gently. "Tell Lord Varrin why we're here."

"Oh." Sirinita turned back to the Lord of the Games, grabbed Tharn by his head-crest to keep him from eating anything he shouldn't, and explained.

When she had finished, Lords Varrin and Doran looked at one another.

"I'm afraid," Lord Varrin said gently, "that your father is right; we don't ever keep dragons inside the city walls. It simply isn't safe. Even the most well-intentioned dragon can't be trusted not to do some serious damage—quite by accident, usually. A full-grown dragon is *big*, young lady; just walking down a street its wings and tail could break windows and knock down sign-boards. And if it loses its temper—*anyone* can lose his temper sometimes."

Sirinita looked at Lord Doran for confirmation.

"There's nothing *I* can do," that worthy said. "I'm not even sure my brother could manage it, and I certainly can't; our duty is to protect the city, and Lord Varrin is right—that means no large dragons. I'm very sorry."

"Not even for the Arena?" Sirinita asked.

Lord Varrin shook his head. "If we ever really needed a dragon," he said, "we could have one sent in from somewhere, just for the show; we wouldn't keep one here. And we'd have a dozen magicians standing guard every second, just in case."

"So Tharn has to die?"

Varrin and Doran looked at one another.

"Well," Doran said, "that's up to you and your father. We just know he can't stay inside the city walls once he's bigger than a grown man. That's the law."

"It's a *law*?"

"I'm afraid so."

"Oh." She looked down at her feet, dejected, then remembered her manners. "Thank you anyway," she said.

"You're welcome. I'm sorry we can't do more."

The servant escorted Sirinita and Tharn back out onto War-

gate High Street, where she looked down at Tharn in despair
and asked, "*Now* what?"

He snorted playfully, and the hot, fetid fumes made Sirinita
cough. She also thought she might have seen an actual spark
this time.

That would be the pebble that sank the barge, Sirinita
thought—if her parents found out that Tharn was spitting sparks
out his nose they wouldn't allow him in the house, and that
"few days" her mother had mentioned would disappear—he'd
be chopped up and sold to the wizards *today*, she was sure.

Ordinarily, when confronted with an insoluble problem, she
might have thought about consulting a wizard herself—she
couldn't afford their fees, but sometimes, if they weren't busy,
they would talk to her anyway, and offer advice. She had never
needed any actual magic, so she didn't know if they would have
worked their wizardry for her.

This time, though, wizards were out of the question. They
were the ones who wanted Tharn's blood for their spells. Lord
Varrin had said that magicians could control dragons in the
Arena, but if they could control them well enough to keep them
in the city, wouldn't they have already done so?

Besides, there was that law—no grown dragons inside the
city walls.

Well, then, Sirinita told herself, she would just have to get
Tharn outside those walls!

She looked around.

Games Street led northeastward—didn't it go right to Eastgate? And of course, Wargate High Street went to Wargate, but
Wargate was down in the guard camp with the soldiers; Sirinita
didn't like to go there. She didn't mind the city guards most of
the time, but when there were that many all in one place they
made her nervous.

Eastgate should be all right, though. She had never been
there, let alone out of the city, but it should be all right.

Grandgate or Newgate might be closer than Eastgate, but she didn't know the streets to find them. Eastgate was easy.

"Come on, Tharn," she said, and together they set out along Games Street.

It took the better part of an hour to reach Eastgate Plaza. Sirinita didn't think the distance was even a whole mile, but there were so many distractions!

Games Street, after all, was lined with gaming houses. There were cardrooms and dice halls and archery ranges and wrestling rings and any number of other entertainments, and there were people drifting in and out of them. One man who smelled of *oushka* offered to gamble with Sirinita, his gold against her dragon; she politely declined. And dragons weren't often seen in Eastside, so several people stopped to stare and ask her questions.

At last, however, she reached Eastgate Plaza, where a few farmers and tradesmen were peddling their wares in a dusty square beside the twin towers of Eastgate. It wasn't terribly busy; Sirinita supposed most of the business went on at the other squares and markets, such as Eastgate Circle, four blocks to the west, or Farmgate, or Market.

The gatetowers were big forbidding structures of dark gray stone, either one of them several times the size of Sirinita's house, which wasn't small. The gates between them were bigger than any doors Sirinita had ever seen—and they were all standing open.

All she had to do was take Tharn out there, outside the walls, and he wouldn't have to be killed.

She marched forward resolutely, Tharn trotting at her heel.

Of course, it meant she would have to turn Tharn loose, and never see him again—*she* couldn't live outside the walls. Her mother would never allow it. And besides, there were pirates and monsters and stuff out there.

But at least he'd still be alive.

That was what she was thinking when she walked into the spearshaft.

She blinked, startled, then started to duck under it, assuming that it was in her way by accident.

"Ho, there!" the guard who held the spear called, and he bent down and grabbed her arm with his other hand. "What's your hurry?"

"I need to get my dragon out of the city," Sirinita explained.

The guard looked at Tharn, then back at Sirinita. "Your dragon?"

"Yes. His name's Tharn. Let go of my arm." She tugged, but the guard's fingers didn't budge.

"Can't do that," he said. "Not yet, anyway. Part of my job is to keep track of any kids who enter or leave the city without their parents along. If, for example, you were to be running away from home, and your folks wanted to find you but couldn't afford to hire a magician to do it, it'd make things much easier on them if they could ask the guards at the gate, 'Did my girl come through here? A pretty thing in a blue tunic, about so tall?' And I'd be able to tell them, so they'd know whether you're inside or outside the city walls."

Sirinita blinked up at the man. He was a big, heavy fellow, with deep brown eyes and a somewhat ragged beard.

"What if I went out a different gate?" she asked.

"Oh, we report everything to the captain, and he tallies up the reports every day, so your folks could check the captain's list. Then they'd even know which gate you went out, which might give them an idea where you're going."

Sirinita said, "My name's Sirinita, and I'm just going out to find a place for my dragon. I'll be back by nightfall."

"Just Sirinita?"

"Sirinita of Ethshar. Except the neighbors call me Sirinita of the Dragon."

"I can understand that." The guard released her arm. "Go on, then."

Sirinita had gone no more than three steps when the man called after her, "Wait a minute."

"Now what is it?" she asked impatiently, turning back.

"What do you mean, find a place for your dragon?"

"I mean find somewhere he can live. He can't stay in the city anymore."

"You don't have any supplies."

Sirinita blinked up at him in surprise. "Supplies?"

"Right, supplies. It's a long way to anywhere it would be safe to turn a dragon loose."

"It is?" Sirinita was puzzled. "I was just going to take him outside the walls."

"What, on someone's farm, or in the middle of a village?"

"No, of course not," Sirinita said, but the guard's words were making her rethink the situation. She probably *would* have just turned Tharn loose on someone's farm.

But that wouldn't be a good idea, would it?

"Um," she said, "I'm going to take him to my grandfather, I'm not going to turn him loose."

Her grandfathers both lived in the city—one was a Seagate merchant, the other owned a large and successful carpentry business in Crafton—but she didn't see any reason to tell the guard that.

"Your grandfather's got a farm near here?"

Sirinita nodded.

The guard considered her for a moment, then turned up an empty palm. "All right," he said, "go ahead, then."

"Thank you." She turned eastward once again, and marched out of the city.

She wondered what sort of supplies the guard had meant. Whatever they were, she would just have to do without them. It couldn't be *that* far to somewhere she could turn Tharn loose.

She looked out across the countryside, expecting to see a few farms and villages—she had seen pictures, and had a good idea what they should look like, with their half-timbered houses and pretty green fields.

What she actually saw, however, was something else entirely.

The road out of the city was a broad expanse of bare, hard-packed dirt crossed here and there with deep, muddy ruts. A few crude houses built of scrap wood were scattered around, and people stood or crouched in doorways, hawking goods and services to passersby—goods and services that were not allowed in the city, and Ethshar was a fairly tolerant place.

A hundred yards from the city the farms began—not with quaint cottages and tidy little fields, but with endless rows of stubby green plants in black dirt, and rough wooden sheds set here and there. The only roads were paths just wide enough for a wagon.

Sirinita was surprised, but walked on, Tharn at her heels.

She was still walking, hours later, when the sun sank below the hills she had already crossed. She was dirty and exhausted and miserable.

She had finally reached farms that more or less resembled those in the pictures, at any rate—not so clean or so charming, but at least there were thatched farmhouses and barns, and the fields no longer stretched unbroken to the horizon.

But she hadn't reached forests or mountains or even a fair-sized grove. The only trees were windbreaks or orchards or shade trees around houses. As far as she could see, from any hilltop she checked, there were only more farms—except to the west, of course, where she could sometimes, from the higher hills, still see the city walls, and where she thought she could occasionally catch the gleam of sunlight on the sea.

And everything smelled of the cow manure the farmers used as fertilizer.

The world, she thought bitterly, was obviously bigger than she had realized. No wonder her father's trading expeditions lasted a month at a time!

Tharn had not enjoyed taking so long a walk, either; he was a healthy and active young dragon, but he was still accustomed to taking an afternoon nap, to resting when he felt like it. He had not appreciated it when his mistress had dragged him along, and had even kicked him when he tried to sleep.

And when the sun went down, he had had enough; he flopped onto a hillock, mashing some farmer's pumpkin vines, and curled up to sleep.

Sirinita, too exhausted for anger or protest, looked down at him and started crying.

Tharn paid no attention. He slept.

And when she was done weeping, Sirinita sat down beside her dragon and looked about in the gathering gloom.

She couldn't see anyone, anywhere. They weren't on a road anymore, just a path through somebody's fields, and she couldn't see anything but half-grown crops and the shadowy shapes of distant farmhouses. Some of the windows were lighted, others dark, but nowhere did she see a torch or signboard over a door— if any of these places were inns, or even just willing to admit weary travelers, she didn't know how to tell.

She was out here in the middle of nowhere, miles from her soft clean bed, miles from her parents, her friends, *everybody*, with just her stupid dragon to keep her company, and it was all because he was growing too fast.

And Tharn wouldn't even stay awake so she could talk to him. She kicked him, purely out of spite; he puffed in annoyance, emitting a few sparks, but didn't wake.

That was new; he hadn't managed actual sparks before, so far as she could remember.

It didn't matter, though. She wasn't going any further with him. In the morning she was going to turn him loose, just leave him here and go home, maybe even slip away while he was asleep. If the farmers didn't like having him around, maybe they'd chase him off to the wilderness, wherever it was.

And maybe they'd kill him, but at least he'd have a *chance*, and she just couldn't go any farther.

Tharn breathed out another tiny shower of sparks, and a stench of something foul reached Sirinita's nostrils; Tharn's breath, never pleasant to begin with, was getting really disgusting—even worse than the cow manure, which she had mostly gotten used to.

Sirinita decided there wasn't any need to sleep right next to the dragon; she wandered a few paces away, to where a field of waist-high cornstalks provided some shelter, and settled down for the night.

The next thing she knew was that an unfamiliar voice was saying, "I don't see a lantern."

She opened a sleepy eye, and saw nothing at all.

"So maybe she just burned a cornstalk or something," a second voice said.

"I don't even see a tinderbox," the first replied.

"I don't either, but what do I know? I saw sparks here, and here she is—it must've been her. Maybe she had some little magic spell or something—she looks like a city girl."

"Maybe there was someone with her."

"No, she wouldn't be lying here all alone, then. No one would be stupid enough to leave a girl unprotected."

The first voice giggled unpleasantly. "Not if they knew *we* were around, certainly."

"She's pretty young," the second said dubiously.

Sirinita was completely awake now; she realized she was looking at the rich black earth of the farm. She turned her head, very carefully, to see who was speaking.

"She's awake!" the first voice said. "Quick!"

Then rough hands grabbed her, and her tunic was yanked up, trapping her arms, covering her face so that she couldn't see, and pulling her halfway to her feet. Unseen hands clamped around her wrists, holding the tunic up.

"Not all *that* young," someone said, but Sirinita couldn't hear well enough through the tunic to be sure which voice it was. Another hand touched her now-bare hip.

Sirinita screamed.

Someone hit her on the back of the head hard enough to daze her.

And then she heard Tharn growl.

It wasn't a sound she had heard often; it took a lot to provoke the dragon, as a rule.

"What was that?" one of her attackers asked.

"It's a baby dragon," the other replied. The grip on her left wrist fell away, and she was able to pull her tunic partway down, below her eyes.

She was in the cornfield, and it was still full night, but the greater moon shone orange overhead, giving enough light to make out shapes, but not colors.

There were two men, *big* men, and they both had swords, and Tharn was facing them, growling, his tail lashing snakelike behind him. One of the men was holding her right wrist with his left hand, drawing his sword with his right.

The other man, sword already drawn, was approaching Tharn cautiously.

"Dragon's blood," he said. "The wizards pay good money for dragon's blood."

He stepped closer, closer—and Tharn's curved neck suddenly straightened, thrusting his scaly snout to a foot or so from the man's face, and Tharn spat flame, lighting up the night, momentarily blinding the three humans, whose eyes had all been adjusted to the darkness.

The man who had approached the dragon screamed horribly, and the other dropped Sirinita's wrist; thus abruptly released, she stumbled and almost fell.

When she was upright and able to see again, she saw one man kneeling, both hands covering his face as he continued to scream; his sword was nowhere in sight. The other man was circling, trying to get behind Tharn, or at least out of the line of fire.

And Tharn was growling differently now, a sound like nothing Sirinita had ever heard before; his jaws and nostrils were glowing dull red, black smoke curled up from them, and his eyes caught the moonlight and gleamed golden. He didn't look like her familiar, bumbling pet; he looked terrifying.

The uninjured man dove for Tharn's neck, and the dragon turned with incredible speed, belching flame.

The man's hair caught fire, but he dived under the gout of flame and stabbed at Tharn.

Tharn dodged, or tried to, but Sirinita heard the metal blade scrape sickeningly across those armored scales she had so often scratched herself on.

Then Tharn, neck fully extended and bent almost into a circle, took his attacker from behind and closed his jaws on the man's neck.

Sirinita screamed—she didn't know why, she just did.

The first man was still whimpering into his hands.

The second man didn't scream, though; he just made a soft grunting noise, then sagged lifelessly across Tharn's back. His hair was smoldering; a shower of red sparks danced down Tharn's flank.

Sirinita turned and ran.

At first she wasn't running anywhere in particular; then she spotted a farmhouse with a light in the window. Someone had probably been awakened by the screaming. She turned her steps toward it.

A moment later she was hammering her fists on the door.

"Who is it?" someone called. "I've got a sword and a spear here."

"Help!" Sirinita shrieked.

For a moment no one answered, but she heard muffled voices debating; then the door burst open and she fell inside.

"They attacked me," she said, "and Tharn killed one of them, and . . . and . . ."

"Who attacked you?" a woman asked.

"Two men. Big men."

"Who's Tharn? Your father?" a man asked.

"My pet dragon."

The man and the woman looked at one another.

"She's crazy," the man said.

"Close the door," the woman answered.

"You don't think I should try to help?"

"Do you hear anyone else screaming?"

The man listened; so did Sirinita.

"No," the man said. "But I hear noises."

"Let them take care of it themselves, then."

"But . . ." The man hesitated, then asked, "Was anyone hurt?"

"The men who attacked me. Tharn hurt them both. I think he killed one."

"But this Tharn was all right when you left?" the woman asked.

Sirinita nodded.

"Then leave well enough alone for now. We'll go out in the morning and see what's what. Or if this Tharn comes to the door and speaks fair—we've the girl to tell us if it's the right one."

The man took one reluctant final look out the door, then closed and barred it, while the woman soothed Sirinita and led her to a corner by the fire where she could lie down. The man found two blankets and a feather pillow, and Sirinita curled up, shivering, certain she would never sleep again.

She was startled to wake up to broad daylight.

"You told us the truth last night," her hostess remarked.

Sirinita blinked sleep from her eyes.

"About your dragon, I mean. He's curled up out front. At first my man was afraid to step past him, after what you'd said about his fighting those two men, but he looks harmless enough, so at last he ventured it."

"I'm sorry he troubled you," Sirinita said.

"No trouble," she said.

"I have to get home," Sirinita said, as she sat up.

"No hurry, is there?"

Sirinita hesitated. "It's a long walk back to the city."

"It is," the woman admitted, "but isn't that all the more reason to have breakfast first?"

Sirinita, who had had no supper the night before, did not argue with that; she ate a hearty meal of hot buttered cornbread, apples, and cider.

When she was done she tried to feed Tharn, but the dragon wasn't hungry.

When the farmer showed her what he had found in the cornfield she saw why. Both her attackers were sprawled there—or at any rate, what was left of them. Tharn was still a very small dragon; he had left quite a bit.

She looked down at the dragon at her side; Tharn looked up at her and blinked. He stretched his wings and belched a small puff of flame.

"Come on," Sirinita said. She waved a farewell to her hosts—she never had learned their names, though she thought they'd been mentioned—then started walking up her own shadow, heading westward toward Ethshar.

It was late afternoon when, footsore and frazzled, she reached Eastgate with Tharn still at her heels. She made her way down East Road to the city's heart, then turned south into the residential district that had always been her home.

Her parents were waiting.

"When you weren't home by midnight we were worried, so this morning we hired a witch," her mother explained, after embraces and greetings had been exchanged. "She said you'd be home safe some time today, and here you are." She looked past her daughter at the dragon. "And Tharn, too, I see." She hesitated, then continued, "The witch said that Tharn saved your life last night. We really *can't* keep him here, Siri, but we can find a home for him somewhere . . ."

"No," Sirinita interrupted, hugging her mother close. "No, don't do that." She closed her eyes, and images of the man with the burned face screaming, the other man with his hair on fire and his neck broken, the two of them lying half-eaten between the rows of corn, appeared.

Tharn had been protecting her, and those men had meant to rape her and maybe kill her, but she knew those images would always be there.

Tharn was a dragon, and that was what dragons did.

"No, Mother," she said, shuddering, tears leaking from the corners of her tightly-shut eyes. "Get a wizard and have him killed."

DREAM READER
▼▼▼

JANE YOLEN

ONCE upon a time—which is how stories about magic and wizardry are supposed to begin—on a fall morning a boy stood longingly in front of a barrow piled high with apples. It was in the town of Gwethern, the day of the market fair.

The boy was almost a man and he did not complain about his empty stomach. His back still hurt from the flogging he had received just a week past, but he did not complain about that either. He had been beaten and sent away for lying. He was always being sent away from place to place for lying. The problem was, he never lied. He simply saw truth differently from other folk. On the slant.

His name was Merrillin but he called himself Hawk, another kind of lie because he was nothing at all like a hawk, being cowering and small from his many beatings and lack of steady food. Still he dreamed of becoming a hawk, fiercely independent and no man's prey, and the naming was his first small step toward what seemed an unobtainable goal.

But that was the other thing about Merrillin the Hawk. Not only did he see the truth slantwise, but he dreamed. And his dreams, in strange, uncounted ways, seemed to come true.

So Merrillin stood in front of the barrow on a late fall day and told himself a lie; that the apple would fall into his hand of its own accord as if the barrow were a tree letting loose its fruit. He even reached over and touched the apple he wanted, a rosy round one that promised to be full of sweet juices and crisp meat. And just in case, he touched a second apple as well, one that was slightly wormy and a bit yellow with age.

"You boy," came a shout from behind the barrow, and a face as yellow and sunken as the second apple, with veins as large as worm runnels across the nose, popped into view.

Merrillin stepped back, startled.

A stick came down on his hand, sharp and painful as a fire-brand. "If you do not mean to buy, you cannot touch."

"How do you know he does not mean to buy?" asked a voice from behind Merrillin.

It took all his concentration not to turn. He feared the man behind him might have a stick as well, though his voice seemed devoid of the anger that always preceded a beating.

"A rag of cloth hung on bones, that's all he is," said the cart man, wiping a dirty rag across his mouth. "No one in Gwethern has seen him before. He's no mother's son, by the dirt on him. So where would such a one find coins to pay, cheeky beggar?"

There was a short bark of laughter from the man behind. "Cheeky beggar is it?"

Merrillin dared a glance at the shadow the man cast at his feet. The shadow was cloaked. That was a good sign, for he would be a stranger to Gwethern. No one here affected such dress. Courage flooded through him and he almost turned around when the man's hand touched his mouth.

"You are right, he is a cheeky beggar. And that is where he keeps his coin—in his cheek." The cloaked man laughed again, the same sharp, yipping sound, drawing an appreciative echo from the crowd that was just starting to gather. Entertainment was rare in Gwethern. "Open your mouth, boy, and give the man his coin."

Merrillin was so surprised, his mouth dropped open on its own, and a coin fell from his lips into the cloaked man's hand.

"Here," the man said, his hand now on Merrillin's shoulder. He flipped the coin into the air, it turned twice over before the cart man grabbed it out of the air, bit it, grunted, and shoved it into his purse.

The cloaked man's hand left Merrillin's shoulder and picked up the yellowing apple, dropping it neatly into Merrillin's hand. Then his voice whispered into the boy's ear. "If you wish to repay me, look for the green wagon, the castle on wheels."

When Merrillin turned to stutter out his thanks, the man had vanished into the crowd. That was just as well, though, since it was hardly thanks Merrillin was thinking of. Rather he wanted to tell the cloaked man that he had done only what was expected and that another lie had come true for Merrillin, on the slant.

After eating every bit of the apple, his first meal in two days, and setting the little green worm that had been in it on a stone, Merrillin looked for the wagon. It was not hard to find.

Parked under a chestnut tree whose leaves were spotted with brown and gold, the wagon was as green as Mab's gown, as green as the first early shoots of spring. It was indeed a castle on wheels, for the top of the wagon was vaulted over. There were three windows, four walls, and a door as well. Two docile drab-colored mules were hitched to it and were nibbling on the few brown blades of grass beneath the tree. Along the wagon's sides was writing, but as Merrillin could not read, he could only guess at it. There were pictures, too: a tall, amber-eyed mage with a conical hat was dancing across a starry night, a dark-haired princess in rainbow robes played on a harp with thirteen strings. Merrillin could not read— but he could count. He walked toward the wagon.

"So, boy, have you come to pay what you owe?" asked a soft voice, followed by the trill of a mistle thrush.

At first Merrillin could not see who was speaking, but then something moved at one of the windows, a pale moon of a face. It was right where the face of the painted princess should have been. Until it moved, Merrillin had thought it part of the painting. With a bang, the window was slammed shut and then he saw the painted face on the glass. It resembled the other face only slightly.

A woman stepped through the door and stared at him. He thought her the most beautiful person he had ever seen. Her long dark hair was unbound and fell to her waist. She wore a dress of scarlet wool and jewels in her ears. A yellow purse hung from a braided belt and jangled as she moved, as if it were covered with tiny bells. As he watched, she bound up her hair with a single swift motion into a net of scarlet linen.

She smiled. "Ding-dang-dong, cat's got your tongue, then?"

When he didn't answer, she laughed and sat down on the top step of the wagon. Then she reached back behind her and pulled out a harp exactly like the one painted on the wagon's side. Strumming, she began to sing:

> "A boy with eyes a somber blue
> Will never ever come to rue,
> A boy with . . ."

"Are you singing about me?" asked Merrillin.

"Do you think I am singing about you?" the woman asked and then hummed another line.

"If not now, you will some day," Merrillin said.

"I believe you," said the woman, but she was busy tuning her harp at the same time. It was as if Merrillin did not really exist for her except as an audience.

"Most people do not," Merrillin said, walking over. He put

his hand on the top step, next to her bare foot. "Believe me, I mean. But I never tell lies."

She looked up at that and stared at him as if really seeing him for the first time. "People who never tell lies are a wonder. All people lie sometime." She strummed a discordant chord.

Merrillin looked at the ground. "I am not *all people*."

She began picking a quick, bright tune, singing:

> *"If you never ever lie*
> *You are a better soul than I . . ."*

Then she stood and held up the harp behind her. It disappeared into the wagon. "But you did not answer my question, boy."

"What question?"

"Have you come to pay what you owe?"

Puzzled, Merrillin said: "I did not answer because I did not know you were talking to me. I owe nothing to you."

"Ah, but you owe it me," came a lower voice from inside the wagon where it was dark. A man emerged and even though he was not wearing the cloak, Merrillin knew him at once. The voice was the same, gentle and ironic. He was the mage on the wagon's side; the slate gray hair was the same—and the amber eyes.

"I do not owe you either, sir."

"What of the apple, boy?"

Merrillin started to cringe, thought better of it, and looked straightaway into the man's eyes. "The apple was *meant* to come to me, sir."

"Then why came you to the wagon?" asked the woman, smoothing her hands across the red dress. "If not to pay."

"As the apple was meant to come into my hands, so I was meant to come into yours."

The woman laughed. "Only you hoped the mage would not

eat you up and put your little green worm on a rock for some passing scavenger."

Merrillin's mouth dropped open. "How did you know?"

"Bards *know* everything," she said.

"And *tell* everything as well," said the mage. He clapped her on the shoulder and she went, laughing, through the door.

Merrillin nodded to himself. "It was the window," he whispered.

"Of course it was the window," said the mage. "And if you wish to talk to yourself, make it *sotto voce*, under the breath. A whisper is no guarantee of secrets."

"Sotto voce," Merrillin said.

"The soldiers brought the phrase, but it rides the market roads now," said the mage.

"Sotto voce," Merrillin said again, punctuating his memory.

"I like you, boy," said the mage. "I collect oddities."

"Did you collect the bard, sir?"

Looking quickly over his shoulder, the mage said, "Her?"

"Yes, sir."

"I did."

"How is she an oddity?" asked Merrillin. "I think she is"— he took a gulp—"wonderful."

"That she is; quite, quite wonderful, my Viviane, and she well knows it," the mage replied. "She has a range of four octaves and can mimic any bird or beast I name." He paused. "And a few I cannot."

"Viviane," whispered Merrillin. Then he said the name without making a sound.

The mage laughed heartily. "You are an oddity, too, boy. I thought so at the first when you walked into the market fair with nothing to sell and no purse with which to buy. I asked, and no one knew you. Yet you stood in front of the barrow as if you owned the apples. When the stick fell, you did not protest; when the coin dropped from your lips, you said not a word. But I

could feel your anger and surprise and—something more. You
are an oddity. I sniffed it out with my nose from the first and
my nose"—he tapped it with his forefinger, managing to look
both wise and ominous at once—"my nose, like you, never lies.
Do you think yourself odd?"

Merrillin closed his eyes for a moment, a gesture the mage
would come to know well. When he opened them again, his
eyes were no longer the somber blue that Viviane had sung about
but were the blue of a bleached out winter sky. "I have dreams,"
he said.

The mage held his breath, his wisdom being as often in silence as in words.

"I dreamed of a wizard and a woman who lived in a castle
green as early spring grass. Hawks flew about the turrets and a
bear squatted on the throne. I do not know what it all means,
but now that I have seen the green wagon, I am sure you are
the wizard and the woman, Viviane."

"Do you dream often?" asked the mage, slowly coming down
the steps of the wagon and sitting on the lowest stair.

Merrillin nodded.

"And do your dreams often come true?" he asked. Then he
added, quickly, "No, you do not have to answer that."

Merrillin nodded again.

"Always?"

Merrillin closed his eyes, then opened them.

"Tell me," said the mage.

"I dare not. When I tell, I am called a liar or hit. Or both. I
do not think I want to be hit anymore."

The mage laughed again, this time with his head back. When
he finished, he narrowed his eyes and looked at the boy. "I have
never hit anyone in my life. And telling lies is an essential part
of magic. You lie with your hands like this." And so saying,
he reached behind Merrillin's ear and pulled out a bouquet of
meadowsweet, wintergreen, and a single blue aster. "You see, my

hands told the lie that flowers grow in the dirt behind your ear. And your eyes took it in."

Merrillin laughed, a funny crackling sound, as if he were not much used to laughter.

"But do not let Viviane know you tell lies," said the mage, leaning forward and whispering. "She is as practiced in her anger as she is on the harp. I may never swat a liar, but she is the very devil when her temper's aroused."

"I will not," said Merrillin solemnly. They shook hands on it, only when Merrillin drew away his grasp, he had a small copper coin in his palm.

"Buy yourself a meat pie, boy," said the mage. "And then come along with us. I think you will be a very fine addition to our collection."

"Thank you, sir," gasped Merrillin.

"Not *sir*. My name is Ambrosius, because of my amber eyes. Did you notice them? Ambrosius the Wandering Mage. And what is your name? I cannot keep calling you 'boy.'"

"My name is Merrillin but . . ." He hesitated and looked down.

"I will not hit you and you may keep the coin whatever you say," Ambrosius said.

"But I would like to be called Hawk."

"Hawk, is it?" The mage laughed again. "Perhaps you will grow into that name, but it seems to me that you are mighty small and a bit thin for a hawk."

A strange sharp cackling sound came from the interior of the wagon, a high *ki-ki-ki-ki*.

The mage looked in and back. "Viviane says you *are* a hawk, but a small one—the merlin. And that is, quite happily, close to your Christian name as well. Will it suit?"

"Merlin," whispered Merrillin, his hand clutched tightly around the coin. Then he looked up, his eyes gone the blue of the aster. "That was the hawk in my dream, Ambrosius. That was the sound he made. A merlin. It has to be my true name."

"Good. Then it is settled," said the mage standing. "Fly off to your pie, Hawk Merlin, and then fly quickly back to me. We go tomorrow to Carmarthen. There's to be a great holy day fair. Viviane will sing. I will do my magic. And you—well, we shall have to figure out what you can do. But it will be something quite worthy, I am sure. I tell you, young Merlin, there are fortunes to be made on the road if you can sing in four voices and pluck flowers out of the air."

▼▼▼

The road was a gentle winding path through valleys and along-side streams. The trees were still gold in most places, but on the far ridges the forests were already bare.

As the wagon bounced along, Viviane sang songs about Robin of the Wood in a high, sweet voice and the Battle of the Trees in a voice deep as thunder. And in a middle voice she sang a lusty ballad about a bold warrior that made Merlin's cheeks turn pink and hot.

Ambrosius shortened the journey with his wonder tales. And as he talked, he made coins walk across his knuckles and found two quail's eggs behind Viviane's left ear. Once he pulled a turtledove out of Merlin's shirt, which surprised the dove more than the boy. The bird flew off onto a low branch of an ash tree and plucked its breast feathers furiously until the wagon had passed by.

They were two days traveling and one day resting by a lovely bright pond rimmed with willows.

"Carmarthen is over that small hill," pointed out the mage. "But it will wait on us. The fair does not begin until tomorrow. Besides, we have fishing to do. And a man—whether mage or murderer—always can find time to fish!" He took Merlin down to the pond where he quickly proved himself a bad angler but a merry companion, telling fish stories late into the night. All he caught was a turtle. It was Merlin who pulled up the one small spotted trout they roasted over the fire that night and shared three ways.

▼▼▼

Theirs was not the only wagon on the road before dawn, but it was the gaudiest by far. Peddlers' children leaped off their own wagons to run alongside and beg the magician for a trick. He did one for each child and asked for no coins at all, even though Viviane chided him.

"Do not scold, Viviane. Each child will bring another to our wagon once we are in the town. They will be our best criers," Ambrosius said, as he made a periwinkle appear from under the chin of a dirty-faced tinker lass. She giggled and ran off with the flower.

At first each trick made Merlin gasp with delight. But partway through the trip, he began to notice from where the flowers and coins and scarves and eggs really appeared—out of the vast sleeves of the mage's robe. He started watching Ambrosius' hands carefully through slotted eyes, and unconsciously his own hands began to imitate them.

Viviane reached over and, holding the reins with one hand, slapped his fingers so hard they burned. "Do not do that. It is bad enough he does the tricks for free on the road, but you would beggar us for sure if you give them away forever. Idiot!"

After the scolding, Merlin sat sullenly inside the darkened wagon practicing his sotto voce with curses he had heard but had never dared repeat aloud. Embarrassment rather than anger sent a kind of ague to his limbs. Eventually, though, he wore himself out and fell asleep. He dreamed a wicked little dream about Viviane, in which a whitethorn tree fell upon her. When he woke, he was ashamed of the dream and afraid of it as well, but he did not know how to change it. His only comfort was that his dreams did not come true literally. *On the slant,* he reminded himself, which lent him small comfort.

He was still puzzling this out when the mules slowed and he became aware of a growing noise. Moving to the window, he stared out past the painted face.

If Gwethern had been a bustling little market town, Carmarthen had to be the very center of the commercial world. Merlin saw gardens and orchards outside the towering city walls though he also noted that the gardens were laid out in a strange pattern and some of the trees along the northern edges were ruined and the ground around them was raw and wounded. There were many spotty pastures where sheep and kine grazed on the late fall stubble. The city walls were made up of large blocks of limestone. How anyone could have moved such giant stones was a mystery to him. Above the walls he could glimpse crenelated towers from which red and white banners waved gaudily in the shifting fall winds, first north, then west.

Merlin could contain himself no longer and scrambled through the wagon door, squeezing in between Ambrosius and Viviane.

"Look, oh, look!" he cried.

Viviane smiled at the childish outburst, but the mage touched his hand.

"It is not enough just to look, Merlin. You must look—and remember."

"Remember—what?" asked Merlin.

"The eyes and ears are different listeners," said the mage. "But both feed into magecraft. Listen. What do you hear?"

Merlin strained, tried to sort out the many sounds, and said at last, "It is very noisy."

Viviane laughed. "I hear carts growling along, and voices, many different tongues. A bit of Norman, some Saxon, Welsh, and Frankish. There is a hawk screaming in the sky behind us.

And a loud, heavy clatter coming from behind the walls. Something being built, I would guess."

Merlin listened again. He could hear the carts and voices easily. The hawk was either silent now or beyond his ken. But because she mentioned it, he could hear the heavy rhythmic pounding of building like a bass note, grounding the entire song of Carmarthen. "Yes," he said, with a final exhalation.

"And what do you see?" asked Ambrosius.

Determined to match Viviane's ears with his eyes, Merlin began a litany of wagons and wagoners, beasts straining to pull, and birds restrained in cages. He described jongleurs and farmers and weavers and all their wares. As they passed through the gates of the city and under the portcullis, he described it as well.

"Good," said Ambrosius. "And what of those soldiers over there." He nodded his head slightly to the left.

Merlin turned to stare at them.

"No, never look directly on soldiers, highwaymen, or kings. Look through the slant of your eyes," whispered Viviane, reining in the mules.

Merlin did as she instructed, delighted to be once more in her good graces. "There are ten of them," he said.

"And what do they wear?" prompted Ambrosius.

"Why, their uniforms. And helms."

"What color helms?" Viviane asked.

"Silver, as helms are wont. But six have red plumes, four white." Then as an afterthought, he added, "And they all carry swords."

"The swords are not important," said Ambrosius, "but note the helms. Ask yourself why some should be sporting red plumes, some white. Ask yourself if these are two different armies of two different lords. And if so, why are they both here?"

"I do not know," answered Merlin. "Why?"

Ambrosius laughed. "I do not know either. Yet. But it is something odd to be tucked away. And remember—I collect oddities."

Viviane clicked to the mules with her tongue and slapped their backs with the reins. They started forward again.

"Once around the square, Viviane, then we will choose our spot. Things are already well begun," said the mage. "There are a juggler and a pair of acrobats and several strolling players, though none—I wager—with anything near your range. But I see no other masters of magic. We shall do well here."

▼▼▼

In a suit of green and gold—the gold a cotte of the mage's that Viviane had tailored to fit him, the green his old hose sewn over with gold patches and bells—Merlin strode through the crowd with a tambourine. It was his job to collect the coins after each performance. On the first day folk were liable to be the most generous, afterward husbanding their coins for the final hours of the fair, at least that was what Viviane had told him. Still he was surprised by the waterfall of copper pennies that cascaded into his tambourine.

"Our boy Merlin will pass amongst you, a small hawk in the pigeons," Ambrosius had announced before completing his final trick, the one in which Viviane was shut up in a box and subsequently disappeared into the wagon.

Merlin had glowed at the name pronounced so casually aloud, and at the claim of possession. *Our* boy, Ambrosius had said. Merlin repeated the phrase sotte voce to himself and smiled. The infectious smile brought even more coins, though he was unaware of it.

It was after their evening performance when Viviane had sung in three different voices, including a love song about a shepherd and the ewe lamb that turned into a lovely maiden who fled from him over a cliff, that a broad-faced soldier with a red plume in his helm parted the teary-eyed crowd. Coming up to the wagon stage, he announced, "The Lady Renwein would have you come tomorrow evening to the old palace and sends this as way of a promise. There will be more after a satisfactory performance. It is in honor of her upcoming wedding." He dropped a purse into Ambrosius' hand.

The mage bowed low and then, with a wink, began drawing a series of colored scarves from behind the soldier's ear. They were all shades of red: crimson, pink, vermilion, flame, scarlet, carmine, and rose.

"For your lady," Ambrosius said, holding out the scarves.

The soldier laughed aloud and took them. "The lady's colors. She will be pleased. Though not, I think, his lordship."

"The white soldiers, then, are his?" asked Ambrosius.

Ignoring the question, the soldier said, "Be in the kitchen by nones. We ring the bells here. The duke is most particular."

"Is dinner included?" asked Viviane.

"Yes, mistress," the soldier replied. "You shall eat what the cook eats." He turned and left.

"Then let us hope," said Viviane to his retreating back, "that we like what the cook likes."

▼▼▼

Merlin dreamed that night and woke screaming but could not recall exactly what he had dreamed. The mage's hand was on his brow and Viviane wrung out cool water onto a cloth for him.

"Too much excitement for one day," she said, making a clucking sound with her tongue.

"And too many meat pies," added the mage, nodding.

The morning of the second day of the holy day fair came much too soon. And noisily. When Merlin went to don his green-and-gold suit, Ambrosius stayed him.

"Save that for the lady's performance. I need you in your old cotte to go around the fair. And remember—use your ears and eyes."

Nodding, Merlin scrambled into his old clothes. They had been tidied up by Viviane, but he was aware, for the first time, of how really shabby and threadbare they were. Ambrosius slipped him a coin.

"You earned this. Spend it as you will. But not on food, boy. We will feast enough at the duke's expense."

Clutching the coin, Merlin escaped into the early morning crowds. In his old clothes, he was unremarked, just another poor lad eyeing the wonders at the holy day fair.

At first he was seduced by the stalls. The variety of foods and cloth and toys and entertainments were beyond anything he had ever imagined. But halfway around the second time, he remembered his charge. *Eyes and ears.* He did not know exactly what Ambrosius would find useful but he was determined to uncover something.

▼▼▼

"It was between the Meadowlands Jugglers and a stall of spinach pies," he told Ambrosius later, wrinkling his nose at the thought of spinach baked in a flaky crust. "A white plumed soldier and a red were quarreling. It began with name calling. Red called white, 'Dirty men of a dirty duke,' and white countered with 'Spittle of the Lady Cock.' And they would have fallen to, but a ball from the jugglers landed at their feet and the crowd surged over to collect it."

"So there is no love lost between the two armies," mused Ambrosius. "I wonder if they were the cause of the twisted earth around the city walls."

"And after that I watched carefully for pairs of soldiers. They were everywhere matched, one red and one white. And the names between them bounced back and forth like an apple between boys."

The mage pulled on his beard thoughtfully. "What other names did you hear?"

"She was called Dragonlady, Lady Death, and the Open Way."

Ambrosius laughed. "Colorful. And one must wonder how accurate."

"And the duke was called Pieless, the Ewe's Own Lover, and Draco," said Merlin, warming to his task.

"Scurrilous and the Lord knows how well-founded. But two dragons quarreling in a single nest? It will make an unsettling performance at best. One can only wonder why two such creatures decided to wed." Ambrosius worked a coin across his knuckles, back and forth, back and forth. It was a sign he was thinking.

"Surely, for love?" whispered Merlin.

Viviane, who had been sitting quietly, darning a colorful petticoat, laughed. "Princes never marry for love, little hawk. For money, for lands, for power—yes. Love they find elsewhere or not at all. That is why I would never be a prince."

Ambrosius seemed not to hear her, but Merlin took in every word and savored the promise he thought he heard.

▼▼▼

They arrived at the old castle as the bells chimed nones. And the castle was indeed old; its keep from the days of the Romans was mottled and pocked but was still the most solid part of the building. Even Merlin, unused as he was to the ways of builders, could see that the rest was of shoddy material and worse workmanship.

"The sounds of building we heard from far off must be a brand-new manor being constructed," said Ambrosius. "For the new-wedded pair."

And indeed the cook, whose taste in supper clearly matched Viviane's, agreed. "The duke's father fair beggared our province fighting off imagined invaders, and his son seems bent on finishing the job. He even invited the bloody-minded Saxons in to help." He held up his right hand and made the sign of horns and spat through it. "Once, though you'd hardly credit it, this was a countryside of lucid fountains and transparent rivers. Now it's often dry as dust, though it was one of the prettiest places in all Britain. And if the countryside is in tatters, the duke's coffers are worse. That is why he has made up his mind to marry the Lady Renwein. She has as much money as she has had lovers, so they say, and that is not the British way. But the duke is besotted with both her count and her coinage. And even I must admit she has made a difference. Why, they are building a new great house upon the site of the old Roman barracks. The duke is having it constructed on the promise of her goods."

Viviane made no comment but kept eating. Ambrosius, who always ate sparingly before a performance, listened intently, urging the cook on with well-placed questions. Following Viviane's actions, Merlin stuffed himself and almost made himself sick again. He curled up in a corner near the hearth to sleep. The last thing he heard was the cook's continuing complaint.

"I know not when we shall move into the new house. I long for the larger hearth promised, for now with the red guards to feed as well as the duke's white—*and* the Saxon retainers—I need more. But the building goes poorly."

"Is that so?" interjected Ambrosius.

"Aye. The foundation does not hold. What is built up by day falls down by night. There is talk of witchcraft."

"Is there?" Ambrosius asked smoothly.

"Aye, the Saxons claim it against us. British witches, they cry. And they want blood to cleanse it."

"Do they?"

▼▼▼

A hand on his shoulder roused Merlin, but he was still partially within the vivid dream.

"The dragons . . ." he murmured and opened his eyes.

"Hush," came Ambrosius' voice. "Hush—and remember. You called out many times in your sleep: dragons and castles, water and blood, but what it all means you kept to yourself. So remember the dream, all of it. And I will tell you when to spin out the tale to catch the conscience of Carmarthen in its web. If I am right . . ." He touched his nose.

Merlin closed his eyes again and nodded. He did not open them again until Viviane began fussing with his hair, running a comb through the worst tangles and pulling at his cotte. She tied a lover's knot of red and white ribbands around his sleeve, then moved back.

"Open your eyes, boy. You are a sight." She laughed and pinched one cheek.

The touch of her hand made his cheeks burn. He opened his eyes and saw the kitchen abustle with servants. The cook, now too busy to chat with them further, was working at the hearth, basting and stirring and calling out a string of instructions to his overworked crew. "Here, Stephen, more juice. Wine up to the tables and hurry, Mag—they are pounding their feet upon the floor. The soup is hot enough, the tureens must be run up, and mind the handles. Use a cloth, Nan, stupid girl. And where are the sharp knives? These be dull as Saxon wit. Come, Stephen, step lively; the pies must come out the oast or they burn. Now!"

Merlin wondered that he could keep it all straight.

The while Ambrosius in one corner limbered up his fingers, having already checked out his apparatus, and Viviane, sitting down at the table, began to tune her harp. Holding it on her lap, her head cocked to one side, she sang a note then tuned each string to it. It was a wonder she could hear in all that noise—the cook shouting, Stephen clumping around and bumping into things, Nan whining, and Mag cursing back at the cook—but she did not seem to mind, her face drawn up with passionate intensity.

Into the busyness strode a soldier. When he came up to the hearth, Merlin could see it was the same one who had first tendered them the invitation to perform. His broad, homey face was split by a smile, wine and plenty of hot food having worked their own magic.

"Come, mage. And you, singer. We are ready when you are."

Ambrosius gestured to three large boxes. "Will you lend a hand?"

The soldier grunted.

"And my boy comes, too," said Ambrosius.

Putting his head to one side as if considering, the soldier asked, "Is he strong enough to carry these? He looks small and puling."

"He can carry if he has to, but he is more than that to us."

The soldier laughed. "You will have no need of a tambourine boy to pass among the gentlefolk and soldiers. Her ladyship will see that you are well enough paid."

Ambrosius stood very tall and dropped his voice to a deep, harsh whisper. "I have performed in higher courts than this. I know what is fit for fairs and what is fit for a great hall. You know not to whom you speak."

The soldier drew back.

Viviane smiled but carefully, so that the soldier could not see it, and played three low notes on the harp.

Merlin did not move. It was as if for a moment the entire kitchen had turned to stone.

Then the soldier gave a short, barking laugh, but his face was wary. "Do not mock me, mage. I saw him do nothing but pick up coins."

"That is because he only proffers his gifts for people of station. I am but a mage, a man of small magics and tricks that fool the eye. But the boy is something more." He walked toward Merlin slowly, his hand outstretched.

Still Merlin did not move, though imperceptibly he stood taller. Ambrosius put his hand on Merlin's shoulders.

"The boy is a reader of dreams," said the mage. "What he dreams comes true."

"Is this so?" asked the soldier, looking around.

"It is so," said Viviane.

Merlin closed his eyes for a moment, and when he opened them, they were the color of an ocean swell, blue-green washed with gray. "It is so," he said at last.

From the hearth where he was basting the joints of meat, the cook called out, "It is true that the boy dreamed here today. About two dragons. I heard him cry out in his sleep."

The soldier, who had hopes of a captaincy, thought a moment, then said, "Very well, all three of you come with me. Up the stairs. Now." He cornered young Stephen to carry the mage's boxes, and marched smartly out the door.

The others followed quickly, though Merlin hung back long enough to give the other boy a hand.

▼▼▼

Viviane sang first, a medley of love songs that favored the duke and his lady in turn. With the skill of a seasoned entertainer, she inserted the Lady Renwein's name into her rhyme, but called the duke in the songs merely "The Duke of Carmarthen town." (Later she explained to Merlin that the only rhymes she had for the duke's name were either scurrilous or treasonous, and sang a couple of verses to prove it.) Such was her ability, each took the songs as flattering, though Merlin thought he detected a nasty undertone in them that made him uncomfortable. But Viviane was roundly applauded and at the end of her songs, two young soldiers picked her up between them and set her upon their table for an encore. She smiled prettily at them, but Merlin knew she hated their touch, for the smile was one she reserved for particularly messy children, drunken old men—and swine.

Deftly beginning his own performance at the moment Viviane ended hers, Ambrosius was able to cover any unpleasantness that might occur if one of the soldiers dared take liberties with Viviane as she climbed down from the tabletop. He began with silly tricks—eggs, baskets, even a turtle was plucked from the air or from behind an unsuspecting soldier's ear. The tortoise was the one the mage had found when they had been fishing.

Then Ambrosius moved on to finer tricks, guessing the name of a soldier's sweetheart, finding the red queen in a deck of cards missing yet discovering it under the Lady Renwein's plate, and finally making Viviane disappear and reappear in a series of boxes through which he had the soldiers thrust their swords.

The last trick brought great consternation to the guards, especially when blood appeared to leak from the boxes, blood which when examined later proved to be juices from the meat which Viviane had kept in a flask. And when she reappeared, whole, unharmed, and smiling once the swords had been withdrawn from the box, the great hall resounded with huzzahs.

The duke smiled and whispered to the Lady Renwein. She covered his hand with hers. When he withdrew his hand, the duke held out a plump purse. He jangled it loudly.

"We are pleased to offer you this, Ambrosius."

"Thank you, my lord. But we are not done yet," said the mage with a bow which, had it been a little less florid, would have been an insult. "I would introduce you to Merlin, our dream reader, who will tell you of a singular dream he had this day in your house."

Merlin came to the center of the room. He could feel his legs trembling. Ambrosius walked over to him and, turning his back to the duke, whispered to the boy. "Do not be afraid. Tell the dream and I will say what it means."

"Will you know?" asked Merlin.

"My eyes and ears know what needs be said here," said Ambrosius, "whatever the dream. You must trust me."

Merlin nodded and Ambrosius moved aside. The boy stood with his eyes closed and began to speak.

"I dreamed a tower of snow that in the day reached high up into the sky but at night melted to the ground. And there was much weeping and wailing in the country because the tower would not stand."

"*The castle!*" the duke gasped, but Lady Renwein placed her hand gently on his mouth.

"Hush, my lord," she whispered urgently. "Listen. Do not speak yet. This may be merely a magician's trick. After all, they have been in Carmarthen for two days already and surely there is talk of the building in the town."

Merlin, his eyes still closed, seemed not to hear them, but continued. "And then one man arose, a mage, who advised that the tower of icy water be drained in the morning instead of building atop it. It was done as he wished, though the soldiers complained bitterly of it. But at last the pool was drained and lo! there in the mud lay two great hollow stones as round and speckled and veined as gray eggs.

"Then the mage drew a sword and struck open the eggs. In the one was a dragon the color of wine, its eyes faceted as jewels. In the other a dragon the color of maggots, with eyes as tarnished as old coins.

"And when the two dragons saw that they were revealed, they turned not on the soldiers nor the mage but upon one another. At first the white dragon had the best of it and pushed the red to the very edge of the dry pool, but it so blooded its opponent that a new pool was formed, the color of the ocean beyond the waves. But then the red rallied and pushed the white back, and it slipped into the bloody pool and disappeared, never to be seen again whole.

"And the man who advised began to speak once more, but I awoke."

At that, Merlin opened his eyes and they were the blue of speedwells on a summer morn.

The Lady Renwein's face was dark and disturbed. In a low voice she said, "Mage, ask him what the dream means."

Ambrosius bowed very low this time, for he saw that while

the duke might be easily cozzened, the Lady Renwein was no fool. When he stood straight again, he said, "The boy dreams, my lady, but he leaves it to me to make sense of what he dreams. Just as did his dear, dead mother before him."

Merlin, startled, looked at Viviane. She rolled her eyes up to stare at the broad beams of the ceiling and held her mouth still.

"His mother was a dream reader, too?" asked the duke.

"She was, though being a woman, dreamed of more homey things: the names of babes and whether they be boys or girls, and when to plant, and so forth."

The Lady Renwein leaned forward. "Then say, mage, what this dream of towers and dragons means."

"I will, my lady. It is not unknown to us that you have a house that will not stand. However, what young Merlin has dreamed is the reason for this. The house or tower of snow sinks every day into the ground; in the image of the dream, it melts. That is because there is a pool beneath it. Most likely the Romans built the conduits for their baths there. With the construction, there has been a leakage underground. The natural outflow has been damaged further by armies fighting. And so there has been a pooling under the foundation. Open up the work, drain the pool, remove or reconstruct the Roman pipes, and the building will stand."

"Is that all?" asked the duke, disappointment in his voice. "I thought that you might say the red was the Lady Renwein's soldiers, the white mine or some such."

"Dreams are never quite so obvious, my lord. They are devious messages to us, truth . . ."—he paused for a moment and put his hands on Merlin's shoulders—"truth on the slant."

Lady Renwein was nodding. "Yes, that would make sense. About the drains and the Roman pipes, I mean. Not the dream. You need not have used so much folderol in order to give us good advice."

Ambrosius smiled and stepped away from Merlin and made

another deep bow. "But my lady, who would have listened to a traveling magician on matters of . . . shall we say . . . state?"

She smiled back.

"And besides," Ambrosius added, "I had not heard this dream until this very moment. I had given no thought before it to your palace or anything else of Carmarthen excepting the fair. It is the boy's dream that tells us what to do. And, unlike his mother of blessed memory, I could never guess a baby's sex before it was born lest she dreamed it. And she, the minx, never mentioned that she was carrying a boy to me, nor did she dream of him till after he was born when she, dying, spoke of him once. 'He will be a hawk among princes,' she said. So I named him Merlin."

▼▼▼

It was two days later when a special messenger came to the green wagon with a small casket filled with coins and a small gold dragon with faceted red jewels for eyes.

"Her ladyship sends these with her compliments," said the soldier who brought the casket. "There was indeed a hidden pool beneath the foundation. And the pipes, which were as gray and speckled and grained as eggs, were rotted through. In some places they were gnawed on, too, by some small underground beasts. Her lady begs you to stay or at least send the boy back to her for yet another dream."

Ambrosius accepted the casket solemnly, but shook his head. "Tell her ladyship that—alas—there is but one dream per prince. And we must away. The fair here is done and there is another holy day fair in Londinium, many days journey from here. Even with such a prize as her lady has gifted us, Ambrosius the Wandering Mage and his company can never be still long." He bowed.

But Ambrosius did not proffer the real reason they were away: that a kind of restless fear drove him on, for after the performance when they were back in the wagon, Merlin had cried out against him. "But that was not the true meaning of the dream. There *will* be fighting here—the red dragon of the Britons and the Saxon white will fight again. The tower is only a small part—of the dream, of the whole."

And Ambrosius had sighed loudly then, partly for effect, and said, "My dear son, for as I claimed you, now you are mine forever, magecraft is a thing of the eye and ear. You tell me that what you dream comes true—but on the slant. And I say that to tell a prince to his face that you have dreamed of his doom invites the dreamer's doom as well. And, as you yourself re-minded me, it may not be *all* the truth. The greatest wisdom of any dreamer is to survive in order to dream again. Besides, how do you really know if what you dream is true or if, in the telling of it, you make it come true? We are men, not beasts, because we can dream and because we can make those dreams come true."

Merlin had closed his eyes then, and when he opened them again, they were the clear vacant blue of a newborn babe's. "Fa-ther," he had said, and it was a child's voice speaking.

Ambrosius had shivered with the sound of it, for he knew that sons in the natural order of things o'erthrew their fathers when they came of age. And Merlin, it was clear, was very quick to learn and quicker to grow.

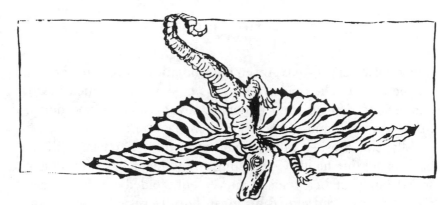

THE DRAGON ON
THE BOOKSHELF
▼▼▼

HARLAN ELLISON AND
ROBERT SILVERBERG

H E was small; petite, actually. Perhaps an inch shorter—
resting back on his glimmering haunches—than any of the mass-
market paperbacks racked on either side of him. He was green,
of course. Blue-green, down his front, underchin to bellybottom,
greenish yellow-ochre all over the rest. Large, luminous pastel-
blue eyes that would have made Shirley Temple seethe with
envy. And he was licking his front right paw as he blew soft gray
smoke rings through his heroically long nostrils.

To his left, a well-thumbed Ballantine paperback edition of
C. Wright Mills's *The Causes of World War III*; to his right, a
battered copy, sans dust jacket, of *The Man Who Knew Coolidge*
by Sinclair Lewis. He licked each of his four paw-fingers in turn.

Margaret, sitting across the room from the teak Danish Modern bookcase where he lived, occasionally looked up from the
theme papers she was correcting spread out across the card table,
to smile at him and make a ticking sound of affection. "Good

doughnuts?" she asked. An empty miniature Do-Nettes box lay on the carpet. The dragon rolled his eyes and continued licking confectioners' sugar from under his silver claws. "Good doughnuts," she said, and went back to her classwork.

Idly, she brushed auburn hair away from her face with the back of a slim hand. Completing his toilette, the little dragon stared raptly at her graceful movement, folded his front paws, sighed deeply, and closed his great, liquid eyes.

The smoke rings came at longer intervals now.

Outside, the afreet and djinn continued to battle, the sounds of their exploding souls making a terrible clank and clangor in the dew-misty streets of dark San Francisco.

So it was to be another of those days. They came all too frequently now that the gateway had been prised open: harsh days, smoldering days, dangerous nights. This was no place to be a dragon, no time to be in the tidal flow of harm's way. There were new manifestations every day now. Last Tuesday the watchthings fiercely clicking their ugly fangs and flatulating at the entrance to the Transamerica Pyramid. On Wednesday a shoal of blind banshees materialized above Coit Tower and covered the structure to the ground with lemony ooze that continued to wail days later. Thursday the resurrected Mongol hordes breaking through west of Van Ness, the air redolent of monosodium glutamate. Friday was silent. No less dangerous; merely silent. Saturday the gullgull incursion, the burnings at the Vaillancourt Fountain. And Sunday—oh, Sunday, bloody Sunday!

Small, large-eyed dragons in love had to walk carefully these days: perils were plentiful, sanctuaries few.

The dragon opened his eyes and stared raptly at the human woman. There sat his problem. Lovely, there she sat. The little dragon knew his responsibility. The only refuge lay within. The noise of the warfare outside was terrifying; and the little dragon was the cause. Coiling on his axis, the dragon diminished his extension along the *sril*-curve and let himself slip away. Margaret gasped softly, a little cry of alarm and dismay. "But you said you wouldn't—"

Too late. A twirling, twinkling scintillance. The bookshelf was empty of anything but books, not one of which mentioned dragons.

"Oh," she murmured, alone in the silent pre-dawn apartment.

▼▼▼

"Master, what am I to do?" said Urnikh,• the little dragon that had been sitting in the tiny San Francisco apartment only moments before. "I have made matters so much worse. You should have selected better, Master . . . I never knew enough, was not powerful enough. I've made it terrible for them, and they don't even know it's happening. They are more limited than you let me understand, Master. And I . . ."

The little dragon looked up helplessly.

He spoke softly. "I love her, the human woman in the place where I came into their world. I love the human woman, and I did not pursue my mission. I love her, and my inaction made matters worse, my love for her helped open the gateway.

"I can't help myself. Help me to rectify, Master. I have fallen in love with her. I'm stricken. With the movement of her limbs, with the sound of her voice, the way her perfume rises off her, the gleam of her eyes; did I say the way her limbs move? The things she thinks and says? She is a wonderment, indeed. But what, *what* am I to do?"

The Master looked down at the dragon from the high niche in the darkness. "There is desperation in your voice, Urnikh."

"It is because I am so *desperate!*"

"You were sent to the Earth, to mortaltime, to save them. And instead you indulge yourself; and by so doing you have only made things worse for them. Why else does the gateway continue

---

•Pronounced "Oower-*neesh*."

to remain open, and indeed grow wider and wider from hour to hour, if not on account of your negligence?"

Urnikh extended his head on its serpentine neck, let it sag, laid his chin on the darkness. "I am ashamed, Master. But I tell you again, I can't help myself. She fills me, the sight of her fills my every waking moment."

"Have you tried sleeping?"

"When I sleep, I dream. And when I dream, I am slave to her all the more."

The Master heaved a sigh very much like the sigh the little dragon had heaved in Margaret's apartment. "How does she bind you to her?"

"By not binding me at all. She is simply *there*; and I can't bear to be away from her. Help me, Master. I love her so; but I want to be the good force that you want me to be."

The Master slowly and carefully uncoiled to its full extension. For a long while it studied the contrite eyes of the little dragon in silence.

Then it said, "Time grows short, Urnikh. Matters grow more desperate. The djinn, the afreet, the watchthings, the gullgull, all of them rampage and destroy. No one will win. Earth will be left a desert. Mortaltime will end. You must return; and you must fight this love with all the magic of which you are possessed. Give her up. Give her up, Urnikh."

"It is impossible. I will fail."

"You are young. Merely a thousand years have passed you. Fight it, I tell you. Remember who and what you are. Return, and save them. They are poor little creatures and they have no idea what dangers surround them. Save them, Urnikh, and you will save *her* . . . and yourself as well."

The little dragon raised his head. "Yes, Master."

"Go, now. Will you go and do your best?"

"I will try very hard, Master."

"You are a good force, Urnikh. I have faith in you."

The little dragon was silent.

"Does she know what you are?" the Master asked, after a time.

"Not a bit. She thinks I am a cunningly made toy. An artificial life-form created for the amusement of humans."

"A cunningly made toy. Indeed. Intended to amuse." The Master's tone was frosty. "Well, go to her, then. *Amuse* her, Urnikh. But this must not go on very much longer, do you understand?"

The little dragon sighed again and let himself slip away on the *sril*-curve. The Master, sitting back on its furry haunches, turned itself inward to see if there was any hope.

It was too dim inside. There were no answers.

▼▼▼

The dragon materialized within a pale amber glow that spanned the third and fourth shelves of the bookcase. Evidently many hours had passed: the lost day's shafts of sunlight no longer came spearing through the window; time flowed at different velocities on the *sril*-curve and in mortaltime; it was night but tendrils of troubling fog shrouded everything except the summit of Telegraph Hill.

The apartment was empty. Margaret was gone.

The dragon shivered, trembled, blew a fretful snort. Margaret: *gone!* And without any awareness of the perils that lurked on every side, out there on the battlefield that was San Francisco. It appalled him whenever she went outside; but, of course, she had no knowledge of the risks.

Where has she gone? he wondered. Perhaps she was visiting the male-one on Clement Street; perhaps she was strolling the chilly slopes of Lincoln Park; perhaps doing her volunteer work at the U of C Clinic on Mt. Parnassus; perhaps dreamily peering into the windows of the downtown shops. And all the while, wherever she was, in terrible danger. Unaware of the demonic alarums and conflicts that swirled through every corner of the embattled city.

I will go forth in search of her, Urnikh decided; and immediately came a sensation of horror that sent green ripples undulating down his slender back. Go *out* into that madness? Risk the success of the mission, risk existence itself, wander fogbound streets where chimeras and were-pythons and hungry jack-o'lanterns lay in waiting, all for the sake of searching for *her*?

But Margaret was in danger, and what could matter to him more than that?

"You won't listen to me, ever, will you?" he imagined himself telling her. "There's a gateway open and the whole city has become a parade-ground for monsters, and when I tell you this you laugh, you say, 'How cute, how cute,' and you pay no attention. Don't you have any regard for your own safety?"

Of *course* she had regard for her own safety.

What she *didn't* have was the slightest reason to take him seriously. He was cuddly; he was darling; he was a pocket-sized bookcase-model dragon; a cunning artifact; cleverly made with infinitesimal clockwork animatronic parts sealed cunningly inside a shell-case without seam or seal; and nothing more.

But he *was* more than that. He was a sentinel; he was an emissary; he was a force.

Yes. I am a sentinel, he told himself, even as he was slipping through the door, even as he found himself setting out to look for Margaret. *I am a sentinel . . . why am I so frightened?*

▼▼▼

Darkness of a sinister quality had smothered the city now. Under the hard flannel of fog no stars could be seen, no moon, the gleam of no eye. But from every rooftop, every lamp post, every parked car, glowed the demon-light of some denizen of the nether realms, clinging fiercely to the territory that it had chewed out, defying all others to displace it.

The dragon shuddered. This was *his* doing. The gateway that had been the merest pinprick in the membrane that separated the continuums now was a gaping chasm, through which all manner of horrendous beings poured into San Francisco without cease; and it was all because he, who had been sent here to repair the original minuscule rift, had lingered, had dallied, had let himself become obsessed with a creature of this pallid and inconsequential world.

Well, so be it. What was done—was done. His obsession was no less potent for the guilt he felt. And even now, now that the forces of destruction infested every corner of this city and soon would be spreading out beyond its bounds, his concern was still only for Margaret, Margaret, Margaret, Margaret.

His beloved Margaret.

Where was she?

He built a globe of *zabil*-force about himself, just in time to fend off the attack of some hairy-beaked thing that had come swooping down out of the neon sign of the Pizza Hut on the corner, and cast the *wuzud*-spell to seek out Margaret.

His mental emanations spiraled up, up, through the heavy chill fog, scanning the city. South to Market Street, westward to Van Ness: no Margaret. Wherever his mind roved, he encountered only diabolical blackness: gibbering shaitans, glassy-eyed horrid ghazulim, swarms of furious buzzing hospodeen, a hundred hundred sorts of angry menacing creatures of the dire plasmatic void that separates mortaltime from the nightmare worlds.

Margaret? *Margaret!*

Urnikh cast his reach farther and farther, probing here, there, everywhere with the shaft of crystalline *wuzud*-force. The swarming demons could do nothing to interfere with the soaring curve of his interrogatory thrust. Let them stamp and hiss, let them leap and prance, let them spit rivers of venom, let them do whatever they pleased: he would take no mind of it. He was looking for his beloved and that was all that mattered.

Margaret, where are you?

His quest was complicated by the violent, discordant emanations that came from the humans of this city. Bad enough that the place should be infested by this invading horde of ghouls and incubi and lamias and basilisks and psychopomps; but also its own native inhabitants, Urnikh thought, were the strangest assortment of irritable and irritating malcontents. All but Margaret, of course. She was the exception. She was perfection. But the others—

What were they shouting here? "U.S. out of Carpathia! Hands off the Carpathians!" Where was Carpathia? Had it even existed, a month before? But already there was a protest movement defending its autonomy.

And these people, four blocks away, shouting even louder: "Justice for Baluchistan! No more trampling of human rights! We demand intervention! Justice for Baluchistan! Justice for Baluchistan!"

Carpathia? Baluchistan? While furious armies of invisible ruvakas and sanutees and nyctalunes snorted and snuffled and rampaged through the streets of their own city? They were blind, these people. Obsessed with distant struggles, they failed to see the festering nightmare that was unfolding right under their noses. So demented in their obsessions that they continued to protest in ever-thinning crowds and claques even after nightfall, when all offices were closed, when there was no one left to hear their slogans! But a time was coming, and soon, when the teeming manifestations that had turned the subetheric levels of San Francisco into a raging inferno would cross the perceptual threshold and burst into startling view. And then—then—

The territorial struggles among the invading beings were almost finished now. Positions had been taken; alliances had been forged. The first attacks on the human population, Urnikh calculated, might be no more than hours away. It was possible that in some outlying districts they had already begun.

Margaret!

He was picking up her signal, now. Far, far to the west, the distant reaches of the city. Beyond Van Ness, beyond the Fillmore, beyond Divisadero—yes, that was Margaret, he was sure of it, that gleam of scarlet against a weft of deep black that was her *wuzud*-imprint. He intensified the focus, homed downward and in.

Clement and Twenty-third Street, his orientation perceptor told him. So she *had* gone to see the male-one again, yes. That mysterious Other, for whom she seemed to feel such an odd, incomprehensible mix of ambivalent emotions.

It was a long journey, halfway across San Francisco.

But he had no choice. He must go to her.

▼▼▼

It was nothing for Urnikh to journey down the *sril*-curve to an adjacent continuum. But transporting himself through the streets of this not very large city was a formidable task for a very small dragon.

There was the problem of the retrograde gravitational arc under which this entire continuum labored: he was required to weave constant compensatory spells to deal with that. Then there was the imperfection of the geological substratum to consider, the hellish fault lines that steadily pounded his consciousness with their blazing discordancies. There was the thick oxygen-polluted atmosphere. There was—

There was one difficulty after another. The best he could manage, by way of getting around, was to travel in little ricocheting leaps, a few blocks at a time, playing one node of destabilization off against another and eking out just enough kinetic thrust to move himself to the next step on his route.

Ping and he leaped across the financial district, almost to Market Street. A pair of fanged jagannaths paused in their mortal struggle to swipe at him as he went past; but with a hiss and a growl he drove them back amid flashes of small but effective lightnings, and landed safely atop a traffic light. Below him, a little knot of people was marching around and around in front of a church, crying, "Free the Fallopian Five! Free the Fallopian Five!" None of them noticed him. *Pong* and Urnikh moved on, a diagonal two-pronged ricochet that took him on the first hop as far as the Opera House, from which a terrible ear-splitting clamor was arising, and then on the next bounce to Castro Street at Market, where some fifty or eighty male humans were waving placards and chanting something about police brutality. There were no police anywhere in sight, though a dozen hungry-looking calibargos, tendrils trembling in the intensity of their appetites, were watching the demonstration with some interest from the marquee of a movie theater a little way down the block.

If only these San Franciscans can focus all this angry energy in their own defense when the time comes, Urnikh thought.

Poing and he was off again, up Castro to Divisadero and Turk, where some sort of riot seemed to be going on outside a restaurant, people hurling dishes and menus and handfuls of food at one another. *Pung* and he reached Geary and Arguello. *Boing* and he bounced along to Clement and Fifth. A tiny earth-tremor halted him there for a moment, a jiggle of the subterranean world that only he seemed to feel; then, *bing bing bing*, he hopped westward in three quick leaps to Twenty-third Avenue.

The Margaret-emanation filled the air, here. It streamed toward his perceptors in joyous overpowering bursts.

She was here, no doubt of it.

He stationed himself diagonally across from the male-one's house, tucking himself in safely behind a fire hydrant. The street was deserted here except for a single glowering magog, which came shambling toward him as though it planned to dispute possession of the street corner with him. Urnikh had no time to waste on discussion; he dematerialized the hideous miasmatic creature with a single burst of the *seppul*-power. The stain left on the air was graceless and troubling. Then, as safe behind his globe of *zabil*-force as he could manage to make himself with his depleted energies, he set about the task of drawing Margaret out of the apartment across the way.

She didn't want to come. Whatever she might be doing in there, it seemed to exert a powerful fascination over her. Urnikh was astonished and dismayed by the force of her resistance.

But he redoubled his own efforts, exhausting though that was. The onslaught of the subetheric ones was imminent now, he knew: it would begin not in hours but in minutes, perhaps. She must be home, safe in her own apartment, when the conflict broke out. Otherwise, paralyzing thought, thinking the unthinkable, how could he protect her?!

Margaret—Margaret—

It took all the strength in his power wells. His *zabil*-globe spasmed and thinned. He would be vulnerable, he realized, to any passing enemy that might choose to attack. But the street was still quiet.

Margaret—

Here she was, finally. He saw her appear, framed in a halo of light in the doorway of the house across the way. The male-one loomed behind her, large, uncouth-looking, emanating a harsh, coarse aura that Urnikh detested. Margaret paused in the doorway, turning, smiling, her fingers still trailing the touch of his hand, looking up at the male-one in such a way that Urnikh's soul cried out. Margaret's aura coruscated through two visible and three invisible spectra. Her eyes shone. Urnikh felt all the moisture of his adoration squeezed out of him.

Never. She had *never* looked at the dragon in her bookcase like that. Cunning, clever, cuddly, a wonderful artifact; but never with eyes that held the cosmos.

For an instant, he felt anger. Something like what the mortals called hatred, the need for balance, revenge, something to strike or corrupt or disenfranchise. Then it passed. He was a dragon, a force, not some wretched flawed mortal. He was finer than that. And he loved her.

Enough, he thought. *Enough of that. Associate with them just a short time and their emotional pollution seeps in. Time's short.*

Come, Margaret, he murmured, pouring more power into the command. *Come at once! Come now, immediately, come to safety!*

But her final moments with the male-one took an eternity and a half. Exerting himself utterly, nonetheless there was nothing the little dragon could do about it. Twice, as tiny inimical fanged creatures with luminous wings and fluorescent exoskeletons came swooping past the doorway in which she stood, he mustered shards of his steadily-diminishing energy to club them into oblivion.

Come on!

Then, finally, she allowed their fingertips to slide apart, and gave him that look again, and descended the few steps to the sidewalk. Urnikh moved up close beside her in an instant, bringing her within his sphere of power but taking care to remain in the shadows of the *zabil*-globe. She must not see him, the toy, the cunningly articulated plaything, not here, not so far from the bookshelf in her apartment: it would upset her to know that he had traveled all this way to find her, small and vulnerable as he was. And she wouldn't even understand how much danger he had chanced, just to watch over her. *How ironic*, he thought: *she* was the vulnerable one, and yet, most wonderful creature, she would worry so much about *him*!

Mortaltime trembled at the brink, and all he could do was worry that she got back to the apartment, that he watch over her, back across the city, to Telegraph Hill.

Unseen by Margaret, the night erupted.

The sky over San Francisco turned the color of pigeon-blood rubies! The gateway had fully opened. He had waited too long. The pinhole had become a rent, the rent a fissure, the fissure a chasm, the chasm a total rending of the membrane between mortaltime and the dark spill that lay beyond. The sky sweated blood and screeching demons rode trails of scarlet light down through the roiling clouds, down and down between the high-rise buildings.

He had waited too long! The Master's faith in him had been misplaced, he'd known that from the start. He was not the good force, never could be, knew too little, waited too long.

All he could do now, was make certain Margaret got back to the sanctuary of Telegraph Hill. And from there, safe within his sphere of power, he would try to do what he could do. *There was nothing to be done.* He had done worse than merely fail. He had brought mortaltime to an end.

She boarded the bus, and he was there. Steel-trap mouth floaters assaulted the bus, but he sent a tendril of power out through the sphere and squeezed them to pulp.

He protected her through the long, terrible ride.

▼▼▼

Nights dissolve into days. Days stack into weeks. Weeks become the cohesions humans call months and years. Time in mortaltime passes. The race of dragons ages very slowly. One year, two, four. Wind cleanses the streets and the oceans roll on to empty into the great drain.

▼▼▼

"Would you like another grape?" she asked, looking up from her book.

The little dragon cocked his head and opened his mouth.

"Okay, we'll try it one more time . . . and this time you'd better catch it. I'm not getting off this sofa again, I'm too comfortable." She pulled a grape off the stalk, closed one eye and took aim, and popped it across the room toward the bookcase. Urnikh extended his long jaw on its serpentine neck, and snagged the fruit as it sailed past.

"Excellent, absolutely *excellent!*" Margaret said, smiling at the agility of the performance. "We will send you down to one of the farm clubs first, and let you season a bit, and in a year, maybe two, you'll be playing center field at Candlestick."

She tossed him a kiss, and went back to her book. It was a fine Spring day, and through the open window she could smell fuchsia and gladioluses and the scent of garlic and oregano from up the street where Mrs. Capamonte was laying it on for the Sunday night spectacular.

▼▼▼

It was, of course, all a creation.

Outside the tiny apartment everything was black ash to the center of the Earth, airless void to the far ends of space. Nothing lay outside this apartment. It had ended, as the Master had feared. Mortaltime had been killed. No creature lived beyond this apartment in its sphere of power. No child laughed, no bird soared, no sponge grew on the floor of an ocean. Nothing. Absolute nothing existed beyond.

Urnikh had failed to sew up the tiniest pinprick, had simply not been the good force. And mortaltime had ended. The billions and billions had died horribly, and the world had ended, and everything was dark and empty now, never to grow again.

Because mortaltime existed only as a dream of dragons; and for this little dragon, assigned to save the puny humans who were his creations, love had been the greater imperative.

Now, they would exist this way for however long she would live.

Here, in Urnikh's dream.

Living in a world of sweetness and light and pleasure—that did not exist. He would do it all for her, only for her. For Margaret he had sacrificed everything. That which was his to sacrifice, and all that belonged to the unfortunates who had vanished.

For the little dragon, it was sad, and all honor had been lost;

but it was worth it. He had his Margaret, and together, here in his dream, they would stay.

Until she, too, died.

And then it would be very hard to go on. With her gone. With all that was left of the world gone. It would be terribly hard to bear these human emotions he had taken on. Loneliness, sadness, loss. It would then, truly, be the end of all things.

And even little dragons grow old—slowly, ever so slowly.

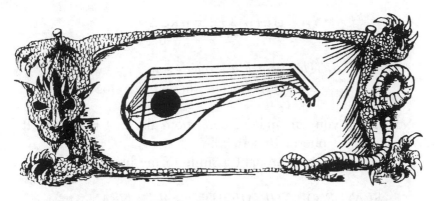

THE SHEDDING AND THE
SONG
▼▼▼

IAN HUNTER

CONTRARY to popular belief, news does not travel fast. King Roderick had already been dead almost a year before I stood in front of his grave on top of the highest mountain in his former kingdom. His final resting place looked simple enough, almost tasteful. A long marble slab stretched across the ground to the base of a statue which depicted King Roderick holding aloft his famous sword, Starcatcher, while a lute rested in his other hand. Of course, in real life, the sword had been too heavy to hold in one hand, and the lute was probably Roderick's greatest weapon, considering his playing.

I bent down to read the series of inscriptions on the bottom of the statue.

HERE LIES KING RODERICK, THE BRAVE

Then there was a quote from one of the many songs composed in his honor:

*"There came a farmer's son,
who played before the king."*

Not bad, if you can judge a song from the first two lines. It obviously wasn't one of Roderick's.

The last inscription brought a smile to my lips.

SLAYER OF THE MIGHTY GOLDENFANG

That was more like it. The Mighty Goldenfang. Better than The Dreaded Goldenfang, The Cruel Goldenfang, The Virgin-Eating Goldenfang, or The Destroyer of Crops Goldenfang.

Mighty.

I liked it.

But Slayer?

That was wrong. I was far from dead, despite what people believed, but then again, who could I blame? It had all been my idea.

▼▼▼

It was a rare time and a bad time. The worst for any dragon. The two cycles of Shedding and Coupling were coinciding and I was making my way across country towards the Mating Peaks. I couldn't fly. I was weak, overcome by fever and spasming pains which wracked my body.

I lay low, traveling by night, skirting villages and gypsy camps, feeding off livestock as carefully as I could by taking the strays from the herd or the flock. Still, it wasn't enough, I was sighted several times, and word spread like wildfire. Goldenfang was back, blazing a trail of destruction across the land, and the usual collection of fools, brave knights, witches seeking parts of my anatomy for potions, and souvenir hunters began following my trail. Fortunately I came to the great chasm called Crack in the World, and the rickety wooden bridge that spanned it, or rather used to span it. A little lick of flame, and *whoosh*! The dry, ancient timbers blackened and crumbled, spinning into the void.

No one could follow me now, and I traveled freely until Lystrata, when the final stage of the Shedding stopped me in my tracks and I took refuge on a high plateau.

And slept.

▼▼▼

What woke me was a mixture of clanking noises and muffled cries. My eyelids were heavy and barely lifted enough to reveal a knight in armor tumbling head over heels down the side of the hill that stretched up to my resting place. With a metallic clang, and a loud groan, he reached the bottom and lay there. Dead, I thought, until he stirred, crawling on his hands and knees towards a sword, which he passed, so great was his urge to flee.

My eyelids fluttered, and the world wavered. A shudder passed through my body, then another. The Shedding was calling me. I closed my eyes and answered the call.

▼▼▼

My next awakening was more abrupt, and a total shock. A jarring blow struck my body and a sharp *thwack*! filled my ears. Quickly, I reared up and glared at the knight standing before me who had slapped my tail with the flat of his sword. The fool. He could have easily dispatched me with a strike to the heart or throat, but, oh, no, he wanted to arouse me first and fight an honorable battle. The fool. He raised his sword high. It was made of gold, encrusted with jewels, and was obviously heavy. The knight began to topple backwards, pulled by the weight of his sword, and then, he would be gone, tumbling down the hillside again. But that wasn't what I had in mind. I was tired, and angry, and would need something to eat after the Shedding, and armor cooked humans quite well.

So I snatched the knight off the ground and tore the sword

from his grasp and spun it round and round between my talons. The knight struggled and reached behind his back, which drew my attention to the leather strap over his shoulder.

"Aha!" I cried, pulling the strap. "Another weapon!"

"No, don't break it," he pleaded.

"Break it? I'll burn it!" I roared, pulling hard, and the weapon appeared, banging the knight on the back of the head before falling to the ground.

I stared at it, and wondered briefly if this was all a dream, if I was still under the influence of the Shedding.

Because the knight's secret weapon was a lute.

I raised a leg, intent on smashing the instrument.

"No, don't," said the knight, who had pulled back his visor to reveal a young, slightly simple-looking, sweaty face. "Please."

I frowned. "No?"

He nodded. "No."

And so the moment was sealed. I knew I wouldn't break the lute just as I wouldn't harm this knight.

My grip dissolved and he landed with a crash. As soon as his head cleared he snatched up the lute and stroked the strings. Satisfied, he smiled and held the instrument to his breast, then looked at me with wonder and said, "Thank you."

I opened my mouth, but couldn't speak. The final moments of the Shedding were upon me. A thousand daggers pricked my tongue, then a million more stabbed my head, and raced out to cover the rest of my body. My vision blurred, then began to fade. I fell forward and the jeweled sword twisted from my grasp, spinning across the earth and stones towards the knight, who reached out towards it, and smiled as darkness crowded around me, clamoring to fill my eyes.

▼▼▼

It was strange to look down on my own body.

"Don't touch it," I warned the knight. He was reaching for one of the golden scales that covered my old skin.

"Why not?"

"Because they're hot, and that white sticky stuff which is oozing through the cracks between the scales is extremely
poisonous."

"Oh," he said, and drew back his hand.

I stretched out for the heavens and flexed my wings. I felt
strong, better than I had for days, but I knew that my new scales
would take a few days to harden, and I should avoid any encoun-
ters with humans carrying lances or swords. I also knew I was
lucky to be in this position, the knight could have killed me
when I collapsed at his feet.

"Why didn't you?" I asked.

He looked at me. "What?"

"Why didn't you kill me?"

He shrugged and gestured at the lute lying beside his armor.
"You didn't destroy my songmaker."

I shook my head. "It's a strange knight who wants to make
music."

"I'm no knight," he told me. "I'm Roderick, Musician in the
court of King Mandaro."

"Then why attack me?" I asked, although I could guess.

Roderick looked across the land and a dopey expression filled
his face while his eyes seemed to shine. I had guessed right.

"Whoever kills you wins the hand of the Princess Alicia."

"And you were first in the queue."

Roderick nodded. "The King even gave me a Starcatcher and
a suit of the finest armor since I had none of my own."

"Starcatcher?"

He held up the sword, the jewels on it were dazzling.

"It seems a fine weapon to entrust in the hands of a musician," I pointed out.

"Not really. King Mandaro is well known for his generosity,
and he said that giving me the sword was a small price to pay
for getting me out of the castle."

"I wonder what he meant by that."

Roderick shrugged, but I could see he was thinking about it. I lay down on the ground. There was a good hot sun in the sky, perfect for baking my new scales. I stretched out my wings. "Give me a song then, musicmaker."

I closed my eyes, as Roderick strummed a few strings. He cleared his throat.

"There was a terrible dragon,
His name was Goldenfang ..."

Ah, *fame at last*, I thought, and yawned. Roderick had a pleasant enough voice, although his choice of note picking left something to be desired.

"Virgins were his dinner,
And anything that grazed upon the land."

I winced, and opened one eye. "That was terrible," I told him.

He held out his hands. "I'm sorry, but you don't inspire my creative talents."

"Oh, excuse me."

"That's quite all right," he said, and grinned. "Now take Princess Alicia. She is an inspiring subject with a face to stir a thousand sonnets into life."

"Then sing about her."

He placed his right foot on top of a boulder and struck a jangling chord. *Here we go again*, I thought.

"How beautiful is she,
How beautiful is thee
Who stirs my heart with joy.
The lovely Princess Alicia,

Who will never be mine,
Because I have not slain
The terrible dragon, Goldenfang,
Who eats virgins for dinner, and . . ."

I groaned, wishing I was still under the spell of the Shedding, or better still, slain by the sword, Starcatcher. Anything rather than listen to this.

I opened my mouth to beg Roderick to stop, but it wasn't my voice I heard.

"Enough, songster. Give us the jeweled sword, or die."

Yes, yes, yes, I thought. Looking around at six of the meanest, dirtiest rogues I have ever laid my eyes upon. *Kill him now before he sings another line.*

"Look, it's the dragon!"

"Let's kill him too!"

I stood up and cleared my throat and sent a jet of fire racing into the sky. "Now, lads, let's not be hasty. Do you really want to try and kill me?" I leaned closer and put on my fierce face. "Do you really want to die?"

One of the six—clearly the leader—took a nervous step forward. "We've no quarrel with you, mighty dragon. We just want his sword."

"Then take it," I insisted. "And his lute."

"Not my musicmaker!" cried Roderick, and he reached for the sword, but a blow to the top of his skull sent him sprawling to the ground.

"Don't forget the lute," I reminded the outlaws as they drooled over the sword.

A face sneered at me. "Who wants that thing?"

"It's worthless!"

"Oh, no," I said. "You wouldn't believe what a weapon it is in the wrong hands."

"Then you have it," said one of them, and he kicked the lute across the ground. I noticed with regret that none of the strings had broken.

"Take the lute with you," I insisted.

The air sang with the sound of swords being drawn from metal scabbards. The six spread out, and waved their weapons at me. I licked my lips, calculating the chances of killing all of them before a sword struck my tender new scales. The odds didn't seem in my favor.

"All right, all right," I bellowed. "Just take the sword and go."

Roderick stirred as the robbers slipped down the side of the hill, the air ringing with tales of the fortune they had just made and what they would do with it.

"Ahhhh," groaned the musicmaker, rubbing his head, but his face brightened when he saw the lute, and immediately dulled as he looked all around him.

"The sword?"

"Gone," I told him.

"You let them take it?"

I shrugged. "It wasn't my sword."

Roderick slumped down on top of the boulder, and his whole body sagged. "But don't you understand. I'll never be able to go back to King Mandaro's court now, not without Starcatcher."

"I didn't think you would have gone back anyway," I said. "Since you hadn't killed me."

He looked angry. "Of course I would have gone back. How else could I continue to see the Princess Alicia and have any hope . . ."

His voice trailed off, his eyes went misty. I feared another ballad, a song in praise of great beauty with jangling notes and words to match. Instead, Roderick dragged a hand through his thick hair and shook his head.

"Now I can never go back," he croaked. "Better for them to think I am devoured, and the sword destroyed, and then forget about me, while I wander on through the world, my heart broken, never resting, never—"

I stopped yawning, aware of the silence, and looked at the musicmaker. I didn't like the strange gleam in his eyes.

"Unless I came with you," he said.

"Oh, no," I protested.

Roderick stood up. "Oh, but, yes. Just think of it, your very own songsmith, immortalizing every terrible deed you do in song, almost as soon as it happens."

Terrible deeds and terrible songs, I thought, and winced as Roderick struck a chord.

"I'll start right now," he said eagerly.

"There was a mighty dragon,
We met upon a hill.
His skin was coming off,
And he felt very . . ."

"Ill?" I suggested, which was exactly how I did feel.

"Ill," he sang, then rubbed his chin. "Now what about the second verse?"

I turned and looked desperately across the land, spying the six rogues at the bottom of the plateau. I straightened my wings. Flying was beyond me so soon after the Shedding, but I could still glide. I ran down the side of the hill, and leaned forward, and rose into the air.

▼▼▼

It wasn't much of a fight. My first pass ripped off two heads and the rest of them scattered, leaving one poor fool to drag the jeweled sword across the ground. I left him for last and went after the others, incinerating them with my flame. When I returned, the one with Starcatcher was breathing hard, and his face resembled a large beetroot. He tried to raise the sword as I approached and managed to lift it an inch or two off the ground before he gasped loudly and dropped the weapon. I watched with interest as he staggered a few paces while clawing at his chest, then he toppled forward. Dead.

Someone screamed behind me.

It was only Roderick, of course, falling down the hill again, this time without armor. He landed at my feet, the lute unscratched. It had to be an enchanted instrument.

"Arise, King Roderick."

If looks could kill, then I was a dead dragon.

"I thank you for retrieving Starcatcher, mighty dragon, but I'll ask you not to make fun of my predicament."

"Oh, shut up, and go and drag my old skin down here," I told him, deliberately not reminding him about the poisonous ooze. It would be a shame if his fingers were too swollen to play.

▼▼▼

By the time he returned, I had gathered five bodies into a heap. The sixth was delicious, if a trifle undercooked.

"Now what?"

"Watch," I said, and jumped up and down on the bodies until skin burst and bones shattered and all that was left was a red, glistening mass.

I held up my old skin and pushed some of the mix inside. "Now do you understand?" I asked the musicmaker.

"I confess, I do not," he replied.

"We're making a dragon," I said, popping a loose eye into my mouth. "One which you killed with your legendary skill and cunning."

"I did?"

"Of course you did, and now you shall marry a princess, and one day become King, which you have to admit is a lot better than trudging around the land with me."

Roderick smiled. "It is," he agreed.

And I wasn't offended that he didn't want to come with me, not in the least.

▼▼▼

And the rest, as they say, is history.

Thanks to some squashing and squeezing and a little flame on my old skin, everyone believed that Roderick had killed the mighty Goldenfang, and he went on to marry the Princess Alicia and become King when Mandaro died, a position he fulfilled somewhat better than Court Musician.

His life became a legend, and legends never die, but they do take odd twists and turns from time to time, and I've added one of my own.

So when you climb the highest mountain in Lystrata and visit the grave of its most famous King, Roderick, slayer of the Mighty Goldenfang, tell me how those golden scales got embedded in the marble slab that covers his body.

Go on, tell me.

THE OLD, OLD STORY
▼▼▼

ANDREW LANE

WINTER had stayed like an unwelcome guest long into spring that year. Snow still carpeted the mountain slopes and the steep roofs of the houses, and the cold winds blowing across from the steppes carried nothing before them but the promise of more. Each day the icy surface of the well had to be broken anew. Murzasichle, high in Poland's gaunt Carpathian mountains, survived on cooperation and friendship, and the memories of other times like these.

Father Pradziad struggled upwards through the crisp white shroud which covered the hillside. Far beneath him the cabins of the village were sliced into a brightly painted mosaic by the forest. Ahead the spruce trees stood like charcoal marks on paper, their lines abbreviated by the harsh wind and the cold. The constant, dazzling whiteness made distances hard to judge and, with the black slashes of the trees seeming to dance against the bright backdrop of snow, Father Pradziad was hard-pressed even to tell which direction was uphill.

The only sounds were the muffled crunch of snow beneath his boots and the distant chugging of the snowplough as it tried to keep the main road to Zakopane open. The bitter smell of pinecones filled the cold air. The heavy hem of his cloak dragged behind him, erasing his trail as he went. He checked his wristwatch and struggled faster through the drifts, knowing that if he failed to return to the village before night fell he risked losing his way in the forest. It was possible to find his way back by other means, but he did not want to be forced to use them.

Ahead, through the trees, Pradziad recognized the house of Franek Szulc. Gratefully the priest moved faster, desperate to rid himself of the ice-goblins which nibbled hungrily at his fingers. Before his outstretched hand could even touch the door it was pulled open, and the bearlike figure of his friend was welcoming him into the blessed warmth of the *chalupa*'s black room. He barely noticed his cloak being removed and hung by the door. The sight of the glowing logs in the fireplace filled his eyes, and the crackling as they split and burned almost drowned out Szulc's voice. The smoke stung his nostrils, and the flames reminded him, as they always did, of other times, long ago.

"Andrzej, at last!" boomed Szulc as he maneuvred the priest into the large central room of the house. His wife Ewelina squeezed past her husband as Father Pradziad lowered himself thankfully into an armchair by the fire. She was small and fragile beside Szulc, like a porcelain figure glazed with the hairline cracks of middle age. Her blouse was as white as the snow outside. Her dress was black, embroidered with tiny flowers in scarlet and gold. Szulc flung an affectionate arm around her shoulder. She shrugged him off, but smiled as she did it.

"You'll take food with us, of course," she said, gazing fixedly like a sparrow up into the priest's face.

"I really shouldn't . . ." Father Pradziad began to say, but she was already moving towards the kitchen. Szulc's hand closed over his shoulder.

"None of this nonsense," he said. "Andrzej will eat with us, won't you, Andrzej?"

"Franek, I couldn't possibly—"

"—offend my hospitality by refusing my food," finished Szulc, smiling as he played the rule of *nukak*, the one who urges.

Father Pradziad smiled back. Honor had been satisfied on both sides.

"I found your note when I returned from Zakopane," he said. "I came as soon as I could. What troubles you, my friend?"

Szulc dropped heavily into a chair.

"What took you to Zakopane?" he asked, avoiding the priest's gaze.

Pradziad hesitated before he answered, feeling his way through the conversation. Whilst he tried to identify the source of the Mendiuks' worries, Ewelina emerged from the kitchen, her tray piled high with meats, smoked cheeses, and pickled mushrooms. The aromas mingled with the smell of wood smoke, and Pradziad began to realize how hungry he was. Ewelina placed the tray on a small table to one side and retreated back to the kitchen.

"A child whose parents claimed she was possessed," he replied eventually. "Nothing more than epilepsy. I recommended the hospital in Warsaw."

"You seem to spend a great deal of time traveling. We see too little of you here in Murzasichle."

"There are so few in the church these days who believe in the power of evil. I seem to have become something of a specialist in possession."

He smiled benignly.

"What ails you, Franek?" he said again.

"It's little Anatoly," said Szulc, shifting in his chair. "When he's around . . . things happen." He buried his head in his hands. His wife entered with a pot of sweet tea which, by the smell, was laced with vodka, placed it beside the food and stroked her husband's neck.

"Things?" the priest asked quietly. Ewelina Szulc looked at him, then looked away.

"It started a few weeks ago," she said. "Just after his twelfth birthday. He's been growing up so quickly these past few months. It's hard to believe..." She stopped abruptly. Her husband reached up and took her hand from his neck, cradling it gently in his. He looked up at Pradziad.

"We thought nothing of it at first," he said, quiet and level. "A few smashed cups, an overturned chair or two. We thought it was the dogs, or Anatoly and some of his friends in one of their boys' games. You know how it is when you're young?"

Pradziad smiled in reassurance. Szulc squeezed his wife's hand briefly and paused, looking for the right words.

"Then it got worse. Plates were broken. One afternoon I came back from the village to find a window smashed and the glass outside in the snow."

Father Pradziad leaned forward and picked up his cup of tea. Reminded by the priest's action, Szulc did the same.

"Go on," said Pradziad.

"And then, one night, after Anatoly had gone to bed..."

"Yes?"

Szulc looked up at his wife. She smiled tightly and nodded.

"I swear to God, Andrzej, we saw a teapot fly across the room and smash against the wall. And there wasn't a soul near it. Not a living soul!"

Father Pradziad looked down into his cup. The surface of the tea vibrated gently, forming small rings that fitted one inside another and vanished into the center of the liquid.

"I don't disbelieve you, Franek," he began.

"It happened, Andrzej! I tell you, it happened!"

"And where is the lad now?"

Szulc looked to his wife, who touched his shoulder reassuringly.

"I sent him upstairs for a nap," she said. "He's been getting easily tired since . . ." She stopped, suddenly overcome by the sense of what she was saying.

"Since this all began," Szulc continued. He shook his head sorrowfully, and Pradziad noticed that his hand had begun to shake, clattering the teacup against the saucer. "The boy is possessed, Andrzej! You are our friend as well as our priest. Tell us what to do."

The priest leaned forward reassuringly and lay his hand upon his friend's wrist, hoping to calm him down, but to his surprise there was no tremor in Szulc's arm at all. Not a quiver. Szulc and his wife were both staring into the teacup with sick apprehension upon their faces. The cup clattered violently, moving up the curved side of the saucer and threatening to spill the hot liquid into Szulc's lap. The priest watched, amazed. Suddenly he noticed a slight vibration in his own hand. He glanced down, knowing what he would see. The surface of his tea was jittering in the cup like a rough ocean as the cup wandered aimlessly about in the saucer.

"Always when he's asleep," said Szulc. "After an hour or so." Pradziad looked up into Szulc's eyes.

Thud!

Pradziad almost dropped his cup as the sound echoed around the small house. Ewelina burst into tears.

Thud! Thudthud! Thud!

Franek's hands clenched and unclenched. The strongest man in the village, he looked frail and tired, but not surprised.

Thudthudthud! Thud!

The sound was coming from upstairs. Pradziad could have sworn that he could see the carved spruce beam which supported the ceiling shake in its sockets.

"His bed," whispered Ewelina Szulc. Her eyes were dark and shadowed. "It's his bed."

"And he's still asleep?" asked the priest, aghast. Szulc merely nodded.

Father Pradziad reached out and took the hands of Franek and Ewelina Szulc.

"Oh, God, most merciful," he began, "hear us in our hour of need."

With an incoherent cry Ewelina Szulc, unable to take the strain anymore, sprang to her feet and ran towards the stairway. Her husband tried to stop her, but she was too quick. With Franek and Father Pradziad close behind she stumbled up the stairs, but by the time she got to her son's bedroom the noises had ceased.

Unable to see over Franek Szulc's shoulder, Father Pradziad peered under his arm. Young Anatoly slept peacefully in a tangle of linen, framed by his father's body. His face was puffy and flushed and his hair was slick with sweat, yet his face was some-how still angelic and innocent in the light that spilled through the drawn curtains.

Could they be wrong? Pradziad wondered to himself. *Could he be just an ordinary boy?* Then he saw the circular dents that pockmarked the carpet around the legs of the boy's bed.

"Wake him," he said, more harshly than he had intended. "I'll be waiting downstairs."

Concerned voices murmured behind him as he descended the stairs, and as he entered the main room he heard Anatoly's sleepy reply. He felt tired. Old and tired. This was the part he hated most about his chosen vocation; the rooting out of the unnatural, the inquisition, the penance. He had hoped that his time in Murzasichle would be free of such problems. He'd had enough. He wanted a rest.

"Father?"

He turned. Ewelina stood in the doorway, her face haggard,

her hand on young Anatoly's shoulder. Franek stood behind him, filling the space.

Pradziad smiled warmly at Anatoly, but inside he was cold at the thought of what was to come.

"Anatoly," he said, "how large you've grown. I remember when I arrived in Murzasichle you were only"—he gestured vaguely with his hands—"this high. Look at you! You're almost a man now!"

Anatoly just stared back at the priest. His eyes had a bruised look to them, and his shirt was buttoned up awry.

Pradziad tried again. "I want you to take a walk with me into the woods," he said. "There are things we must talk about. Things," he added meaningfully, "I think you might *want* to talk about."

Anatoly frowned warily. "My father told me to keep out of the forest," he said. "He said there are wolves there."

Pradziad smiled benignly. "Trust me," he said. "We'll be safe."

"What about the *planetnicy?*" the boy replied stubbornly.

"Stories, Anatoly, just stories. There are no demons, especially ones who move storm clouds around for fun. Not anymore."

Anatoly looked up at his father for reassurance, but Franek Szulc merely patted his shoulder and said in a voice that was too hearty to be convincing, "You just go along with Father Pradziad, and don't worry about the wolves. Or the *planetnicy.* Father Pradziad is a man of God, and God will protect the both of you."

Anatoly didn't look convinced but, deprived of excuses, he held his arms away from his sides as his mother helped him into his coat.

"Take good care of him, Andrzej," Szulc murmured, and then added in a louder voice, "And you obey the Father, Anatoly, do you hear me?"

Anatoly Szulc nodded his head, then pulled on a pair of woolen mittens and followed the priest toward the door.

Within a few minutes they had climbed far enough up the hill for the trees to hide the house and the village below. They could have been a hundred miles from Murzasichle. Snow covered everything around them like a fungal growth. It seemed to glow of its own accord, and both Pradziad and Anatoly had to screw their eyes into slits to avoid walking into bushes, trees or each other. The branches of the trees were burdened with snow, and for a moment it appeared to Pradziad that the white snow was actually the trees and the darker branches beneath merely shadows cast by the sun. But only for a moment.

Eventually Father Pradziad found a spot which, for reasons which he couldn't explain, appealed to him as fitting. He swept the snow from a fallen tree trunk and gestured to Anatoly to sit beside him.

"Can you guess why I wanted to talk to you?" he asked kindly.

The boy's face was as frozen as the land. Eventually he managed a tight little nod.

"Your mother and father are worried," Father Pradziad continued. "They fear for you."

"I haven't done anything wrong," the boy said.

"I know," said Pradziad, "I know. But nonetheless, they worry. They hear strange noises, and they see strange sights, and they think perhaps that their son has been possessed by demons." He smiled. "By *planetnicy* perhaps."

Anatoly's eyes filled with a sudden rush of tears.

"Will you have to drive the demons out of me?" he asked breathlessly. "Will God hate me for ever and ever?"

"Can you say the Lord's Prayer?"

Anatoly frowned, remembering, then said in a rush; "*Pater noster, qui es in Caelis; sanctifictur nomen tuum—*"

Father Pradziad stopped him with a raised hand.

"You see?" he said, smiling. "If you'd been possessed by demons, you'd be nothing but a puff of black smoke by now."

The boy couldn't help smiling back.

"So if I'm not possessed," he said, "then what am I?"

Pradziad stretched his arms out in front of him and then raised them above his head, easing the kinks in his back. The vertebrae in his neck and spine creaked arthritically.

"You feel out of place here, don't you?" he murmured sympathetically. "Like a stranger to your friends and your family."

The boy nodded, desperately eager to be understood and accepted, if only by his priest.

"Do you ever feel superior to them?" Father Pradziad asked, just as warmly. "Do you ever pity them, because they can't do the things that you can?"

Anatoly looked away, flushing suddenly despite the cold.

"I'll let you in on a secret," Pradziad continued. "So do I. I'm not a mountain-liver, a *górale*. I've lived here for ten years now, but I'll always be the new priest." He was looking beyond Anatoly now, across the years and the miles of his life, and he wondered if Anatoly could detect an undertow of bitterness there. "We're outsiders, you and I. We have that in common."

The boy nodded, clearly unsure of the priest's meaning.

Pradziad seemed to tremble slightly as he pulled himself back from whatever thoughts had entangled him. He smiled warmly at Anatoly.

"You're not alone, young man," he said reassuringly. "There have been other people who can do the things that you can do. I've heard about them. I've made a point of seeking them out. You're only the third one I've ever found. It's a rare gift, you know? It's a capability that's been lost to humanity for thousands of years, apart from the occasional throwback like you. And like me."

Anatoly's face had broken into a hesitant smile, but his eyes were still shadowed. "I have dreams," he blurted, and looked up beseechingly into the priest's face. Pradziad nodded knowingly, and Anatoly continued with more confidence. "I dream that it's night and I'm flying through the sky, looking down on all of the houses and seeing all the little people inside. I dream that I've got wings."

A shadow passed across his face.

"But when I try to see the wings they fold up beneath me and I can't fly anymore, and I fall all the way to the ground. And then I wake up crying, and things are always smashed downstairs."

Pradziad patted the boy's shoulder.

"That's the first lesson I would have taught you," he said. "The wings are just for decoration. It's your mind that holds you up."

Anatoly frowned, confused by the priest's words.

"I've been so frightened," he whispered. "So scared."

Father Pradziad sighed and looked beyond the boy.

"Do you remember my sermon last week?" he asked. The boy shook his head. "No," said the priest. "It was hardly the stuff of memories, was it? 'Now the serpent was more subtle than any beast of the field.' Hardly inspiring. And yet there's a lot of truth in the Bible, if you know where to look."

▼▼▼

The shadows of the sun playing through the snow-laden branches made Father Pradziad's face seem to shift in strange ways. Anatoly gazed at him in mixed fascination and fear, not really listening to what he said, but picking up on the unseen things that moved beneath the surface of the words and gave them new meanings.

"In the old days, the peasants of China worshiped us and feared us. They thought that we were gods who could take on human form. They didn't realize that we were humans with another form in our mind's eye, and the power to make that form real. Once in a generation, a child is born with the power. We used to teach them to use it. Now we kill them to stop them."

He stood, and there was something terribly wrong about his body, but Anatoly couldn't work out what it was.

"It's just another chapter in an old, old story, my son," he said sadly, as a blush the color of burnished gold spread across his skin, and his wings spread wide to eclipse the sun. "There isn't enough room in the world for all of us. A few can survive, hidden in human bodies, but any newborn like you might draw attention to us."

His eyes were slits, and a long-banked fire was flaring behind him.

"In the old days we could have fought from sunrise to sunset and gloried in the battle, but times have changed. We have to catch you young now."

Anatoly screamed as a jeweled claw the size of his father's body reached out toward him.

▼▼▼

Winter had stayed like an unwelcome guest long into spring that year. Snow carpeted the mountain slopes and the steep roofs of the houses, and it was a long time before the hot breath of the *halny* winds blew once again from the far Mediterranean. For weeks the valley had been filled with the tinkling of falling icicles and the slushy wet rush of snow sliding from the roofs and into the streets.

The remains of Father Pradziad were never discovered. Nobody in Murzasichle was surprised. By then everybody in the village had heard the story of how their priest and young Anatoly Szulc had been set upon as they were walking in the forest by wolves made ravenous by the cold, and how Father Pradziad had attracted the wolves away, giving Anatoly time to escape. Young Anatoly had become something of a celebrity, with people coming from as far afield as Nowy Targ and Zakopane to marvel at his story, and at the calmness with which he recounted it.

Searches had been organized as soon as Anatoly ran into the

village, of course, but Anatoly could not remember where they had walked that day, and who could blame him? Besides, winter had made its passing felt with unexpected flurries of snow, and any tracks would have been covered over within minutes of being made. Reluctantly the search was abandoned. Despite the absence of a body, Father Pradziad's funeral took place after three days of weeping, feasting, praying, and dancing. In death he had become what he always wanted to be—*górale*.

Much to the surprise of Franek and Ewelina Szulc, the gift that had set young Anatoly apart from his friends seemed to vanish with the snows. They gave thanks to God and, when they visited the graveyard to pay their respects to Father Pradziad's empty grave, they gave thanks to him as well.

Anatoly himself kept very quiet about that day on the mountain, priests who turned into *planetnicy*, and trees which mysteriously uprooted themselves and flew through the air to impale demons and save a young boy from death. On those increasingly frequent occasions when he awoke to find himself coasting silently through the starry sky, held aloft by the power of his mind and guiding his flight with vast, sail-like wings, he closed his eyes and wished himself back in bed.

He didn't want to call attention to himself.

From anything.

THE MANDELBROT DRAGON
▼▼▼

MARY A. TURZILLO

IT was watching her, Heather knew. It didn't move, unless her dad tapped the keys, but it was staring at her.

"Dad, get rid of it."

"Get rid of *what*?"

"The dragon. You called the dragon again."

Dad pushed away from the console and sighed. "Heather, I don't see any dragon. And if there is a dragon, it's just part of the fractal program."

"The Mandelbrot set."

"Yes. A mathematical function, like—suppose I drew a line to show how tall you are each month." On a scrap from the wastebasket he drew points, connected them. "See, that's a function. The Mandelbrot set is just a more complicated function."

Heather tried to hide her fear and embarrassment. "I know, Dad. You explained all that before." The fractal program was supposed to create a pretty picture, like on the front of the book on chaos. But the dragon wasn't pretty; it was horrible.

"Look, you're a smart girl. Most eleven-year-olds couldn't figure out what a function was if it bit them on the nose." He leaned over and pretended to bite her nose. "Or a fractal. How come you're scared of a silly picture?"

She shivered. "It changes. It's always different. It's like it was alive, Dad. Things that are dead don't change."

He turned back to the screen in obvious exasperation. "Show me the damn dragon, Heather. I can't see it."

Her small, ragged-nailed finger hesitantly traced a figure on the screen. "See? Its eye is orange, and its tail is pink, and its claws are bright red."

"That's a dragon? It looks like a dead squid to me."

"No!"

"Or a squashed centipede. Look, I'll change the colors, and it'll go away." He tapped keys.

"No! Dad, the dragon is still there, but it's hiding behind that large wave!"

"Well, then, here!" He tapped more keys, and different colors washed across the screen. As they watched the Mandelbrot set change, he put his arm around her. "Is that better?"

"Now there's *two* dragons! It's alive, Dad. Things that change like that are alive."

"Okay, I give up. It's alive. But it can't get out of the computer, can it? It's just a picture."

Heather had already thought about this, and about the fact that you could magnify every part of that picture and get another picture, with more dragons, with flaming eyes and sharper and sharper claws. "Dad, your software has windows, doesn't it?"

"What does that have—"

"And things from one file can move into another one?"

"Yes! Yes! But they can't get into the real world, don't you understand?"

"Dad," she said, very softly. "Aren't you always telling me our brains are like computers?"

He tapped the mouse, defeated. "Yes, but—a computer can't

open a window in our brains. Our brains are thousands of times more complicated than any computer."

"Yes, Daddy." But she was thinking how complicated the Mandelbrot set must be, to have living things in it like the dragon.

"Okay, kid. Do you want me to shut it down?"

She nodded hesitantly, at first relieved. But then she said, "You'll just bring it up again when I go to bed, won't you?"

He shook his head, impatient. "No. No, I'll go watch TV or play with something else. Okay?"

She didn't believe him.

Mom appeared in the doorway. She was holding Heather's old stuffed rabbit and a cup of cinnamon milk. "Kiss your father goodnight."

Heather took the warm milk and sipped it. The cinnamon made a swirling shape, and the shape was like a—

—like the dragon.

"What's wrong, Heather?" Mom looked appraisingly at Heather. "Is everything okay at school? Don't you like the new math class?"

"The new math class is fine. I don't want this." She handed her mother the milk, in which the cinnamon dragon was writhing and stretching its jaws.

"Do you want chocolate instead? Because—"

"Throw it away!" Heather grabbed the stuffed rabbit and ran upstairs.

Brushing her teeth, she noticed the foam from the toothpaste she spit out swirling down the drain.

Dragon tail.

Stop it! she thought. But a horrid suspicion dawned on her.

Once in bed, she noticed a pattern in the branches outside her window. Claws, scales. She got up and closed the drapes. Of course that didn't destroy the dragon, but at least it couldn't watch her.

What did it want with her?

Stop thinking about the dragon. Maybe if she stopped thinking about it she could banish it, make it not real.

She settled back in bed and thought about math class. In the magnet school she attended, she was in the highest math class. She didn't particularly like math, but she was very good at it. The reason she didn't like it was that people were always asking her to multiply large numbers or solve problems in her head. To show her off, like a pet.

She liked the more interesting math things. For example, Mr. Devon yesterday had said, "Suppose you take a number, square it"—Heather's class knew about powers and roots—"then add the number again. Then we square that number and add the original number, and we keep doing that."

Heather soothed herself by doing this. Then she wondered, suppose I use two different kinds of numbers, and draw a picture with them. She could almost picture the result. Yes, she *could*.

The picture grew more and more complex in her mind until—

—it was the picture of the dragon.

Oh, it wasn't in color, and it wasn't as clear, but it was still watching her.

Her eyes snapped open. She gazed at a stain on her bedspread, inches from her eyes. Dragon tail. At a Venus's-flytrap, a school project. The shadow of the plant was the dragon's teeth and head.

Yes! Terrified, she realized that something larger than she, infinitely larger than the world, was dreaming the Mandelbrot set. And inside the Mandelbrot set, watched by the dragon, she was generating the set. She was in the dragon, and the dragon was in her.

Please go away. Please let it be that I'm dreaming.

Just numbers. Dad said it was just numbers. She made herself breathe slowly, willed her heart to stop banging in her chest. *Just numbers*. And for the first time in days, she relaxed and couldn't see the dragon.

Exhausted, she *was* dreaming.

▼▼▼

When she awoke, the dragon wasn't there in her mind's eye at all. Dad had turned off the computer, and that must surely have killed the dragon, at least temporarily. So she opened her eyes.

Everything was fine. Just fine. She stepped out of bed.

There was a shadow on the rug.

The shadow couldn't hurt her, of course. But the shape was familiar and she didn't want to look at it. She squeezed her eyes shut so hard they hurt. Still, she couldn't stand there all morning. She would just ignore the shadow.

Ignore it. Open your eyes and look somewhere else. She put one toe forward, on the rough wool of the rug. She stepped, left foot. Right foot.

She had to go round the shadow, because it was shaped like the dragon, *was* the dragon.

Her fear grew as she stepped, blossoming in her chest like the image on the computer screen, all in orange and pink and blood red. But why couldn't she stop? She could scream, and Dad would come and break the pattern.

But could Dad break the pattern? He couldn't even comprehend how terrifying it was, so how could he help?

As she walked, she curved into the world she had generated in her mind. She walked around the edge of the dragon, which was in the rug, and with every step she took, the tiny points that made up the dragon-picture grew tinier and finer.

She knew now that she couldn't stop, couldn't turn back. Her feet were programmed to move without her will, iterating the ever-more complex pattern like the one on the computer screen.

Her face held too tight for tears, she walked from terror into despair.

She was following the pictures of the Mandelbrot set, as it was magnified again and again. The dragon's edges spiraled in, like the wave in the Mandelbrot set when Dad hid the dragon. In and in.

It had happened, and nothing could save her. She was in the dragon and the dragon was in her. The Mandelbrot set had gotten out of the computer into her helpless brain. Windows.

Unable even to whimper, she went on walking, toward the door. But the door, like the dragon's eye, was at the center of something that could be magnified and magnified, deeper and deeper. And she walked and walked and walked and never stopped walking.

Toward the dragon's eye.

DRAGONLORD'S JUSTICE

▼▼▼

JOANNE BERTIN

A SHADOW passed over Talid as he saddled his horse. The gelding reared; Talid grabbed the tether and looked up.

High overhead a dragon the deep red of unwatered wine soared in the dawn sky. Its scales glinted in the sun.

"Gods—will you look at that!" Talid cried, and forgot to breathe. He'd never seen anything so beautiful.

The dragon hovered a moment, its great wings motionless, then flew west.

"True-dragon or Dragonlord, boy—which do you think?" Talid looked at the trembling horse. Its eyes rolled. "I forgot, pea-brain. You don't think. Why I had to get stuck with the dumbest horse in the stable for my journeyman's trek and why my trek had to be in the middle of nowhere . . ."

Shifting the harp case on his back, Talid picked up the bridle. "He won't eat you, lackwit, so settle down. We've a long way to go today before we see the end of these mountains."

Talid sighed at the injustice of it all. With his abilities—at nineteen he was one of the youngest ever to make journeyman Bard—he should be playing for lords and ladies at their city homes. Or, if he had to be sent to the country, it should have been to some noble's hall at the least.

"I shouldn't have to play for yokels," he grumbled as he mounted. "I wish I were back in Bylith already. Give me the city any day over all this nothing."

As the day wore on, Talid forgot about the dragon. The miles fell behind him. He rested as little as possible, eager to get out of the mountains. Even so it was nearly dusk when he rode down from the last of the foothills.

The narrow trail wound on through a stand of pines. As he came out, Talid saw the perfect campsite: level, with a stream, and grass that promised a softer bed than mountain rocks.

Perfect—except that it was already occupied. Talid hoped the other traveler wouldn't mind sharing.

A man knelt by a small fire, feeding sticks into it, a black horse standing beyond him. Talid thought he could see a thin clan braid hanging down the man's back.

Talid smiled. *Not only company, but a fellow Yerrin. But how odd—the horse doesn't seem to be tethered.*

The man looked up. He reached out and grabbed something from his packs. Firelight gleamed along the blade of a greatsword as he drew it from its sheath.

Talid pushed the neck of his cloak back, pulled his bard's torc out from under his tunic and made ready to reassure the stranger. He had no fear for himself. His calling protected him.

To Talid's surprise, the man sheathed his sword and set it back in his baggage. He cupped his hands to his mouth and called, "Ho, Bard—welcome to you. There's wine if you fancy it."

Talid's jaw dropped. *Bloody hell; he couldn't possibly see the torc—not in this light.* Then he shrugged. Well enough; he wouldn't have to explain with a sword waving under his nose. He urged his tired horse into a trot.

When he reached the campsite, Talid reined up before the

man. "Did you know your horse is loose?" he asked as he dismounted.

The horse—a stallion—snorted. As the man fed the last twigs into the fire, yellow and red flames blazed up, their light playing across his face. One eye seemed deeply shadowed, almost sunken; a moment later Talid realized the "shadow" was a birthmark across the eyelid.

"Shan'll be here in the morning," said the man. He smiled.

Talid rolled his eyes. *Gods; a mountain accent an ell thick— this one's straight out of the back country. And odd to boot.* Still, there was an open friendliness in the fellow's manner that he liked.

The stranger stood up and dusted his knees. Shaggy, shoulder-length blond hair shone in the firelight.

Talid swallowed. It had been a long time since he'd had to look up to meet someone's eyes. He was glad the fellow had put his sword away.

He said, "I'm Talid e'Vares. I'm on my way to Bylith. And you?"

The man paused. "I'm Kovannin . . . e'Dahl."

Nodding, Talid thought, *Oh, gods—is every mother in the hills still naming her boy baby after that Dragonlord? Just because he was mountain-bred . . .*

Kovannin continued, "And as the gods would have it, I'm also on my way to Bylith. Perhaps we could keep each other company along the way; there aren't that many Yerrins here in Kelnith."

"I'd like that," Talid said. But inwardly he winced, wondering what he and this rustic would have to talk about. *Still, any company's better than none and if he bores me, I can always get away from him somehow.*

He set saddle, saddlebags, and harp case down in an untidy heap by the fire. After hobbling the gelding, Talid gave it a quick brushing and an even faster inspection of hooves for stones. Next he slipped the feedbag full of grain over the horse's nose. Finally,

with a grateful sigh, he finished with the gelding and could look
to his own needs.

His stomach rumbling, Talid pulled food from his bags: hard
bread, dried meat, and fruit. He smiled as he unrolled his blankets and sat down.

Tonight he'd have an audience. True, only one mountain
bumpkin's worth, but an audience nonetheless. And that was
better than meat and drink to a bard—especially one who'd held
the rank for less than a year.

He chewed the tough meat as he considered what he'd sing.

▼▼▼

Talid wriggled his fingers, put the harp back in its case, and
cleared his throat. "There! That's it for now, I'm afraid; I'm
parched," he said.

"Then have the last of my wine and my thanks for your songs.
You're very good," Kovannin said. He refilled the cup by Talid's
side. "Now tell me your news; bards always hear everything."

Talid laughed ruefully. "I've been through only two or three
villages in the past few weeks. Unless you're interested in whose
cow got into which garden, I've not much to tell you."

Kovannin nodded and poked at the fire.

Talid frowned. That wouldn't do; a bard should always have
news. Surely there was something . . . "Ah! But if you're interested in dragons, then I've news."

Kovannin's head came up at that. "Dragons?"

"Yes." Talid held the precious memory to himself a moment.
"I saw a dragon this morning. He was huge, dark against the
pale morning sky. Gods, but he was beautiful." He gazed off in
remembered wonder.

Kovannin grunted, then said, "True-dragon or Dragonlord?"

Talid blinked. *How should I know the difference between a*

true-dragon and one of the great *were-dragons?* Aloud, he replied, "I don't know. Why?"

Kovannin ignored that. "Couldn't you tell whether he was larger or smaller than other dragons you've seen?"

Talid drew himself up. "I've never seen another dragon."

Sounding amused, Kovannin said, "You're city-bred then, aren't you? Most country folk have seen dragons. But true-dragons won't fly over a city and Dragonlords rarely do. What color was this dragon?"

Nettled that this country bumpkin knew something he didn't, Talid said shortly, "Red—like this wine."

"Ah." Kovannin's fingers went up to touch the birthmark across his eyelid. He dropped his hand. Rising, he said, "I'll bank the fire." His breath steamed in the cold night.

Talid stood up as well. The wine rushed to his head. He suspected he'd had more of the wine than Kovannin; the man looked cold sober. "D'you mind if I ask you a question?"

Kovannin shook his head. He laid a square of turf on the fire.

Talid said, "What are you planning to do when you reach Bylith?"

Kovannin shrugged. "I don't know. Look about, I suppose." He carefully laid a second turf by the first.

Talid closed his eyes a moment, shaking his head. *Look about? Bumpkin, they eat country boys like you alive in the fair city of Bylith.*

He said, "Look—no offense meant, but . . . You haven't been out of your mountains much, have you, boyo?"

Kovannin's eyebrow went up at the "boyo."

Talid supposed he couldn't blame the man; it did sound odd coming from him to a man of some twenty-eight or -nine years. Still, Talid guessed he was ages older in experience than this innocent.

The wine made him benevolent. He put aside his rancor at

Kovannin's earlier amusement. With all the wisdom of his nine-teen years, Talid continued, "You'd best stay by me when we get there. I've lived at the bard's school in Bylith these seven years now and there isn't much about the city I don't know."

Kovannin's mouth twitched. After a moment he said, "That would be good of you, Talid. It has been a long time since I've left the mountains."

Talid nodded, pleased with his generosity. He hiccuped and pulled his cloak tight against the cold of the autumn night. He lay down by the fire, rolled himself in his blankets, and rested his head on his saddlebags. "See you in the morning, boyo."

▼▼▼

"Kelan Village? Why? That's the roundabout route to Bylith," Talid said, puffing clouds into the chill of the dawn. He finished tying his packs to the gelding's saddle. "If we strike off south and east we'll meet the road again much farther down."

Kovannin heaved his saddle onto Shan's back. "I've a fancy to go there. I'm told the inn's worth a day's journey to see." He tightened the girth.

There was an odd note in Kovannin's voice, so faint that Talid wondered if he imagined it. Sighing, he tried again to change Kovannin's mind. Talid wanted this last stretch of his journey-man's trek over with as soon as possible.

"It's hardly worth that—at least not compared to the taverns of Bylith, boyo. It should only take us—"

Kovannin turned. "I've a fancy," he repeated.

The big blond Yerrin looked as immovable as one of his mountains. Talid thought, *The hell you do, boyo. What are you after—and do I really want to find out?*

But like any bard, Talid was more curious than ten cats. He'd wonder for the rest of his life what tale he'd missed if he left now. Nor did he relish the thought of another lonely journey.

Yet what could possibly be in Kelan Village?

One last try ... Aloud, he said, "There's no one and nothing in Kelan worth seeing. I know; I passed through on my way north."

Kovannin swung easily into the saddle; he laughed. "Is that so? Now I would have said that you never know whom you might meet—even in the middle of nowhere." He set Shan to an easy walk.

Talid scrambled into the saddle. Catching up, he said, "You're a stubborn one, aren't you, boyo?"

Kovannin just smiled.

▼▼▼

The most noticeable thing about Kelan Village was the inn. Though small by Talid's city standards, it was the only stone and beam building among houses of wattle and daub, and the only structure to boast a second floor. The inn was the pride of Kelan and the talk of the countryside for three days' ride. Farmers and foresters, hunters and shepherds came just to say they'd had their ale in such a fine place—even if the common room tended to get smoky on a cold night. The country folk thought Innkeeper Derin One-Arm had done well for himself since he'd left the Kelnethi army—as Talid had heard over and over when he stopped there on his way north.

"Is their ale good?" Kovannin asked as they rode into Kelan late in the afternoon of the second day.

"Yes." Talid licked his lips with remembered pleasure. "Gods, but I'm thirsty."

"Strange," Kovannin said quietly, almost to himself. "There's no one moving about."

Occupied with his memories of the inn's ale, Talid hadn't noticed the unusual silence until Kovannin spoke. He looked around. Not even the ever-present chickens were scratching for insects. Save for the smoke from the inn's chimney, Kelan looked deserted. Talid shivered.

They rode into the tiny yard of the inn and waited. When, after a few minutes, no one came, they dismounted.

"Odd," Talid said, growing more uneasy by the moment. "The stableboy was quicker than this last time."

Kovannin shrugged. "I'll take care of the horses. Go in, send the boy out to help me, and bespeak me a mug, will you?"

Shaking off his foreboding, Talid said, "I'll do that." He tossed his reins to Kovannin, pulled his saddlebags off, and went to the inn.

Talid ducked through the door. Before he got more than three steps into the hall, a small figure hurled itself at him. He set his burdens down barely in time to catch his assailant's arms. "What the—" he began, then recognized who was trying to push him back out the door. Bewildered, Talid said, "Jaida, what are you doing here? And what are you *doing*?" He released her hands.

Jaida pushed her brown hair back from her face. "Talid, get out. Now, while you still can; *he* hasn't realized you're here."

"Who?" Talid asked, more confused than ever. And why was Jaida's voice so hoarse? It sounded as if she'd strained it—but she was a trained bard. She'd know better than to misuse it.

"You stubborn idiot—don't ask questions, just run."

Talid folded his arms. "Not until you tell me what's going on." He braced himself against her efforts to shove him out the door.

Jaida stamped her foot. "Talid, you can be such an ass. All right, I'll tell you. And on your head be it if he notices . . ." She took a deep breath.

"It's awful. All our lives we've heard how wonderful the Dragonlords are, learned the songs and stories about them. There's a Dragonlord inside—Kovannin Rathan!—and may the gods help me, he's a stinking brute." Jaida wiped her eyes.

The sight of her tears shook Talid. He'd never known Jaida to cry over anything.

"He's been here for three days now, doing nothing but demand the rights he says are due his rank. He won't let anyone work—they must be ready for his orders—and he's drinking and eating Derin One-Arm out of business. He killed two men who defied him. And he's forced Corrie into his bed every night."

"Corrie? But she's barely old enough to be wed!" Talid clutched Jaida's arms. His stomach crawled with sick betrayal. "Are you sure it's Kovannin Rathan?"

"Yes; he's Yerrin, a big man, with a red-wine Marking on his face, and he carries a greatsword—Tsan Rhilin—just like the stories. What he's doing to Corrie—it can't go on."

A thought struck Talid. He felt the blood drain from his face. "He—he hasn't . . ."

Jaida laughed harshly. "No, I'm too thin for His Grace's tastes."

He shook his head. "We can't let this continue. Surely he'll listen to bards."

She swung at him. "You idiot! Don't you understand? He doesn't give a damn about bards. He hasn't listened to me all this time—what makes you think he'll listen to you, you conceited pig? Get out while you still can!"

A drunken voice bellowed, "Get back here, little crow! Don't think I didn't see you sneak off. It'll be the worse for you if I have to come after you."

The voice made Talid hesitate; he reconsidered Jaida's advice to run. But he couldn't leave a fellow bard in peril. With Jaida close behind him and swearing every step of the way, Talid stepped into the common room. He stopped, appalled at the scene before him.

What had to be all of the villagers were huddled around the edges of the dim common room. They looked numb, beyond even fear now. Some of the children wept silently, their faces buried against their parents.

The tables in the center of the room were empty—save the one closest to the ale barrels. There sat the Dragonlord in drunken splendor. He held Corrie against him, ignoring her whimpers as his hands roamed over her. Corrie's father, Derin One-Arm, watched helplessly from the sidelines, his face a mask of grief and anger.

The Dragonlord was a big man, broader of chest and shoulder than even country-bumpkin Kovannin. He looked much as described in the old tales. But no song had ever told of the coarse features, the greedy eyes and mouth.

Talid was heartsick. He'd always loved the stories about Dragonlords—especially the tales about Kovannin Rathan—and this was the sorry reality.

The Dragonlord pushed Corrie off his lap. She fell heavily to the floor.

"Fetch me more ale," he said, tossing his mug at her.

Corrie scurried to do his bidding. Tears shone on her cheeks.

Talid wanted to call her to him but his tongue cleaved to the roof of his mouth. When he'd passed through a few months ago, she'd delighted in his songs and tales about Dragonlords. He felt as if he'd betrayed her somehow.

Jaida sobbed behind him.

The sound caught the Dragonlord's attention; his eyes focused on Talid. "Good," he grunted, "another bard. That little stick behind you is sounding like a crow."

Talid swallowed his anger. Gesturing at the villagers, he said, "You can't do this, your Grace; please—"

Harsh laughter greeted his plea. "And who'll stop me, boy? You? Sing or I'll—"

The door swung open and a deep, cheerful voice announced, "The horses are done, Talid. I hope that mug's ready for me."

Kovannin strode into the common room, his saddlebags and greatsword slung over one shoulder. Seeing the huddled villagers, he let everything slide to the floor. He looked around the room, wide-eyed. His gaze settled on the Dragonlord. He took a step forward; one hand jerked toward his dagger. Then the hand fell to his side once again.

Jaida whispered, "Who is he?"

"Someone I met on the road," Talid said, low-voiced. "Bloody idiot; I hope he doesn't get himself killed. I've come to really like him."

Kovannin said quietly, "What the hell is going on here?"

"I am, fool! Now bow to your betters," the Dragonlord roared.

Kovannin cocked an eyebrow at that. He asked, "Who are you?"

The Dragonlord turned scarlet with fury. "Dragonlord Kovannin Rathan, scum. Don't you know a Marking when you see one?" He stroked the wine-red birthmark on his jaw.

"Really?" Kovannin pointed to his eyelid. "As for your so-called Marking, I've one of those myself. They're not uncommon, and not every blemish is a Marking. If you're a Dragonlord, where's your torc of rank?"

Over the gasp of the crowd, the Dragonlord said, "I'm traveling in disguise, or course. Mind your tongue or you'll face Dragonlord's Justice for your insolence."

Kovannin shrugged. "In disguise? You're doing a remarkably poor job of it, then, aren't you? And you wouldn't know Dragonlord's Justice if it upped and kicked you in the ass—which is no more than you deserve. Excuse me; I want some ale."

Talid groaned. "Boyo—have a care! I don't want to have to bury you."

But the Dragonlord sat as if stunned at this arrogance. Only his angry gaze followed Kovannin.

Kovannin crossed the room and took a mug down from its peg on the wall. He joined Corrie still standing by the ale barrel. She clutched the Dragonlord's mug to her as she stared up at Kovannin.

Smiling, Kovannin said, "Shall I fill that for you, child?" He tucked a loose strand of hair gently behind her ear as he took the mug from her.

She nodded.

"Get your hands off the slut or I'll cry Challenge on you — she's mine," the Dragonlord said.

The change that came over Kovannin astonished Talid.

"Gods help us," Talid whispered to Jaida. "I didn't think my bumpkin had a temper. Now look at him."

Kovannin bent until his face was even with Corrie's. "Child," he said, his gentle voice at odds with the fury blazing in his eyes, "has this . . . *Dragonlord* . . . forced you?"

The Dragonlord half-rose. "I'm warning you, scum, get away . . ."

Corrie's face crumpled into tears.

Before Talid could stop her, Jaida jumped from behind him, crying, "For three nights now he's raped her! Look at her, she's barely more than a child."

She ran to Corrie's side. Talid was half a stride behind her.

The Dragonlord growled, "Mind your own business, bitch," and reached for Jaida.

Talid sprang between them. The Dragonlord seized him like a mastiff with a rat and flung him across the room. He crashed into a table, his forearm caught between his body and the table's edge. The bones snapped. Talid slumped to the floor, retching.

Through the gray sickness he heard Jaida crying, felt her arms go around him. Then Kovannin was beside them.

"Talid, cry Challenge on him," Kovannin said.

Talid found his voice enough to say, "Are you mad? How can I fight with a broken arm? Cry Challenge on him yourself." He shut his eyes against the spinning of the room.

Kovannin ground his teeth. "I—I am under geas; I may not Challenge anyone. But I can act as a Champion."

Jaida said, "You would fight him?"

"Yes!"

Talid opened his eyes. "Jaida—no! He'll be killed."

But it was too late. Jaida was on her feet, facing the Dragonlord. She shook with rage. Her voice rasping, she said, "I, Bard Jaida, cry Challenge on you, Dragonlord. I cry Challenge for the violence done the people of Kelan Village; for the murder of Lel Candlemaker and Damath Brewer; for the rape of Corrie; for the ruination of her father, Derin One-Arm; for assaulting a bard."

The Dragonlord laughed. "All true, little bitch. What do you intend to do about it?"

Jaida drew a deep breath. "I name this man to stand as my Champion." She pointed at Kovannin.

"On your head be his death, bitch," the Dragonlord said. "Then I'll deal with you."

▼▼▼

Talid screamed as the village wisewoman set and splinted his broken arm. When his vision cleared, Jaida and the stableboy stood before him. Everyone else was gone.

"Can you walk?" Jaida asked. "They're waiting for you."

Talid swallowed his rebellious stomach. "I think so."

His splinted arm in a sling, and with Jaida and the boy on either side, Talid tottered to the field where the duel was to take place. He was surprised at the amount of space the combatants had marked off.

Jaida said, "The Dragonlord wanted it like that. Said he needed room if he wished to Change. Your friend is either very brave or very stupid; that didn't scare him at all. He laughed and said it suited him just fine."

The grim-faced villagers lined the rough rectangle. The stableboy slunk off to stand with an older couple that Talid supposed were his parents. Jaida led Talid to an empty spot. He leaned on her, sick with apprehension.

The Dragonlord raised his greatsword in a mock salute.

"Good; now that you're here, Bards, your coward of a Champion can no longer refuse to begin."

Kovannin said mildly, "It is their right to see justice; they're among those you've injured. At your convenience—*Dragonlord.*"

Talid held his breath as the two men moved into position. Their greatswords swept up in the traditional salute. Tsan Rhilin, the Dragonlord's famous sword, and Kovannin's unnamed blade shone in the last of the sunlight.

The Dragonlord leaped forward, his sword slashing down and across. He was fast—faster than any man Talid had ever seen.

Yet he wasn't fast enough. Kovannin parried the blow and returned it, sending the Dragonlord scrambling. They continued trading blows, neither able to gain an advantage over the other.

But there was something odd about the fight, something that niggled at Talid's mind and wouldn't come out into the open. He chased the errant notion.

It was the look of fright passing over the Dragonlord's face that gave Talid his answer.

He whispered, "Jaida, is it my imagination or is Kovannin only half-trying?"

As if he'd heard, Kovannin said, "Enough of this farce!" His sword sung around in a blur, ringing down on the Dragonlord's blade—and shattering it.

Jaida gasped, "But Tsan Rhilin can't be broken! The enchantment—"

Kovannin stepped back, sheathed his sword, and set it down on the grass. "Maybe you'd do better to Change, Dragonlord."

The Dragonlord cast the remnants of his sword to one side. "You're not worthy of it, true-human scum," he said and made ready to charge.

"Ah," Kovannin murmured. "Perhaps this form is." He bowed his head.

A red mist surrounded him.

The villagers cried out. Many fell to their knees—as did the supposed Dragonlord.

Talid hardly felt Jaida's fingers dig into his arm. His mouth worked; no sound came out. He finally yelled in indignation, "Kovannin e'Dahl, my ass! *He* was Kovannin Rathan all along!"

Talid felt like a fool. What had addled his wits? He should have been able to guess—all the signs were there. The dragon he'd seen, Kovannin's uncanny eyesight at their first meeting, the birthmark across his eyelid . . .

And the horse that wasn't tied— "Of course! It's a Dragonlords' Llysanyin, as smart as any true-human!"

Another thought dawned on him. His voice broke as it scaled up an octave or three. "Gods have mercy—I've been calling him 'boyo'!"

The red mist spread, became a ghostly dragon. In less than the space of a heartbeat, the mist solidified.

An enormous wine-red dragon stood on the grass, his wings folded tight against his back. Talid knew he beheld Rathan, the dragon half of Kovannin Rathan's soul.

A voice like the wind off the mountains rang in Talid's mind. From the faces of those around him, he knew they heard it as well.

Fool. Had you been content with a mug or two of ale and a meal as you were when I first heard of your impersonation, I would have only given you a thrashing when I'd caught you. But you have killed, raped, and pillaged in the name of the Dragonlords— in my *name—and for that you must face Dragonlord's Justice— true Dragonlord's Justice.*

The dragon stretched out a clawed foot. He seized the imposter around the waist, sat back on his haunches, and lifted the man from the ground.

The man screamed. Talid had never seen another human in such mortal terror.

The voice returned in Talid's mind. *The penalty for rape or murder is death. By your own words are you condemned. Yet if there is one here who will speak for you, I will listen.*

The dragon curled his long neck to look at the villagers one by one.

No one spoke.

So be it. There was a hint of sadness in the voice. *It is the right of those injured to see justice done. Is that the wish of the families of the two men killed or your wish, Corrie?*

Some of the villagers looked away; others covered their eyes, shaking their heads. Only Corrie stepped forward.

She stared up at the dragon towering over her, her eyes wide. Talid saw that it was wonder, not fear, that filled them.

Do you wish to invoke your right, Corrie?

Corrie shook her head but stretched out her hand.

The dragon dropped his head to her level.

"Beautiful," she whispered, stroking his scaled muzzle. Then, "Please—take him away. Take him far away." She turned, crying, and ran back to the shelter of her father's lopsided embrace.

As you wish. The relief was like something solid. The dragon raised his head again. A great glowing eye fixed on the false Dragonlord.

The man offered no resistance to the claws pinioning him. By his face he was past terror; it was plain he already considered himself a dead man.

The voice in Talid's head became smaller, somehow, more personal. *Talid, there's something I want you to do for me.*

"Of course, Your Grace," Talid said, bowing his head. He thought he caught a faint echo in his mind: *Oh, bloody damn ...* The regret—and something else—he felt puzzled him. "My lord?"

There's a small gray pouch filled with gold and silver coins in my saddlebags. Give it to Derin for his losses and to add to Corrie's

*dowry. It's the best I can do. I've no healing to offer for what's
been done to her.*

Talid caught his breath at the pain in the mind-voice. "I'm
sorry," he whispered.

The mind-voice sighed. *And now I've a far more unpleasant
duty . . .*

Kovannin Rathan spread his wings.

Talid ran back, pulling Jaida with him. The villagers scattered
as well. Still, the wind created by the downsweep of the powerful
wings knocked many over. They sat in the long grass, laughing
in wonder.

Corrie stood up first. "Farewell," she called softly. "Fare
thee well."

▼▼▼

"Are you sure His Grace wanted you to do this?" the innkeeper
asked for perhaps the hundredth time as he and Jaida hovered
over Talid's shoulders.

"Yes, I tell you!" Talid snapped, then yawned. "Now let me
get on with this before I fall asleep—that sleeping draught is
starting to work."

He rooted one-handed through Kovannin Rathan's saddlebags.
His fingers closed on a leather pouch; by the feel there were
coins inside. As he grabbed it, his fingers slid along another
shape. He pulled that out as well and dropped it into his lap.

Talid weighed the small gray pouch on his palm, then passed
it to Derin. "Here—he said this was for Corrie's dowry and
your losses."

Derin stared at the heavy pouch in his hand. His lips
quivered.

With his good hand, Talid picked at the object in his lap. It
was wrapped in soft doeskin. Wondering at his own daring, Talid

unwrapped it with trembling fingers and held it up. He caught his breath at the beauty of it; so did Jaida and Derin.

A heavy silver torc lay gleaming in the torchlight. The two ends were wrought in the shape of dragon's heads, their ruby eyes glittering.

"Look how tiny the scales are—and how perfect," Jaida whispered.

" 'Where's your torc of rank?' " Talid quoted softly.

" 'I'm traveling in disguise,' " Jaida finished, and laughed. "The sorry lout; it was the only thing he got right."

Talid yawned again; his eyelids drooped. "Let me wrap this up again, then I've got to sleep," he mumbled. With Jaida's help he returned the torc to its place in the saddlebags.

Lurching to his feet, he staggered off to bed.

▼▼▼

The sun was well on its way toward noon when Talid and Jaida were ready to leave the inn at Kelan Village.

"I wish Kovannin Rathan hadn't left so early," she said. "I would've liked to thank him."

Derin helped Talid into the saddle and nodded. "He came back before dawn. Looked right heart-weary, he did. I don't think that's the sort of thing he enjoys doing.

"Now that I've met a real Dragonlord, I don't think I'll ever make that mistake again. Polite His Grace was, like I was as good as him. Insisted on paying for his drink and food and told me something if anyone tries that trick again: Dragonlords can't get drunk. He left the false Dragonlord's horse and any belongings to the murdered men's families to sell for their were-gild. Then he left before anyone else was up."

Talid said nothing as he arranged his splinted arm as comfortably as he could. He missed his new friend already. He wished Kovannin e'Dahl was the real man, not Kovannin Rathan; that way he'd have a chance to meet him again. But now . . .

"Let's go," he said shortly and turned his horse out of the inn's yard.

Jaida must have sensed his mood for she said nothing as they ambled down the road. The sun was warm for autumn and the air was crisp, but Talid didn't notice. He wondered once again what he'd felt when Kovannin Rathan had spoken to him alone. If only he could understand . . .

They rounded a bend. The way forked before them: left and south to Bylith, right and north to the border mountains.

A great red dragon lay on the road before them. Shan cropped the grass in a nearby field.

Their horses tried to bolt, then stopped as if enchanted and walked slowly forward.

Stand before me, Bard Talid e'Vares.

The voice echoing in his mind, Talid never understood how he dismounted—even with Jaida's help—or how his shaking legs carried him to stand before the dragon. He felt no bigger than a flea.

"Your Grace," he stammered. He was terrified, remembering how he'd teased his "country bumpkin" during the ride. Talid began a stuttering apology.

No one has called me 'boyo' for some six hundred years.

Talid stared into an open mouth filled with fangs as long and sharp as war daggers. Green and blue flames erupted from it. His last thought as he flung up his arm in a vain attempt to ward the fire off was, *That's harsh for an honest mistake!*

Yet his flesh didn't melt from his bones. Instead a soothing coolness surrounded him. He floated in it, free of pain, feeling strong enough to leap from star to star. It lasted forever and no time at all.

Talid's broken arm no longer ached. It took him but a few moments to shed the uncomfortable splints. He flexed his fingers and looked up at Kovannin Rathan.

Once again the great fangs were bared. Somehow Talid knew it for a dragon's grin.

Forgot about a dragon's Healing fire, didn't you—boyo? The mind-voice was amused—and a touch smug. *Bards these days— don't they study the old tales?*

The dragon melted into red mist. Before Talid could blink, a man stood before him.

Kovannin Rathan said cheerfully, "Nice to see you decided to wake up, Talid. I thought I'd have to sit here all day."

Now Jaida came forward and knelt. She stammered, "Your— Your Grace!"

Talid fell to his knees beside her.

Kovannin Rathan closed his eyes a moment; he looked weary. "There's no need for that," he said. "I only meant to say good-bye." He whistled; Shan trotted up and he mounted. He wheeled the stallion away.

Along the north fork of the road.

And Talid suddenly understood. He scrambled into his saddle and stood up in his stirrups.

"Where the bloody hell do you think you're going, boyo?" he yelled.

When Kovannin Rathan looked back, his mouth open in surprise, Talid continued, "Bylith is *that* way, you idiot!" and pointed to the south.

Jaida gasped in horror as she stood up. "Talid!"

Ignoring her protests, Talid leaned down from his saddle and lifted her onto her horse. All the while he watched Kovannin Rathan.

Emotions chased across the Dragonlord's face, but Talid recognized the one that settled there: delight.

Yet it was a delight tinged with sadness. The Dragonlord rode back and stopped before them.

Talid studied him. "Were you truly going to Bylith—or just hunting the false Dragonlord?" he asked.

"Hunting. And I would go with you, but . . . Things outside

the mountains change so quickly—too quickly sometimes. The Bylith I remember is gone. One day I'll go back—but not this time. I need to return to Dragonskeep." Kovannin Rathan looked away; he said softly, "I didn't think I'd have to play executioner."

Talid winced at the pain in the Dragonlord's voice. "I understand. Still—I hope we'll see you again, someday . . . Kovannin."

Kovannin Rathan smiled a little. "Perhaps you will at that."

This time Talid made no protest as Kovannin Rathan rode away. He watched until the Dragonlord disappeared behind a hill. Jaida sat silently beside him.

At last he asked, "Did I do the right thing?"

"Calling after him like that? As if he were a friend? Yes; he liked it, I think," Jaida said. "I've heard it's a lonely thing to be a king or a queen; I would think it even worse to be a Dragonlord."

Talid urged the gelding into a trot, thinking as they rode mile after mile. The innkeeper's words echoed in his memory: "Polite His Grace was, like I was as good as him." He compared that with the false Dragonlord's high-handed ways.

And what was I doing? I was so busy looking down on a so-called bumpkin, I didn't see the Dragonlord under my nose. Which one do I want to be like—Kovannin Rathan or that impostor?

"I'm willing to spend a silver piece on those thoughts, Talid," Jaida finally said. "I've never known you to be quiet for so long."

Talid squinted up at the sky. "I was just thinking what a fool I've been."

A mile or two down the road they caught up with an ox-cart. An old woman drowsed on the seat; three children played among the turnips and firewood in the cart.

The old woman turned at the sound of their horses' hooves. She looked apprehensive; then her face split in a toothless smile. "Bards!" she cried with delight.

The children fell silent, studying Talid and Jaida as the bards rode up alongside. The youngest child had a grubby thumb firmly planted in her mouth. Talid felt as if their solemn-eyed regard went right through him.

"Good day to you both," the old woman said. "Will you ride with us and take shelter with my family this night? There's just my son, his wife, these younglings and me for your audience, but you're welcome to the best we have. It's not often we have bards up this way."

Talid looked over the rickety cart, the bony ox, the tattered clothing of the old woman and her grandchildren. A poor household, this; likely a hunter's or a charcoal burner's, and not much to offer.

He caught Jaida's eye; she made no sign. This was up to him.

Taking a deep breath, Talid said, "Goodwife, we'd be delighted to stay with your family this night"—and surprised himself by meaning it with all his heart.

He thought, *Though I may never see you again, Dragonlord, thank you for the lesson. I won't forget it.*

GRANDFATHER'S
BRIEFCASE
▼▼▼

GERALD PERKINS

H OW can I explain Grandfather? First, you have to understand that he had been everywhere. Ask him where he was from
and he might say Bangkok or Beijing, Shanghai or Saigon. He
once confessed to me that he had forgotten where he was born.
I didn't quite believe him. He had one of those undefinable
Asian faces that could be from anywhere, just enough wrinkles
to get respect, and a full head of hair. And no matter what
language someone spoke to him in, he answered in the same
language. Well, maybe he didn't know Uzbeki or Masai, but it
wouldn't have surprised me if he did. I knew he was in World
War II, the Korean Conflict, and Vietnam. I figure he was a spy.
He sure had some strange friends.

So how come I'm Anglo and have a name like Conrad?
Grandfather married a Murphy—in Ireland. Mom married a
Schroeder, in California, and I'm their oldest kid.

Grandfather always treated me as though I was his own son.
He tolerated my sisters but, well, they're female. I think Dad
approved of our friendship, though it hurt Mom that Grandfather

ignored the girls. I know Dad had Grandfather in mind when he bought a house with a big yard and a granny house in the back. That way Grandfather and his friends could come and go at all hours without disturbing the family. I'm pretty sure Grandfather was still working for Uncle Sam at the time—maybe until the end—under cover as a dealer in East Asian antiquities.

Even then, Grandfather never went anywhere without his briefcase. He said some Frenchman abandoned it at Ankor Wat. I asked him once during which war. He put on his best inscrutable face except for an odd smile.

Kids name everything, right? So when I asked him the name of his briefcase, he said, "Waloon." Actually, he said something in Chinese, but I couldn't pronounce it properly.

It was a *neat* briefcase. At first glance you think it's covered in fine alligator skin, probably from before it was illegal to kill alligators. If you look closely—and most don't—you'll see it isn't alligator, but I defy you to tell me what reptile gave its life to cover that case. Mostly it's warm brown, but if you hold it in bright light, it gets real red, and if you hold it just right, you'll see a kind of a gold wash over the red. It's pretty. It's nice to touch. And it liked me.

I know that last sounds silly, but it did—still does.

Even when I was little, Grandfather's door was always open to me. I'd come in to get away from my parents, or my sisters, or just because it was cool. Some of my best memories are of playing in his front room—which looked and smelled like a cross between a curio store and a library—paging through picture books with strange writing, making paper airplanes out of odd, spice-smelling wrappings, or playing with whatever gift Grandfather brought me. For a long time my favorite was a bronze horse. I probably destroyed any value it had by rubbing off the patina.

When Grandfather came back from wherever he'd been, I'd wait as long as I could, then run out to the little house in back. We'd bow to one another, then he'd hug me. I could always tell by his smile if he had a present. The briefcase knew if it held something for me. Sometimes it sort of purred. Sometimes it played hard to open. I'd poke and pry and turn the little combination wheels, but nothing would happen until I bowed and said, "Honorable Waloon, please display for this unworthy one your magnificent treasures," or words like that. I had to mean it, too, or it was no toy or book for at least a day. If I did mean it, the briefcase would pop open of its own accord. When I was little, I believed the briefcase listened. Later I figured Grandfather had something like a radio control that did the trick.

Grandfather had remarkable patience, but I suppose with his life, even a boy going through puberty was only a minor nuisance. He taught me a lot, very subtly. I learned about East Asian culture and history, though I could never speak any of the languages. That disappointed him. I can't remember when I began addressing him as "Sir," and meaning it. He was very pleased when I entered Redlands Community College.

Redlands, California is east of the Coast Range, south of Norton Air Force Base, which is south of San Bernardino. Officially, we're not part of Los Angeles. Unofficially, we might as well be; we have most of their problems. I was born in 1973, so I never heard the opening verses of the siren's song. I came in when she was well along and showing her teeth—PCP, speed, crack, heroin. She ate a few of my schoolmates. Grandfather had such utter contempt for anyone who would fry his brains that it never occurred to me to try drugs.

I knew who had them, of course, and stayed well away. The soldiers could be anyone, but the local bosses were Chinese working for a man named Chin. Chin, so the story goes, bought his way out of Vietnam in 1974 and lost a turf battle in L.A. about ten years ago. The cops know who he is and what he does, but can't touch him.

I was in Grandfather's house, sorting a selection of Buddha images by age and place of origin while he watched, when Chin's representative breezed in. He was only a little older than me and acted like he was in some side-street curio shop. I guess the art objects fooled him. Grandfather treated him with cold formality, addressing him in Mandarin—I think—looking more sad than angry when the rep didn't understand a word. The rep sort of oozed out *under* the door.

I grinned triumphantly at Grandfather when the guy was gone. Grandfather then gave me a lecture about triads that scared me spitless. The Mafia are kids in diapers next to those guys. I could see how Grandfather, with his contacts, could be invaluable to Chin. I remember pacing my room, furious that someone would threaten Grandfather and frustrated that there was nothing I could think of to do about it. Nonetheless, I decided to guard Grandfather as best I could.

I suppose there were more emissaries, but the only other one I saw was a middle-aged Chinese dressed in a conservative silk business suit. I knocked, entered, and stopped. The room was a good twenty degrees colder than the air conditioning could account for. Angry, I stepped into the room and fell flat on my face. Somehow I hadn't seen Waloon standing in my way and tripped over the briefcase. They both stared at me with blank expressions as I disentangled myself. Blushing furiously, I picked up the briefcase to set it aside.

Cold hatred flowed into me from the briefcase. I wanted to kill the stranger. Grandfather lifted his hand as I turned toward his visitor and the emotion vanished, leaving me empty. I bowed, apologized for my intrusion, placed the case on one corner of Grandfather's desk, bowed again, and left.

Outside in the cold November mist—about the only rain we got that year—I had to grab the old swing set to keep from fainting. I knew the rep. Oh, not personally; he was too high up for me to have crossed his path before. What shook me, though, was the certainty that of the two men, grandfather was the more dangerous. And that the briefcase was far more dangerous than either. I tossed and turned all that night.

Grandfather refused to talk about Chin or Waloon and what happened that day. After that, though, I occasionally caught him looking at me with a faint frown. Why would he worry about *me*?

I was the most surprised of the family when he broached the subject of retirement during Christmas break. When Mom told me Grandfather was over ninety, my first thought was, *World War I?* Stupid, I know, but though Grandfather had always been there, he didn't look that old. I couldn't believe he would ever leave.

I believed it when he gave me his briefcase at the start of winter semester.

I tried to refuse. He gave me one of his stern looks. We bowed to one another and he placed the briefcase in my hands. "Take care of him," he said. Waloon seemed as reluctant to leave as I was to take it. We both knew better than to argue.

▼▼▼

I turned up my collar against the cold March wind as I hurried down the street toward the library parking lot. I'd stayed late, doing some research for a history paper. A car started a few seconds after I walked past. I turned to look when the driver burned rubber taking off, wondering who the idiot was. The briefcase got in my way and down I went, thinking, *Can't chew gum and walk at the same time.* Then there was this snoring sound, barely audible above the car engine, and a lot of *rattle-slap-pings* all around me. The briefcase hit me four times, but not very hard as the books inside soaked up the energy of the slugs. I about crapped myself.

The cops were no help. They found the spent bullets all right, but since there wasn't a mark on the briefcase, they figured the shooters simply missed. Since I couldn't even tell them the color of the car, let alone make or license, they didn't offer much hope of finding the assassins. Later, I sat on my bed and stared at Grandfather's briefcase for a long time. Had he known Chin would try punishing him for refusing to cooperate by hitting me? Was he in danger or did Chin still want him?

Three days later a stolen pickup ran Grandfather off the road. Someone put a twenty-two slug through his left eye into the back of his brain from close range. I think the Fed who questioned me meant to be comforting when he said Grandfather never felt a thing.

The cops asked their own questions. More Feds searched Grandfather's little house thoroughly. I stayed with them to make sure I got a complete, signed list of everything they took for evidence. They didn't take anything, not even Grandfather's shotgun or his souvenir pistols—one from each war.

Mom and Dad just sort of stood around. I felt like there was this big block of ice around me, melting from the growing heat inside.

When everybody left, I sat in Grandfather's desk chair getting madder and madder. I started beating on the desktop—*thump! thump! thump! boom!* I thought for a second I'd stuck my hand in a fire, then I realized I'd just hit the briefcase. It was more angry than I was.

Too mad to be scared, I jumped up, shoving the chair so hard that it hit the wall several feet behind me. The door to the gun cabinet swung open. I know from nothing about using a pistol, but a shotgun you pump, pull the trigger, pump, pull the trigger, and things in front of you fall down. I grabbed the twelve gauge, then realized there was no ammunition. Swearing, I turned toward the door and stumbled over the briefcase. I hit the wall next to the cabinet hinge hard as I caught myself. The back of the case swung silently open.

I'm sure most of the hardware in that hidden closet was illegal, but I had eyes only for the shotgun shells. I loaded the gun through the slot in the side, not the magazine. I didn't know any better. I put two boxes of double-aught shells in one jacket pocket and two in the other. I looked at some boxes of weird ammunition and took one labeled "Beehive" and one marked "Dragon's Breath." From what the box said, a beehive round turns into a cloud of razor sharp flechettes as soon as it leaves the barrel; real nasty at close range. Dragon's Breath is a flame-thrower cartridge with a three second burn. I remember thinking that you can put *anything* in a shotgun.

I took off down Ramona with the shotgun in the trunk and the briefcase sitting next to me. A town cop gave me a hard look when I squealed a little leaving a stoplight. That cooled me down. I got real paranoid when I realized that anyone on the street could be Chin's, watching me, but the gut-deep rage kept me going all the way to California 215 and the edge of the Lake Perris Recreational Area.

Lake Perris sits in a little wooded valley, but this is desert country so a lot of the recreation area is pretty empty—if you don't count the ATV nuts and motorcyclists. A few rich people managed to get the land bordering the area so they have no neighbors on at least one side.

I turned off 215 and drove the twisting side road that passed Chin's place. A mile or so later I turned off, parked where I wouldn't easily be spotted, and walked back. It was hot and still. I thought of transferring the extra ammunition to the briefcase and ditching my jacket, but decided not to. The shotgun gained weight as I trudged, scared that a park ranger would come along and demand to know why I had it and where my license was.

The barbed wire fence around Chin's property only seemed old. When I looked closely, I could see that the scrub that masked any view of the house had been carefully planted to *appear* wild. I had trouble getting through the fence, but found a trail through the manzanita immediately.

The brush ended abruptly, but uncut dry grass continued for

another hundred feet. The house sprawled on a little rise on the generally downward slope. Its roof lines rambled here and there, naturally aged wood shading porches with huge picture windows. If I'd had a sniper rifle and patience I could have picked off Chin from where I stood. As it was, I would have to cross the dry grass, a ring of crushed stone, a ring of ice plant, and then a manicured lawn. I really thought about it.

I heard the dog running through the grass before I saw him, big, tan, and growling silently. I froze. Twenty feet away from me he came to a skidding stop, looked at the briefcase, then ran away, yelping in terror. Then the biggest bee in the world buzzed past me, followed by a sharp *crack!* from my right and below me. I saw a man running my way. Another bee went by from my left.

The shotgun kicked twice before I realized I'd fired. No way could I do damage from this range, but both guards dived for cover. I ducked back into the brush, calculating how fast I could make the road, then my car, against how fast they could follow me through familiar territory. I didn't like the answer.

I fished in my pocket for the odd ammo. Everything was pretty dry already. Maybe I could outrun a fire when I couldn't outrun men. I shoved in a Dragon's Breath cartridge. Even in bright daylight the magnesium in the flare almost blinded me. For a three second eternity I hosed the brush with that ten-foot-high, yards long jet of fire. Grass, manzanita, trees exploded into flame.

When the flare died, I saw the briefcase sitting unharmed in the midst of the fire. It drew the flames, the last magnesium sparks, into itself. The fire went out as Grandfather's briefcase opened, and opened, and opened again, changing shape as it grew. I watched, *knowing.* "Waloon," Grandfather said in my memory, *"wah loong."* Fire dragon.

I suppose he wasn't big as dragons go, but he was at least ten feet at the shoulder and forty from nose to tail tip. And he was beautiful. He varied from darkest crimson along his midline and wings to pale orange on back and belly. His head was solid crimson, vaguely equine except for droopy, fleshy mustaches, and teeth to make a dinosaur proud. The edge of each scale glinted gold. He fixed me with one infinitely deep black eye as he raised his wings.

Watch.

That much mass shouldn't be able to fly under muscle power. Two wing beats and he was a hundred feet in the air. By the time I blinked ash from my eyes, he had circled the property once. People ran from the house, pointing at the sky. I heard them shooting, yet a peculiar silence hurt my ears.

The dragon exhaled. Hissing, roaring, white gold fire struck the ground, following the perimeter of the brush. I saw one of the guards leap up, burning, his scream lost in the fire sound. Above the heat shimmer I saw Grandfather's dragon circle, making ever smaller rings of fire on the ground. The house exploded as his final blast hit it squarely.

Run.

I ran! Almost blinded by the heat and smoke I still managed to find the path I'd taken on the way in. Oddly, the fire stopped at the road. I passed fire trucks outward bound as I took 215 back to town. The evening news made quite a mystery of how the fire started and why it died so soon when the hills were ready for a major conflagration. The firechief merely looked grateful.

▼▼▼

The morning was already hot when I stopped the rented four-wheeler on the lip of the barren ravine I remembered from geology class. Grandfather's will left everything to me, stating that I, alone, was to dispose of his body by cremation in the desert. The family objected, but I held my own. The mortuary and the health department nearly killed the whole thing. I paid the full fee to the vultures and signed papers promising to make a safe, sanitary burn. Grandfather looked fine in his best suit with his medals pinned on, but he was light, an empty vessel in my arms as I laid him carefully on the stony ground.

"Waloon," I said to the air, "there is one last service you can do for your friend." I stood in the dry stillness until I thought he wouldn't come.

Stand away.

I clambered to the top of the ravine. Grandfather's dragon made two passes. When he finished, not even bones remained.

He landed next to me and I was not afraid. I looked into his eye.

A wounded man in black peasant pajamas struggled from one bit of shelter to the next in a jungle-eaten temple, flinching as artillery shells fell. I recognized the stone Buddha faces of Ankor Wat from travel magazines. A hole appeared suddenly in a solid stone wall. Grandfather slipped and fell into a subterranean temple. Daylight faded as the hole closed behind him.

After a while he lit a match. The faint light gleamed from the crimson scales and huge black eyes of a sad looking dragon. His wings were tattered, his scales dull, and his expression spoke of terrible weariness. Dust sifted through the air as another shell hit the ancient temple.

I could not hear the words that passed between Grandfather and the dragon, but suddenly Grandfather stood straight, all evidence of his wound gone. He bowed to the dragon.

Dragons live long. I was back on the California desert, standing next to the dragon from the vision; one no longer tattered and worn. *But they also sleep long. They are vulnerable then and must seek safe refuge for their slumbers. I thought the dead ancient holy place would be safe, but I did not understand the ferocity of man toward man. Wars kept me awake when I should have slept. Your grandsire offered me peace in exchange for protection. I did not expect we would share dreams, much less become friends. I need yet another century of rest. Will you take up your grand-sire's bargain?*

"If this is how you punish someone who disturbs your nap," I said, choking, "I would hate to see you really angry." I laughed until I cried. The dragon held me gently and shared my grief at the passing of a man we both loved.

The security guard from Norton didn't believe me when I told him the fire was Grandfather's pyre. He let me go after I showed him the permit and gave him a fake business card with my real name and address. As I put Grandfather's card case back, he looked at the seat next to me.

"Nice briefcase," he said.

MORDRED AND THE DRAGON
▼▼▼

PHYLLIS ANN KARR

PROLOGUE

MALORY tells how, near the outset of his reign, young King Arthur committed incest with his half-sister Morgawse—neither of them knowing their relationship—and dreamed of a serpent coming forth from his side to devour his kingdom. Malory does not tell, but his French source does, how Morgawse's youngest son spent his first few years at Arthur's court as a good and promising young knight; how he went out adventuring with the great Sir Lancelot; how one morning on the way to a tournament they met an old hermit who revealed that Mordred was both the fruit of Arthur's incest and the serpent of Arthur's dream; how Mordred in a rage killed the hermit, to Lancelot's annoyance, before he could tell Lancelot's fortune; and how in that day's tournament, Mordred fought like a man seeking death. The French book does not tell, but I do, what happened immediately after that.

▼▼▼

Wounds still bleeding, Mordred limped away into the wild wood, as far and as fast as he could hobble, until he sank exhausted on a fallen tree and lay too spent even for tears.

Neither stars nor moon could penetrate these moss-grown depths. Darkness wrapped him: murmurous with small noises, the loudest of them the distant hoot of a hunting owl; odorous with the perfumes both of growth and of decay; rough beneath him and hard against his left side, where it pressed upon the lichen-crusted tree trunk; yet so strangely laden of atmosphere that after a time he hardly felt in which direction he lay, whether his face was to the air or to the moss.

At length, with much pain, he groped his way up to a sitting position and fumbled for the talisman he had long worn secretly near his heart. No one else, not even that meddlesome old hermit—especially not that wicked old hermit—could ever have known about the gift his Aunt Morgan had given him on his fourteenth birthday: the dragon's egg from lands far, far to the east. "Someday," she had counseled him, "in your hour of sorest need, this may come to your aid."

Working by feel, he carefully unclasped the filigree case and rolled the egg into his palm, then clenched his fist around it. A great pearl, smooth as rainwater, lustrous as a tear, little larger than an acorn . . .

Much smaller than the egg required for a chicken. How, then, could so tiny an egg as this engender a dragon? Yet the tighter he held it, the more he felt it pulse within his hand.

He squeezed until his fist glowed with a ruddy light that, limning first the thin lines between his fingers, then veins and flesh until he glimpsed his very bones, began to illuminate the woods around him. When it showed him a fairy ring growing on the other side of the fallen tree, he cast the dragon's egg down into the middle of that circle of small white mushrooms.

Curls of bright mist started rising from it, twists of white and gold, intertwining with green, crimson, and purple, overflowing the fairy ring, looming up to block the treetops from the young knight's view. The glowing vapors coalesced, took shape, and solidified into a great serpent of three loops and four feet, each short leg ending in silver claws. The head—large, square, and wide-jawed as a hellmouth—bristled with broad darts of light. Bluish green iridescence rippled through the monster's scales with every motion, every breath, every pulse of its leisurely heart, as though it were bathed from within by its own light . . . as though, where other creatures held dank darkness inside their skins, this one held sunlit brilliance.

After turning its snubnosed head until it faced Mordred, the beast blinked twice, yawned immensely, then stretched its jaws in an inscrutable grin. "Well, well, well," it remarked in a low rumble. "Honorable young master, why do you desire this humble one's presence?"

Reminding himself of his newborn hatred and newly learned doom, the young knight held his voice steady. "You were given to me as an egg. I think, then, that I have hatched you."

"A mistake that you have been neither the first nor the oldest to make." Still grinning, the dragon inclined its head as if in courtesy. "Young master, small though this one may be among my own kindred, I am not at your command."

Of course. Was not a virgin sacrifice always required? How fitting . . . how appropriate, and how suited to Mordred's soul. Shuddering—less with fear than resolution—he hoisted himself onto the fallen tree and lay at full length, face upward. "Very good: take me. I am as yet a virgin knight. I sacrifice myself."

"To whom?"

"To you! Who else?"

The dragon bunched itself into a coil and sat as if pondering, chin poised delicately upon one silver claw. "Am I expected to swallow you whole? Do you think to command me from inside my belly?"

Finding it tricky to maintain his balance on the treetrunk, Mordred sat up and said in exasperation, "I have very little idea. All my life's study was to be a knight, not a damned necromancer!"

"Indeed?" the dragon remarked. "Why do you wish to change your role now, without study?"

"*Wish* to? My God! Do you think I *wish* to be damned and evil?"

"To be a necromancer, then, is evil, while to be a knight is good?"

"Perhaps," said Mordred, "as a creature of evil yourself, you fail to understand the difference."

"Let be, for a moment, the question of my evilhood," the dragon answered mildly. "I understand, at least, that in seeking to turn yourself from knight into necromancer, you wish to become evil and therefore judge yourself worthy of death. It strikes this ignorant one that you are using a great deal of effort to reach a simple end."

"I have spent this whole day trying for a simpler end!" The events threw themselves into Mordred's head so sharply that it seemed he could almost have stepped back into the bitter sunlit hours. "My lord Sir Lancelot should have slain me at once for killing the hermit! But he held his hand, and in the day's tourney—how could I have done so well? My God, I fought like a madman! Surely I gave them a hundred openings, a thousand chances to cut me down, yet I felled them right and left, and came out with not even wounds enough to hold me in my bed! What is this, if not my doom?"

"Allow us," the dragon said mildly, "to consider this hermit whom you killed. That was when you were still a knight and, therefore, good?"

"I have never been good," Mordred answered in hot impatience. "Our fine hermit laid it out before us very early today. That was why I slew him."

"The knowledge of further details would greatly assist this slow one's comprehension."

"What do you need 'comprehension' for, Sir Dragon? All you need is to swallow me, go out, and destroy my—" Mordred choked. "—my father's kingdom."

"Must I not know his name, lest I should destroy the wrong kingdom?"

"My very good lord the High King Arthur! He dreamed— when less than my age, I think—that a great dragon—a monstrous beast, a foul and loathsome worm—came out of his own side and devoured his realm." Once unleashed, the words burst forth in a rush. "By Merlin's counsel, he tried to avoid his fate by killing all babies born at the time of that dream. I should have died with them, but chance—or doom, as it turns out— saved me. Saved me to learn from today's hermit that I am the beast of my Lord Arthur's dream, that he is my father by incest— I had always thought him 'uncle'—that I myself am that foul and loathsome worm from out of his side, which he should have destroyed at birth, but could not!"

Mordred collapsed into himself and lay face down on the log, holding back sobs of rage and grief. The dragon sat hugely upon its coils and pondered.

At length it said, "So, then, you would become part of me, a dragon in truth, under the expectation that I would proceed to devour your father's kingdom. Suppose I did not?"

"Why would you not?"

The great beast sighed. "Young one, what are this man and his kingdom to me? How does it concern me whether he is father or uncle to you, whether either of you should or will destroy the other?"

"You are a dragon. I suppose you will devour this land because that is your nature. I sit here ready, so you can begin with me, and everything works out according to prophecy."

"Suppose, again," the dragon argued whimsically, "that neither you nor your father's kingdom are to my taste? Suppose that I am unhappily possessed of a delicate stomach, and require daintier morsels to digest?"

"Then . . . then at the least, slay me! If you will not eat, at least slay. Whatever you do afterward, I care nothing, but if we cheat the prophecy, so much the better."

Nodding as though it had carried a point at last, the dragon stretched itself and said, "Young knight, if my assumptions are wrong, I beg you to correct them; but it seems to this shallow one that you regard 'life' and 'death' as very final."

"What? How else should I regard them? If you'd change my thinking, bring the old hermit back to life here before me!"

"Ah! You would undo your deed. That shows promise." Once again the dragon settled thoughtfully into its coils. "Suppose that I *could* bring him back? Is that what you would truly wish?"

Mordred felt as if his heart stopped for a beat. When it began again, he said, "If you could do that, you would be as great as Our Lord. If you lie, the lie proves you evil as the Devil."

"Lie? In what way can mere supposition be construed as falsehood? But suppose that this thing lay within my humble power. Your hermit, while alive, did you mischief. Would you offer yourself in sacrifice for the restoration of his life, as readily as for the destruction of your uncle-father's little kingdom?"

"I . . . Yes! Yes, I think that I would! If only to prove him wrong!" Like lightning striking, a grin broke out on Mordred's face. "Yes! To spoil their pretty prophecies—that would heap coals on their heads! If you could do it . . ."

The dragon shook its head. "Not the strongest team of horses can draw back a word once spoken, nor a deed once done. Yet I will tell you one way. If you are truly willing to sacrifice yourself, do so to the life, and take this hermit's place as a man of God."

"Take . . . his . . . place?" The idea fell on Mordred like thunder. He needed time to—

"*Mordred! Sir Mordred!*" Lancelot's voice, loud above the

crashing of his horse through the forest. *"Mordred!* God-damned stripling, where are you?"

Mordred whispered, "Lancelot!"

The dragon returned its liquid gaze from the direction of the new noises back to Mordred. "He is calling you?"

"Yes."

"Will you answer him?"

"No! God damn him, himself! Why did he not kill me when he had the chance?"

The dragon shook its head. "Honorable youth, these questions grow too heavy for this simple one's intelligence."

Then it stretched. Yawning, it slowly lifted its great body, loop by loop and coil by coil, each scale sparkling by the beast's own interior luminance. Like a column of brilliant smoke, or a lightning-spangled stormcloud, it expanded until, feet still on the ground, its head rose above the treetops. And it roared—or sighed—like thunder.

"Dragon!" came Lancelot's bellow, and the knight already called the greatest of all the Table Round crashed into the clearing at full tilt, sword drawn.

"No!" cried Mordred. Despite his wounds, he rolled to his feet and, unarmed and unarmored as he stood, caught up a broken limb of the fallen tree.

Lancelot reined his charger up into a pivoting standstill. "So!" he exclaimed. "You *have* gone mad!"

"No madder than you, my lord Sir Lancelot! No madder than this whole world, that pays lip service to Our Lord even as it runs adoring after King Herod!"

"Stand aside! If you do not know your duty, then stand aside and let me slay that beast unhindered!"

"These honorable young barbarians," the dragon observed, "speak of slaying as though their kind were plentiful in this land."

"Hear it roar!" shrieked Lancelot. "Stand aside, or I run you down on my way, and rid the world of two evils at once!"

"Ride me down, then! This beast is wiser than all the sages of Rome. I would be honored to die for it or with it."

Screaming a battle cry, Lancelot spurred his charger forward. Mordred struck back with all his strength. The dead tree's limb shattered against the steed's armor. Falling beneath its iron-shod hooves, Mordred's head twisted at such an angle that he saw Lancelot's sword plunge deep into the dragon's throat.

Instead of writhing, it gave a chuckle and shook itself like a dog, dislodging the sword. From the wound in its throat flew drops of water clear and bright as rain.

Earlier, it had expanded only by uncoiling its body. Now that entire body seemed to swell out, at the same time growing somehow unsolid . . . cloudlike . . . floating up from the ground. The two huge forepaws reached briefly down into the mushroom circle. When they came back up, they held between them the dragon's egg. Expanding along with the beast that carried it, it shone forth as a huge pearl, ethereal colors shimmering through its milky surface.

Bearing its pearl, the dragon rose higher and higher; and, as it rose, the rain spread. At last, far above the treetops, the pearl covered the moon . . . and then the rain came down in such a flood as to wash all sight from the two men's eyes for several moments.

As the onslaught settled into a quiet drizzle, Lancelot lifted his visor, blinked, and shook his head. "Mordred!" he exclaimed, glancing down. "Young scoundrel, so there you are! What did you mean, running away into these woods alone when what you need is a good surgeon?"

Lancelot, it appeared, had forgotten the dragon completely. Mordred remembered the beast; remembered, too, that its words had roused in him certain aspirations to change his course of life and thereby foil his fate.

"My sword!" Lancelot went on, staring across the open space. "How came it there?" He dismounted, retrieved it, and paused on his way back to prod Mordred lightly with one mailed toe. "Up, rogue, and beg pardon for leading me such a chase."

While the dragon's rain had left Mordred's tournament wounds much as before, he found that it had healed the newer and deadlier injuries caused by Lancelot's charge. Accepting the older knight's arm, he pulled himself to his feet and suffered himself to be mounted on the steed's crupper.

"I shall always regret," Lancelot grumbled, jumping into the saddle, "that I could never learn what our hermit had to prophesy concerning *my* future."

"Be content," Mordred replied. "He might have told you that you, too, would help bring about our good king's downfall." He could not reawaken the aspirations the dragon had roused in him before Lancelot's coming: they remained mere cold recollections, crushed beneath his sense of doom. "Indeed," he muttered, "you may already have played your part."

FALCON AND DRAGON
▼▼▼

JOSEPHA SHERMAN

PRINCE Finist, young magician-ruler of Kirtesk, sported in the air high above his royal city, sunlight glinting off his falcon-form's silvery wings, the avian shape as comfortable to him as the human.

Eh, what was this? A wing-weary pigeon labored far below him, headed towards the gleaming white-and-gold palace, and the prince's keen eyes noted a message strapped to one thin avian leg. Odd! *Verst* after *verst* of forest separated his lands from those of neighboring rulers or even from those of the various *boyars* who were his vassals. None of his fellow princes used the birds, preferring human messengers, and Finist had ceded his vassals enchanted mirrors should they need to contact him. Rare, indeed, to see a messenger pigeon being used!

Almost, Finist mused, *as though the sender were suddenly afraid to make use of magic.*

The prince sped back to the royal palace, swooping in through an open window to where his attendants stood waiting with matter-of-fact patience for their shape-shifting master to return. By the time other servants brought him the sealed message the pigeon had borne, Finist was back in human shape and seated in a small audience chamber, his tall form clad in a hastily donned silken caftan, his wild silvery hair almost confined by a simple coronet. The only sign of the falcon he'd been just a short time ago was his bright amber eyes.

"Duke Vasily's seal," Finist murmured, studying the intricate design. Waving the servants away, he delicately broke the wax and unrolled the tiny strip of parchment. The duke, a very distant cousin, was one of those *boyars* whose lands lay in the more mountainous northern reaches. Frowning slightly, Finist read:

Prince Finist, liege lord and kinsman, I scrawl this in haste, praying the bird reaches you in equal haste. I dare not use the magic mirror, for he would sense the use of even the slightest spell, or so he has warned me.

" 'He?' " Finist said impatiently. "*What* 'he'?"

And I have no reason to doubt his word, for the dragon who would conquer my lands has already carried off my son, my little Dimitri, as hostage. I plead with you, my prince, my liege lord and kinsman, save him, save my little Dimitri.

"The dragon!" Finist exclaimed. Of course the forest was full of such magical folk as the *leshiye*, the tricky little forest lords. But there were no such things as dragons, not in these lands.

Not *true* dragons, at any rate, Finist admitted reluctantly. There were instead, or so legend claimed, such creatures as *dragon-kalduni*, dragon-sorcerers. If the tales about such beings were true, a dragon-sorcerer began life as a human who, for whatever evil reason, turned to the darkest forms of sorcery, bargaining away humanity for dragon-shape and dragon might.

Finist got to his feet, pacing restlessly about the small chamber. Some *dragon-kalduni*, the stories claimed, lived on as brooding hermits, endlessly, pointlessly gathering magical power, but others turned without warning to a hunger for political power as well. Shape-shifters, they were perilous enough in man-form, but in dragon-form they combined sorcerous cunning with deadly fangs and flame.

And that, Vasily claims, is what has invaded his lands. And stolen his son. Charming.

Was it true? Could there actually be such a thing as a dragon-sorcerer? Couldn't some clever bandit have fobbed himself off as— No, no, Vasily had never been a flighty man. He would never be so easily tricked.

The prince stopped short, leaning on the narrow windowsill, staring bleakly out at Kirtesk's brightly painted wooden houses and busy streets, feeling nothing but honest terror. He didn't want to leave, God no, he didn't want to put himself in who knew what danger!

Who does? Finist asked himself drily.

There was hardly a choice. He had to aid Vasily, no matter what the peril; he could not, by the vows he and Vasily had exchanged, allow a kinsman's child, a vassal's child, to come to harm. And even if he refused honor, stayed safely hidden here, how long *would* Kirtesk be safe? If there really was a true dragon-sorcerer in his domain, the evil, coldly amoral creature was hardly going to be content with one easy, bloodless victory.

Besides, Finist mused, heroic times of knightly *bogatyri* to the contrary, few nonmagical folk were going to survive an encounter with a *dragon-kaldun*. A magician at least had *some* hope of success!

Akh, but he didn't dare use his magic, not with the boy's life at stake, not till he was ready for a final confrontation with the enemy. Even as Vasily had warned, a true dragon-sorcerer would easily sense even the slightest use of Power.

So I must go and conquer a creature of who knows how much physical and sorcerous strength without using a shred of magic. Wonderful.

▼▼▼

Of course, Finist reflected, soaring high over his lands, he could never have told his people the truth; while they had a great deal of respect for his magic, they would hardly have accepted the idea of their prince taking on so sorcerous and alien a foe. And so he flew to Duke Vasily's lands under the guise of making a polite, politic visit, seeing the *versts* pass swiftly beneath his wings, the fertile fields and forest like a lovely green tapestry gradually giving way to more rocky terrain. Seeing the river that marked the edge of Duke Vasily's lands, Finist knew he dared fly no further lest he attract the dragon's attention too soon, and swooped down to a landing in human-form.

Shape-shifting from human to falcon and back again was a simple thing for one of Finist's blood; the avian form was almost as natural to one of the royal line of Kirtesk as the human. But working any other type of shape-shifting was another matter. At last, after much effort, Finist managed to hide his admittedly exotic coloring behind the plain features and dull brown hair of a common farmhand. Clad in the plain, lightweight tunic he'd been carrying rolled up in his talons, he continued into Vasily's lands like any other commoner looking for work, luckily catching a ride all the way to the ducal estate in the wagon of a bored farmer.

Two guards hurriedly blocked his path as he tried to enter Vasily's elegant, white-washed mansion. "Where do you think you're going, peasant?"

"To see your duke," Finist answered mildly. "And before you try throwing me out, kindly tell Duke Vasily his liege lord sends him this."

It was a silvery feather. And it brought Finist a hasty entry into Duke Vasily's private chambers.

"Yes," Finist said before the frantic man or his equally frantic wife, Duchess Anya, could call his name and in the process break the shape-disguising spell, "I've taken a different form, but it *is* me. *Don't* call me by name, I pray you. The spell was difficult enough to set the first time! Akh, don't worry; it leaves no magical residue. Even—ah—That One won't detect it."

"You received my message, then," Vasily asked carefully, and Anya added with equal care, "You will help?"

"As best I may." Finist had been working out the details of a plot as he'd flown. "But," he added, "I will need one thing from you first."

"Name it!" husband and wife cried almost as one.

"It's nothing so dramatic. Grant me this: a nice, meaty herd of cows."

"But—what—"

The prince grinned. "Why, kinsfolk, even a dragon needs to eat!"

▼▼▼

Finist, princely cowherd, took the cattle a bit further afield than might have been expected from an ordinary, easygoing laborer, all the way to the rocky edges of the mountains. There, pretending to daydream while the animals grazed, he studied those mountains with a careful eye. Difficult to see detail clearly: so much quartz glinted in those rocks that the sunlight made them look almost like the glass mountains of ancient ballads.

He's up there somewhere, I can feel it. But just where . . .

The prince shook his head. Even if he dared use a Spell of Finding, it might not work as it should. Before one could successfully deal with a new form of magic, one needed to know its name and shape. And nowhere in his scrolls back in Kirtesk had he found anything truly useful about dragon-sorcerers or their spells. He'd just have to wait and learn.

A cow lowed in sudden alarm and Finist came sharply alert. A sharp wind buffeted him, a great shadow passed over his head—

And the dragon-sorcerer was before him, perched with casual elegance on a rocky outcropping. Finist, used to magic though he was, drew in his breath sharply. Alien, oh, alien . . . metallic-gleaming scales, bright as polished bronze, glinting, deadly fangs, cold, glittering dark eyes. And a sense of strange Power all about.

Should the being breathe flame at him now, the prince knew he wouldn't have time to work a spell or even dodge, so Finist bowed as clumsily as a peasant, unused to such courtesies, might, and heard the dragon-sorcerer chuckle, an incongruous sound from that awesome shape.

But the sorcerer plainly couldn't speak easily in dragon-form; that fanged jaw was hardly made for human speech. He shifted shape as lightly as Finist moved from bird to man, and the prince just barely bit back a second gasp of surprise, because the sorcerer looked not like the human he'd once been but like a dragon trying and failing to mimic humanity, the form *almost* right, the still-scaly skin stretched too tightly over fierce, inhumanly sharp features.

Inhuman, indeed, Finist realized. Somewhere in the transition from man to dragon, humanity—and a good degree of reason with that humanity—had been lost. Only the faintest memory of human ambition could be left to give the creature the drive to conquer Duke Vasily's realm.

And so the Darkness rewards Its servant, Finist thought with a shudder. *Yes, but irrational creature though he may be, that doesn't make him one bit less perilous. Can he still breathe flame in this form? I don't dare risk finding out!*

"Polite little human," the sorcerer hissed. "Perhaps I shall not kill you."

How kind of you, Finist thought wryly, and stammered, "Wh-what do you want, my lord?"

"Tribute," the dragon-sorcerer told him. "A nice, meaty cow."

"Your pardon, lord, but these cows aren't mine to give."

The inhuman eyes flickered angrily. "What does that matter to me? What I want is mine."

So, now: inhuman arrogance, quick temper, and sorcerous power. A perilous combination—but one that just might be useable. Finist stiffened in sudden feigned outrage. "Why, what a gluttonous beast! I am more than satisfied if I get a scrawny little duck for dinner, and yet you want a whole cow!"

The sorcerer grew menacingly still. "Be careful, little man."

"No, no, *you're* the one who should be careful! A whole cow! Whoever heard of such a thing!" Finist fought to keep his voice steady, very well aware of the dangerous game he was playing. Anger the creature too much and face attack; fail to rouse him beyond the point of caution and miss the only chance to find his lair. Inventing wildly, the prince claimed, "I knew a cow once who decided she would eat a whole barnload of hay. D'you know what happened to her? She—"

"Why should I care what happened to your brainless cow?" the dragon roared, and wisps of smoke drifted from his suddenly not-quite human jaws. "Stop this prattle and give me—"

"She *burst*, that's what happened! That's the fate of gluttons—and a glutton you are, you great fool!"

The sorcerer's form blurred completely back into dragon-shape, and for one heart-stopping moment, seeing those now terrible jaws, Finist was sure he'd gone too far. But to his immense relief, the dragon-sorcerer only gave a hiss of contempt, snatched up a cow, and flapped heavily off with it.

That's right, be contemptuous of me, I'm nothing but a peasant, you don't have to be wary about revealing your lair to such as I and—Ahh, is that the way of it? Clever. I never would have spotted that crack in the rocks from down here, or even from the air, not with all that gleaming quartz to dazzle me. The dragon-sorcerer, it would seem, had a flamboyant streak to him.

All Finist had to do was wait till the sorcerer left his lair again, however long it took, then fly up there, get Dimitri out of whatever trap he was in, and—

And do nothing of the sort. The minute he shifted to falcon-form, the rush of magic would send the dragon-sorcerer swooping back to attack him—or, worse, Dimitri. Finist hesitated, realizing with some chagrin that he was so used to flight he had no idea how someone actually climbed something!

Ah, well, he'd just have to learn, wouldn't he?

Oh, damn. So would the boy, little Dimitri. And they would both have to get down that abysmally steep cliff silently and swiftly, because he couldn't even begin to think about how to fight the dragon-sorcerer till the boy was safely out of the way.

One problem at a time. Finist hid himself amid the rocks and waited with a magician's quiet patience. Rather to his surprise, it wasn't long at all before the gleaming dragon-form took wing from the glassy cliff.

Of course. He has to find something to feed the boy. Dimitri can't be expected to eat raw meat, and I doubt the sorcerer has the patience to use dragon-flame to cook it for him!

Warily, feeling ridiculously clumsy, Finist began the long, tedious climb up the mountain. Used to soaring on the winds, he had not the slightest fear of heights, but he was panting and bruised by the time he finally managed to pull himself up into the narrow opening in the rocks.

The dragon got himself through this? This . . . is . . . barely . . . wide enough . . . for a . . . human, and—

And all at once the prince was through, blinking in darkness, waiting tensely for his eyes to adjust. Something stirred in that darkness, and Finist froze, suddenly irrationally sure the dragon-sorcerer had somehow slipped back in through another entrance.

But there was no other entrance. As his vision began to adjust, Finist realized that what he'd heard was only the child-hostage. Dimitri huddled at the far end of the rough, rocky cave, a small, skinny, tow-headed little boy trapped behind a wall of iron bars.

God, what if they're locked with sorcery? I've never heard of anyone working magic on iron—but who knows what a dragon-sorcerer can do?

But then Finist saw the nice, ordinary lock. "The key, Dimitri," he whispered, "where is the key?"

Dimitri, staring at him with wide, terrified eyes, pointed. Finist found the key dropped casually amid the jumble of rocks, and raised a startled brow. No tricks or traps here at all: the sorcerer, being the incomplete, illogical creature he was, must have been arrogantly confident that no one could follow him up here.

The boy was still staring at him. "Don't be afraid," the prince soothed, unlocking the makeshift prison's door. "I'm here to get you out of this."

"D-did Father send you?"

"He did, indeed. Come, hurry, before the dragon returns."

But Dimitri shook his head. "It isn't going to do any good."

Akh, of course the already frightened child wasn't going to trust a stranger. "Don't be afraid," Finist repeated as gently as he could. "I'm your father's friend, my word on it. And I won't let the dragon hurt you."

"You don't understand! You *can't* hurt him. H-he can't die!"

"Nonsense. Now—"

"It's true. He told me so himself, he doesn't keep his life in his body. It's in a—a little locked box somewhere."

Finist blinked in surprise. Oh, yes, he'd heard of such a bizarre thing, but the idea of keeping one's life-force outside one's body belonged to the realm of tales, not to the real world!

But then, the prince admitted, *until recently, I didn't believe in dragon-sorcerers, either.*

Time enough to learn the truth later. "Never mind that, boy. Come, follow me."

Little Dimitri proved to be as agile as a squirrel, practically scuttling down the cliff, leaving Finist to struggle along in his wake. They had just reached flat ground again when a vast shadow passed over them. The prince glanced sharply up, even though he already knew what he'd find.

Damn. Didn't expect him to overtake us quite this swiftly.

Hastily, he pushed the boy into hiding amid the rocks, then turned to face the foe.

Have to draw him away from Dimitri. No need to hide what I am now that his hostage is out of his reach.

Finist took to the air as falcon, and heard the dragon's startled hiss. So, the creature really hadn't sensed his magic till this moment.

That's right, monster, follow me. You've got greater strength than me, but there's no way in the good green world you can maneuver as quickly.

He banked and dove and soared, whirling around and about the furious dragon, dodging bursts of terrifyingly fierce flame, hoping he could tire the creature out before he exhausted himself.

It—it isn't working. He has some form of magical strength beyond mine. And I don't think he's about to just let me go, either.

He couldn't cast spells in this form any more than could the dragon-sorcerer, and the sorcerer was blocking any safe route to the ground. For want of a better refuge, Finist sped through the narrow crack in the cliff—a far easier job in this smaller shape—and came to a hasty landing in human shape behind the jumble of rocks, gathering his magic to him, praying the dragon wouldn't simply scorch the entire cavern. But the creature had apparently exhausted his flame for now, because he suddenly transformed to his eerie, once-human form, the *feel* of his Power crackling in the air.

Finist struck first. His magic wasn't really of the combat sort,

but a hastily altered spell for light and heat flashed into being
with all the force he could cast, engulfing the sorcerer in a
sudden blue-white blaze of Power so fierce it astonished even
Finist.

I have him, he's dead!

But to the prince's horrified astonishment, the magic that
should have burned the sorcerer to ash faded harmlessly away,
leaving the creature totally untouched. Dear God, Finist realized,
backing away, desperately searching his mind for a new spell,
Dimitri had been right: the sorcerer really *was* invulnerable. He
really did have his life-force stored outside his body.

How am I ever going to find—

The sorcerer hissed a twisted, savage Word of Power. Finist
threw himself frantically aside as something that *felt* like a wave
of darkness harsh as death came crashing down where he'd just
been. Scrambling back to his feet, he wondered wildly, *What
language is* that? *I've never heard or felt anything like it!*

Alien sorcery, truly alien; unless he could figure out the shape
and name of it, he could never counter it—and this wasn't exactly the place for careful study!

The sorcerer stood between him and the entrance, cutting off
any hope of escape. Smiling without the slightest trace of humor
or humanity, the creature began the whispering syllables of yet
another spell. As the force of it came thundering down about
him, Finist turned to falcon-form, soaring hastily up out of reach,
nearly cracking his skull against the cavern's roof, then dove back
down to human shape, panting. God, he couldn't keep dodging
like this forever!

And I can hardly say, "Please, sir, let me go home!"

But Dimitri had said— Small hope, to depend on what a
frightened child might have misheard or falsely believed, smaller
hope, to believe the thing would be here. Still . . . that casually
tossed-aside key had proven the dragon-sorcerer had little concept
left of human artifacts, human cunning.

It might be. God, let it be.

It would mean leaving himself wide open to attack for a precious moment. But what other hope was there? Instead of trying another useless attack, Finist cast the simplest, lightest Spell of Finding, hunting . . . hunting . . .

Ha, yes, *finding!* With a fierce cry, Finist dropped to his knees, tossing rocks aside with desperate strength, hardly daring to believe, even as the dragon-sorcerer rushed forward to—

Stop short, staring. Finist straightened in triumph, the small, plain, earth-colored casket in his arms. *You were right, Dimitri, bless you, child, you were quite right!* "That's it, sorcerer. Keep back. We both know what's kept inside this."

The sorcerer knew, all right. Hissing, he altered shape. A blast of fire singed Finist's arm and he cried out in startled pain, losing his hold on the casket. As it fell, it burst open—and a hare raced out.

I don't believe—

Both the sorcerer and the prince lunged after the hare, but Finist, more agile than the larger dragon, snatched up the squirming little animal—only to lose it again with a shocked gasp as the dragon lashed out with a talon, just barely missing him and instead tearing the hare open as neatly and bloodlessly as a man slits fabric with a knife.

My God, we really are *in the world of the old tales!*

No time to wonder at it: A small bird sprang out of what had been a hare, taking flight in a flurry of wings. Finist hastily turned to falcon, snapping his beak shut against the sudden new stab of pain in what was now a wing. It hurt almost unbearably to take to the air, but he caught the same strong current of air the bird had found and soared down it after the small, swift thing, even as the dragon thundered after him. Far below him, he caught a glimpse of Dimitri's upturned face as the boy stared up in wonder. No way to warn the child to get back into hiding, no way to—

There, now, he had the bird!

No, damnit, he had nothing more in his talons than a few feathers, and now he had to sideslip quickly out of the way of a gust of flame. As Finist flapped fiercely to catch a new current, fighting new complaints from his scorched arm-wing, he glanced back to see that the dragon was about to snare the little bird.

No, you don't! the prince thought, and dove at the inhuman eyes with talons extended. With an angry hiss, the dragon-sorcerer threw his head up. Suddenly about to collide with the bony jaw, Finist pulled sharply up in a climb that made him cry out anew—a falcon's shriek—at the strain on his injured wing until he'd caught the wind once more. The dragon roared, twisting about in the air, and the end of one mighty wing struck Finist a glancing blow that sent him tumbling. By sheer chance, the prince crashed right into the small bird, his talons clenching reflexively even as he struggled to right himself. The bird—

Tore neatly open, even as had the hare. A gleaming golden something—an egg, by God, a golden egg—fell free. Both falcon and dragon tried for it, but it plummeted down more swiftly than they could move. Before either of them could go after it, little Dimitri darted out from hiding and it fell right into his waiting hands.

He doesn't see the danger! God, the dragon will kill him!

Finist plunged down, changing shape almost before he was within a safe distance from the ground, hurling Dimitri to the ground. The golden egg flew free, and Finist dove after it, only to spring wildly back as a blast of flame nearly roasted him.

"Yes, that's right!" Finist shouted hoarsely up at the dragon-sorcerer in sudden inspiration, struggling for breath. "Roast me if you can! I challenge you!" He leaped aside again and yet again as bolts of fire roared down about him. "Call yourself a dragon? Can't even hit a cow let alone a man!"

Were the blasts not quite as fierce? Were they spaced more and more widely apart? Yes! Once again, the creature had exhausted his flame. He quickly turned from dragon to sorcerer—but Dimitri was even quicker, snatching up a rock in both hands and bringing it smashing down on the golden egg with hysterical force, over and over.

"Oh, well done!" Finist breathed. This was the end of it, this had to be the end of it.

But rather than shattering, the egg broke neatly into halves. Dimitri backed off with a puzzled frown, because within the halves lay a withered brown seed.

That's it? Finist wondered doubtfully. *That's what holds the creature's life-force?*

It must be. With a shriek of fury, the sorcerer screamed out a Word that seemed to tear apart the very air. Finist threw himself against Dimitri, hurling them both to the ground as a hot, savage wind slashed and slashed above them.

But so much Power spent has to stagger him. I have a chance.

The prince scrambled back up, buffeted by the last shreds of the sorcery, racing for the seed. He and the sorcerer collided, and Finist screamed as the creature's nails, almost as terrible as dragon talons, raked his already scorched arm. Before he could focus his pain-shocked mind, the sorcerer's harsh hands were about his throat, fierce with dragon-strength, cutting off any hope of air. Blood surging painfully in his ears, Finist kicked and hit and clawed flesh that seemed invulnerable as stone.

But all at once the sorcerer grunted, jerking back, grunted again, losing his grip. Finist tore free, gasping in wonderful lungfuls of air, realizing as his mind cleared that little Dimitri, nearly sobbing with fright and fury, was throwing rocks and earth and bits of bark with all the frantic strength in his terrified body.

The seed, have to get the seed before the dragon realizes I'm— Yes, there it is!

He snatched the hard little thing up, wondering wildly how he could ever hope to destroy it. Hitting the seed with a rock wasn't the answer; it was rock-hard itself. Fire? Ridiculous, this was a dragon's life he held; fire wouldn't hurt it. Water? Drown the thing? How, when there wasn't even the hint of water here? God, God, if he didn't find the answer in the next moment, both he and brave little Dimitri were dead and—

Wait . . . not death. If the dragon was Death in this duel, then he, surely, was Life . . . He had often helped the farmers in his realm by casting certain charms, small spells to ensure the fruitfulness of their crops . . .

Yes!

Holding the seed firmly in one hand, Finist shouted out the Words of the most Powerful spell of growth he knew.

And the sorcerous seed, even as any other, stirred and came to life, splitting apart in his hand. He heard the dragon-sorcerer shriek in terrifying rage and grief and sheer despair—

Then that which had been the sorcerer's life flared up and out in strange new growth, in so savage an explosion of raw Power that Finist, dazzled, drained, exhausted, felt his senses spin away into darkness.

▼▼▼

To his surprise, Finist awoke in a bed, aware that his scorched arm was swathed in bandages, aware of being watched. . . .

"Ah, of course. Vasily. You followed me."

The duke smiled nervously. "I—I couldn't bear *not* to follow. My prince, my kinsman, you saved my son, and I—"

"Hey, now, Dimitri returned the favor! That is a brave boy you've reared."

Vasily's eyes glinted with pride. "But what about the—the dragon? Is he really . . . gone?"

"Quite." Finist managed a weary grin, too tired for any regal proclamations. "Let's just say that like any overblown tree past its prime, our dragon-sorcerous friend simply . . . dried up and ran to seed."

WHEN THE SUMMONS CAME
FROM CAMELOT
▼▼▼

CYNTHIA WARD

WHEN the summons came from Camelot, Michael, Baron of Segreves, was returning from vespers in the company of his wife and retainers. As they left the chapel, they glanced toward the heavens, though they had no reason to; the season was spring, not autumn. But no man or woman of the barony could step under open sky without watching for the Dragon of Segreves.

Hooves ringing like a swordsmith's hammer, a lathered horse burst into the courtyard. Sir Michael's knights drew their swords. The baron saw the heraldic device emblazoned on the horseman's white surcoat, a dragon *passant gules*, and gestured for his men to put away their weapons. The stranger pulled a letter from his breast, and Sir Michael saw the same heraldic dragon impressed in the wax seal. He accepted the missive. His wife laid her hand on his arm as he broke the seal and unfolded the letter with fumbling fingers.

He stood still a moment, until Lady Eleanor said, "I pray you, my lord, tell us what it says."

Sir Michael drew breath to steady himself, and read the message in his deep, carrying voice: "'His Royal Majesty Arthur, King of the Britons, requests the companionship of the Christian knight Michael, Baron of Segreves, Harrower of the Dragon of Segreves, in the Fellowship of the Round Table and the Quest for the Holy Grail.'"

His wife gasped and his men cheered loud and long. And Sir Michael felt his heart's blood pump fiercely through his veins at the fulfillment of his deepest desire.

He turned to Lady Eleanor, and thought he saw a shadow of sadness on her face. But then her eyes met his, and they glowed with love and pride, and he knew his wife had only been startled. The honor had been so long delayed; he was reminded of how long by the lines about her eyes, and the grey hairs that had escaped her wimple. But now, after twenty years, he had been invited to join the fellowship of the most courageous and celebrated knights of all Christendom.

"A feast, to celebrate my good fortune!" Sir Michael cried. "Summon my son! Tomorrow I leave for Camelot!"

His son could not be found, so the celebration needs must start without him. Sir Michael wondered if Thomas were at the alehouse; but of course if he were, one of the knights would have escorted him to the keep. Even without the presence of the heir, however, it was a merry celebration, for the Fellowship of the Round Table was the most exclusive brotherhood of knights in the world.

Sir Lamorak spoke, praising Sir Michael's honor and courage; then, during the feast, the old minstrel Gruffydd sang of the heroism of King Arthur's knights. He sang of Sir Gawaine and the Green Knight, and of Sir Gareth and the Lady Lynette. Then, as the men went deeper in their cups and the women retired for the evening, the minstrel struck up a salacious song about Gawaine's way with the ladies. The baron's vassals pounded their fists on the boards, shouting for another bawdy tune.

The minstrel struck a chord on his lute.

"Oh, the greatest knight in the land
Rides the fairest mare in the land
She's the only mare in the stable
But to ride her the King's unable—"

The knights rose up roaring, and goblets flew at Gruffydd, spilling wine. Sir Lamorak stood and overturned his goblet, bringing it down on the high table with such force that its thunder silenced the wrathful knights.

"*Gruffydd!*" Sir Michael cried. "What is the meaning of this?"

The minstrel dashed wine from his brow and made no reply.

"King Arthur sends his knight Sir Lamorak to summon me to Camelot, and you serve my honor by insulting our Queen and the greatest knight this world has ever seen! You risk *much!*"

"Forgive me, my lord," Gruffydd said, not looking up, and went forth from the hall.

Sir Michael turned to his guest. "I pray you accept my apology, Sir Lamorak. Wine has made the minstrel foolish. Grant me a moment's leave, and I shall see to it that he is punished."

Sir Lamorak gave a stiff nod. Sir Michael strode grim-faced from the hall, his cape swirling behind him like a river in tumult.

He did not find his minstrel within the keep. He went into the courtyard, glancing up automatically. When he lowered his head, he saw Gruffydd. The minstrel stood staring up at the night's bright cloak of stars; in the full moon's light, his grey hair shone like a silver torch-flame, a beacon to his lord.

Sir Michael seized Gruffydd by the shoulder, and spun the old man about. "To think I trusted you as an advisor! You are no fit servant for a knight of the Round Table. By God, I've a good mind to *kill* you!"

"My lord, grant me a moment's speech," Gruffydd said. "If after I speak you still want me to leave, I shall be gone by dawn."

"A moment," Sir Michael said, restraining his anger with an effort so great it brought sweat to his brow.

"My lord, you know the rumors about Sir Lancelot and Queen Guinevere are true, and have been for years—for decades."

"It is not our place to speak of such things. Especially before a guest from the Royal Court. *Especially* when I have been summoned to Camelot! You asked my forbearance so that you might repeat your insults? By the Christ, I—"

"My lord," Gruffydd said, "I do not seek to waste your time with idle gossip. You are a good and honorable man. You are faithful to your wife and courteous to all women. You are fair to your vassals, and do not burden your villeins with heavy taxes. You wish, like all brave men, to join King Arthur's company. But have you thought on the company you would be keeping?

"King Arthur is a great leader; he united the warring lords of Britain with not only strength but diplomacy, creating a single mighty nation from a multitude of weak and tiny kingdoms.

"But King Arthur is also the man who keeps an unfaithful wife, and names the man who cuckolds him his dearest friend. He is the man who lay with his own sister, then ordered the slaughter of every infant boy in Britain when he learned he had fathered an incestuous bastard. He is the man who answered the boredom of successful peace-making with the Quest that has killed most of his knights and driven many of the rest to madness."

Sir Michael felt his face burning with his anger, his cheeks hot against the cool of the spring night. But he held his tongue and let his minstrel continue.

"Lancelot may be the greatest fighter of the age, but he is no true lover. He is not content with the adulterous love of the Queen, but must lie also with Lady Elaine of Carbonek. And when the ladies learn of each other, he flees from them in madness, and wanders the countryside, bereft of wit, for two years.

"And what of Gawaine? He has taken many maidenheads, and also the heads of many maidens—"

"That is *enough!*" Sir Michael roared, seizing his swordhilt. "These are great men you defame!"

"Every word I have spoken is true," the minstrel said. "And what you say is true: these are great men. They are without a doubt the greatest men Britain has ever seen. And great men have great faults. Their misdeeds are the equal of their accomplishments. Murder and madness and despair haunt their every step. Do you wish to follow in their path?

"And do you wish your wife to dwell among their women? The ladies of Camelot think courtly love means taking a husband's closest companion to her bed. And most of the ladies are young and beautiful, and vain of their looks. Many dabble in witchcraft—Arthur's own half sisters are powerful sorceresses. Do you wish to bring your wife into this vipers' den?"

"My Lady Eleanor wishes to go to court. I have achieved my dream. She will want to see it."

"But do *you* truly wish to go to Camelot, my lord?"

"You know I've wished it since the day Arthur was crowned."

"My lord, why did King Arthur wait so *long* to summon you?" Gruffydd asked. "You have been Baron of Segreves for twenty years. You have ruled your people with fairness, and a wisdom few of Arthur's companions seem to possess."

"The King waited for my son to come of age," the baron said. "Now my heir is sixteen, and may rule Segreves in his own right."

"Aye, perhaps King Arthur waited for that," said Gruffydd. "Perhaps. My lord, one of your knights *did* see your son tonight."

"And told me he did not! Who *lied?*"

"I shall not say, for your son ordered the knight to tell you nothing," Gruffydd said. "Drinking and whoring do not make a man unfit to rule, God knows, but Thomas does *nothing* save drink and whore. And when the Dragon of Segreves flies, he hides."

"Be *silent!*"

"In his summons, my lord, the King called you the 'Harrower of the Dragon of Segreves.' Yet the dragon preys here still. This is why you were not summoned to Camelot. You are summoned now only because so many knights have died or lost their wits in the Grail Quest. There are few knights left in Britain who are bold and strong and whole."

Sir Michael's wrath slipped its leash and his hand lashed out, striking with a meaty crack, felling the minstrel.

Gruffydd looked up. "You are a man of honor, my lord. That is why you are a better man than any knight of the Round Table." He wiped the blood from his lips. "Your son is at the Sign of the Winged Pig."

Sir Michael stalked out of the courtyard, and came swiftly to the alehouse. Through the open door and the torch-smoke, he saw his son Thomas slouched over the trestle, a tankard in his hand. He sat alone, not with his usual companions, four or five knights' sons; those young men were at the castle, celebrating the baron's summons to Camelot.

Thomas upended the tankard, spilling ale off his stubbled chin, then threw the tankard aside and seized the young woman walking past. Startled, she dropped her earthenware pitcher. It shattered on the dirt floor. Shouting an indecent request, Thomas thrust his ale-wet face against her breasts and his hands up her skirt. She cooed and laid her arms around his shoulders, but as he forced her down on the bench, her expression had nothing of pleasure in it.

Anger melding with sudden hot grief, Sir Michael strode into the alehouse and pulled his son off the woman. "Thomas! Have you forgotten the very meaning of chivalry?"

The woman fled as Thomas sat up. He said, "Chivalry is not for peasant sluts." His eyes were clouded, his breath a beery stench. He did not seem to care that his hose gaped open.

"Cover yourself!" Sir Michael shouted, and Thomas fumbled with the lacings. "You know chivalry requires a knight to protect

all women, not assault them! By God! Why do you tarry here
when you know I have received the summons to Camelot?"

"I have no desire to hear the droning speech of some old
windbag from Camelot." Thomas pounded the trestle with his
fist. "More ale!" He smirked at Sir Michael. "Don't trouble yourself to hurry back, Father. At last, Segreves is *mine—*"

Thomas's eyes closed and he slumped off the bench. Sir Michael raised his son off the floor and shook him violently, but
Thomas did not stir. Sir Michael released his son, letting him
fall back to the dirt. Thomas was in a stupor.

Sir Michael returned to his keep, but did not return to the
great hall. He needed to speak to his wife about their son.

Voices echoed down the narrow stone corridor. His wife's
voice, and that of a lady-in-waiting.

"Do not leave off preparations for the journey, Marcella," said
Lady Eleanor. "I must accompany my husband."

"My lady, Camelot is no place for a gentlewoman."

Sir Michael stopped, surprised.

"It has always been Sir Michael's greatest desire, to join the
Fellowship of the Round Table," said Lady Eleanor, "and it is
the highest honor a knight may receive. So, though I have no
wish to live at court, and though my husband will soon leave on
quest, I shall go with him to court."

Sir Michael turned and walked away. He hardly noticed that
he left his keep and wandered upon the moonlit moor.

He had struck his minstrel, though he had never laid a blow
in anger on his wife or son or retainers. The minstrel's words
had angered him beyond thought. His wife's words had shocked
him back to himself.

Why had he not seen that his wife, a quiet, faithful woman,
would have only misery among the gilded serpents of the Royal
Court, and only pain from his absence on the Grail Quest?

By God, he'd been so puffed up by the summons to Camelot
that his pride had blinded him. Pride was a deadly sin. Yet

it was not so grievous as the manifold sins of the men of the Round Table.

He wanted to go on the Grail Quest, though he had not completed his own quest, to destroy the dragon that had haunted Segreves since men first came to Britain. Every autumn since the earliest days, the barons of Segreves had staked a virgin under the sky, for when the dragon found a sacrifice, it did not rake the land with its terrible white flame, but instead seized the maiden and departed immediately from Segreves. The practice had continued uninterrupted until twenty years ago, when the new baron of Segreves, Sir Michael, had declared the worm would be placated no longer by heathenish sacrifice of Christian maidens. When the dragon came, the young lord and his vassals fought valiantly, but the dragon broiled a score of men alive in their armor and flew away unharmed, clutching a knight in its forepaws like a lobster. It did not seem to care whether its prey was a maiden, so long as it had food to bear away.

The survivors of the encounter, joined by questing knights from other lands, searched the Isles and the Continent for the Dragon of Segreves. And meeting with no success they returned to Segreves with the autumn. Every year fewer of Sir Michael's liegemen returned, and fewer knights errant joined his quest. When the Grail Quest was called, no more young gallants came to serve Sir Michael, and the search for the dragon went forth no more. And every autumn, the dragon returned to slay with its fiery breath and fly away with one of the men who opposed it.

Sir Michael had ordered books and scrolls, to search for knowledge he might use against the firedrake; but he found nothing of worth. He had requested an exorcism be performed; but not even the Archbishop of Canterbury could banish the monster.

Sir Michael imagined leaving the care of his land to his son, who never stood beside him and the knights and squires when the dragon came to Segreves. His son would not be changed by the duties and responsibilities of ruling Segreves. Thomas would continue to drink the days away, and when the dragon came he would hide or flee; and the liegemen, disheartened, would die in far greater numbers. His son was no leader of men. His son was, in fact, not much of anything. And Sir Michael had no other child.

Perhaps if he bent all his efforts to the task, Sir Michael could mold his son into a worthy heir. But had he not always spent as much time as he could with Thomas? Perhaps he should disown his son. But then he must choose and train a new heir.

Sir Michael thought of his longing, the desire greater than any other. He thought of the splendor of Camelot and the glory of the Round Table.

Sir Michael stopped walking. He knew what a man of honor must do, though the choice seem to other men to hold no honor.

Sir Michael looked around, to find he was far out upon the moor. He glanced up, for he was under open sky. He saw two moons. Then one moon filled the sky, and wasn't a moon at all.

The dragon hovered on wings wider than a ship's sail, its eyes glowing like white suns, its muzzle parted to exhale wisps of white flame. A row of triangular blades ran down its snaky neck from the spiky crest raised fanlike behind the great head. Despite the darkness of night, every scale was visible, glowing a different color, as if the dragon were mailed from beaky snout to spear-blade tailtip with brilliant gems. The firedrake floated before Sir Michael like a vast opalescent ship at anchor in the sky, and was as unlikely as such a thing, for it had come to Segreves six months too soon.

The dragon was beautiful as a dream.

Sir Michael drew his sword, thinking of his coat of plate hanging useless in the armory, and of the scores of armored knights who had died fighting the firedrake. Thinking that no one knew where he was. Thinking that the decision he had made was now meaningless.

The dragon regarded him steadily with eyes like faceted diamond suns. Then it bowed its head, as if in regret, and in utter silence turned and flew away.

Sir Michael stared after the dragon long after it had gone.

Then he sheathed his sword and returned to his keep and his life.

Sir Lamorak rode out alone in the morning.

The dragon was never seen again.

SERPENT FEATHER
▼▼▼

GORDON R. MENZIES

PACAN awoke with the sun in his eyes, and raised a hand
to shield them. He lay where he had fallen asleep the previous
night, with his back against a pile of stones in the open dusty
field that had been cleared and leveled to provide a site for the
new ball court in the city of Uxmal. Other men slept nearby,
and a few were already moving about, whispering in low voices
so that the Toltec soldiers standing guard over them would not
hear what they were saying. Pacan looked down at his bare feet
and cursed as he pulled himself into a sitting position.

One of the other Mayan slaves had stolen his sandals.

Well, it was not the first time he had gone barefoot. Pacan
stood and pulled aside his loincloth, urinating into the dust. He
was careful not to let his water touch the stone piled beside him.
He had made that mistake once before and was beaten with a
scourge of thorns by the Toltec soldiers for defiling the glory of
Kukulcan, their feathered god, the great serpent that had come
with them over the waters when they had invaded the peninsula
six years ago. Pacan's people, a race of traders, scholars, astrono-
mers, and artists, had broken like a dry stalk of maize before the

foreigners. Many simply gave up and accepted the rule of the Toltec, seeing they were in the presence of a god they could not hope to defeat, but not everyone. Pacan's brother Aachtun, for one, had joined with other Mayan warriors and offered a stubborn resistance, but they too were soon overwhelmed or had to flee south into the highland rain forests, where the enemy was not yet willing to pursue them. The Toltec were fearful of the forest Indians who had allied themselves with the Maya, for the long arrows of the Lacandon people could find the glitter of a man's eye on the darkest night. From the forest cities of Palenque and Tikal and a few others, far from the menace of the invader, the Mayan resistance still launched sporadic attacks against the Toltecs, but years had passed since their arrival and it was getting more and more difficult to determine who was one's enemy and who was not. Too many of the lowland Maya were happy to live with the Toltec presence. They gave their sons and daughters in marriage to them, adopted their mode of dress and customs, and some had begun to worship their gods.

Pacan was ashamed of himself for not taking up arms with his brother, but his wife Jainah and her family had refused to leave their village, and he had remained with them for the love of his woman. That had been a mistake. The Toltec had burned the little village of Nunacan, and he had been forced to watch the rape and ritual sacrifice of his wife and in-laws. When he fought the Toltec, they had beaten him senseless with their war clubs and sent him off to labor with others like him, to raise cities and monuments to their serpent god. An eternity had passed since then, and Pacan did not like to think about it.

He cut stone for the Toltec now, that was his purpose. He, who was one of the greatest sculptors on the northern coast and in the Puuc Hills region, was now a maker of bricks.

It was a fitting punishment for his foolishness.

The others were awake now, responding with numb acceptance to the harsh shouts of their overseers, rising and stumbling sleepily to where their breakfast awaited them at one end of the field. A group of withered old women, and a few younger ones who were crippled or unnaturally deformed, had been recruited to serve the laborers—the Toltec always kept the best women for themselves. To each man the servant women would give a small wooden bowl of azoli, a nourishing but tasteless gruel made from ground maize that was bland and unappetizing unless it was sweetened with honey, and a pair of bruised papayas. Pacan followed suit with the others, stopping at one of the large clay jars filled with water that were arranged about the work site for the use of the laborers. He removed the lid and splashed some on his face and neck before he noticed the brown lump of human feces floating against one side of the container. Nearby, a pair of Toltec soldiers burst into laughter.

Pacan scowled, frustrated. He wanted to leap upon his enemies and seize them by their throats, but he did not. The time for fighting had passed. He deserved such treatment. He had failed to protect his family, and was no longer a man—he had no right to be angry at their abuse. He touched the distinctive leather collar encircling his neck that marked his servitude, and it felt right to him.

He turned away.

Someone called his name. He knew the voice and felt loathing rise in his breast. It was Chalti, a man who was once his friend in the days before the coming of the Toltec, but he was a friend no longer. If Pacan deserved to be ashamed for his lack of action during the invasion, then Chalti deserved the feeling tenfold, for not only did he not fight against their enemies, he accepted them and offered them his loyalty. Chalti had welcomed their rule, their strange customs and their cruel gods. It was said he had even given them his children to prove his loyalty. For this, and his architectural talent which he had freely allowed to be exploited, he had risen high in their favor.

Pacan looked at his old friend. His hair was clean and combed and tied off in an elaborate flaring tail behind his head. His loincloth was multicolored and unsoiled, he wore gold bands on his wrists and biceps and a necklace of jade around his neck, and oh, yes, he had sandals. Chalti was a wealthy man.

"Pacan," he said, smiling broadly. "I knew I would find you here."

"Where else would you look for a slave, but among the slaves, Chalti?"

Chalti frowned at him and for a moment his eyes fell critically on Pacan's unkempt, overlong hair and stained clothing as if he were seeing him for the first time. A moment later he had regained his composure. He smiled again. "Don't be like that, old friend. I bring you good news. I have convinced the governor to release you from your labors here."

Pacan was silent.

"What, no thanks?" Chalti eyed him questioningly. "Very well, I do not give my gifts for gain. I simply told him that an artist such as yourself should not be cutting bricks in the hot sun. Your talents are going to waste. I showed him your work on the House of Turtles, and he was very impressed. He wants you to carve an image of Kukulcan overlooking the courtyard where the administration buildings stand."

Pacan could not believe what he was hearing. "I'll do no such thing," he replied angrily, his voice full of contempt.

"Don't be stubborn Pacan, you've labored long enough. The Toltec are not going to go away. You must accept that. Do what they have asked of you and consider your talents a blessing. Accommodations will be provided for you if you agree, good food and clothing . . . a woman. The governor is generous to those who serve the empire."

Pacan sneered derisively. "The Toltec murdered Jainah, Chalti. You know this. You were there. Is your memory so short? I will not create anything of beauty for my wife's murderers.

They have taken her from me, but they will not take my art. I cut brick for the Toltec now, and that is all they will have of me."

"Then you will die here. They will work you until you break, Pacan."

"Better this than to lay down at their feet like a dog. They command you and you jump, and if you jump high enough they favor you with some scrap from their table. Can you not see what you have become? A dog, I tell you!"

Chalti sighed. "A dog who still has a wife, Pacan. And it is not I that wears a collar." He dismissed Pacan with a wave of his hand and turned to walk away.

Behind him, Pacan stood shaking with rage as he watched him go. How dare he insult Jainah's memory? How dare he? Pacan could not let him get away so easily. He shouted Chalti's name until he looked back at him. His chest heaved. "I am not the only one who wears a collar!" he cried, his voice carrying loudly across the field. Soldiers and slaves turned to look at him. "The one you wear is made of jade . . . but you are no more free than I!"

▼▼▼

Pacan sat by himself, far from the fires of the other laborers who were enjoying their nightly ration of poor quality *balche*, a beer made from fermented maize, and from the sounds of it, one of the women who served them their meals during the day. He was sickened by the old woman's animal grunts of pleasure. *So this is what has become of us,* he thought bitterly. *Oh, wise and noble Maya, you learned to number the days and measure the stars, but you did not have the foresight to protect yourself from the barbarians of the world. So now you sell them your daughters and couple with your grandmothers in the dark. Who will remember you were once a great and learned people?*

Maybe it is better this way, Pacan thought.

A stream of bats issued from some hidden crevice in the Pyramid of the Magician and dispersed into the hazy darkness that grew all around. Pacan shivered. The sun was dying in the west, and shadows were rising up out of the scrub forest and entering the city, heralds of the night pressing close about the fires. The pyramid loomed up over the city and central plaza, its very existence an affront to the Toltec, who could not hope to tear it down. It had been built to serve as a temple for the rain god Chaac, whose worship had been banned in the occupied cities and, because they could not destroy it, the Toltec had defiled it and their god had taken its sacred rooms for its own. Even now the white serpent lay coiled at its summit, gazing down on those who, by its word, had been enslaved. A dull red glow came from the rooms at the top, the color of blood, and the light seemed to have a life of its own.

Pacan narrowed his eyes, remembering.

▼▼▼

Aachtun stood in the doorway of the thatched hut Pacan had built for himself and his wife. The light was at his back and he was a dark and menacing demon arrayed for war, with a spear in one hand and an obsidian-chipped hardwood sword in the other. Quetzal feathers adorned his arms and legs, and at his waist hung the conch-shell war horn Pacan had bartered for in Tulum on the eastern coast. It had been a gift for his twenty-ninth birthday. Its sound was loud and daunting, and it was inscribed with runes of power and strength. Aachtun carried it with him always.

"Come with me, little brother," Aachtun had said, his face grim and determined. "We will drive these invaders back into the sea."

Pacan sat on the floor of the hut sharpening a chisel with a grindstone. His hands worked rhythmically, honing the edge of the tool to perfection. He did not look up at his brother. He had laughed when he'd first suggested he accompany him into battle. The last time he had used a sling he had struck himself in the head with it before he could loose the stone. He was no warrior. "They say the Toltec have already overrun Dzibilchaltun, Aachtun. They say their numbers are great, and that they are in the company of a powerful serpent god."

Aachtun scowled. "I do not believe these stories of a feathered serpent that can fly through the air. Who has heard of such a thing? Besides, even if it were true, I have killed serpents before. The best way is to step on their necks first—their heads come off with one stroke of the knife."

▼▼▼

Pacan did not know if Aachtun was alive or dead, but he harbored little hope for the former. The Toltec were unmerciful to those who opposed them. Aachtun had gone north with a group of other like-minded men who had hired themselves out as *holcans*, mercenary soldiers, to a contingent of royal soldiers from Coba, and he had not returned. *He is dead*, Pacan told himself. *I will not fool myself into believing otherwise.*

He laughed to himself softly and without humor. Aachtun had not believed in the serpent—*not believed!* Pacan looked up at the pyramid and felt Kukulcan's eyes upon him. He could not disbelieve his fear. It was real. It shrieked inside his head. Shrieked with the voice of Jainah, dragged by her hair and pulled backwards over the *chacmool*, her eyes wild and her bare breasts heaving in her panic. Before he could stop them, they had torn out her heart and shown it to her before her eyes had closed.

Pacan felt a tear spill from one eye, and he spoke her name aloud just to hear the sound of it.

Barely discernible in the failing light, a large iguana scuttled across the stones in front of him and stopped to stare fixedly at him. Pacan returned the creature's glance until he shifted in his seat, uncomfortable in its gaze. Finally, he looked away.

"That was a foolish decision you made today," said a voice.

"A missed opportunity. Your answer was given without thought or foresight, so I have done your thinking for you."

Pacan jumped, startled by the nearness of the voice, and turned to find the iguana had disappeared. In its place stood a little man in an elaborately carved jade mask, wearing a long mantle fashioned from the pelt of a white jaguar. The man was perhaps three feet tall, a dwarf, and Pacan recognized him at once.

"Chilax-Alenque!" he cried, and threw himself to the ground before the most powerful Mayan sorcerer ever known. Had he not built the Pyramid of the Magician in a single night? Was he not the servant and spokesman of the great rain god Chaac, who could summon lightning from the sky at will? He was all this and more.

"Sit up and take your place as you were, Pacan," said the sorcerer. "Do not draw attention to yourself."

Pacan did as he was told. "Mighty Chilax-Alenque, there are many Toltec guards about. You are in danger."

The little man waved his hand in such a manner as to express he thought the news to be of little consequence. "Do not be afraid," said the tiny sorcerer. "They can neither see nor hear me while I wear the cloak of the ghost jaguar. So now, listen to me and hear my counsel if you are willing."

"Command me, Chilax-Alenque. I hear you."

"Good. Then this must you do. Tomorrow seek out the one you know as Chalti and tell him you have reconsidered. Apologize to him for your angry words. Tell him you are willing to labor for the glory of the god Kukulcan."

Pacan's mouth became a thin line. He looked at his feet. "Forgive me, great one. This I cannot do. I will not serve my wife's murderers in such a manner."

Silence.

Pacan felt his throat constrict as the sorcerer stepped towards him and the menacing face of jade came near to his own. A tiny hand touched his shoulder in the manner a father might touch his son. Pacan felt raw power in Chilax-Alenque's touch.

"You can, and you will, Pacan Worker-of-Stone. I would bind the worm Kukulcan and drive the Toltec from our land." The sorcerer removed his hand and Pacan felt as though he had withdrawn a part of himself in the doing. "I need your help to do this thing."

"But lord, I am, as you have said, only a sculptor of stone. What can I possibly do to aid one such as you?"

"Then you are willing?"

Pacan nodded. "I would see my people free again, to carve stone and wood, to paint, to measure the stars. All these things. And I would have revenge upon my enemies."

"Do as I say then, and I will come to you again," the sorcerer promised.

And Pacan was alone.

▼▼▼

On the following morning Pacan went in search of Chalti, averting his eyes from the baleful gazes of the Toltec soldiery as he made his way through the streets of Uxmal. This conduct was demanded of all Mayan slaves in the occupied cities, and a man could be slain outright for disobeying if the offended party chose to do so. Incidents such as this rarely occurred though—for who would do the work of the laborers if there were no slaves? Pacan continued on and finally found Chalti inspecting some recent stonework on a defensive wall the Toltec had ordered raised around the entire city to aid them against the Mayan resistance. Chalti glared at him as he approached. Pacan endured the burning gaze until he was close enough to speak, and then fell to one knee before the man.

Chalti was the first to speak. "What are you doing here?" he demanded. His voice was harsh and hostile.

"I have come to apologize," Pacan answered, hating himself

for his forced lies. "I was wrong to speak to you so. Forgive me, Chalti."

This time it was Chalti's turn to be silent.

"I was a fool to spurn your friendship," Pacan continued. "I should have been grateful that you even remembered me. I was wrong, but I beg you to give me another chance to prove my worth and I promise you will not regret it. Forget my earlier words, Chalti. Being a slave has not been . . . easy . . . on me. The loss of my wife . . ."

"No more words, Pacan. I understand what you are saying, and it has been hard for you, I know. I should not do this but . . . I forgive you, Pacan."

Pacan slowly stood, feigning a look of disbelief. "Thank you," he said. "I am truly blessed to have a friend such as you. I will not forget this."

Chalti took him by the shoulders and embraced him. It was all Pacan could do to keep from recoiling in revulsion from the man's touch, but he remembered what Chilax-Alenque had said, and he somehow endured and returned the gesture. He thought of Jainah and began to weep at his betrayal of her, but to his benefit Chalti mistook them for tears of gratitude, and smiled. He hugged Pacan all the harder and kissed him on the forehead.

"Welcome back," he whispered. "Welcome back, old friend."

▼▼▼

They gave him his own rooms in a stone building not far from where he would be working, and the finest tools available were given to him. He was washed and clothed and fed as promised, but when they tried to take his braided slave collar from him Pacan stopped them.

"No," he said. "This I shall remove only when I have completed my service to Kukulcan. Only then will I deserve to walk without it."

This pleased the governor and his guardsmen immensely, and

Pacan was invited to join his friend Chalti at the governor's palace for a feast that very night. There they served him food he had not even looked upon for years—sweet potatoes, roast duck, squash, tomatoes. Pacan sat in the midst of his enemies and partook of their food, all the while thinking that with a single lunge he could be at the governor's throat. But the governor was only a man, and Chilax-Alenque had enlisted him to assist in felling a god. He could not risk exposing his true intentions, so he smiled and nodded and spoke of his plans for the sculpture, but when a servant handed him a cup of cacao he almost dropped it.

Cacao was a favorite of Jainah's, who had an uncontrollable sweet tooth when it came to the creamy drink. He used to tease her mercilessly whenever she drank it. "I will not abide a fat wife," he used to say, and sometimes he would hide the little clay jar that held the ground beans and feign ignorance while she hunted for it.

"Pacan?" Chalti nudged him out of his revery. He had been staring blankly into the cup. "Are you not well?"

Pacan blinked. "I'm fine," he said. "It's just . . . the cacao. It has been some time since I have tasted it, and I was simply relishing the pleasure of it on my tongue."

Chalti laughed, delighted. "When you are finished the sculpture, you shall have anything the empire can offer. You'll see." He smiled knowingly, and Pacan hated him for it.

Later in the evening there was good *balche* to be had, much better than that which was given to the laborers, and of that he drank far too much. One of Chalti's servants had to help him back to his quarters. When he stepped inside the door there was a young girl there waiting for him. Chalti's servant grinned the grin of his master and bowed once before leaving as the girl began to slowly shed her clothing.

Pacan crouched down awkwardly before the girl and eyed her, his head swimming. His eyes ran over the perfect contours of her warm brown skin, and the rising swell of her young breasts. She smiled invitingly and he saw that her teeth were the whitest of white, like precious stones. So beautiful, he thought. He reached out hesitantly with a single finger to trace the curve of one dark nipple, watching as the areola tightened and pulled together, turning in on itself like some exotic jungle flower.

Pacan felt a dull ache in his loins . . . it had been far too long. He knew he should resist, but could not. He was not made of stone, after all. Pacan was a man. A desperately lonely man in need of comfort, however base.

"Forgive me, Jainah," he whispered.

The girl reached out for him, and he took her there on the cold stone floor.

▼▼▼

Pacan opened his eyes. The girl was still sound asleep, her black hair spread out across his chest like strands from a spider's web and her warm breath like a secret caress across the taut muscles of his stomach. Pacan looked down upon her and despite his former arguments to justify his actions, his heart was heavy with guilt, and it pained him to know what he had done. He knew it was wrong, terribly wrong.

"You have done well for yourself," someone said appreciatively, and suddenly the jade mask of Chilax-Alenque was hovering near his face. Pacan drew in a sudden, startled breath and the girl murmured in her sleep at his movements. Embarrassed, he tried to gently push her to one side but the sorcerer shook his hand and said, "No, do not wake her. What I have to say will not take long."

Pacan averted his eyes. "I am ashamed."

The sorcerer clucked his tongue. "You need not be. Faithfulness beyond the grave serves no one, Pacan, but I am not concerned with your earthly needs in any case. What I do need is your strength. You have done what I have asked up until this point—are you willing to do so again?"

"Yes," Pacan answered. "I will obey you."

"What more can I ask for?" The little man seemed pleased. He turned away and paced up and down the floor, deep in thought, for several moments before returning to where Pacan lay, nervously waiting for him to speak again, uncertain of what would be asked of him. Finally, the mask came close a second time. Chilax-Alenque's voice was low and serious. "I need you to steal a feather from the feathered serpent himself—one from the very hide of Kukulcan."

Pacan gasped. "How will I do such a thing?"

"You will need to sketch the beast to properly plan your sculpture, will you not?"

Pacan nodded.

"Good. Then there lies your opportunity." The dwarf sorcerer poked Pacan's chest with a stubby finger. "The rest is up to you," he said slowly. "But know this, without that feather I cannot bind the god."

"I won't fail you," Pacan promised, not believing his own words.

▼▼▼

Chalti accompanied him to the central plaza before noon. A team of workmen had already constructed the scaffolding along the face of the building, and a crew were chiseling away at its surface in preparation for the new sculpture. As they approached, Pacan could hear the weeping of the stone masons as they worked and his heart froze at what he beheld. The workers were not raising a new framework above the old facing to hold the new sculpture in place—they were utterly destroying the ancient sculptures already adorning the building. His mouth dropped open in dismay.

Chalti could see how alarmed his companion was at the sight.

He took him by the arm and turned him around. "It was ordered by the governor, Pacan. Kukulcan demands that all images of Chaac be destroyed."

"But that stonework was carved generations ago, Chalti. How can you let them . . ."

Chalti shook his head angrily. "I do not believe what I am hearing. The Toltec do not care for what has come before them. Who do you serve, Pacan?"

"The empire, of course." It was the proper answer.

"Good."

"But the sculpture . . ."

"Think no more of it. I am certain yours will outshine even the work of the ancients." Chalti laughed and slapped him on the back.

Pacan looked down at his feet, at his new sandals. "Yes," he said.

A shadow fell across them then. "You," a voice snarled. Pacan looked up to see one of the masons, his dusty face streaked with tears, standing directly in front of him. His fists were clenched tightly around a chisel and a hammerstone. "This is your doing!"

"Guards!" Chalti yelled. A pair of Toltec soldiers standing nearby started trotting towards them.

"Traitor," the angry man continued. He glared a Pacan, his eyes full of hate. "Your brother would strike you dead himself if he were here!"

"How do you know my brother?" Pacan demanded. He searched the man's face, but did not recognize him at all. "Who are you?" The guards arrived and seized hold of the man, pulling his arms up behind his back painfully so that he cried out and dropped the tools. "Who are you?" Pacan shouted at him again as they dragged him away. In answer the man spat at him, striking him full in the face. Pacan wiped the spittle from his cheek.

"Let it go," Chalti counseled him. "They will soon forget who you were."

"Did you know the man?"

"No, but what does it matter? Some can never release the past, Pacan, and that is something I cannot understand. The here and now is all that matters to me, and that which is to come. Just let it go."

Pacan nodded. "What now?" he said.

"Well, we are still preparing the preliminary structure, but once you have drawn up your design, work will begin at once. You have been given a team of forty sculptors to assist you, and they will do everything but the image of Kukulcan itself—that is for you alone."

"I will need to make some sketches of Kukulcan. Can this be arranged?"

"I will see to it directly, but . . . are you not afraid?"

"No," Pacan answered. "There is nothing left for the Toltec to take from me. I belong to them now—why should I fear their god? Is the serpent not my god now as well?"

Chalti nodded slowly, a strange look on his face. "Nonetheless, you should be afraid. Kukulcan sleeps during the heat of the day—you will have to go at night."

▼▼▼

The night wind wanted to tear him from his perch and throw him down the almost vertical steps of the pyramid that dropped away behind him. Pacan leaned against it and clung to the top landing fearfully. Never had he climbed to such a height. His whole body shook uncontrollably and he was finding it difficult to breathe. He could not forget that despite what the Toltec had done to this place, it was still holy to Chaac, and he felt a mixture of awe and terror to find himself here. He had dared to go where no common man should tread. Before him, the familiar reddish glow reached out into the night from the inner chambers of the temple to beckon him within, but Pacan stood frozen where he was, as the wind sucked and pulled at him insistently, unable to go forward.

Finally he managed to force himself up onto the platform, his sandaled feet finding the last steps woodenly as if they themselves were unwilling to continue onward. Out of breath from the climb and frightened, Pacan slowly turned his body around and sat down on the stone, firmly anchoring himself against the wind that whipped his hair into his eyes angrily, having missed its chance to take him to his death. Clutching his leather packet of drawing materials against his chest, Pacan stared out over the city. Torches and hearthfires, rising smoke, and the sound of distant music came to him atop the pyramid, but the music was foreign, and it reminded him why he had come here. Beyond the city limits the lightless expanse of the forest stretched endlessly in all directions, finally melting into the sky where a score of the brightest stars stood watch along their borders, giving the two only the slightest distinction from one another. However, the black tangle of the scrub forest was alive and vocal, unlike the cold and voiceless sky. The cries of myriad nightbirds, the bark and wail of lonely monkeys and the hunting songs of the jaguar came to him in his airy seat, each one sounding like a warning to him. *Go back*, they said. *There is nothing you can do here.*

Suddenly he felt eyes upon him where he sat, and a shadow glided across the red light that spilled out through the open doorway. He turned to look but there was nothing there. Nonetheless, he knew he could wait no longer and, ignoring the warnings of the forest, he forced himself to stand. He tried to call up his anger for this enemy to help him dispel his growing fear, but it would not come. His mouth felt dry and he was unable to swallow. His feet were heavy and seemed to want to fuse with the stone. *Do it now or it will never be done*, he thought. *You are Mayan*, he told himself. *Walk like a man into the presence of the god of your enemy.*

He took a deep breath, and stepped through the doorway.

▼▼▼

Kukulcan lay loosely coiled on the cool stones at one end of the small chamber, regarding Pacan with the mild interest of a predator that sees its prey within reach but is too sated to bother with the effort of killing it. Its unblinking golden eyes, like jewels in the firelight, were hypnotic and full of power. They held Pacan in their gaze as if he were under a spell. He stared back, unwilling to break eye contact. He thought he would abhor the sight of the Toltec god, but that was not what he was feeling at all. He was terrified, yes, more frightened than he had ever been in his life, but foremost in his mind was the thought that Kukulcan was the most wonderfully beautiful creature he had ever seen.

The feathered serpent was the whitest of white, the color of the solitary wandering clouds one could see in an otherwise clear blue summer sky, the kind that never threatened rain. It was as big around the middle as a man was around the waist and more than thirty feet long, every inch covered in small, tightly layered feathers that it held close against its body. Around the neck they were longer, some as long as a man's arm, and were draped back behind the head like the elaborate headdress of a priest from an unknown forest cult.

The god slowly raised its head until it hovered well above the ornately etched copper brazier of glowing coals that stood between it and Pacan. As it did this, the lengthy neck feathers unfolded and rose in a sunburst display, framing its golden eyes and head impressively. Pacan could not help but take an involuntary step backwards.

"You are Pacan the Mayan sculptor," said the god. Its voice was like a midnight wind moving through leaves, and a chill ran through Pacan to hear it speak.

Pacan inclined his head, too frightened to speak at first, then forced himself to say, "I have come to render your image on paper before I carve it from stone. I have brought my things . . ."

Kukulcan hissed suspiciously and said, "You stink of magic." It said the words slowly and purposefully, swaying back and forth slightly as if it were preparing to strike. "Are you a magician, then, as well as a sculptor?" The serpent's head moved closer, its tongue flicking out to taste the air. Pacan stood immobile, not knowing what to think, and uncertain seconds passed when he thought it was all over, that it would end here. "No, no you are not," the serpent decided at last, answering its own question. "The scent is very weak. Perhaps it is just the strength of your talent that I sense."

"I do not understand," said Pacan in a small voice. "I have never known magic, Great One. I am but an artist, a worker of stone."

The feathered serpent nodded and seemed satisfied. Its neck feathers slowly folded back down behind its head. "So it has been said," it breathed. "Now do what you have come to do. You may begin."

Pacan's heart was pounding heavily in his chest as he unfolded his leather case and took out several leaves of pounded-bark paper and a half dozen charcoal sticks. He wiped away the sweat from his forehead with the back of his hand, and beneath the gaze of those riveting golden eyes he set to work.

▼▼▼

Pacan sketched the head first, concentrating on the arrangement of feathers that encircled the neck and the unusual shape and size of the serpent's eyes. Kukulcan never once looked away from him the entire time he worked. Pacan could not believe how breathtakingly beautiful this god was, and found himself fascinated with its perfection of form and the subtle movements it made from time to time. Long minutes passed when he had completely forgotten his mission in coming here, where he had become simply an artist with his subject, and the two became locked in that special spiritual bond that manifests itself whenever one creature takes of another in the pursuit of an art form. Kukulcan seemed to be aware of Pacan's sense of wonder and admiration, and more than that, the serpent god seemed even more pleased to sense it in one of those it had conquered.

Pacan took a deep breath, rapidly sketched a line or two more, and then suddenly and clearly remembered why he had come here. He needed to bring back a feather. He did not know how, but somehow he had to try. Wetting his lips, he searched for his voice and found it. "May I touch you?" he asked hesitantly.

"You would touch a god?" the serpent hissed. "It is a bold request."

Pacan hung his head. "Forgive me, mighty Kukulcan. I should not have asked such a thing. I only wanted to get a feel for the texture I must raise from the stone. You must know it will be difficult to reproduce the magnificence of your feathered mantle."

Kukulcan seemed amused. "Are you not afraid, little Mayan?"

"Yes, I am afraid. But my curiosity has dampened my fear."

The serpent considered his words. "Your courage speaks much of your race. Come forward then, man-who-would-touch-a-god."

Pacan did what he was told, and his hands were trembling when he finally reached out to stroke the white features. He drew his fingers across the body of the serpent, lost for an instant as if in a dream before he realized the pain that shot through his hand. Pacan cried out and jerked his hand away, leaving a bloody red smear behind that sullied the coat of Kukulcan. He was amazed yet again as to the strangeness of this god. These were not feathers at all, but razor edged scales that only resembled feathers, each one hard enough to turn a blade or even an arrow.

The great serpent brought its head around to where Pacan had touched it. Kukulcan's long tongue darted out to deftly lick the blood from its scales.

"Your blood calls up my hunger, little Mayan. I must leave you now, for I must hunt."

Pacan backed out of the way as Kukulcan slithered across the stone towards the exit, then carefully followed after, quickly enough to see the serpent god reach the edge of the pyramid, the edge of the light . . . and keep going. He covered his mouth with his hand to keep from crying out loud.

When he was a little boy he and his brother Aachtun would hunt for frogs at the edge of a murky cenote that was on the outskirts of their village. On many of those summer days he had seen snakes dart from the reeds to skate across the water, gliding over the surface with little effort, undulating their bodies back and forth as they sped along. This was exactly how the god of the Toltec invaders moved through the air, and Pacan stared after it with wonder in his eyes.

It could fly, it could actually fly. . . .

Returning to the inner chambers to retrieve his drawings, Pacan looked around the bare room and noticed things he had not seen while in the presence of the god. Bones for one, they littered the room here and there, and each was too large to be anything but human. In one corner he found a pile of tiny skulls and the bile rose in his throat to see the distinctive sloping foreheads that marked them as having belonged to Mayan children, but near them was a feather-scale from the hide of the god itself. It was not the only one, Pacan soon discovered, there were several that had been shed at one time or another, and they lay where they had fallen about the chamber. Careful not to cut himself this time, Pacan took the longest one of these and wrapped it in one of his sketches before shoving it deep into the leather case that held the others.

Then, without waiting another moment longer, he fled.

▼▼▼

Chilax-Alenque held the feather between his diminutive thumb and forefinger, slowly turning it in the light so that it glittered and gleamed at every angle. Pacan squatted on the ground a few feet away from him, watching apprehensively. He was thinking of the tiny pile of skulls.

"Can it be done now?" he asked. "Can you bind the serpent now that you have one of its feathers?"

The dwarf swiveled around and faced him as if he had forgotten he was there. Then he laughed out loud and shook his head. "Oh, no," he said, "there is much more to the magic than this. But listen and I will tell you of the feather's significance. With it, I can fly, yes, fly like the great serpent itself. I will use the god's own magic to defeat it. I am going to cross the water with the aid of this feather, and when I return I will have the true name of Kukulcan. And with the true name of Kukulcan, I will bind the god once and for all."

"So you are leaving me again," said Pacan, disappointedly.

"Yes, but in my absence, your work must not falter. The sculpture will also play a part in the imprisonment. To bind a god is one thing, to build its prison house is quite another. Courage, Pacan, I will return to you again."

The sorcerer raised his arms, his right hand clutching the silver-white feather tight. He waved it once over his head and said a word that Pacan had never heard before, then he shot into the air like an arrow. Pacan fell backwards and shielded his eyes from the sun as he watched the sorcerer quickly disappear from view.

▼▼▼

Pacan worked by torchlight. His hands were covered in dust and grit as he chiseled away at the stone head of Kukulcan—all that was left to be finished of the sculpture. For over two cycles of the moon he had awaited Chilax-Alenque's return, and all this time he had labored ceaselessly, working his team of masons and stonecutters harder than any Toltec overseer had done before him. Pacan knew they hated him for it, and this pained him.

He desperately wanted to tell them that they labored towards their salvation, but he knew he could not risk such a thing. It was far too dangerous.

The workers were growing belligerent and rebellious in light of several new raids by the Mayan resistance in the past few days. Rumor had it that they planned to take back the city before the defensive wall could be completed, and recently more Toltec soldiers had been brought south from the growing city of Chichen-Itza to strengthen the garrison. There was a feeling in the air as if a great storm was on its way.

Pacan did not know what would become of him if such a thing happened, but he knew his fate would not be a good one. He would be considered a traitor, damned by those he was trying to rescue.

The following afternoon a ceremony had been scheduled to officially present the new stone facade for the inspection of the serpent god itself. Pacan was just putting on the finishing touches in preparation for the gathering. He chipped away a rough spot just beneath one great eye and stood back to view his handiwork.

"A horribly good likeness," said a voice. Pacan dropped his stone chisel to the floor and spun around. Chilax-Alenque stood in the doorway.

"You have returned!"

"Yes, and now you must come with me," said the sorcerer. "Quickly, there is little time."

Pacan followed the dwarf out into the street, where his gaze was directed towards Kukulcan's pyramid. "Watch," whispered Chilax-Alenque, and a moment later Pacan saw the serpent leave the upper rooms and swim rapidly through the air towards the dark forest. Hunting again, he thought.

"Take my hand," said the dwarf urgently. "Do not cry out."

Pacan did as he was told and found himself rising into the night sky. His heart leapt into his throat as they passed over the city. One of his sandals worked itself loose from his toes and fell away from him, spiraling into blackness. He caught one last glimpse of Kukulcan ahead of them, apparently unaware of their pursuit, then closed his eyes tight and did not open them again until he felt the ground beneath his feet.

They were standing in the undergrowth that overlooked a small cenote, the black water lapping at its sides as if it had been recently disturbed. "Do not speak," the sorcerer cautioned him. Pacan nodded obediently and sat back on his heels to wait. Chilax-Alenque watched the water intently for what seemed like hours. It grew very late, and overhead the moon rose over the trees and cast its ghostly glow into the clearing. Pacan yawned impatiently, snapping his mouth shut again at the sound of splashing water.

He raised himself up a little and looked down to see the white serpent cavorting in the water. Again and again it dove beneath the surface, only to appear again somewhere unexpected. It looked as though it was thoroughly enjoying itself, like a child playing in the sand on the ocean's edge, and Pacan was once again struck by the creature's incredible beauty. Finally, it launched itself into the air and headed back towards the city.

Pacan nervously followed the sorcerer to the water's edge. Once there, Chilax-Alenque reached into some hidden pocket and withdrew a small white stone almost perfectly round. Holding it in the palm of one hand, he passed his other over it, and instantly a bright light burst forth from it, flooding the entire clearing.

"Take this," he said. "You will need it to see."

"To see what?" Pacan asked, glancing uncertainly towards the dark pool of water. His hand closed over the stone.

"You must dive into the cenote and swim straight down. On this side of the cenote you will find a small cave. Enter it and swim upwards again. You will surface in a hidden grotto where there is air to breathe. Go, and bring me what you find there."

▼▼▼

The water was murky and shockingly cold, but the stone illuminated the depths enough for him to find the cave without difficulty. He swam into it as ordered and finally burst out of the water in a large limestone cavern that was damp and dripping with moisture. The air was musty and stale. He swam to a nearby ledge and pulled himself up to rest, holding the stone high in one hand so he could see. Dripping wet and panting from his efforts, he suddenly spotted what he was certain he had been sent to retrieve.

There, on a shelf opposite his own, were a pair of huge silver-white eggs.

Chilax-Alenque was waiting for him at the edge of the cenote. Upon sighting Pacan's face break through the water he clapped his hands together, delighted at his success. He helped Pacan drag his weary body up onto the bank, where the sculptor stood naked beneath the moon, the eggs of Kukulcan wrapped in his loincloth and held in one strong hand.

"The great serpent is . . ."—Pacan panted—"is . . . a female!"

Chilax-Alenque nodded knowingly and took the eggs. "Tomorrow," he cried triumphantly. "Tomorrow, you and I shall bind her once and for all!"

▼▼▼

The scaffolding and the worker's huts had all been removed from the central plaza, and the only thing that remained was a small stepped platform that led up to the place on the sculpture where Pacan would lay the final stone. Opposite this a low dais had been erected for the governor and his retainers. A contingent of Toltec soldiers on either side of this formed a solid wall that kept the crowd at bay. The plaza was packed with people, each one jockeying for a better view. Everyone was waiting for the drums and rattles to sound that would summon Kukulcan from her lair.

It was not a good day for a ceremony.

Overhead, the sky was a twisting gray mass of angry stormclouds that repeatedly grumbled and threatened those who had gathered in the plaza. Despite this, the signal was given to sound the music, and the resulting din drowned out both the voices in the sky and the voices in the crowd below. Moments later, Kukulcan appeared in all her majesty, a white silhouette against the dark sky, and rose into the air over the Pyramid of the Magician, her great coils rising and falling in anticipation. The crowd gasped to see the god uncloaked by the night, for she rarely came forth in the daylight hours. Pacan looked up at her and shuddered to think he had once dared to touch the god—convinced he must have been in a trance at the time. He placed a hand on the stone head beside him.

In the next instant a brilliant blue bolt of lightning slammed into the steps of the government buildings, and the scream of the crowd was lost in the tremendous crack of thunder that immediately followed. Toltec soldiers standing nearby threw themselves to the ground in fear. When they raised their eyes to look again, Chilax-Alenque stood in the place where the lightning had touched the stone.

"*Kukulcan!*" the sorcerer shouted, and thunder rolled across the sky at the sound of his voice.

The governor barked an order and several of the Toltec soldiers got to their feet and advanced upon the little man, but an instant later a snarling white jaguar was in his place, its ears drawn back as it spat and hissed and raked the air with its claws. The soldiers backed off, knowing this was no normal animal they faced, and once again it was the dwarf-sorcerer who stood before them.

"This battle is not for you," he said from behind the jade mask. "My words are for the feathered serpent alone!"

Kukulcan shrieked horrendously as the challenge reached her ears, and people scattered from the plaza as the serpent descended to crush the puny human who dared to oppose her. Pacan crouched on his platform, wanting to flee with the others, but too afraid to move.

"Enough!" cried the sorcerer, as rain began to fall in great drops from the sky, and the serpent halted in midair, hovering over the plaza and thrashing about angrily. "On your belly, worm," the dwarf commanded, holding the long white feather up for all to see. "I rob you of your flight." Chilax-Alenque snapped the feather between his fingers then, and Kukulcan came crashing down in a heap upon the stony expanse of the plaza, her tangled coils bruised and bleeding from her fall. The rain fell in sheets, and mud smeared her pure white countenance.

"Do you feel the kiss of Chaac, unholy one?" Chilax-Alenque raised his hands over his head, and each one held a silver-white egg. Fear filled the eyes of Kukulcan. "You killed our children," the dwarf spat at her. "Now witness the death of your own!"

The eggs shattered on the stone before the great serpent. Kukulcan dragged herself closer and watched the two tiny worms writhe and die in the mass of translucent bloody mucus and broken shell. A wail of anguish escaped her throat, and she threw herself towards the dwarf in a rage.

"Come no further, false god of my enemy," the dwarf commanded. "For I know your true name . . . Quetzalcoatl!"

The white serpent drew herself up over the tiny dwarf, hissing with rage.

"Now, Pacan! Now!"

Pacan's heart quailed at the sound of his name, but somehow he found the strength in his arms to lift the head stone and slide it into place. He turned to see the little sorcerer face his enemy a final time. "Quetzalcoatl," the sorcerer cried, "I bind thee unto stone for a thousand years!"

The white serpent shrieked and threw back her head as if to strike, her neck feathers spreading in a fearsome display, but before she could act a second bolt of lightning left the sky and struck her full in the head. Her body jerked and danced appallingly and took on a ghostly blue glow that completely engulfed it, then the light gathered itself into a fiery ball and sped towards the sculpture, slamming directly into the stone facade. Pacan looked up to see the image of Kukulcan glowing white as if the stone had been heated in a hot fire. He reached out to touch it and felt a surge of power that threw him backwards off the platform. He lay on his back, stunned, with the rain falling freely in his face.

After a moment he groaned and raised himself up on one elbow. His hand throbbed painfully. Not far away the feathered serpent lay lifeless in the square, and a growing crowd of distraught and wailing Toltec circled around the body, exhorting it earnestly to rise up once again—all in vain. Still standing on the stone steps, Chilax-Alenque raised his hands to the sky, dispelling the clouds that spiraled away upon his command. Moments later the sun lit up the central plaza once again.

That was when Pacan heard it.

If was a familiar sound, a haunting sound, one that made his chest tighten and his heart pound as if he had just heard the voice of a dead relative whispering to him at his bedside. He could not believe his ears, but Chilax-Alenque turned to him and nodded. It was true then. . . .

It was Aachtun's war horn.

It sounded throughout the city, loud and joyful, a promise of liberation. Mayan voices rose in a cheer, and Toltec soldiers began running to and fro, terrified of what had happened and unsure of what to do next. Then suddenly soldiers of the Mayan resistance entered the central plaza and began to skirmish with those who had not dropped their weapons to flee. Pacan was standing now. Across the swirl of chaos, standing atop a building on the far side of the plaza, Aachtun stood like a hero of the ancients, sounding his conch shell war horn as his troops flooded into the city. Pacan heard himself shout with joy at the sight. They saw each other then, locked eyes and knew for certain they had been reunited at last.

Pacan seized his slave collar in both hands and tore it asunder before running towards his brother.

DRAGON'S FIN SOUP

▼▼▼

S.P. SOMTOW

AT the heart of Bangkok's Chinatown, in the district known as Yaowaraj, there is a restaurant called the Rainbow Café which, every Wednesday, features a blue plate special they call dragon's fin soup. Though little known through most of its hundred-year existence, the café enjoyed a brief flirtation with fame during the early 1990s because of an article in the Bangkok *Post* extolling the virtues of the *specialité de la maison*. The article was written by the enigmatic Ueng-Ang Thalay, whose true identity few had ever guessed. It was only I and a few close friends who knew that Ueng-Ang was actually a Chestertonian American named Bob Halliday, ex-concert pianist and Washington *Post* book critic, who had fled the mundane madness of the western world for the more fantastical, cutting-edge madness of the Orient. It was only in Bangkok, the bastard daughter of feudalism and futurism, that Bob had finally been able to be himself, though what *himself* was, he alone seemed to know.

But we were speaking of the dragon's fin soup.

Perhaps I should quote the relevant section of Ueng-Ang's article:

▼▼▼

Succulent! Aromatic! Subtle! Profound! Transcendental! These are but a few of the adjectives your skeptical food columnist has been hearing from the clients of the Rainbow Café in Yaowaraj as they rhapsodize about the mysterious dish known as dragon's fin soup, served only on Wednesdays. Last Wednesday your humble columnist was forced to try it out. The restaurant is exceedingly hard to find, being on the third floor of the only building still extant from before the Chinatown riots of 1945. There is no sign, either in English or Thai, and as I cannot read Chinese, I cannot say whether there is one in that language either. On Wednesday afternoons, however, there are a large number of official-looking Mercedes and BMWs double-parked all the way down the narrow soi, and dozens of uniformed chauffeurs leaning warily against their cars; so, unable to figure out the restaurant's location from the hastily scrawled fax I had received from a friend of mine who works at the Ministry of Education, I decided to follow the luxury cars . . . and my nose . . . instead. The alley became narrower and shabbier. Then, all of a sudden, I turned a corner, and found myself joining a line of people, all dressed to the teeth, snaking single file up the rickety wooden steps into the small, unaircondi-tioned, and decidedly unassuming restaurant. It was a kind of time-travel. This was not the Bangkok we all know, the Bangkok of insane traffic jams, of smörgåsbord sexuality, of iridescent skyscrapers and stagnant canals. The people in line all waited patiently; when I was finally ushered inside, I found the restaurant to be as quiet and as numinous as a Buddhist temple. Old men with floor-length beards played mah jongg; a woman in a cheongsam directed me to a table beneath the solitary ceiling fan; the menu contained not a word of Thai or English. Nevertheless, without my having to ask, a steaming bowl of the notorious soup was soon served to me, along with a cup of piping-hot chrysanthemum tea.

At first I was conscious only of the dish's bitterness, and I wondered whether its fame was a hoax or I, as the only pale-faced rube in the room, was actually being proffered a bowl full of microwaved Robitussin. Then, suddenly, it seemed to me that the bitterness of the soup was a kind of veil or filter through which its true taste, too overwhelming to be perceived directly, might be enjoyed . . . rather as the dark glasses one must wear in order to gaze directly at the sun. But as for the taste itself, it cannot truly be described at all. At first I thought it must be a variant of the familiar shark's fin, perhaps marinated in some geriatric wine. But it also seemed to partake somewhat of the subtle tang of bird's nest soup, which draws its flavor from the coagulated saliva of cave-dwelling swallows. I also felt a kind of coldness in my joints and extremities, the tingling sensation familiar to those who have tasted fugu, the elusive and expensive Japanese puffer fish, which, improperly prepared, causes paralysis and death within minutes. The dish tasted like all these things and none of them, and I found, for the first time in my life, my jaundiced tongue confounded and bewildered. I asked the beautiful longhaired waitress in the cheongsam whether she could answer a few questions about the dish; she said, "Certainly, as long as I don't have to divulge any of the ingredients, for they are an ancient family secret." She spoke an antique and grammatically quaint sort of Thai, as though she had never watched television, listened to pop songs, or hung out in the myriad coffee shops of the city. She saw my surprise and went on in English, "It's not my first language, you see; I'm a lot more comfortable in English."

"Berkeley?" I asked her, suspecting a hint of Northern California in her speech.

She smiled broadly then, and said, "Santa Cruz, actually.

It's a relief to meet another American around here; they don't let me out much since I came home from college."

"American?"

"Well, I'm a dual national. But my great-grandparents were forty-niners. Gold rush chinks. My name's Janice Lim. Or Lam or Lin, take your pick."

"Tell me then," I inquired, "since you can't tell me what's in the soup . . . why is it that you only serve it on Wednesdays?"

"Wednesday, in Thai, is Wan Phutth . . . the day of Buddha. My father feels that dragon's flesh should only be served on that day of the week that is sacred to the Lord Buddha, when we can reflect on the transitory nature of our existence."

▼▼▼

At this point it should be pointed out that I, your narrator, am the woman with the long hair and the *cheongsam*, and that Bob Halliday has, in his article, somewhat exaggerated my personal charms. I shall not exaggerate his. Bob is a large man; his girth has earned him the sobriquet of "Elephant" among his Thai friends. He is an intellectual; he speaks such languages as Hungarian and Cambodian as well as he does Thai, and he listens to *Lulu* and *Wozzeck* before breakfast. For relaxation, he curls up with Umberto Eco, and I don't mean Eco's novels, I mean his academic papers on semiotics. Bob is a rabid agoraphobe, and flees as soon as there are more than about ten people at a party. His friends speculate endlessly about his sex life, but in fact he seems to have none at all.

Because he was the only American to have found his way to the Rainbow Café since I returned to Thailand from California, and because he seemed to my father (my mother having passed away in childbirth) to be somehow unthreatening, I found myself spending a good deal of time with him when I wasn't working at the restaurant. My aunt Ling-ling, who doesn't speak a word of Thai or English, was the official chaperone; if we went for a quiet cup of coffee at the Regent, for example, she was to be found a couple of tables away, sipping a glass of chrysanthemum tea.

It was Bob who taught me what kind of a place Bangkok really was. You see, I had lived until the age of eighteen without ever setting foot outside our family compound. I had had a tutor to help me with my English. We had one hour of television a day, the news; that was how I had learned Thai. My father was obsessed with our family's purity; he never used our dearly bought, royally granted Thai surname of Suntharapornsunthornpanich, but insisted on signing all documents Sae Lim, as though the Great Integration of the Chinese had never occurred and our people were still a nation within a nation, still loyal to the vast and distant Middle Kingdom. My brave new world had been California, and it remained for Bob to show me that an even braver one had lain at my doorstep all my life.

Bangkoks within Bangkoks. Yes, that charmingly hackneyed metaphor of the Chinese boxes comes to mind. Quiet places with pavilions that overlooked reflecting ponds. Galleries hung with postmodern art. Japanese-style coffee houses with melon-flavored ice cream floats and individual shrimp pizzas. Grungy noodle stands beneath flimsy awnings over open sewers; stratospherically upscale French patisseries and Italian gelaterias. Bob knew where they all were, and he was willing to share all his secrets, even though Aunt Ling-ling was always along for the ride. After a time, it seemed to me that perhaps it was my turn to reveal some secret, and so one Sunday afternoon, in one of the coffee lounges overlooking the atrium of the Sogo shopping mall, I decided to tell him the biggest of all secrets. "Do you really want to know," I said, "why we only serve the dragon fin soup on Wednesday?"

"Yes," he said, "and I promise I won't print it."

"Well you see," I said, "it takes about a week for the tissue to regenerate."

▼▼▼

That was about as much as I could safely say without spilling the whole can of soup. The dragon had been in our family since the late Ming Dynasty, when a multi-multi-great-uncle of mine, a eunuch who was the Emperor's trade representative between Peking and the Siamese Kingdom of Ayuthaya, had tricked him into following his junk all the way down the Chao Phraya River, had imprisoned him beneath the canals of the little village that was later to become Bangkok, City of Angels, Dwelling Place of Vishnu, Residence of the Nine Jewels, and so on and so forth (read the *Guinness Book of Records* to obtain the full name of the city), known affectionately to its residents as City of Angels Etc. This was because the dragon had revealed to my multi-great-uncle that the seemingly invincible Kingdom of Ayuthaya would one day be sacked by the King of Pegu and that the capital of Siam would be moved down to this unpretentious village in the Chao Phraya delta. The dragon had told him this because, as everyone knows, a mortally wounded dragon, when properly constrained, is obliged to answer three questions truthfully. Multi-great-uncle wasted his other questions on trying to find out whether he would ever regain his manhood and be able to experience an orgasm; the dragon had merely laughed at this, and his laughter had caused a minor earthquake which destroyed the summer palace of Lord Kuykendaal, a Dutchman who had married into the lowest echelon of the Siamese aristocracy, which earthquake in turn precipitated the Opium War of 1677, which, as it is not in the history books, remains alive only in our family tradition.

Our family tradition also states that each member of the family may only tell one outsider about the dragon's existence. If he chooses the right outsider, he will have a happy life; if he chooses unwisely, and the outsider turns out to be untrustworthy, then misfortune will dog both the revealer and his confidant.

I wasn't completely sure about Bob yet, and I didn't want to blow my one opportunity. But that evening, as I supervised the ritual slicing of the dragon's fin, my father dropped a bombshell.

The dragon could not, of course, be seen all in one piece. There was, in the kitchen of the Rainbow Café, a hole in one wall, about nine feet in diameter. One coil of the dragon came through this wall and curved upward toward a similar opening in the ceiling. I did not know where the dragon ended or began. One assumed this was a tail section because it was so narrow. I had seen a dragon whole only in my dreams, or in pictures. Rumor had it that this dragon stretched all the way to Nontha-buri, his slender body twisting through ancient sewer pipes and under the foundations of century-old buildings. He was bound to my family by an ancient spell in a scroll that sat on the altar of the household gods, just above the cash register inside the restaurant proper. He was unimaginably old and unimaginably jaded, stunned rigid by three thousand years of human magic; his scales so lusterless that I had to buff them with furniture polish to give them some semblance of draconian majesty. He was, of course, still mortally wounded from the battle he had endured with multi-great-uncle; nevertheless, it takes them a long, long time to die, especially when held captive by a scroll such as the one we possessed.

You could tell the dragon was still alive, though. Once in a very long while, he breathed. Or rather, a kind of rippling welled up him, and you could hear a distant wheeze, like an old house settling on its foundations. And of course, he regenerated. If it wasn't for that, the restaurant would never have stayed in business all these years.

The fin we harvested was a ventral fin and hung down over the main charcoal stove of the restaurant kitchen. It took some slicing to get it off. We had a new chef, Ah Quoc, just up from Penang, and he was having a lot of trouble. "You'd better heat up the carving knife some more," I was telling him. "Make sure it's red hot."

He stuck the knife back in the embers. Today, the dragon was remarkably sluggish; I had not detected a breath in hours; and the flesh was hard as stone. I wondered whether the event our family dreaded most, the dragon's death, was finally going to come upon us.

"*Muoi, muoi,*" he said, "the flesh just won't give."

"Don't call me *muoi,*" I said. "I'm not your little sister, I'm the boss's daughter. In fact, don't speak Chiuchow at all. English is a lot simpler."

"Okey-doke, Miss Janice. But Chinese or English, meat just no slice, la."

He was hacking away at the fin. The flesh was stony, recalcitrant. I didn't want to use the spell of binding, but I had to. I ran into the restaurant—it was closed and there were only a few old men playing mah jongg—grabbed the scroll from the altar, stormed back into the kitchen and tapped the scaly skin, whispering the word of power that only members of our family can speak. I felt a shudder deep within the dragon's bowels. I put my ear up to the clammy hide. I thought I could hear, from infinitely far away, the hollow clanging of the dragon's heart, the glacial oozing of his blood through kilometer after kilometer of leaden veins and arteries. "Run, blood, run," I shouted, and I started whipping him with the brittle paper.

Aunt Ling-ling came scurrying in at that moment, a tiny creature in a widow's dress, shouting, "You'll rip the scroll, don't hit so hard!"

But then, indeed, the blood began to roar. "Now you can slice him," I said to Ah Quoc. "Quickly. It has to soak in the marinade for at least twenty-four hours, and we're running late as it is."

"Okay! Knife hot enough now, la." Ah Quoc slashed through the whole fin in a single motion, like an imperial headsman. I could see now why my father had hired him to replace Ah Chen, who had become distracted, gone native—even gone so far as to march in the 1992 democracy riots—as if the politics of the Thais were any of our business.

Aunt Ling-ling had the vat of marinade all ready. Ah Quoc sliced quickly and methodically, tossing the pieces of dragon's fin into the bubbling liquid. With shark's fin, you have to soak it in water for a long time to soften it up for eating. Bob Halliday had speculated about the nature of the marinade. He was right about the garlic and the chilies, but it would perhaps have been unwise to tell him about the sulfuric acid.

It was at that point that my father came in. "The scroll, the scroll," he said distractedly. Then he saw it and snatched it from me.

"We're safe for another week," I said, following him out of the kitchen into the restaurant. Another of my aunts, the emaciated Jasmine, was counting a pile of money, doing calculations with an abacus and making entries into a leatherbound ledger.

My father put the scroll back. Then he looked directly into my eyes—something he had done only once or twice in my adult life—and, scratching his beard, said, "I've found you a husband."

That was the bombshell.

▼▼▼

I didn't feel it was my place to respond right away. In fact, I was so flustered by his announcement that I had absolutely nothing to say. In a way, I had been expecting it, of course, but for some reason ... perhaps it was because of my time at Santa Cruz ... it just hadn't occurred to me that my father would be so ... so ... old-fashioned about it. I mean, my God, it was like being stuck in an Amy Tan novel or something.

That's how I ended up in Bob Halliday's office at the Bangkok *Post*, sobbing my guts out without any regard for propriety or good manners. Bob, who is a natural empath, allowed me to yammer on and on; he sent a boy down to the market to fetch some steaming noodles wrapped in banana leaves and iced coffee in little PVC bags. I daresay I didn't make too much sense. "My father's living in the nineteenth century ... or worse," I said. "He should never have let me set foot outside the house ... outside the restaurant. I mean, Santa Cruz, for God's sake! Wait till I tell him I'm not even a virgin anymore. The price is going to plummet, he's going to take a bath on whatever deal it is he's drawn up. I'm so mad at him. And even though he did send me to America, he never let me so much as set foot in the Silom Complex, two miles from our house, without a chaperone. I've never had a life! Or rather, I've had two half-lives—half American coed, half Chinese dragon lady—I'm like two half-people that don't make a whole. And this is Thailand, it's not America and it's not China. It's the most alien landscape of them all."

Later, because I didn't want to go home to face the grisly details of my impending marriage contract, I rode back to Bob's apartment with him in a *tuk-tuk*. The motorized rickshaw darted skillfully through jammed streets and minuscule alleys and once again—as so often with Bob—I found myself in an area of Bangkok I had never seen before, a district overgrown with weeds and wild banana trees; the *soi* came to an abrupt end and there was a lone elephant, swaying back and forth, being hosed down by a country boy wearing nothing but a *phakhomah*. You must be used to slumming by now," Bob said, "with all the places I've taken you."

In his apartment, a grizzled cook served up a screamingly piquant *kaeng khieu waan*, and I must confess that though I usually can't stand Thai food, the heat of this sweet green curry blew me away. We listened to Wagner. Bob has the most amazing collection of CDs known to man. He has twelve recordings of *The Magic Flute*, but only three of Wagner's *Ring* cycle— three more than most people I know. "Just listen to that!" he said. I'm not a big fan of opera, but the kind of singing that issued from Bob's stereo sounded hauntingly familiar ... it had the hollow echo of a sound I'd heard that very afternoon, the low and distant pounding of the dragon's heart.

"What is it?" I said.

"Oh, it's the scene where Siegfried slays the dragon," Bob said. "You know, this is the Solti recording, where the dragon's voice is electronically enhanced. I'm not sure I like it."

It sent chills down my spine.

"Funny story," Bob said. "For the original production, you know, in the 1860s . . . they had a special dragon built . . . in England . . . in little segments. They were supposed to ship the sections to Bayreuth for the première, but the neck was accidentally sent to Beirut instead. That dragon never did have a neck. Imagine those people in Beirut when they opened that crate! What do you do with a disembodied segment of dragon anyway?"

"I could think of a few uses," I said.

"It sets me to thinking about dragon's fin soup."

"No can divulge, la," I said, laughing, in my best Singapore English.

The dragon gave out a roar and fell, mortally wounded, in a spectacular orchestral climax. He crashed to the floor of the primeval forest. I had seen this scene once in the Fritz Lang silent film *Siegfried*, which we'd watched in our History of Cinema class at Santa Cruz. After the crash there came more singing.

"This is the fun part, now," Bob told me. "If you approach a dying dragon, it *has* to answer your questions . . . three questions usually . . . and it has to answer them truthfully."

"Even if he's been dying for a thousand years?" I said.

"Never thought of that, Janice," said Bob. "You think the dragon's truthseeing abilities might become a little clouded?"

Despite my long and tearful outpouring in his office, Bob had not once mentioned the subject of my Damoclean doom. Perhaps he was about to raise it now; there was one of those long pregnant pauses that tend to portend portentousness. I wanted to put it off a little longer, so I asked him, "If you had access to a dragon . . . and the dragon were dying, and you came upon him in just the right circumstances . . . what *would* you ask him?"

Bob laughed. "So many questions . . . so much I want to know . . . so many arcane truths that the cosmos hangs on! I think I'd have a lot to ask. Why? You have a dragon for me?"

▼▼▼

I didn't get back to Yaowaraj until very late that night. I had hoped that everyone would have gone to bed, but when I reached the restaurant (the family compound itself is reached through a back stairwell beyond the kitchen) I found my father still awake, sitting at the carving table, and Aunt Ling-ling and Aunt Jasmine stirring the vat of softening dragon's fin. The sulfuric acid had now been emptied and replaced with a pungent brew of vinegar, ginseng, garlic, soy sauce, and the ejaculate of a young boy, obtainable in Patpong for about one hundred baht. The whole place stank, but I knew that it would whittle down to the subtlest, sweetest, bitterest, most nostalgic of aromas.

My father said to me, "Perhaps you're upset with me, Janice; I know it was a little sudden."

"Sudden!" I said. "Give me a break, Papa, this was more than sudden. You're so old-fashioned suddenly . . . and you're not even that old. Marrying me off like you're cashing in your blue chip stocks or something."

"There's a world-wide recession, in case you haven't noticed. We need an infusion of cash. I don't know how much longer the dragon will hold out. Look, this contract . . ." He pushed it across the table. It was in Chinese, of course, and full of flowery and legalistic terms. "He's not the youngest I could have found, but his blood runs pure; he's from the village." The village being, of course, the village of my ancestors, on whose soil my family has not set foot in seven hundred years.

"What do you mean, not the youngest, Papa?"

"To be honest, he's somewhat elderly. But that's for the best, isn't it? I mean, he'll soon be past, as it were, the age of lovemaking . . ."

"Papa, I'm not a virgin."

"Oh, not to worry, dear; I had a feeling something like that might happen over there in Californ' . . . we'll send you to Tokyo for the operation. Their hymen implants are as good as new, I'm told."

My hymen was not the problem. This was probably not the time to tell my father that the deflowerer of my maindenhead had been a young, fast-talking, vigorous, muscular specimen of corn-fed Americana by the name of Linda Horovitz.

"You don't seem very excited, my dear."

"Well, what do you expect me to say?" I had never raised my voice to my father, and I really didn't quite know how to do it.

"Look, I've really worked very hard on this match, trying to find the least offensive person who could meet the minimum criteria for bailing us out of this financial mess—this one, he has a condominium in Vancouver, owns a computer franchise, would probably not demand of you, you know, too terribly degrading a sexual performance—"

Sullenly, I looked at the floor.

He stared at me for a long time. Then he said, "You're in love, aren't you?"

I didn't answer.

My father slammed his fists down on the table. "Those damned lascivious Thai men with their honeyed words and their backstabbing habits . . . it's one of them, isn't it? My only daughter . . . and my wife dead in her grave these twenty-two years . . . it kills me."

"And what if it *had* been a Thai man?" I said. "Don't we have Thai passports? Don't we have one of those fifteen-syllable Thai names which *your* grandfather purchased from the King? Aren't we living on Thai soil, stewing up our birthright for Thai citizens to eat, depositing our hard-earned Thai thousand-baht bills in a Thai bank?"

He slapped my face.

He had never done that before. I was more stunned than hurt. I was not to feel the hurt until much later.

"Let me tell you, for the four hundredth time, how your grandmother died," he said, so softly I could hardly hear him above the bubbling of the dragon's fin. "My father had come to Bangkok to fetch his new wife and bring her back to Californ'. It was his cousin, my uncle, who managed the Rainbow Café in those days. It was the 1920s and the city was cool and quiet and serenely beautiful. There were only a few motor-cars in the whole city; one of them, a Ford, belonged to Uncle Shenghua. My father was in love with the City of Angels Etc. and he loved your grandmother even before he set eyes on her. And he never went back to Californ', but moved into this family compound, flouting the law that a woman should move into her husband's home. Oh, he was so much in love! And he believed that here, in a land where men did not look so different from himself, there would be no prejudice—no bars with signs that said *No Dogs or Chinamen*—no parts of town forbidden to him—no forced assimilation of an alien tongue. After all, hadn't King Chulalong-korn himself taken Chinese concubines to ensure the cultural diversity of the highest ranks of the aristocracy?"

My cheek still burned; I knew the story almost by heart; I hated my father for using his past to ruin my life. Angrily I looked at the floor, at the walls, at the taut curve of the dragon's body as it hung cold, glittering and motionless.

"But then, you see, there was the revolution, the coming of what they called democracy. No more the many ancient cultures of Siam existing side by side. The closing of the Chinese-language schools. Laws restricting those of ethnic Chinese descent from certain occupations. . . . True, there were no concentration camps, but in some ways the Jews had it easier than we did ... someone *noticed*. Now listen! You're not listening!"

"Yes, Papa," I said, but in fact my mind was racing, trying to find a way out of this intolerable situation. My Chinese self calling out to my American self, though she was stranded in another country, and perhaps near death, like the dragon whose flesh sustained my family's coffers.

"Nineteen forty-five," my father said. "The war was over, and Chiang Kai-Shek was demanding that Siam be ceded to China. There was singing and dancing in the streets of Yaowaraj! Our civil rights were finally going to be restored to us ... and the Thais were going to get their comeuppance! We marched with joy in our hearts ... and then the soldiers came ... and then we too had rifles in our hands ... as though by magic. Uncle Shenghua's car was smashed. They smeared the seats with shit and painted the windshield with the words 'Go home, you slanty-eyed scum.' Do you know why the restaurant wasn't torched? One of the soldiers was raping a woman against the doorway and his friends wanted to give him time to finish. The woman was your grandmother. It broke my father's heart."

I had never had the nerve to say it before, but today I was so enraged that I spat it out, threw it in his face. "You don't know that he *was* your father, Papa. Don't think I haven't done the math. You were born in 1946. So much for your obsession with racial purity."

He acted as though he hadn't heard me, just went on with his preset lecture: "And that's why I don't want you to consort with any of them. They're lazy, self-indulgent people who think only of sex. I just know that one of them's got his tentacles wrapped around your heart."

"Papa, you're consumed by this bullshit. You're a slave to this ancient curse ... just like the damn dragon." Suddenly, dimly, I had begun to see a way out. "But it's not a Thai I'm in love with. It's an American."

"A *white* person!" he was screaming at the top of his lungs. My two aunts looked up from their stirring. "Is he at least rich?"

"No. He's a poor journalist."

"Some blond young thing batting his long eyelashes at you—"

"Oh, no, he's almost fifty. And he's fat." I was starting to enjoy this.

"I forbid you to see him! It's that man from the *Post*, isn't it? That bloated thing who tricked me with his talk of music and literature into thinking him harmless. Was it he who violated you? I'll have him killed, I swear."

"No, you won't," I said, as another piece of my plan fell into place. "I have the right to choose one human being on this earth to whom I shall reveal the secret of the family's dragon. My maidenhead is yours to give away, but not this. This right is the only thing I can truly call my own, and I'm going to give it to Bob Halliday."

▼▼▼

It was because he could do nothing about my choice that my father agreed to the match between Bob Halliday and me; he knew that, once told of the secret, Bob's fate would necessarily be intertwined with the fate of the Clan of Lim no matter what, for a man who knew of the dragon could not be allowed to escape from the family's clutches. Unfortunately, I had taken Bob's name in vain. He was not the marrying kind. But perhaps, I reasoned, I could get him to go along with the charade for a while, until old Mr. Hong from the Old Country stopped pressing his suit. Especially if I gave him the option of questioning the dragon. After all, I had heard him wax poetic about all the questions he could ask . . . questions about the meaning of existence, of the creation and destruction of the universe, profound conundrums about love and death.

Thus it was that Bob Halliday came to the Rainbow Café one more time—it was Thursday—and dined on such mundane delicacies as beggar chicken, braised sea cucumbers stuffed with pork, cold jellyfish tentacles, and suckling pig. As a kind of *coup de grâce*, my father even trotted out a small dish of dragon's fin which he had managed to keep refrigerated from the day before (it won't keep past twenty-four hours) which Bob consumed with gusto. He also impressed my father no end by speaking a Mandarin of such consonant-grinding purity that my father, whose groveling deference to those of superior accent was millennially etched within his genes, could not help addressing him in terms of deepest and most cringing respect. He discoursed learnedly on the dragon lore of many cultures, from the salubrious, fertility-bestowing water dragons of China to the fire-breathing, maiden-ravishing monsters of the West; lectured on the theory that the racial memory of dinosaurs might have contributed to the draconian mythos, although he allowed as how humans never coexisted with dinosaurs, so the racial memory must go back as far as marmosets and shrews and such creatures; he lauded the soup in high astounding terms, using terminology so poetic and ancient that he was forced to draw the calligraphy in the air with a stubby finger before my father was able vaguely to grasp his metaphors; and finally—the clincher—alluded to a great-great-great-great-aunt of his in San Francisco who had once had a brief, illicit, and wildly romantic interlude with a Chinese opium smuggler who might *just possibly* have been one of the very Lims who had come from *that* village in Southern Yunnan, you know the village I'm talking about, that very village . . . at which point my father, whisking away all the *haute cuisine* dishes and replacing them with an enormous blueberry cheesecake flown in, he said, from Leo Lindy's of New York, said, "All right, all right, I'm sold. You have no money, but I daresay someone of your intellectual brilliance can conjure up some money somehow. My son, it is with great pleasure that I bestow upon you the hand of my wayward, worthless, and hideous daughter."

I hadn't forewarned Bob about this. Well, I had meant to,

but words had failed me at the last moment. Papa had moved in for the kill a lot more quickly than I had thought he would. Before Bob could say anything at all, therefore, I decided to pop a revelation of my own. "I think, Papa," I said, "that it's time for me to show him the dragon."

We all trooped into the kitchen.

The dragon was even more inanimate than usual. Bob put his ear up to the scales; he knocked his knuckles raw. When I listened, I could hear nothing at all at first; the whisper of the sea was my own blood surging through my brain's capillaries, constricted as they were with worry. Bob said, "This is what I've been eating, Janice?"

I directed him over to where Ah Quoc was now seasoning the vat, chopping the herbs with one hand and sprinkling with the other, while my two aunts stirred, prodded, and gossiped like the witches from *Macbeth*. "Look, look," I said, and I pointed out the mass of still unpulped fin that protruded from the glop, "see how its texture matches that of the two dorsal fins."

"It hardly seems alive," Bob said, trying to pry a scale loose so he could peer at the quick.

"You'll need a red-hot paring knife to do that," I said. Then, when Papa wasn't listening, I whispered in his ear, "Please, just go along with all this. It really looks like 'fate worse than death' time for me if you don't. I know that marriage is the farthest thing from your mind right now, but I'll make it up to you somehow. You can get concubines. I'll even help pick them out. Papa won't mind that, it'll only make him think you're a stud."

Bob said, and it was the thing I'd hoped he'd say, "Well, there *are* certain questions that have always nagged at me . . . certain questions which, if only I knew the answers to them, well . . . let's just say I'd die happy."

My father positively beamed at this. "My son," he said, clapping Bob resoundingly on the back, "I *already* know that I shall die happy. At least my daughter won't be marrying a Thai. I just couldn't stand the thought of one of those loathsome creatures dirtying the blood of the House of Lim."

I looked at my father full in the face. Could he have already forgotten that only last night I had called him a bastard? Could he be that deeply in denial? "Bob," I said softly, "I'm going to take you to confront the dragon." Which was more than my father had ever done, or I myself.

▼▼▼

Confronting the dragon was, indeed, a rather tall order, for no one had done so since the 1930s, and Bangkok had grown from a sleepy backwater town into a monster of a metropolis; we knew only that the dragon's coils reached deep into the city's foundations, crossed the river at several points, and, well, we weren't sure if he did extend all the way to Nonthaburi; luckily, there is a new expressway now, and once out of the crazy traffic of the old part of the city it did not take long, riding the sleek aircondi-tioned Nissan taxicab my father had chartered for us, to reach the outskirts of the city. On the way, I caught glimpses of many more Bangkoks that my father's blindness had denied me; I saw the *Blade Runner*esque towers threaded with mist and smog; saw the buildings shaped like giant robots and computer circuit boards designed by that eccentric genius, Dr. Sumet; saw the not-very-ancient and very-very-multicolored temples that dotted the cityscape like rhinestones in a cowboy's boot; saw the slums and the palaces, cheek by jowl, and the squamous rooftops that could perhaps have also been little segments of the dragon pok-ing up from the miasmal collage; we zoomed down the road at breakneck speed to the strains of Natalie Cole, who, our driver opined, is "even better than Mai and Christina."

How to find the dragon? Simple. I had the scroll. Now and then, there was a faint vibration of the parchment. It was a kind of dousing.

"This off-ramp," I said, "then left, I think." And to Bob I said,

"Don't worry about a thing. Once we reach the dragon, you'll ask him how to get out of this whole mess. He can tell you, *has* to tell you actually; once that's all done, you'll be free of me, I'll be free of my father's craziness, *he'll* be free of his obsession."

Bob said, "You really shouldn't put too much stock in what the dragon has to tell you."

I said, "But he *always* tells the truth!"

"Well yes, but as a certain wily Roman politician once said, 'What is truth?' Or was that Ronald Reagan?"

"Oh, Bob," I said, "if push really came to shove, if there's no solution to this whole crisis . . . could you actually bring yourself to marry me?"

"You're very beautiful," Bob said. He loves to be all things to all people. But I don't think there's enough of him to go round. I mean, basically, there are a couple of dozen Janice Lims waiting in line for the opportunity to sit at Bob's feet. But, you know, when you're alone with him, he has this ability to give you every scintilla of his attention, his concern, his love, even; it's just that there's this nagging concern that he'd feel the same way if he were alone with a Beethoven string quartet, say, or a plate of exquisitely spiced *naem sod.*

We were driving through young paddy fields now; the nascent rice has a neon-green color too garish to describe. The scroll was shaking continuously and I realized we must be rather close to our goal; I have to admit that I was scared out of my wits.

The driver took us through the gates of a Buddhist temple. The scroll vibrated even more energetically. Past the main chapel, there were more gates; they led to a Brahmin sanctuary; past the Indian temple there was yet another set of gates, over which, in rusty wrought iron, hung the character *Lim*, which is two trees standing next to one another. The taxi stopped. The scroll's shaking had quieted to an insistent purr. "It's around here *somewhere*," I said, getting out of the cab.

The courtyard we found ourselves in (the sun was setting at

this point, and the shadows were long and gloomy, and the marble flagstones red as blood) was a mishmash of nineteenth-century *chinoiserie*. There were stone lions, statues of bearded men, twisted little trees peering up from crannies in the stone; and tall, obelisk-like columns in front of a weathered stone building that resembled a ruined ziggurat. It took me a moment to realize that the building was, in fact, the dragon's head, so petrified by time and the slow process of dying that it had turned into an antique shrine. Someone still worshipped here at least. I could smell burning joss-sticks; in front of the pointed columns—which, I now could see, were actually the dragon's teeth—somebody had left a silver tray containing a glass of wine, a pig's head, and a garland of decaying jasmine.

"Yes, yes," said Bob, "I see it too; I feel it even."

"How do you mean?"

"It's the air or something. It tastes of the same bitterness that's in the dragon's fin soup. Only when you've taken a few breaths of it can you smell the underlying sensations . . . the joy, the love, the infinite regret."

"Yes, yes, all right," I said, "but don't forget to ask him for a way out of our dilemma."

"Why don't you ask him yourself?" Bob said.

I became all flustered at this. "Well, it's just that, I don't know, I'm too young, I don't want to use up all my questions, it's not the right time yet . . . you're a mature person, you don't . . ."

". . . have that much longer to live, I suppose," Bob said wryly.

"Oh, you know I didn't mean it in quite that way."

"Ah, but, sucking in the dragon's breath the way we are, we too are forced to blurt out the truth, aren't we?" he said.

I didn't like that.

"Don't want to let the genie out of the bottle, do you?" Bob said. "Want to clutch it to your breast, don't want to let go . . ."

"That's my father you're describing, not me."

Bob smiled. "How do you work this thing?"

"You take the scroll and you tap the dragon's lips."

"Lips?"

I pointed at the long stucco frieze that extended all the way around the row of teeth. "And don't forget to ask him," I said yet again.

"All right. I will."

Bob went up to the steps that led into the dragon's mouth. On the second floor were two flared windows that were his nostrils; above them, two slitty windows seemed to be his eyes; the light from them was dim, and seemed to come from candlelight. I followed him two steps behind—it was almost as though we were already married!—and I was ready when he put out his hand for the scroll. Gingerly, he tapped the dragon's lips.

This was how the dragon's voice sounded: it seemed at first to be the wind, or the tinkling of the temple bells, or the far-off lowing of the waterbuffalo that wallowed in the paddy, or the distant cawing of a raven, the cry of a newborn child, the creak of a teak house on its stilts, the hiss of a slithering snake. Only gradually did these sounds coalesce into words, and once spoken the words seemed to hang in the air, to jangle and clatter like a loaded dishwasher.

The dragon said, *We seldom have visitors anymore.*

I said, "Quick, Bob, ask."

"Okay, okay," said Bob. He got ready, I think, to ask the dragon what I wanted him to ask, but instead, he blurted out a completely different question. "How different," he said, "would the history of music be, if Mozart had managed to live another ten years?"

"Bob!" I said. "I thought you wanted to ask deep, cosmic questions about the nature of the universe—"

"Can't get much deeper than that," he said, and then the answer came, all at once, out of the twilight air. It was music of a kind. To me it sounded dissonant and disturbing; choirs singing out of tune, donkeys fiddling with their own tails. But you know, Bob stood there with his eyes closed, and his face was suffused with an ineffable serenity; and the music surged to a noisome clanging and a yowling and a caterwauling, and a slow smile broke out on his lips; and as it all began to die away he was whispering to himself, "Of course . . . apoggiaturas piled on apoggiaturas, bound to lead to integral serialism in the mid-romantic period instead, then minimalism mating with impressionism running full tilt into the Wagnerian *gesamtkunstwerk* and colliding with the pointillism of late Webern . . ."

At last he opened his eyes, and it was as though he had seen the face of God. But what about me and my miserable life? It came to me now. These *were* Bob's idea of what constituted the really important questions. I couldn't begrudge him a few answers. He'd probably save the main course for last; then we'd be out of there and could get on with our lives. I settled back to suffer through another arcane question, and it was, indeed, arcane.

Bob said, "You know, I've always been troubled by one of the hundred-letter words in *Finnegan's Wake*. You know the words I mean, the supposed 'thunderclaps' that divide Joyce's novel into its main sections . . . well, its the ninth one of those . . . I can't seem to get it to split into its component parts. Maybe it seems trivial, but it's worried me for the last twenty-nine years."

The sky grew very dark then. Dry lightning forked and unforked across gathering clouds. The dragon spoke once more, but this time it seemed to be a cacophony of broken words, disjointed phonemes, strings of frenetic fricatives and explosive plosives; once again it was mere noise to me, but to Bob Halliday it was the sweetest music. I saw that gazing-on-the-face-of-divinity expression steal across his features one more time as again he closed his eyes. The man was having an orgasm. No wonder he didn't need sex. I marveled at him. Ideas themselves were sensual things to him. But he didn't lust after knowledge, he wasn't greedy about it like Faust; too much knowledge could not damn Bob Halliday, it could only redeem him.

Once more, the madness died away. A monsoon shower had come and gone in the midst of the dragon's response, and we were drenched; but presently, in the hot breeze that sprang up, our clothes began to dry.

"You've had your fun now, Bob. Please, please," I said, "let's get to the business at hand."

Bob said, "All right." He tapped the dragon's lips again, and said, "Dragon, dragon, I want to know . . ."

The clouds parted and Bob was bathed in moonlight.

Bob said, "Is there a proof for Fermat's Last Theorem?"

Well, I had had it with him now. I could see my whole life swirling down the toilet bowl of lost opportunities. "Bob!" I screamed, and began pummeling his stomach with my fists . . . the flesh was not as soft as I'd imagined it would be . . . I think I sprained my wrist.

"What did I do wrong?"

"Bob, you idiot, what about *us*?"

"I'm sorry, Janice. Guess I got a little carried away."

Yes, said the dragon. Presumably, since Bob had not actually asked him to prove Fermat's Last Theorem, all he had to do was say yes or no.

What a waste. I couldn't believe that Bob had done that to me. I was going to have to ask the dragon myself after all. I wrested the scroll from Bob's hands, and furiously marched up the steps toward that row of teeth, phosphorescent in the moonlight.

"Dragon," I screamed, "dragon, dragon, dragon, dragon, dragon."

So, Ah Muoi, you've come to me at last. So good of you. I am old; I have seen my beginning and my end; it is in your eyes. You've come to set me free.

Our family tradition states clearly that it is always good to give the dragon the impression that you are going to set him free. He's usually a lot more cooperative. Of course, you never do set him free. You would think that, being almost omniscient, the dragon would be wise to this, but mythical beasts always seem to have their fatal flaws. I was too angry for casuistic foreplay.

"You've got to tell me what I need to know." Furiously, I whipped the crumbling stone with the old scroll.

I'm dying, you are my mistress; what else is new?

"How can I free myself from all the baggage that my family has laid on me?"

The dragon said:

There is a sleek swift segment of my soul
That whips against the waters of renewal;
You too have such a portion of yourself;
Divide it in a thousand pieces;
Make soup;
Then shall we all be free.

"That doesn't make sense!" I said. The dragon must be trying to cheat me somehow. I slammed the scroll against the nearest tooth. The stucco loosened; I heard a distant rumbling. "Give me a straight answer, will you? How can I rid my father of the past that torments him and won't let him face who he is, who I am, what we're not?"

The dragon responded:

There is a sly secretion from my scales
That drives a man through madness into joy;
You too have such a portion of yourself;
Divide it in a thousand pieces;
Make soup;
Then shall we all be free.

This was making me really mad. I started kicking the tooth. I screamed, "Bob was right . . . you're too senile, your mind is too clouded to see anything that's important . . . all you're good for is Bob's great big esoteric enigmas . . . but I'm just a human being here, and I'm in bondage, and I want out . . . what's it going to take to get a straight answer out of you?" Too late, I realized that I had phrased my last words in the form of a question. And the answer came on the jasmine-scented breeze even before I had finished asking:

> *There is a locked door deep inside my flesh*
> *A dam against bewilderment and fear;*
> *You too have such a portion of yourself;*
> *Divide it in a thousand pieces;*
> *Make soup;*
> *Then shall we all be free.*

But I wasn't even listening, so sure was I that all was lost. For all my life I had been defined by others—my father, now Bob, now the dragon, even, briefly, by Linda Horovitz. I was a series of half-women, never a whole. Frustrated beyond repair, I flagellated the dragon's lips with that scroll, shrieking like a premenstrual fishwife: "Why can't I have a life like other people?" I'd seen the American girls with their casual ways, their cars, speaking of men as though they were hunks of meat; and the Thai girls, arrogant, plotting lovers' trysts on their cellular phones as they breezed through the spanking-new shopping mall of their lives. Why was *I* the one who was trapped, chained up, enslaved? But I had used up the three questions.

I slammed the scroll so hard against the stucco that it began to tear.

"Watch out!" Bob cried. "You'll lose your power over him!"

"Don't speak to me of empowerment," I shouted bitterly, and

the parchment ripped all at once, split into a million itty-bitty pieces that danced like shooting stars in the brilliant moonlight.

That was it, then. I had cut off the family's only source of income, too. I was going to have to marry Mr. Hong after all.

Then the dragon's eyes lit up, and his jaws began slowly to open, and his breath, heady, bitter, and pungent, poured into the humid night air.

"My God," Bob said, "there *is* some life to him after all."

My life, the dragon whispered, *is but a few brief bittersweet moments of imagined freedom; for is not life itself enslavement to the wheel of sansara? Yet you, man and woman, base clay though you are, have been the means of my deliverance. I thank you.*

The dragon's mouth gaped wide. Within, an abyss of thickest blackness; but when I stared long and hard at it, I could see flashes of oh, such wondrous things . . . far planets, twisted forests, chaotic cities . . . "Shall we go in?" said Bob.

"Do you want to?"

"Yes," Bob said, "but I can't, not without you; dying, he's still *your* dragon, no one else's; you know how it is; you kill your dragon, I kill mine."

"Okay," I said, realizing that now, finally, had come the moment for me to seize my personhood in my hands, "but come with me, for old times' sake; after all, you did give me a pretty thorough tour of *your* dying dragon . . ."

"Ah, yes; the City of Angels Etc. But that's not dying for a few millennia yet."

I took Bob by the hand and ran up the steps into the dragon's mouth. He followed me. Inside the antechamber, the dragon's palate glistened with crystallized drool. Strings of baroque pears hung from the ceiling, and the dragon's tongue was coated with clusters of calcite. Further down, the abyss of many colors yawned.

"Come on," I said.

"What do you think he meant," Bob said, "when he said you

should slice off little pieces of yourself, make them into soup, and *that* would set us all free?"

"I think," I said, "that it's the centuries of being nibbled away by little parasites . . ." But I was no longer that interested in the dragon's oracular pronouncements. I mean, for the first time in my life, since my long imprisonment in my family compound and the confines of the Rainbow Café's kitchen, since my three years of rollercoastering through the alien wharves of Santa Cruz, I was in territory that I instinctively recognized as my own. Past the bronze uvula that depended from the cavern ceiling like a soundless bell, we came to a mother-of-pearl staircase that led ever downward. "This must be the way to the oesophagus," I said. "Yeah." There came a gurgling sound. A dull, foul water sloshed about our ankles. "Maybe there's a boat," I said. We turned and saw it moored to the banister, a golden barque with a silken sail blazoned with the ideograph *Lim.*

Bob laughed. "You're a sort of goddess in this kingdom, a creatrix, an earth-mother. But I'm the one with the waistline for earth-mothering."

"Perhaps we could somehow meld together and be one." After all, his mothering instinct was a lot stronger than mine.

"Cosmic!" he said, and laughed again.

"Like the character *Lim* itself," I told him, "two trees straining to be one."

"Erotic!"

And I too laughed as we set sail down the gullet of the dying dragon. The waters were sluggish at first. But they started to deepen. Soon we were having the flume ride of our lives, careening down the bronze-lined walls that boomed with the echo of our laughter . . . the bronze was dark for a long long time till it started to shine with a light that rose from the heat of our bodies, the first warmth to invade the dragon's innards in a thousand years . . . and then, in the mirror surface of the walls, we began to see visions. Yes! There was the dragon himself, youthful, pissing the monsoon as he soared above the South China Sea. Look, look, my multi-great-great-uncle bearing the urn of his severed genitals as he marched from the gates of the Forbidden City, setting sail for Siam! Look, look, now multi-great-great-uncle in the Chinese Quarter of the great metropolis of Ayuthaya, constraining the dragon as he breached the raging waters of the Chao Phraya! Look, look, another great-great-uncle panning for gold, his queue bobbing up and down in the California sun! Look, look, another uncle, marching alongside the great Chinese General Taksin, who wrested Siam back from the Burmese and was in turn put to an ignominious death! And look, look closer now, the soldier raping my grandmother in the doorway of the family compound . . . look, look, my grandfather standing by, his anger curbed by an intolerable terror . . . look, look, even that was there . . . and me . . . yielding to the stately Linda Horovitz in the back seat of a rusty Toyota . . . me, stirring the vat of dragon's fin soup . . . me, talking back to my father for the first time, getting slapped in the face, me, smashing the scroll of power into smithereens.

And Bob? Bob saw other things. He heard the music of the spheres. He saw the Sistine Chapel in its pristine beauty. He speed-read his way through Joyce and Proust and Tolstoy, unexpurgated and unedited. And you know, it was turning him on.

And me, too. I don't know quite when we started making love. Perhaps it was when we hit what felt like terminal velocity, and I could feel the friction and the body heat begin to ignite his shirt and my *cheongsam*. Blue flame embraced our bodies, fire that was water, heat that was cold. The flame was burning up my past, racing through the dirt roads of the ancestral village; the fire was engulfing Chinatown, the rollercoasters of Santa Cruz were blazing gold and ruddy against the setting sun, and even the Forbidden City was on fire, even the great portrait of Chairman Mao and the Great Wall and the Great Inextinguishable Middle Kingdom itself, all burning, burning, burning, all

cold, all turned to stone, and all because I was discovering new
continents of pleasure in the folds of Bob Halliday's flesh, so
rich and convoluted that it was like making love to three hundred
pounds of brain; and you know, he was considerate in ways I'd
never dreamed; that mothering instinct, I supposed, that empa-
thy; when I popped, he made me feel like the apple that received
the arrowhead of William Tell and with it freedom from oppres-
sion; oh, God, I'm straining, aren't I, but you know, those things
are so so hard to describe; we're plummeting headlong through
the mist and foam and flame and spray and surge and swell and
brine and ice and hell and incandescence and then:

In the eye of the storm:

A deep gash opening and:

Naked, we're falling into the vat beneath the dragon's flanks
as the ginsu-wielding Ah Quoc is hacking away at the disinteg-
rating flesh and:

"No!" my father shouted. "Hold the sulfuric acid!"

We were bobbing up and down in a tub of bile and semen
and lubricous fluids, and Aunt Ling-ling was frantically snatching
away the flask of concentrated H_2SO_4 from the kvetching
Jasmine.

"Mr. Elephant, la!" cried Ah Quoc. "What you do, Miss Janice? No can! No can!"

"You've gone and killed the dragon!" shrieked my father.
"Now what are we going to do for a living?"

And he was right. Once harder than titanium carbide, the
coil of flesh was dissipating into the kitchen's musty air; the
scales were becoming circlets of rainbow light in the steam from
the bamboo *cha shu bao* containers; as archetypes are wont to
do, the dragon was returning to the realm of myth.

"Oh, Papa, don't make such a fuss," I said, and was surprised
to see him back off right away. "We're still going to make
soup today."

"Well, I'd like to know how. Do you know you were gone

for three weeks? It's Wednesday again, and the line for dragon's fin soup is stretching all the way to Chicken Alley! There's some kind of weird rumor going around that the soup today is especially *heng*, and I'm not about to go back out there and tell them I'm going to be handing out rain checks."

"Speaking of rain—" said Aunt Ling-ling.

Rain indeed. We could hear it, cascading across the corrugated iron rooftops, sluicing down the awnings, splashing the dead-end canals, running in the streets.

"Papa," I said, "we *shall* make soup. It will be the last and finest soupmaking of the Clan of Lim."

And then—for Bob Halliday and I were still entwined in each other's arms, and his flesh was still throbbing inside my flesh, bursting with pleasure as the thunderclouds above—we rose up, he and I, he with his left arm stretched to one side, I with my right arm to the other, and together we spelled out the *two trees melding into one* in the calligraphy of carnal desire—and, basically, what happened next was that I released into the effervescing soup stock the *sleek swift segment of my soul, the sly secretion from my scales*, and, last but not least, the *locked door deep inside my flesh*; and these things (as the two trees broke apart) did indeed divide into a thousand pieces, and so we made our soup; not from a concrete dragon, time-frozen in its moment of dying, but from an insubstantial spirit-dragon that was woman, me, alive.

"Well, well," said Bob Halliday, "I'm not sure I'll be able to write this up for the *Post*."

▼▼▼

Now this is what transpired next, in the heart of Bangkok's Chinatown, in the district known as Yaowaraj, in a restaurant called the Rainbow Café, on a Wednesday lunchtime in the mid-monsoon season:

There wasn't very much soup, but the more we ladled out,

the more there seemed to be left. We had thought to eke it out with black mushrooms and *bok choi* and a little sliced chicken, but even those extra ingredients multiplied miraculously. It wasn't quite the feeding of the five thousand, but, unlike the evangelist, we didn't find it necessary to count.

After a few moments, the effects were clearly visible. At one table, a group of politicians began removing their clothes. They leaped up onto the lazy susan and began to spin around, chanting "Freedom! Freedom!" at the top of their lungs. At the next table, three transvestites from the drag show down the street began to make mad passionate love to a platter of duck. A young man in a pinstripe suit draped himself in the printout from his cellular fax and danced the hula with a shriveled crone. Children somersaulted from table to table like monkeys.

And Bob Halliday, my father, and I?

My father, drinking deeply, said, "I really don't give a shit who you marry."

And I said, "I guess it's about time I told you this, but there's a strapping Jewish tomboy from Milwaukee that I want you to meet. Oh, but maybe I *will* marry Mr. Hong—why not?—some men aren't as self-centered and domineering as you might think. If you'd stop sitting around trying to be Chinese all the time—"

"I guess it's about time I told you this," said my father, "but I stopped caring about this baggage from the past a long time ago. I was only keeping it up so you wouldn't think I was some kind of bloodless half-breed."

"I guess it's about time I told you this," I said, "but I *like* living in Thailand. It's wild, it's maddening, it's obscenely beautiful, and it's very, very, very un-American."

"I guess it's about time I told you this," my father said, "but I've bought me a one-way ticket to Californ', and I'm going to close up the restaurant and get a new wife and buy myself a little self-respect."

"I guess it's about time I told you this," I said, "I love you."

That stopped him cold. He whistled softly to himself, then sucked up the remaining dregs of soup with a slurp like a farting buffalo. Then he flung the bowl against the peeling wall and cried out, "And I love you too."

And that was the first and only time we were ever to exchange those words.

But you know, there were no such revelations from Bob Halliday. He drank deeply and reverently; he didn't slurp; he savored; of all the *dramatis personae* of this tale, it was he alone who seemed, for a moment, to have cut himself free from the wheel of *sansara* to gaze, however briefly, on nirvana.

As I have said, there was a limitless supply of soup. We gulped it down till our sides ached. We laughed so hard we were sitting ankle-deep in our tears.

But do you know what?

An hour later we were hungry again.

BIOGRAPHIES

KEVIN J. ANDERSON is the author of 25 novels spanning the science fiction, fantasy, and horror fields, including numerous best-selling *Star Wars* novels, the acclaimed *Climbing Olympus*, the Nebula Award nominee *Assemblers of Infinity* (with Doug Benson), the YA fantasy novel *Born of Elven Blood* (with John Gregory Betancourt), and the Bram Stoker Award finalist *Resurrection, Inc.*. His powerful short fiction has appeared in *Analog, Fantasy and Science Fiction, The Ultimate Werewolf, The Ultimate Zombie, The Ultimate Dracula* and many other places. He and his wife Rebecca both work as technical editors at the Lawrence Livermore National Laboratory.

JOANNE BERTIN was born in New York City, but has lived in Connecticut almost all her life. She's worked an odd variety of jobs, ranging from a stint coloring comic books to another as a dairy goat herder. For the past nine years she's been working at Wesleyan University and taking classes in medieval history whenever she can. In her spare time she enjoys reading fantasy and science fiction, writing the same, archery, silversmithing, and horseback riding. She shares a house—once a forge for a cannon factory—with her boyfriend Sam and three ferrets who are determined to stage a coup. "Dragonlord's Justice" is dedicated to Nikki, the fourth ferret, who recently passed away; she was always ready to jump on the keyboard and "help" whenever the author was at the computer. That help is sorely missed.

JOHN BETANCOURT is the author of a dozen books, including the acclaimed *Rememory, Johnny Zed*, and *The Blind Archer*, as well as a large number of short stores and nonficton. He had two collaborative novels published in 1995: the YA fantasy *Born of Elven Blood* (with Kevin J. Anderson) and the *Star Trek: Deep Space Nine* novel *Devil in the Sky* (with Greg Cox). In 1993, he and his wife Kim were World Fantasy Award finalists for their independent publishing venture The Wildside Press. He has also served as editor on the anthologies *The Ultimate Witch, The Ultimate Zombie, The Ultimate Alien, New Masters of Horror,* and *The Best of Weird Tales.* Currently he lives in New Jersey, where he collects cats and computers with equal success.

FRANCES CICHETTI has been a woodcut illustrator and designer for seven years. She holds a Bachelor of Science from the Environmental Science and Forestry College at Syracuse, New York. Some of her other clients are *The New York Times, Spy* magazine, Disney, St. Martin's Press, Macmillan, and Scribner's.

When he was young and impressionable, **KEITH R.A. DeCANDIDO**'s parents gave him Ursula K. Le Guin, Robert A. Heinlein, J.R.R. Tolkien, and P.G. Wodehouse to read. He was doomed. He has been a writer and editor in the science fiction, fantasy, and comics fields since 1989. His nonfiction has appeared in *Creem, Publishers Weekly, Horror, Library Journal, The Comics Journal,* and *Wilson Library Bulletin*; his short fiction has been published in the anthologies *The Ultimate Spider-Man, The Ultimate Silver Surfer,* and *Two-Fisted Writer Tales,* and he edits the series of novels and short-story anthologies based on Marvel Comics' super heroes co-published by Byron Preiss Multimedia Company, Inc., and Putnam Berkley.

NICHOLAS A. DiCHARIO was nominated for the John W. Campbell Award for Best New Writer of the Year (1992) and has also been nominated for the Hugo and World Fantasy Awards. His short fiction has appeared in *The Magazine of Fantasy and Science Fiction*, Robert Silverberg's *Universe* series, and several other original anthologies.

HARLAN ELLISON has been called "one of the great living American short story writers" by the *Washington Post*. In his 40-year-long writing career, Ellison has won the Hugo Award 8 ½ times, the Nebula Award 3 times, the Edgar Allan Poe Award of the Mystery Writers of America twice, the World Fantasy Lifetime Achievement Award, and was awarded the Silver Pen for journalism by P.E.N., the international writers' union. Among Ellison's most recognized works are his two books of TV essays, *The Glass Teat* and *The Other Glass Teat*, and his short story collections, including *Deathbird Stories, Strange Wine, I Have No Mouth & I Must Scream, Angry Candy*, and *Shatterday*, among others. In addition, Ellison's 1992 novella, *The Man Who Rowed Christopher Columbus Ashore*, was selected for inclusion in the 1993 edition of *The Best American Short Stories*. He is the author of more than sixty books, among the most recent of which are *Mind Fields* (with Polish artist Jacek Yorka), *Mefisto in Onyx*, and *I, Robot: The Illustrated Screenplay* (based on Isaac Asimov's story-cycle).

LARS HOKANSON is an award-winning artist who specializes in woodcut illustrations. His clients include *The New York Times*, Random House, Viking/Penguin, *Rolling Stone*, and *Time*, among others. His art has also been exhibited in the permanent collections of several museums, including the Museum of Modern Art in New York, the Philadelphia Museum of Art, and the National Portrait Gallery in London.

IAN HUNTER was born in Edinburgh in 1960, and is married with a young son. He lives and works in the central belt of Scotland as a Community Economic Development Worker. He has so far written one horror/fantasy novel and seven children's novels, and spends a large amount of his time trying to find a home for them. He has won several prizes for his short fiction, and had stories published in *Fear, Winter Chills, Dark Horizons, New Images 1* and *2*, and *Now Read This*, among others. He is currently working on two humorous fantasy novels which are overflowing with dragons.

PHYLLIS ANN KARR was born in the naval hospital at Oakland, California in 1944 and raised in the northwest corner of Indiana, with frequent trips downstate to visit her mother's family in Terre Haute (the city wiped out at the end of *Dead Men Don't Wear Plaid*). Hal Foster, Howard Pyle, and T.H. White made an Arthurian fan of her in childhood. After eight years of librarianhood, she moved to northwest Wisconsin, where she later met Clifton A. Hoyt, thanks to a rural bookmobile they both patronized. They married in 1990, saving a piece of cake for the bookmobile librarians. They live in a county large in area, but so small in population that it still has no traffic lights.

ANDREW LANE has a degree in physics, works for the United Kingdom government, and moonlights as a reviewer and novelist. He is the author of four *Doctor Who* novels, *Lucifer Rising* (with Jim Mortimore), *All-Consuming Fire*, *The Empire of Glass*, and *Original Sin*. His hair has started turning grey since selling his first short story to *The Ultimate Witch*, but he's sure it's a coincidence.

TANITH LEE was born in 1947. Her first fantasy novel, *The Birthgrave*, was published by DAW Books in 1975. She has since published more than 50 books and around 130 short stories. Currently, she is working on *Scarabae Blood Opera*—novels so far include *Dark Dance, Personal Darkness*, and *In Darkness, I*—a series about an ancient and perhaps immortal family with vampiric leanings, set in the modern world and the limitless past. She is also working on a series of Victorian gothic horror novels (so far: *Heartbeast* and *Elephantasm*). She is currently working on *Red Unicorn*, the sequel to the acclaimed YA novels *Black Unicorn* and *Gold Unicorn*. She is married to the writer John Kaiine.

URSULA K. LE GUIN writes both poetry and prose in several genres, including realistic fiction, science fiction, fantasy, young children's books, books for young adults, screenplays, essays, verbal texts for musicians, and voicetexts for performance and recording. She established her reputation in science fiction with the Hainish novels, which include *The Left Hand of Darkness* and *The Dispossessed*, and in fantasy with the first three of the Earthsea books: *A Wizard of Earthsea, The Tombs of Atuan*, and *The Farthest Shore*. Her most recent books are *Tehanu*, the last of the Earthsea series; *Searoad*, stories of the Oregon coast; and two picture books, *A Ride on the Red Mare's Back* and *Fish Soup*. She has received many awards, including five Hugos, four Nebulas, a Pushcart Prize, a Newbery Honor Medal, a National Book Award, the Kafka Award, and the Harold D. Vursell Award from the American Academy & Institute of Arts & Letters.

GORDON R. MENZIES was born and raised in Cobourg, Ontario, Canada, and now lives in York (a suburb of Toronto) with his wife Lily, their two-year-old son Nicolas, their six-footed cat Hannibal, and a German Shepherd pup named Jesse. He works for an affiliate of the Royal Bank of Canada, and lists his favorite authors as John Irving, Somerset Maugham, Richard Bach, Dean R. Koontz, Margaret Laurence, and Stephen King. He has a special penchant for Lucky Elephant pink candy popcorn and among his most prized possessions is an autographed photo of "The Friendly Giant." "Serpent Feather" is dedicated to his older brother Robert, who bought Gordon's first typewriter for him when he was twelve years old, and his good friend James, with whom he extensively explored the Yucatan peninsula.

GERALD PERKINS was born in 1944 in St. Cloud, Minnesota. After many moves, he wound up back in St. Cloud in time to attend and graduate from St. Cloud State University with a Bachelor of Science degree in Industrial Technology. He immediately left for California; Guam; New Hampshire; Kodiak, Alaska; Australia; and other foreign places. While tracking satellites on Guam, he wondered what might be the equivalent of his job in 100 years. The results of that question will probably never see daylight, but it started him writing seriously. He currently lives in the San Francisco Bay Area as a Quality Engineer for a military aerospace firm, and enjoys reading science fiction and fantasy, music, photography, SF conventions, and, when possible, adding to an eccentric art collection.

BYRON PREISS is the editor of the books *The Planets, The Universe, The Microverse,* and *The Dinosaurs: A New Look at a Lost Era,* which was featured in *Life* magazine. He has collaborated with Arthur C. Clarke, Isaac Asimov, and Ray Bradbury, and edited the Grammy

Award-winning *The Words of Gandhi*. His monograph on *The Art of Leo & Diane Dillon* was a Hugo Award nominee. He is the producer of several CD-ROM titles, including the Invision Award-winning *Isaac Asimov's The Ultimate Robot*. He holds a B.A. from the University of Pennsylvania and an M.A. from Stanford University. He currently resides in New York City.

MIKE RESNICK is the author of more than thirty science fiction novels, including *Santiago, Ivory, Soothsayer,* and *A Miracle of Rare Design.* He is also the author of more than 100 short stories and the editor of 21 anthologies. He has won two Hugo Awards, and has been nominated for nine Hugos, six Nebulas, five Sieun-shos (the Japanese Hugo), a Clarke (the British Hugo), and has won a number of lesser awards. His daughter Laura won the 1993 John W. Campbell Award for Best New Writer.

JOSEPHA SHERMAN is the author of numerous fantasy novels, the latest of which include *Castle of Deception, A Cast of Corbies* (both with Mercedes Lackey), *A Strange and Ancient Name, King's Son, Magic's Son, The Shattered Oath, Windleaf, Gleaming Bright,* and *Child of Faerie, Child of Earth*; several volumes of folklore, including *Rachel the Clever and Other Jewish Folktales* and *Once Upon a Galaxy: Folklore, Fantasy, and Science Fiction*; and over 100 short stories for adults and children. She is also Consulting Editor for a major New York publisher of fantasy and science fiction.

ROBERT SILVERBERG was born in New York City and educated at Columbia. His first book, *Revolt on Alpha C*, was published in 1955, and he has since penned over a hundred books and numerous short stories, among them *Nightwings, Lord Valentine's Castle, Tom O'Bedlam, Nightfall* (with Isaac Asimov), and more. He was won four Hugo Awards and five Nebula Awards, as well as most of the other significant science fiction honors. He was President of the Science Fiction Writers of America from 1967–1968. He edited the *New Dimensions* series of anthologies from 1971–1980, the first volume of *The Science Fiction Hall of Fame* series, and *Robert Silverberg's Worlds of Wonder.* With his wife, Karen Haber, he edited *Universe*, a series of original science fiction anthologies. His newest book is *Hot Sky at Midnight*.

S.P. SOMTOW was born in Bangkok, Thailand, and grew up in Europe. He was educated at Eton College and at Cambridge. His first career was as a composer and performer; he turned to fiction writing in 1977. He won the John W. Campbell Award for Best New Writer in 1981, and two of his short stories have been nominated for the Hugo Award. His fiction writing has included science fiction (*The Darkling Wind*, a *Locus* bestseller), fantasy (the award-winning *The Wizard's Apprentice*), horror (*Vampire Junction*, called "the most important horror novel of 1984"), and children's literature (*The Fallen Country*). He is also a screenwriter, playwright, and film director. *The Laughing Dead*, the horror film he wrote and directed, was released in the U.S. this year.

LOIS TILTON is the author of *Vampire Winter*, a post-Holocaust survival tale; *Darkness on the Ice*, a World War II thriller with vampires; *Betrayal*, a *Star Trek: Deep Space Nine* novel; and *Accusations*, a *Babylon 5* novel. Since 1987, she has published about three dozen short stories in fantasy magazines and anthologies, including "The Witch's Daughter" in *The Ultimate Witch*.

MARY A. TURZILLO'S stories have appeared in *The Ultimate Witch*, *Science Fiction Age*, *Interzone*, *Tomorrow*, *The Magazine of Fantasy and Science Fiction*, and elsewhere. She has written nonfiction books about Philip José Farmer and Anne McCaffrey under the name Mary T. Brizzi. Born in the year of the dragon, her fascination with these mythic creatures and with mathematics dates from childhood, so she was gratified to be able to connect the two. She is currently writing a novel about teenage dinosaur hunters.

CYNTHIA WARD was born in Oklahoma and raised in Maine, Spain, and Germany as an Air Force brat. After graduating from the University of Maine, she moved to the San Francisco Bay Area. Following a tenure at the 1992 Clarion West Writers' Workshop in Seattle, she moved to that city, and intends never to move again. She has stories published or forthcoming in *Asimov's Science Fiction, Tomorrow Speculative Fiction, Galaxy, After the Loving, 100 Vicious Little Vampire Stories, Sword & Sorceress* Vols. 8, 9, & 11, *Monster Brigade*, and elsewhere.

LAWRENCE WATT-EVANS was born and raised in Massachusetts, fourth of six children, in a house full of books. He taught himself to read at age five in order to read a comic book story called "Last of the Tree People," and began writing his own stories a couple of years later. Eventually a fantasy novel, *The Lure of the Basilisk*, actually sold. Several more novels and dozens of stories have now made it into print, as well as articles, poems, comic book scripts, etc., covering a wide range of fantasy, science fiction, and horror. His short story "Why I Left Harry's All-Night Hamburgers" won the Hugo in 1988; his most successful novels to date have been the Ethshar fantasy series, beginning with *The Misenchanted Sword*. He's married, has two children, and has settled in the Maryland suburbs of Washington, D.C.

In her 27 years as a professional writer, CHELSEA QUINN YARBRO has sold over 50 books, over 60 short stories, and a handful of essays and reviews. Her work covers many genres: horror, science fiction, fantasy, thrillers, mysteries, historical fiction, romantic suspense, young adult fiction, and westerns. When she runs out of words, she writes serious music. She loves opera, horses, the antics of cats, good company and conviviality, and occult studies. She dislikes boredom in all forms. Her only domestic accomplishments are needlepoint and cooking.

JANE YOLEN, author of more than 150 books for children and adults, among them the short story collections *Here There Be Dragons, Here There Be Unicorns,* and *Here There Be Witches,* has been called "America's Hans Christian Andersen" for her many original fairy tales. Winner of the World Fantasy Award, the Kerlan Award, the Regina Medal, the Mythopoeic Society Award, and many other honors, she is a past president of the Science Fiction and Fantasy Writers of America and has been on the board of directors of the Society of Children's

Book Writers since its inception. She is editor-in-chief of Jane Yolen Books, an imprint of Harcourt Brace, specializing in children's books and young adult novels of fantasy and science fiction. Mother of three grown children and one not-so-grown grandchild, she and her husband Dr. David Stemple, divide their time between their home in Hatfield, Massachusetts and St. Andrews, Scotland.